MISS FLIBBERTIGIBBET AND THE BARBARIAN

A CYNSTER NEXT GENERATION NOVEL

STEPHANIE LAURENS

ABOUT MISS FLIBBERTIGIBBET
AND THE BARBARIAN

#1 New York Times bestselling author Stephanie Laurens returns with a story of two people thrown together on a journey of discovery that defines what each most want of life, love, and family.

A gentleman wishing to buy a fabulous horse and a lady set on protecting her family find common ground while pursuing a thief who upends both of their plans.

Nicholas Cynster rides up to Aisby Grange determined to secure the stallion known as The Barbarian for his family's Thoroughbred breeding stable, only to be turned away by the owner's daughter. Nicholas retreats, but is not about to be denied by any lady, no matter how startlingly beautiful and distracting.

Lady Adriana Sommerville knows Nicholas will be back and resigns herself to having to manage his interaction with her aging father. She successfully negotiates that potential quagmire only, at the very last moment, to discover the horse is missing.

Stunned, Addie insists on setting out in pursuit and is not so silly as to refuse Nicholas's support.

But as they follow on the heels of The Barbarian, their adventures and encounters open both their eyes to the prospect of a more enduring partnership. Yet before they can follow that trail farther and before they can lay hands on the horse, through shock after shock, their pursuit uncovers a complicated plot that strips away masks and rescripts everything Addie and her siblings thought they knew about the Sommerville family.

A classic historical romance of adventure, discovery, and reconciliation set in the English countryside. A Cynster Next Generation novel. A full-length historical romance of 103,000 words.

OTHER TITLES BY STEPHANIE LAURENS

The Lady Chosen
A Gentleman's Honor
A Lady of His Own
A Fine Passion
To Distraction
Beyond Seduction
The Edge of Desire
Mastered by Love

Black Cobra Quartet

The Untamed Bride
The Elusive Bride
The Brazen Bride
The Reckless Bride

The Adventurers Quartet

The Lady's Command
A Buccaneer at Heart
The Daredevil Snared
Lord of the Privateers

The Cavanaughs

The Designs of Lord Randolph Cavanaugh
The Pursuits of Lord Kit Cavanaugh
The Beguilement of Lady Eustacia Cavanaugh
The Obsessions of Lord Godfrey Cavanaugh

Other Novels

The Lady Risks All
The Legend of Nimway Hall – 1750: Jacqueline

Medieval (As M.S.Laurens)

Desire's Prize

Novellas

Melting Ice – from the anthologies *Rough Around the Edges* and *Scandalous Brides*

Rose in Bloom – from the anthology *Scottish Brides*

Scandalous Lord Dere – from the anthology *Secrets of a Perfect Night*

Lost and Found – from the anthology *Hero, Come Back*

The Fall of Rogue Gerrard – from the anthology *It Happened One Night*

The Seduction of Sebastian Trantor – from the anthology *It Happened One Season*

Short Stories

The Wedding Planner – from the anthology *Royal Weddings*

A Return Engagement – from the anthology *Royal Bridesmaids*

UK-Style Regency Romances

Tangled Reins

Four in Hand

Impetuous Innocent

Fair Juno

The Reasons for Marriage

A Lady of Expectations An Unwilling Conquest

A Comfortable Wife

MISS FLIBBERTIGIBBET AND THE BARBARIAN

MISS FLIBBERTIGIBBET AND THE BARBARIAN

Copyright © 2023 by Savdek Management Proprietary Limited

ISBN: 978-1-925559-56-9

Cover design by Savdek Management Pty. Ltd.

Cover couple photography by Period Images © 2023

First print publication: March, 2023

Savdek Management Proprietary Limited, Melbourne, Australia.

www.stephanielaurens.com

Email: admin@stephanielaurens.com

CHAPTER 1

JULY 8, 1854. NEWMARKET,
CAMBRIDGESHIRE.

hatever you have to do, get that horse!
Nicholas Cynster reread the words with which his
sister Prudence had concluded her reply to his urgent inquiry. His lips
twisted wryly. Pru had underlined the last three words several times. In
his imagination, he could hear her voice forcefully and determinedly
uttering the injunction.

He was seated in solitary splendor at the breakfast table in the early-
morning quiet of the Cynster farmhouse. Currently, he was the only
member of the family in residence. Indeed, if Pru had been in England,
sitting at the table opposite him as she had for so many years, he had no
doubt she would be preparing to leave in pursuit of said horse herself. But
luckily or unluckily—at times like this, he wasn't sure which—Pru was
now married and living in Ireland with her husband, Deaglan Fitzgerald,
the Earl of Glengarah. More, at present, she was heavily pregnant with
their second child. Consequently, Nicholas and Pru's parents had traveled
to Ireland to assist in keeping Pru and Deaglan's firstborn, Dougal, a
rambunctious toddler, entertained.

Nicholas slumped back in his chair, tossed the letter onto the table
beside his emptied plate, and with reluctant but growing resignation,
contemplated the missive that had been delivered by courier mere
minutes before.

Given that his father, legendary Thoroughbred racehorse owner and
trainer Demon Cynster, would have been privy to Pru's assessment—

Nicholas's inquiry had been addressed to them both—he had to accept that Pru's directive carried his father's imprimatur. Although Nicholas now ran the Cynster racing stable, his father's opinion on such a matter wasn't something he—or indeed, anyone in the Thoroughbred racing world—would ignore.

Several days ago, Nicholas's groom, Young Gillies, had picked up a rumor in a smoky corner of the local tavern to the effect that an exceptional Thoroughbred stallion that had vanished from the Jockey Club's records some years ago, whereabouts unknown, had recently been sighted on the Earl of Aisby's estate.

Unfortunately, Nicholas's younger brother, Toby, who had succeeded Pru as manager of the Cynster breeding stable, was presently off on some mission for Drake Varisey and, consequently, was not available to pursue the horse.

Nicholas's youngest sibling, Meg, was also away from home, spending summer with friends while their parents were in Ireland. Not that Meg, being the only one in the family who was not horse-mad, would have been of much assistance. She certainly wouldn't have agreed to go haring off to Aisby to persuade the earl to sell the stallion known as The Barbarian to the Cynsters.

On learning of the rumor and being of a cautious nature, especially when it came to matters of horseflesh—there were too many shysters in the game—after ascertaining the known particulars of the horse, Nicholas had sent a courier racing to Ireland to seek Pru's advice. He had plenty to keep him occupied at Newmarket, running the Cynster racing stable and filling in for Toby in overseeing the breeding stable. He really didn't want to tear off on some goose-chase—stallion-chase—after a horse that, in the end, proved to be not worth his and the family's time.

"However"—he tapped Pru's letter with one fingertip—"it seems The Barbarian is a horse we have to have."

There was no getting around it; he would have to go to Aisby Grange in Lincolnshire—the earl's principal seat—and negotiate to buy the horse. As part of that, he would need to clarify just why the horse had vanished from the Thoroughbred register for several years before turning up in the earl's stable.

Nicholas sighed and pushed away from the table. "At least it's summer. With any luck, the earl will be rusticating at Aisby Grange."

∽

Two days later, astride Tamerlane, his big gray hunter, Nicholas trotted up the gravel drive of Aisby Grange. Debrett's had informed him that the current earl was a Sommerville, but Nicholas knew little beyond that; he didn't know anyone in the Sommerville family and hadn't had time to visit his grandmother in London to learn more.

Given that he habitually eschewed the capital and paid ton gossip no heed at all, he was, therefore, venturing into unknown territory. When he emerged from the avenue of trees, currently in heavy leaf, and the house came into full view, he reined in and scanned the façade for any clues as to its owner.

Built of pale-yellow stone, with two full stories plus dormers beneath a slate roof, Aisby Grange was an impressive, earl-worthy residence. From this vantage point, the house appeared to be a substantial rectangular block. The front doors faced south, looking over an expanse of gently sloping lawn to the shores of a large lake.

Everything about the place appeared neat and in excellent repair. The stone frame around every long window was crisp and clean, and diamond-shaped panes sparkled in the summer sunshine. The many chimneys stood tall and straight, their pots aligned in perfect symmetry, while the canopies of the ancient trees behind the house swayed and danced, ruffling in the intermittent breeze and forming a living frame for the structure.

A large porte-cochere extended outward over the front steps and the carriage drive, rendering the edifice even more imposing.

Sudden movement in the shadows of the porte-cochere, around the open front doors, accompanied by muffled shouts from within captured Nicholas's attention. He squinted against the sun's glare, trying to see what was happening.

∾

Summoned by a cacophony of shrieks, screams, and yells, Lady Adriana Sommerville rushed into the Grange's front hall and skidded to a stop at the sight that met her eyes.

Her ever-widening eyes.

Their butler, Merriweather, two footmen, and one of the parlormaids were scrambling to assist her three younger siblings—Mortie, fourteen years old, Angie, twelve, and Benjamin, ten—who, apparently, had decided that creating a game involving flying flour bombs was a good idea.

To that end, they'd attached paper sacks stuffed with flour to several conglomerations of rubber balloons—one, two, or three balloons, multiple examples of each. In addition, some of the sacks-plus-balloons were attached to kites. As usual on warm summer days, the front doors were propped wide, and there was enough breeze flowing through the hall to keep the kites-plus-balloons aloft. As for the balloon-only efforts, even without the kites, they were soaring and bobbing in the high-ceilinged hall, wafting this way and that on the currents that swept through whenever a door almost anywhere in the house was opened.

The creations with kites had long strings attached, which were now trailing on the floor, but the balloon-only efforts had strings that might have been long enough to be caught in other rooms or in the house's corridors, but the ceiling in the front hall soared much higher, and the balloons were now bobbing free, despite the best efforts of the footmen, who were leaping up, trying to catch the strings.

The entire scene was comical and would have been amusing had the sacks of flour not started to leak.

Drips of flour now liberally splattered the black-and-green floor tiles and decorated the heads and shoulders of Merriweather and the footmen.

Argh! Lips setting, Addie strode forward. "Mortie! Angie! Benjamin!"

The three culprits swung to face her, identical expressions of guilt on their faces.

She pointed to the kites' trailing strings. "Pull the kites in first. Now!"

Her brothers leapt to obey.

"My lady." Merriweather looked guilty, too. He waved at the chaos. "I'm afraid the contraptions got away from us."

"No need to apologize, Merriweather. Please have"—Addie glanced at the footmen—"Tom and Trevor take charge of the kites and associated balloons. We don't want them to get loose again. I suggest taking the contraptions"—that was as good a name for the things as any other—"to the kitchen, where I'm sure Cook will have an implement sharp enough to puncture the balloons, and she'll want to retrieve her flour." Addie caught Angie's eyes. "I wonder if Cook even knows she's missing several pounds of her best flour, hmm?"

Her expression reminiscent of a startled doe, Angie whirled to help her brothers gather in the kite-attached balloons with their dangling, dripping sacks of flour.

While her siblings dealt with half the problem, planting her hands on her hips, Addie stared upward at the significantly more intractable half. Six balloon-only sacks continued to randomly drip flour across the hall. Without kites attached, the contraptions seemed even more susceptible to every little breeze. They dipped and swayed this way and that.

The sound of a door slamming somewhere on the upper floors of the house reached her.

A second later, a gust of air blew into the hall. For an instant, the balloons dipped low, forced down by the sudden pressure from above. Tom leapt and caught one, only to have the sack of flour burst in his hands, showering him with fine white dust.

"Oh no!" burst from several throats.

Most eyes were on Tom, sputtering and gasping, but Addie's gaze remained locked on the remaining five balloon-and-flour-sack combinations as they swept low across the hall and out through the tall front doors.

Not yet relieved, she hurried to the doorway. It would be a fine thing if the five contraptions escaped into the wide blue sky, but...

She halted on the threshold, looked out, and sighed in disappointment. Glancing back into the hall, she confirmed that the kite-attached flour bombs had been retrieved and were being carted off to the kitchen in the arms of the maid, Trevor, and poor flour-bedecked Tom.

"Right, then!" Imperiously, she beckoned her siblings to join her.

All three responded with an alacrity that suggested the outcome of their latest "experiment" had not, thus far, been a disappointment. Along the way, Mortie and Benjamin swooped and picked up their bows and arrows, apparently set aside on the floor while they'd leapt to catch their contraptions.

Merriweather followed rather more cautiously.

When the children clustered about her, Addie pointed into the porte-cochere, directing their gazes upward into the high, deep-raftered roof. The five contraptions were now lodged between the rafters and cross-beams and, despite the quite gusty breeze, showed no sign of moving again.

Far from being downcast, Mortie, Angie, and Benjamin clattered down the steps. Their faces alight, they peered upward at their handiwork.

Addie studied the contraptions, noting that, from the level of the drive, the attached strings were nowhere near long enough to be caught. She followed her siblings down the steps and onto the gravel and joined them in staring up at the five flour bombs.

"I say!" Mortie exclaimed. "What an excellent notion!" Eagerly, he turned his wide-eyed gaze on Angie and Benjamin. "If our enemies come calling and we have this already set up, we can shoot holes in the sacks and rain...well, something nasty down on the attackers' heads." He looked up at the porte-cochere's ceiling. "They'd never guess the bombs were there."

Addie refrained from pointing out that any archer would have to be visible in the doorway or, worse, down on the drive to shoot at the sacks. She crossed her arms and studied her siblings. "What, exactly, was this in aid of?"

They turned ardent faces her way. "We thought," Mortie explained, "that if the house was under siege—"

"Like it was during the War of the Roses," Angie put in, and Benjamin nodded solemnly.

"Then," Mortie continued, "we could use flying bombs to defend the place. That was our original idea."

Benjamin brandished his bow. "We were going to let the kites and balloons free over the front lawn, then shoot holes in the sacks."

"As a trial," Mortie said, "to see if the idea would work."

"But I tripped in the hall," Angie morosely admitted, "and lost hold of the strings, and the kites and balloons flew up, and we couldn't catch them."

Having witnessed the outcome, Addie fought to keep her lips straight. She looked up at the errant balloons. "Very well. One has to acknowledge that defending the house is a laudable enterprise. But how are you going to get those down?"

All five remaining bombs were intermittently dripping flour.

The trio studied their no-longer-flying bombs, then offered several half-hearted and distinctly improbable suggestions, all of which obviously would not work.

In light of the difficulties, more to herself than to anyone else, Addie mused, "Perhaps we can just leave them. Eventually, the flour will run out, and the balloons will deflate and come down low enough to be caught."

"Or to blow away," Angie said.

Addie nodded. "Indeed."

Merriweather, who had halted on the porch's top step and, until then, had remained a silent observer, cleared his throat.

Addie glanced his way; character-wise, the man was a rock, and he was built like one as well, a stout, solid presence in butler's black. "Yes, Merriweather?"

"If I might comment, my lady, leaving the bombs to drip until empty will hardly do. It will risk the embarrassment of inconveniencing anyone who comes to call."

Addie smiled reassuringly. "But no one is likely to call, at least not over the next days."

"Ahem." Merriweather looked pointedly left, along the drive.

Swiveling, Addie followed his gaze...to the gentleman who was riding up on a magnificent gray hunter.

The gentleman, Addie noted, was rather magnificent, too.

She blinked at the thought, then promptly banished it. She glanced at her siblings, only to see that, judging by their expressions, they shared her assessment. She returned her gaze to the rider and was forced to admit that, with his nut-brown hair touched by the sun, clean-cut, strong, and austere features, broad-shouldered horseman's build, and the relaxed, loose-limbed posture of one born to the saddle, he was the epitome of a gentleman-god approaching on a magnificent steed.

"Such lines," Mortie breathed.

"He's very handsome," Angie whispered. "And such a lovely pearly color."

"Has to be a Thoroughbred," Benjamin announced.

Another glance at her siblings confirmed that their eyes were all for the horse. Hers, on the other hand...

Addie looked back at the rider as he drew the horse to a halt. A nice enough horse, no doubt, but her attention was all for his master.

He dismounted with the fluid grace of an expert horseman, and she discovered her mouth had gone dry.

She felt faintly stunned. Since when had any man affected her like that? And he was still yards away!

Disconcerted by such unexpected—unprecedented—susceptibility, she stiffened her spine and strengthened her defensive shield. No matter what had brought such a gentleman to Aisby Grange, such vulnerability was not a good sign.

As he strolled toward them, closing the distance with distractingly graceful strides, the threat that any such gentleman inherently posed to her family and their ongoing battle to keep her father's condition hidden, concealed from all the ton, bloomed in her mind.

Nicholas saw hostility flare in the lady's eyes and wondered at its cause.

Had she recognized him? Should he have recognized her? Was she one of those tiresome females he'd slipped away from at some ball or other?

Over recent years, he'd avoided ton events, yet she looked to be in her early twenties, some years past her come-out, so it was possible she was one of those to whom, in the past, he'd given social short shrift.

Then again... As he took in her appearance, something within him stirred, and he was suddenly acutely aware that if they had met before, he would have remembered her.

She was of average height and slight build, her curves definite yet sleek and understated. Her blue cambric day dress was of fashionable cut, yet surprisingly unadorned. Most notably, however, the lady possessed a face that was a cross between a female cupid and an angel, with a truly flawless, almost pearlescent complexion combined with large, wide, *huge* periwinkle-blue eyes fringed by impossibly long, lush, golden-brown lashes. Her nose was short and straight, and her finely drawn brown eyebrows were perfectly arched, while her lips—ripe, full, and the color of a blush rose—were the sort to distract any red-blooded male and lead his mind into illicit arenas. Overall, her face was heart-shaped, and her chin was almost pointy but, somewhat unsettlingly, presently set in stony firmness.

Regardless, the wealth of pale-blond curls that clustered like a frame about her face gave her the superficial appearance most—including him —associated with feminine vacuousness.

If he hadn't detected the clear-eyed determination in her blue gaze and the underlying stubbornness in the set of her chin, he might have been fooled into taking her at face value.

Indeed, in many ways, her features and coloring reminded him of his mother, but even at her most youthful innocent, he doubted his mother had ever looked so like the stereotypical artist's rendition of a flighty, witless, yet well-born lady.

He halted before her and politely inclined his head, but before he could speak, one of the boys asked, "I say, do you ride him to hounds?"

Given the direction of the boys' gazes, there was no doubt who "he" was. "Sometimes," Nicholas allowed. "But mostly, I ride him on Newmarket Heath."

"Newmarket?" To say that the older lad's ears perked up would be understating his reaction.

"What's his name?" The girl seemed almost as eager as her brothers.

"Tamerlane."

The younger boy's face scrunched in thought. "Wasn't he some emperor?"

Nicholas grinned. "In the Far East."

He glanced at the lady—and saw a dribble of white descending from above her head.

He had two sisters. He didn't stop to think. He clamped his hands about the lady's shoulders and jerked her forward, out of the line of danger and all but into him.

He felt the galvanizing shock that passed through her—saw it in her blue, blue eyes.

Felt an answering reaction streak though him, leaving him stunned and equally shaken.

He stared into her eyes, and for that moment, the world ceased to turn. She stared back.

Both of them had stopped breathing.

"Oh! Oh!" The children leapt into action, ducking behind the lady, brushing at the back of her skirts, pushing her even farther forward, almost into Nicholas's arms, effectively shattering the moment. "We'll take care of it!" the trio chorused.

Nicholas hauled in a breath and forced himself to take a single step back and release the lady.

Instantly, she swung around to look at the puddle of what appeared to be flour on the ground.

For a second, they both stared at it, then he gestured at the patch. "I saw it falling and thought you would prefer not to have"—*any unnecessary adornment*—"a dusting."

She didn't glance his way, but drew in a tight breath and managed, "No. Indeed." Stiffly, she dipped her head to him. "Thank you."

The children were staring upward.

The younger boy plaintively asked, "How do we get them down?"

As he'd approached, Nicholas had glimpsed some of what had been going on. He could remember his cousins doing something similar at

Somersham Place. He walked under the edge of the porte-cochere and looked up. "Flour bombs?"

"Yes." The older boy glanced at him. "It was a trial to see if we could use something along these lines to defend against marauders."

Solemnly, Nicholas nodded. "A noble cause."

"But now they're stuck, and we have to get them down." The girl fixed blue eyes—not as blue as the lady's but pretty eyes, nonetheless—on Nicholas's face. "Do you know how?"

A spirited discussion ensued. Despite his active participation, Nicholas remained highly aware of the silent figure beside him. With her arms crossed, she watched and listened—specifically, she watched him through narrowed eyes and listened to every word he said—but made no comment, even when he regretfully informed the children that the only way to remove the balloons was to shoot them rather than the flour sacks.

"It might be wise," he suggested, "to attach strings to your arrows, in case they become lodged in the rafters."

The trio appealed to the butler, who had watched the performance with a quietly relieved air, and he dispatched a minion to fetch a ball of twine.

While they waited and the children studied the best angles for their shots, from beside Nicholas, the lady murmured, "Is that the voice of experience speaking?"

He grinned and shot her a glance. "You might say that."

Their eyes met, and a frisson—a definite frisson of attraction—sparked between them.

In unison, they stopped breathing again.

A footman appeared in the doorway, proffering a ball of string. Nicholas glanced at the man and, ruthlessly smothering the unmistakable flare of desire and steadfastly ignoring the more rapid beat of his heart, took the string and proceeded to show the children how to tie the twine in front of the fletching of each arrow. Once all the arrows had strings attached, he stood back and allowed the boys to try their hand at puncturing the balloons.

The older lad managed to nick one enough to have it deflate. It was a minor victory and, it seemed, not one that was going to be repeated.

Nicholas waited patiently until both boys had grown weary of shooting and missing, then asked if he could try his hand and was promptly handed a bow.

He made short work of the remaining four clusters of balloons, much to the children's relief. They glanced at the lady, then gathered up the debris and looked hopefully her way.

She nodded in absolution. "You should tender your heartfelt thanks to Mr....?" She glanced inquiringly at Nicholas.

He met her gaze, then smiled at the children. "Cynster." He held out a hand. "Mr. Nicholas Cynster."

∾

While her siblings eagerly shook Nicholas Cynster's hand and sincerely thanked him for his assistance, Addie seized the moment to rein in her whirling wits, reclaim her senses, and regain her breath, all lost during that charged moment when she'd all but fallen into the distracting man's rich-brown eyes.

And then she had to quell the panic sparked by hearing his name, especially uttered in that deep, dark voice that did very strange things to her insides.

But he was a Cynster, for heaven's sake! Admittedly not one she'd met before, yet even so, she knew the family well enough to know how much of a threat he posed.

"Miss Sommerville?"

She blinked to attention and found him studying her face. The children were scanning the gravel, picking up the last pieces of their wrecked experiment. The trio appeared reconciled to the failure of their grand plan, and she knew she owed their relative equanimity to the way he'd handled the past minutes.

But his question—his guess—confirmed that he wasn't sure who she was...

It was tempting to sound sweet and flighty, to cloak herself in her social persona and shamelessly use it to drive him off, but with the children still there and having spoken as she had to them and him... And she owed him, enough at least to hear why he'd come.

Regretfully setting aside her customary shield, she tipped up her chin and coolly confirmed, "Lady Adriana."

He half bowed. "I'm here to see the earl."

No matter how much in charity with him she ought to feel, that was something she wouldn't allow. Calmly, she responded, "Is my father expecting you?" She knew he wasn't.

Nicholas Cynster frowned slightly. "Given the subject of my inquiry, I didn't feel it necessary to write for an appointment."

No, he wouldn't, not least because he was a Cynster. "And the subject of your inquiry is...?"

"I—my family—have an interest in a horse that I understand is presently gracing your father's stable. The Barbarian."

The children had cleared the gravel and, burdened with the detritus of their experiment, glanced at her. She arched a brow at them, and they dutifully thanked Cynster again and made their farewells, to which he responded in a way that underscored that he was accustomed to dealing with youngsters. When the trio again looked to her, she nodded in dismissal, and they trooped up the steps and into the house, leaving her to deal with their wholly unexpected guest. Merriweather hovered in the doorway, ready to respond to any instruction.

Nicholas Cynster had returned his gaze to her face. "In short," he continued, "assuming The Barbarian is, indeed, a horse your father owns, the Cynster Stable would like to discuss purchasing the stallion."

She searched his expression, wondering... "Why?"

Somewhat to her surprise, he willingly elucidated, explaining his family's wish to add the horse to their stud at Newmarket, which was attached to their famous racing stable that, apparently, he oversaw. He was open and direct and even hinted at how valuable the horse might be.

While she'd enjoyed riding The Barbarian over the months the horse had been at Aisby Grange, given the condition of the estate's accounts, she couldn't overlook such an unexpected source of additional funds, much less dismiss Cynster's offer out of hand.

Yet she'd already seen enough of Nicholas Cynster to know that he was both shrewd and observant—witness the way he'd handled her sometimes difficult siblings. And being a Cynster, he would have all the connections one might expect of a member of that family, which was to say more than enough for him, inadvertently or otherwise, to pose a very real risk to her family's ongoing and exceedingly necessary subterfuge.

All in all, shielding her father from exposure was more important than gaining further funds.

Having reached the end of his explanation, he'd fallen silent, waiting for her response. She forced herself to meet his unrelentingly intent brown gaze and haughtily state, "Regardless, Mr. Cynster, I fear The Barbarian is not for sale."

Of course, he didn't accept that; she hadn't expected he would.

"I can't imagine," he stated, "that such a horse would be easily handled other than by those accustomed to dealing with Thoroughbred stallions."

He was right. The Barbarian was dangerously temperamental, an altogether difficult beast.

"Your stablemen must have their hands full, what with the exercise such a horse requires on a constant basis. You can't have the setup to cope easily with such demands."

As that was true, she said nothing.

His jaw tightening, Cynster continued to press his case, but she was accustomed to dealing with difficult males. She did him the courtesy of hearing him out, then flatly informed him, "Unfortunately, my father isn't of a mind to sell the horse. It was bequeathed to him by a very dear friend."

Nicholas studied Adriana's beautiful blue eyes and accepted those statements were true. Her gaze wasn't guileless—far from it—and her tone and her expression confirmed that, in making such declarations, she felt she stood on absolutely solid ground.

Such grounds could change, but…

He recognized that in Adriana Sommerville, he'd met a lady of adamantine will. She was not going to be swayed, certainly not easily and, very likely, not that day. The set of her lips and chin and the regal way she held her head conveyed that unequivocally.

That meant he was going to have to retreat and come at her—or more precisely, at the earl—from a different angle.

He manufactured a heartfelt sigh. "Very well. As your father is so set on keeping the horse, I can do nothing more than bid you a good day. If, however, he should change his mind, you'll be able to find me at the Angel in Grantham for the next few days."

Her eyes faintly narrowed, but she readily inclined her head. "I'll bear that in mind, but I doubt Papa will have a change of heart."

They exchanged the usual civil phrases in farewell. She knew how to play the social game as well as he; they might be at odds, yet neither of them allowed any of that to show.

Leaving her at the bottom of the steps, he strode to Tamerlane and mounted. Wheeling the big gray, he saluted Lady Adriana, then tapped his heels to Tamerlane's sides and rode quickly down the drive.

Addie watched him go and chided herself for feeling deflated. "What is it with him?" She had no answer. Nevertheless, she allowed herself to enjoy the sight of him riding away until the trees lining the drive cut off the view. It wasn't often that she got the chance to enjoy such a pleasant and, if she was honest, stirring distraction from her daily travails.

Finally, she turned, climbed the steps, and set about soothing Merriweather's still faintly ruffled feathers before commending him and the staff for so swiftly restoring the dignity of the great hall of her ancestors.

~

Nicholas rode through the small village of Aisby and onto the road to Grantham. As one of the horse-mad Cynsters, he was well acquainted with the nearby town, having stayed at its inns numerous times when riding with the local hunts.

While cantering along, he reviewed what little he'd learned and what more he would like to know prior to making another attempt to purchase The Barbarian. He wasn't about to be denied by a pretty face and a pair of periwinkle-blue eyes.

He clattered into the yard of the Angel Inn to find his groom, Young Gillies—so named to distinguish him from Gillies, Nicholas's father's groom and Young Gillies's father—waiting to take Tamerlane's reins.

"Well?" Of less than average height and wiry with it, Young Gillies had a round, open face framed by brown curls. "Did you get the horse?"

His eagerness was understandable; it was Young Gillies who'd brought Nicholas the rumor of The Barbarian's current location, and the groom understood the potential value of such a stallion.

Nicholas grunted and swung down from the saddle. "I've confirmed Aisby has the horse. However, getting him to part with it"—*getting past the dragon at his door*—"is going to take a little more effort."

"Oh?" Young Gillies accepted Tamerlane's reins. "So what's next, then?"

Nicholas paused, then, eyes narrowing, replied, "Before I return to storm Aisby's gates with an offer the earl can't refuse, I believe it would be wise to assure ourselves that The Barbarian is all he's purported to be." Nicholas met Young Gillies's eyes. "In other words, that Pru has it right and we really do want this horse."

CHAPTER 2

*I*t was after nine o'clock the next morning before Nicholas and
Young Gillies located The Barbarian in a strongly fenced
paddock some distance away from the Aisby Grange stable.

They were deep inside the earl's property, but had managed to stick to
the local right of ways that passed between the estate's fields, so they
weren't actually trespassing. They'd been noticed by several groups of
workers, but when, with understated assurance, Nicholas had raised a
hand in salute, the workers had merely waved back and resumed their
toil.

From two fields away, Nicholas had spotted the huge bay stallion
racing about his enclosure. Wise in the ways of stallions, he and Young
Gillies had left their geldings tied to a tree a field away before walking to
the corner of the stallion's paddock, where they could stand at the chest-
high hedge and study the beast.

Staring at the massive bay, Young Gillies breathed, "Cor! Will you
just look at him!"

Nicholas didn't take his eyes from the stallion, who had seen them
and was putting on a display. Sleek muscles bunched and flowed beneath
a glossy bay coat, then the horse pushed off with its powerful hindquar-
ters and raced around the field, his dark mane and tail streaming. "He's a
great deal more impressive than his registration details suggested."

Before he'd left Newmarket, Nicholas had paid a visit to his mother's
cousin, Dillon Caxton, currently the Keeper of the Breeding Register and

the Stud Book, the official tomes of the Jockey Club that effectively ruled the breeding and racing of Thoroughbred horses in England. From those registers, Nicholas had gleaned a technical description of The Barbarian and learned of his background, as far as it was known.

Young Gillies glanced at him. "You said his last registration was some time back."

Nicholas nodded. "More than five years ago. Then The Barbarian disappeared from the register. The theory is that he was sold, then sold again before being reregistered, and the new owner wasn't interested enough to notify the Jockey Club and renew the registration."

Young Gillies's eyes had returned to the prime horseflesh currently kicking up his heels before them. "So how old is he then? Eight?"

"He's turned nine years old."

"Perfect for breeding, then."

"Indeed." Nicholas drank in the horse's lines. "The description for a renewed registration will need to be significantly updated."

They continued to study the horse, which finally grew bored with them and settled to crop grass.

Young Gillies sighed. "He really is a magnificent beast. Your sister was right. We definitely want him."

Nicholas nodded. "We do." Having seen the horse, he no longer harbored the slightest doubt. "Now, I just have to work out the right offer to tempt the earl."

He was already calculating. He had to wonder what it would take to get past the dragon guarding the earl's door.

"Hsst!" Young Gillies ducked and tugged at Nicholas's sleeve. "Someone's coming."

Nicholas ducked, too. Crouching beside Young Gillies, he peered through the hedge.

On the other side of the paddock—the side closer to the house and stable—a groom carrying a side-saddle and leading an already saddled hack swung open a gate and held it for a slender female figure.

Garbed in a teal riding habit with her face shaded by the brim of a fashionable shako, the lady waited for the groom to shut the gate and tie his horse to the rail, then she led him down the paddock toward the stallion. In her gloved hand, she carried a quirt and a bridle and bit.

The Barbarian raised his huge head and watched the pair approach.

Nicholas expected some dramatics, but surprisingly, the horse took a step forward to eagerly greet the lady, who, now she was closer, Nicholas confirmed was Lady Adriana Sommerville.

She smiled, raised a hand, ran her palm down the horse's long nose, and crooned something that the big horse clearly considered his due while she expertly fitted the bridle to his big head. The massive beast shook out his mane, but otherwise stood calmly, allowing the groom to place the side-saddle on his back and secure the strap.

When the groom nodded his satisfaction and stepped back, Lady Adriana led the horse to a stile farther along the hedge behind which Nicholas and Young Gillies were hiding.

Having noticed a gate in the hedge beyond the stile, even farther from their position, and guessing that Lady Adriana would use that exit to leave the paddock and ride out across her father's fields, Nicholas tweaked Young Gillies's sleeve. When the groom glanced his way, Nicholas tipped his head along the right of way, then, still crouching so as not to be seen, led the way back to their mounts.

Halfway there, an overhanging tree and a bend in the track hid them from those in the stallion's paddock. Nicholas straightened and strode quickly for his horse.

∾

As Lady Adriana had waited for her groom to return to his horse and mount before leading the way out of the paddock, Nicholas and Young Gillies soon had the pair in their sights.

At first, Nicholas had wondered at the wisdom of a female—a not-terribly-strong-looking female at that—riding such a powerful horse, but then images of his mother and of Pru rose in his mind, and he could all but hear them telling him not to be stupid.

An excellent rider could manage any well-broken horse.

That certainly seemed to be the case with Lady Adriana and The Barbarian. They flowed over the sward in an effortless canter, the big horse's stride relaxed and graceful. The teal-clad figure on his back moved smoothly with each stride, her long rippling train a bright splash of color against the horse's gleaming hide.

Her groom increasingly lagged behind.

Nicholas caught Young Gillies's eye, nodded toward the other groom, then tapped his heels to Tamerlane's sides. The big gray responded with a surge of speed that carried Nicholas past the startled groom, who was immediately distracted by Young Gillies coming up on his other side.

A few more paces and Nicholas saw Lady Adriana, still some way ahead, tap The Barbarian's shoulder with her quirt. Obediently, the stallion lengthened his stride and shifted into a ground-eating gallop. Whether she'd realized Nicholas was approaching, he couldn't have said, but he and Tamerlane were more than up to the challenge.

Twenty yards farther on, they drew level, and he held Tamerlane parallel to The Barbarian, keeping the gelding a respectful three yards from the huge stallion.

The Barbarian rolled a baleful eye at Tamerlane and snorted a tentative challenge, to which Tamerlane, too accustomed to the vagaries of stallions to rise to such bait, snorted in mildly contemptuous reply.

That seemed to satisfy The Barbarian, at least enough for the massive beast to continue his steady gallop.

Indeed, the horses fell into stride, and the thud of their hooves merged into one steady drumbeat.

Nicholas risked a swift glance at the horse and rider alongside. He could read nothing in Lady Adriana's expression, shadowed as it was by the brim of her hat, and lowered his gaze to the horse; as they thundered on, he endeavored to confine his interest to the stallion's points rather than ogle hers.

That said, it was obvious that she was an accomplished rider; her lack of concern despite their pace was telling.

Eventually, they reached the end of the long glade they'd been following, and she slowed The Barbarian to a walk and twisted in the saddle to look back.

Nicholas knew she would see her groom, now some distance behind them, engaged in a comradely exchange with Young Gillies, yet the pair would still be following in Adriana and Nicholas's wake.

After considering the sight for several seconds, with the horses continuing to walk on, she shifted her attention to him.

Nicholas felt her gaze, but continued to keep his trained on The Barbarian, ostensibly noting the ease with which the horse moved at the slower pace, yet he was so aware of her, he knew when she narrowed her eyes on him.

"You haven't gone away."

None-too-subtle accusation colored her tone.

"No." He nodded at the stallion. "I wanted to see him before I decided whether he was worth the effort of persuading you to take my offer to your father."

Her brows rose. "So you trespassed?"

He raised his gaze to her face. "Right of way."

Predictably, she humphed.

He smothered a grin and added, "At least until you started to gallop, and if that wasn't an invitation to join you, I stand corrected."

To that, she reacted not at all, which led him to suspect she had, indeed, known he was following before she set off on her gallop.

Interesting. Who has been testing whom?

After a moment, she asked, "What was your verdict?" She raised her gaze to his face and drily added, "Regarding the horse."

Hiding his amusement was growing harder by the minute; she seemed to unerringly strike some heretofore unsuspected chord of camaraderie within him. Shifting his gaze forward, he replied, "I've concluded that the Cynster Stable should, indeed, pursue the purchase of The Barbarian." He met her gaze. "Which means I'll need to negotiate with your father, given he's the horse's owner."

Her eyes slowly narrowed.

Seeking to distract her from whatever resistance she was assembling, he added, "Indeed, I'm surprised the earl isn't the one riding him."

Addie accepted what was patently a diversion; anything to gain a little more time to think—to drag her mind from the undeniable thrill of pounding along in tandem with him. "As it happens, I'm the only person, male or female, the devil will allow on his back."

"Really?" His gaze returned to The Barbarian. "That suggests he wasn't well trained."

"Perhaps you should rethink your offer."

He threw her an amused look. "We want him for breeding, not for riding."

And that was enough of that. Addie couldn't believe how much trouble she was having reining in her senses, let alone her thoughts. Then again, Nicholas Cynster was the only gentleman she'd ever met who had subsequently appeared in her dreams.

She didn't want to think what that might mean.

Concentrate!

Given his persistence, she had to weigh the risks of attempting to deny him—and him refusing to accept her dismissal and somehow forcing his way in to see her father—against her remaining in control and managing any interaction.

No choice. Not really.

She heaved a suitably dramatic sigh, then shook The Barbarian's reins and set the big horse trotting.

Naturally, Nicholas Cynster kept his powerful gray alongside.

She dipped her head his way. "As it seems you're so determined, perhaps you might give me an outline of your offer."

He proceeded to do so. While she might have zero experience in the selling of horses, she'd overseen the estate accounts for long enough to have some idea of the sums her father and her older brother Dickie paid for their mounts. And while Nicholas deferred stating any actual figure as his price, indicating that was a point for negotiation, he did make it plain that he was willing to offer, at the very least, the going rate for a Thoroughbred stallion.

Addie hoped her father or Dickie would know what that amount was. Dickie was due home any day; she suspected he would be her most reliable source of information.

Nicholas painted his offer in the best possible light, but was careful to leave himself room to negotiate. "One point I'm not yet clear on is how your father came to own The Barbarian. You mentioned a bequest." A thought occurred, and he met her gaze. "I assume your father has the horse's papers? His bloodlines?"

She blinked, then to his relief, nodded. "I've seen them. I did wonder why a horse had such formal and important-looking documents. Like a birth certificate."

"Trust me, the horse's value lies in those papers. That's why they're so important." He looked at The Barbarian. "Without them, he's just a good-looking horse."

"I see."

She'd led them on a circuitous route that would, eventually, return them to The Barbarian's paddock; Nicholas could see the gate some way ahead.

"To answer your question," she went on, "my father was left the horse by a longtime friend, the late Viscount Wisthorpe. He often came to stay during hunting season and would ride out with Papa. Papa had admired The Barbarian when last he'd visited Wisthorpe, so it wasn't a huge surprise that the late viscount left the horse to him."

"Wisthorpe." Nicholas frowned. "Where exactly is the viscount's seat?"

"In Yorkshire." Her lips quirked. "Not exactly horse-racing or hunting country, not compared to Newmarket or Lincolnshire or Leicestershire, but..." She shrugged. "The late Viscount Wisthorpe appreciated good horseflesh."

"Apparently. I don't suppose you know from where he got the horse?"

Addie shook her head. "I don't believe I ever heard." *My father might know.* She bit the words back. The last thing she needed was for Nicholas to test her father's memory. Then again, these days, her father's recollection of times long gone seemed much more certain than those of five minutes past.

Nicholas's question served only to underscore that she needed to remain in control of any interaction between him and her father, and the only certain way to do that... "I'll take your offer to Papa." She glanced sidelong at Nicholas. "I promise I'll relate all you've said regarding your offer exactly as you've put it to me."

He inclined his head. "Thank you."

"I'll send a message to the Angel—"

"It's barely midmorning." He glanced at the sky. "Why don't you put my offer to your father over the next several hours, and I'll call again this afternoon." He returned his gaze to her face. "Shall we say after two o'clock?"

She searched his brown eyes and saw nothing but granitelike determination.

Then his expression eased, and he faced forward. "How are your brothers and sister today? Have they recovered from their disappointment over the failure of their barrage balloons?"

"The children are fully recovered," she coolly replied. Apparently, he wasn't above using the fact that he'd helped avert disaster to pressure her. Regardless, arguing with him might not be wise. There was really no reason she couldn't give him her father's response in person.

No reason other than my leaping nerves and swooning senses.

Luckily, being forced to deal with him had largely distracted her from those less-than-welcome effects of his presence.

"Very well," she conceded. "Let's say two-thirty. That will give me time enough to discuss the matter in detail with Papa."

They'd reached the open gate to the paddock, and they both drew rein.

She glanced at him and saw he was smiling. Genuinely, spontaneously smiling. She fought not to blink, not to show any reaction to the quite devastating transformation.

"Excellent!" He turned his smile on her, and she stopped breathing. "Two-thirty, then." His gaze roved her face, and his expression softened. He inclined his head to her. "Until then, Lady Adriana."

With that, he shook his reins, and his horse trotted on down the track.

Addie sat and watched him ride away. Again. But given that once the matter of the sale of The Barbarian was concluded one way or the other, she was unlikely to see Nicholas Cynster again, where was the harm?

His groom had parted from hers and followed his master.

Once they'd both disappeared along the old right of way, Addie stifled a sigh and steered The Barbarian through the gate and into his paddock.

The next several minutes went in dismounting and waiting for her groom, Rory, to unsaddle the big horse, then with Rory carrying her saddle and leading his own mount, they set off toward the stable.

"What were you and Mr. Cynster's groom talking about?" she asked.

Rory shrugged, but his expression showed a degree of excitement. "This and that. He—Young Gillies is his name—works with Mr. Cynster at the Cynster Stable."

The place was named with awe and reverence.

Her lips twitched. "So I'd supposed."

Tall, lanky, and several years older than she, Rory had been her groom since she'd emerged from the schoolroom, but while they'd grown easy in each other's company, neither were the chatty sort. Consequently, the walk to the stable and the house beyond gave her time to review Nicholas Cynster's offer and how she should handle placing that before her poor father as well as considering the rather unsettling effect Nicholas had on her.

She'd hoped his impact would have faded—that yesterday had been an aberration, possibly occasioned by not having encountered any gentleman quite like him before—but no. If anything, the leaping of her nerves and the tendency of her senses to swoon and her wits to focus far too intently on him had only grown worse.

It must be because I couldn't put on my usual mask with him. I'm not accustomed to having gentlemen react to me as me rather than as my alter ego.

Sadly, she didn't have the option of donning that mask now, not after he'd seen her without it, not once but twice.

With Rory half a step behind her, she strode along the path and considered how she felt about not being able to retreat behind her customary persona and reluctantly admitted that it was, in fact, refreshing to deal openly with a gentleman, to behave normally rather than have to craft and monitor her every gesture and word to support her façade.

That had always been wearying and had only grown more so with the years.

Still, once she gave him her father's answer, she wouldn't see Nicholas Cynster again.

That thought led to her weighing up his offer. As far as she could judge, it fell on the better side of fair.

Although occasionally she complained about having to be the one to exercise the stallion, she would miss having The Barbarian to ride. Galloping on his broad back, with all that power beneath her—at her beck and call, so to speak—had grown to be something of a quiet thrill.

Hauling her mind from such thoughts, she focused on the best way to lay Nicholas's offer before her father and whether she should encourage him to accept or decline.

She was counting on Nicholas accepting either outcome. If her father agreed and parted with the horse, Nicholas would ride off with The Barbarian, and most likely, that would be the last she would see of man or beast. Alternatively, if her father refused the offer, despite Nicholas's demonstrated doggedness, she doubted he was the sort to push the matter further. He might suggest that the offer remain on the table, but otherwise, he would leave them alone.

Either way—acceptance or refusal—he would be gone.

And given the way she'd been reacting to him, that was an outcome she would be wise to welcome.

Stifling a sigh, she reached the stable yard. With a nod, she parted from Rory and continued toward the house.

As she neared the side door, she frowned and gave herself a mental shake. Really, she had to stop mooning over Nicholas Cynster! It was a *good thing* that she wouldn't see him beyond that afternoon. Such wishy-washy fiddle-faddling was not at all like her.

With a huff of impatience, she opened the door and stalked into the house, determined to find her father and, without further ado, lay the matter of Nicholas Cynster's offer for The Barbarian before him.

~

After changing out of her riding habit into a practical yet flattering day dress of turquoise cambric—one that bolstered her confidence—Addie went downstairs for her daily meeting with Merriweather and Mrs. Merriweather, who filled the role of housekeeper. In more normal times, her mother would have managed the household, but Addie had stepped in so that her mother could devote herself to the necessary task of keeping her father company.

Once the menus had been agreed and Addie had given permission for Merriweather to replenish the cellar, she climbed the stairs again and headed down the family wing to her father's private sitting room. As she neared the door and all but unconsciously steeled herself to deal with whatever she might find, she reflected that, despite the challenges, thus far the family, supported by the entire staff, indoors and out, had succeeded in keeping her father's condition a complete and absolute secret.

Everyone understood what was at stake.

On reaching the door at the end of the corridor, she gripped the knob, drew in a breath, then opened the door and, fixing a brilliant smile on her face, breezed inside with a cheery "Good morning!"

As they often were, her parents were sitting in twin armchairs before the window at the end of the room. Both looked her way and smiled in welcome.

"Addie, my dear." Her father held out a hand.

Smiling, she went forward and, clasping his hand firmly, bent and kissed his cheek. "Good morning, Papa." Still smiling, she glanced at her mother. "Mama."

What she saw in her mother's eyes confirmed her conclusion, based on her father's voice and clear gaze, that today was one of his "good days." Those were the days when his wits were engaged and his thought processes remained lucid and rational.

Relieved herself—if she was going to discuss Nicholas's offer, she needed her father in a capable state—she pulled up an ottoman and sat between them.

These days, her mother rarely left her father's side. Either she or her father's valet, Oswald, were always in attendance. Ever since the afternoon four months ago when the earl had disappeared and had only been located hours later after an estate-wide hunt, they quite simply didn't let him out of someone's sight. On that occasion, he'd been found wandering the meadows south of the lake, with no memory of how he'd got there or why he'd set out in the first place.

His confusion had been disturbing and not just for him. As, physically, he remained remarkably hale and strong, the sudden and unexpected bout of mental frailty had shaken everyone.

Sadly, there'd been other incidents since, destroying any hope that the first had been just a single, inexplicable interlude. So now they watched, waited, and hoped and made the most of days like today.

Banishing all negative thoughts, Addie ventured, "I took The Barbarian out this morning."

Her father glanced at the pleasant summer day beyond the window. "A fine day for a gallop. How's the horse doing?"

"Still a handful, but it appears that the news we have him here has spread."

"Is that why Mr. Cynster called yesterday?" her mother inquired.

Addie blinked.

Her father smiled. "The youngsters told us about his visit just now, when they came to ask permission to go out on the lake."

"Ah… Yes. He was quite helpful yesterday in managing one of the children's experiments that had gone awry." She met her father's eyes and smiled. "Balloon-assisted flour bombs. They got stuck among the rafters of the porte-cochere."

Her father grinned. "I see."

"But," Addie rolled on, "more to my point, Mr. Cynster joined me this morning while I was out riding The Barbarian. He was interested in viewing the horse in action, and long story short, he—on behalf of his family's business—wishes to make an offer to buy the horse."

"Is that so?" Her father's gaze sharpened.

"The children seemed quite taken with Mr. Cynster," her mother put in.

Addie wryly replied, "I suspect they were more taken with his horse and, perhaps, his ability to shoot down their balloons."

"The imps said the gentleman was Mr. Nicholas Cynster." Her father frowned. "Is that correct? Not Tobias?"

"No," Addie said. "It was Nicholas. If I have the family tree straight, he's Toby's older brother."

"Yes, that's right." Her mother glanced at the earl, presumably to see if he was following the connections.

"So," her father obligingly reiterated, "Mr. Nicholas Cynster spoke with you this morning about buying The Barbarian. Did he impart any details as to what arrangement he has in mind?"

Addie drew breath and launched into a concise description of the elements of Nicholas's offer. "He was willing to include a to-be-negotiated number of offspring, which, from what I gathered, might be quite valuable in themselves. In addition, of course, to the purchase price, but as to that, he would only say that he would at least match the market rate for such a horse."

The earl nodded sagely. "He'll want the final price to be part of our negotiations."

"So I understood." Briefly, Addie met her mother's eyes, then refocused on her father. "Consequently, my question to you is do you wish to sell The Barbarian, or should I politely decline Cynster's offer?"

The earl glanced at her mother, then looked back at Addie. "Well, my dear, the truth is that I've never felt that The Barbarian is actually my horse. He was always Henry's horse, and even though Henry bequeathed the beast to me, I haven't had a chance to ride him more than once, and what with one thing and another, I can't see me taking up riding to hounds again."

He smiled rather wistfully at Addie. "All of that is to say that I have no attachment to the animal, and I suppose he's been eating his head off in the stable these past months. And you've had to be the one to give up time to exercise him, which is just another duty laid on your plate. As it now seems the horse might be valuable and Cynster is apparently prepared to pay well for him, then…" Her father held up his hands. "Perhaps we should consider his offer seriously, as it seems that, for us, The Barbarian is costing us more than he's worth. In terms of the family and the estate, that horse's scales are definitely not balanced."

Addie nodded. "That's an excellent way to put it." She was relieved to find her father able to think so clearly.

"There's also the consideration," her father continued, "that if we sell The Barbarian to the Cynster Stables, we can be certain the horse will be valued for what he is and well looked after. In terms of honoring Henry's memory and his trust in bequeathing the horse to me, that will be quite comforting."

Struck by that insight, Addie nodded again. "So really, we'll be doing right by the horse, Henry, and ourselves by entertaining and accepting Cynster's offer."

"It certainly seems that way," her mother agreed.

"Very well." Addie placed her palms on her knees and swiftly scanned her father's face. Would he want to meet Cynster himself? It would be better for the family if they could avoid that. "If you're willing, I'll meet with Cynster and negotiate the best price—the best deal all around."

To her relief, her father sank back in his chair. He glanced at her mother and waved vaguely at Addie. "Please, my dear. I really don't feel up to discussing details. I would be grateful if you would handle it. I've been distant from the world of horses for so long that I really have no idea what the beast might be worth, and your wits are sharper than mine in such matters."

"Thank you for your confidence, Papa." Addie pushed to her feet. "Oh—Cynster mentioned papers. Documents about the horse."

Her father nodded. "Yes, indeed. Being a Thoroughbred, The Barbarian came with a full set of bloodlines and such. The papers—all of them—should be in the safe in the study."

"Yes, I've seen them there." Addie hesitated, then added, "Cynster is staying at the Angel in Grantham. He said he would return after luncheon to hear your thoughts on his offer."

Her father waved her off. "I'll leave the matter in your capable hands, my dear."

"In that case…" With a last smile for her parents, Addie turned for the door. "I'll see you at luncheon in a little while. I want to spend some time looking into the going rate for top-class horseflesh."

As she closed the door behind her, she reviewed the past half hour and was relieved at how well it had gone. With the path before her clear, she headed for the study.

Once there, the first thing she did was to open the safe and extract the papers pertaining to The Barbarian. She discovered several sale notes pinned together and what looked like a detailed pedigree bearing the stamp of the Jockey Club. After rifling through all the other loose papers and confirming she had retrieved everything relevant to the horse, she stacked The Barbarian's papers neatly to one side of the blotter, closed the safe, then went to the shelf on which the estate ledgers for the past several years were housed. She selected several, carried them to the desk, and settled in the chair to peruse them.

Both her father and Dickie had bought prime hunters within the past five years. The prices they'd paid gave her a place to start in estimating The Barbarian's potential value.

"Given the Cynsters want him for breeding, presumably, he'll be worth considerably more."

Eventually, she settled on a base price of two and a half times what the estate had paid for Dickie's new hunter. She studied the figure she'd jotted on a scrap of paper, then softly snorted. "If Cynster will pay that or more..."

Such a sum would greatly assist in keeping the estate on an even keel financially. There were always repairs, some of which were inevitably unexpected, on top of the routine household expenses, the boys' school fees, and Dickie's expenses, even though, as young gentlemen born to noble families went, her brother was no profligate. He didn't gamble, which was a huge relief, being more interested in horses and hunting than anything else. Indeed, although Dickie was still in what she thought of as the typical hedonistic phase through which young gentlemen of the ton invariably passed, underneath, he was a sensible man, and in her heart, Addie knew she could rely on him to stand with her through any disaster.

Unfortunately for them all, Dickie wasn't her father's heir.

That honor fell to Phillip Sommerville, her father's eldest son and his only child by his first marriage. Her father's first countess had died when Phillip was a child, and Phillip had never reconciled himself to his father's second marriage. In actuality, Phillip's relationship with the earl had grown only more strained with the years, in tandem with the expansion of the earl's second family and their relatively happy family life.

Phillip had grown nastier and meaner, falling out with his father, ignoring the current countess entirely, and cutting his half siblings dead.

The staff hadn't fared much better, and gradually, the estate as a whole had washed its hands of Phillip, as he had with it.

"Estranged" didn't come close to describing the gulf that now existed between the earl and his current family and his heir.

After a moment of dwelling darkly on what couldn't be fixed, at least not by her, Addie shook aside all thoughts of Phillip and focused, instead, on the matter before her.

All in all, she'd definitely warmed to the idea of selling The Barbarian to the Cynsters. Concluding the sale was shaping in her mind as a pleasant prospect; all that was required to achieve that reality was for her to meet with Nicholas Cynster and agree on a price.

She tried to imagine how subsequent events would play out. No doubt, once they'd agreed on the deal, he would leave and, subsequently, send a bank draft with a groom, who, after handing over the draft, would take possession of the horse.

After their meeting this afternoon, she would, very likely, not see Nicholas Cynster again.

Her reaction to that scenario was unsettling. Some part of her wanted and demanded that she engineer more time with him, which was ridiculous given she'd only met him less than twenty-four hours ago.

Regardless, instead of feeling relieved that their interaction would be so limited, some heretofore unsuspected part of her was wishing she had time to explore...

Explore what?

Exasperated, she shook her head. She was becoming nonsensical. Foolish even, and she really had no time to waste on such mental maundering. She had more than enough on her plate, what with steering her family and the estate through the unfolding drama occasioned by her father's encroaching illness.

If only her half brother wasn't such a threat.

Phillip—or more specifically, Phillip learning of her father's developing infirmity—was what they had to guard against. That meant they couldn't afford her father's condition to become widely known, sufficiently widely known that it reached Phillip's ears.

To that point, they'd managed, but...

A chill touched Addie's nape.

Nicholas Cynster and Phillip were, she judged, of similar age. Were they acquainted?

As far as she knew, Phillip had never shown any huge interest in horses. In contrast, horses seemed to be the center of Nicholas's life.

In the distance, the gong for luncheon bonged. Addie pushed back from the desk. "Pray God, Phillip and Nicholas aren't friends."

If they were...

Her lips setting, Addie rose and headed for the door. "Just as well Papa has left the sale of The Barbarian in my hands."

CHAPTER 3

*A*ddie was waiting in the front hall, standing before the large, ornately carved, and presently empty fireplace when Nicholas Cynster arrived. She'd spent the hour since luncheon reviewing her approach to the upcoming negotiations and rehearsing safe replies to any queries regarding her father.

Today was as fine as the previous day, and the front door was propped wide, allowing her to watch as, having handed his horse's reins to a groom, Nicholas swiftly climbed the front steps and strode into the house.

She'd been waiting to assess her response to him, having almost convinced herself that her previous reactions had been primarily due to surprise and would not occur again, but when, after exchanging a nod with Merriweather, Nicholas crossed the tiles toward her, such naive hopes were dashed.

The instant she'd set eyes on him, her senses had leapt; as his gaze settled on her, they almost seemed to salivate. As for her nerves, they tensed and tightened in a most peculiar way, as if she—they—were waiting, anticipating...

Such anticipatory tension, so intense and focused, had never afflicted her before. Fueled by a giddy-making blend of curiosity, expectation, and undefined, unacknowledged hope, the resulting sensations twined into a rope and cinched about her lungs, leaving her faintly, irritatingly breathless.

Through all her years of waltzing through the ton, no other man had affected her like that. Then again, she'd never met Nicholas Cynster in the ballrooms.

Not even his brother, Toby, whom she had met several times, had so much as caused her to blink.

Regardless...

As Nicholas drew near, she tipped up her chin and met his gaze. "Good afternoon, Mr. Cynster. You'll be pleased to know that my father has agreed to part with The Barbarian, provided, of course, that we can agree on a price."

His lips lightly curved, and he studied her for several seconds before saying, "Am I to take it that you will be acting for the earl in negotiating our agreement?"

"Indeed. My father is currently engaged with other matters and has delegated arranging the sale of The Barbarian to me."

"I see." He paused, then went on, "In that case, the broader details of my offer remain as I outlined them this morning. Regarding the issue of offspring, I believe three offspring, one from each of the first three years of The Barbarian standing at our stud, would be appropriate. Either colts or fillies, to be selected by the earl from the offspring remaining after the Cynster Stable requirements are met." He held her gaze. "Is such an arrangement satisfactory to you?"

She'd questioned her father over the luncheon table, and he'd stated he would be happy with one offspring. Three... She nodded. "That's acceptable."

He inclined his head. "That leaves only the purchase price itself to be decided. As to that..." He glanced toward the open doorway, then returned his gaze to her. "I would like to examine the horse more closely before finalizing my offer."

Her father had warned her to expect such a request. Smoothly, she gestured to the door. "Of course. Shall we?"

She stepped out, and he fell in beside her, adjusting his long strides to her shorter paces.

"Is the horse in the same paddock?"

"Yes. As you can imagine, he doesn't always behave well in the stable."

Nicholas smothered a snort. Given what he'd already seen of The Barbarian's temperament, that assessment was a gross understatement.

They left the house through the front door and walked along the front façade in the direction of the stable.

As they rounded the corner of the house, he slanted a sidelong glance at Adriana. The turquoise gown became her, sheathing her sleek figure from neck to waist before the full skirts cascaded over her shapely hips. The skirts swung as she walked, her stride free and easy and inherently graceful. She possessed a regal posture, queenly and confident. Despite this being the third time he'd been in her company, his awareness had, once again, flared and focused intently on her.

For some strange reason, she'd captured his attention and awoken his desire with an ease, a facility, he hadn't before encountered.

That fact alone made him even more intent, more curious, and more determined to learn a great deal more about her. Instinct crawled just beneath his skin, and it wasn't something he could readily ignore. In the circumstances, the best he could do was hold himself back from acting on it, and at that moment, he was hanging onto those reins for all he was worth.

Because finally, he'd realized who Lady Adriana Sommerville was.

He'd been slow to make the connection, not least because, on the face of it, the identification hadn't seemed plausible. He was no Louisa, with all information on the ton at his fingertips, but finally, he'd followed all the dots and found himself facing the utterly bizarre not to say incomprehensible conclusion that Adriana was, indeed, the female known throughout the ton as Miss Flibbertigibbet.

Miss Flibbertigibbet was universally acknowledged as the most flighty, frippery, and foolish female currently gracing ton ballrooms. She was patently silly, her conversation inconsequential, her observations vacuous in the extreme.

In fact, now he thought of it, Miss Flibbertigibbet's personality and behavior matched—exactly—what one would expect of a female of Adriana's physical appearance.

Yet the Adriana he'd met at Aisby Grange was nothing like Miss Flibbertigibbet. The lady pacing beside him at that very moment was coolly intelligent, collected and focused, able, determined, sensible, capable, and with a will that was as pliable as granite.

There was strength in her, that sort of feminine strength with which he was exceedingly familiar, given it was a characteristic of virtually all the females in his family.

So now, to his already heightened focus on her he could add a burgeoning, driving, intensely compelling curiosity as to why she seemed to have two such contradictory sides to her.

As the house fell behind and they walked on across the open fields toward the paddock where The Barbarian was housed, he glanced her way again.

Her attention was fixed ahead, and she seemed wholly focused on the matter at hand.

He shifted his gaze forward and told himself he needed to take a leaf from her script. He'd come there to buy The Barbarian. Once he'd accomplished that...

That would be the time to pursue learning more about Lady Adriana Sommerville.

∾

In the earl's sitting room, the earl and countess stood before the window that looked out over the gardens to the distant fields and watched their older daughter walking beside Nicholas Cynster.

"Well, my dear." The earl gently squeezed the countess's hand where it rested on his sleeve. "That was easier than we'd expected. I have to say that old Wisthorpe leaving me that horse was a bit of luck in more ways than one."

The countess's gaze remained on the pair steadily crossing the fields. "Indeed," she murmured. "Without The Barbarian, I don't know how we might have managed this." She cast her spouse a warm glance. "It was an inspired idea to spread that rumor so it reached Cynster's man in particular."

"Hmm. Took a bit of doing that, but"—the earl nodded at the distant couple—"with luck, it'll be well worth the effort." After a moment, he added, "Our venture's certainly borne fruit, old thing, but I have to say I was rather surprised it was the older brother who turned up. We were expecting the younger one, weren't we?"

"Indeed, but"—the countess studied the faraway pair—"I'm not sure the substitute won't prove a better fit for our purpose."

The distant couple rounded a hedge and vanished from sight, and the countess sighed and turned from the window. "Now, we'll have to wait and see what more, if anything, comes of this." She moved to claim her customary seat. "I do think they will suit."

"We can but hope." The earl walked to his armchair and sank into its comfort. After a moment, he admitted, "I'll feel very much more comfortable once Addie is married to a gentleman who values and deserves her."

"You and me both, my dear." The countess leaned across and patted his hand. "You and me both."

The earl sighed. "I do so want to walk down the aisle and give away at least one of my daughters."

The countess's gentle smile was crooked as she squeezed his hand. "And if Fate is kind and smiles on our endeavors, you will, my dear. You will."

Covertly, Nicholas continued to study the lady pacing beside him. He remained confounded by the contradiction between her reputation and the reality, for he had no doubt that the real Adriana was the lady with him now. The lady who, possibly unintentionally, he'd been allowed to meet courtesy of the odd circumstances of their first encounter.

Obviously, her beauty and the full sum of her appearance remained the same in both incarnations, and he could see that her outward appearance might lead people to assume…

But that didn't explain why she'd encouraged people—indeed, the entire ton—to so thoroughly misjudge her character, as she must have done.

In the end, he couldn't resist asking, "What happened to Miss Flibbertigibbet?"

The narrow-eyed look she shot him left him steeling himself to weather a stern set down—that or outright denial or deflection—but instead, after a moment of staring straight ahead, she evenly replied, "For the most part, Miss Flibbertigibbet remains in London."

He considered that answer; it only made him even more curious.

Addie had determined that, given she was unlikely to see Nicholas Cynster after today, her best way forward was to keep him at a distance. She certainly didn't want to engage in a discussion of the whys and wherefores of her alter ego, and she now had confirmation that he had heard of Miss Flibbertigibbet and knew that lady was her.

Hoping to avoid any further exchange on that subject, she lengthened her stride.

The Barbarian's paddock lay just ahead. She reached the gate, opened it, and walked into the grassy field. Searching all around for the large bay horse, she strode toward the middle of the rectangular enclosure.

No glossy brown hide met her eyes.

Halting and putting her hands on her hips, she methodically scanned the field, slowly turning in a circle to take in every corner.

Confusion welled. She frowned. There were a few trees, but unless the horse had tucked himself behind them and even then...

She whistled. The stallion always came when she whistled.

But no welcoming whinny or drum of hooves eventuated.

Slowly, she turned, scanning again as Nicholas Cynster came to stand beside her. "Where is he?" She looked up and met Nicholas's brown eyes.

His jaw was tight, his expression impassive. "Let's quarter the field in case he's down."

The grass was long enough that it was just possible the horse might lie concealed...

She didn't ask why the horse would be lying down, but promptly set off for one corner, while Nicholas strode in the opposite direction.

It didn't take long to confirm that the horse wasn't in the paddock.

They met again at the upper gate.

That Adriana's mystification was genuine was writ large in her face. "Perhaps," Nicholas suggested, sensing her rising panic, "your stablemen took the horse in. They might have heard you were arranging to sell him and thought to be helpful."

Her features eased, but her frown remained. "I didn't order it, and nor did Papa, but it's possible Merriweather—our butler—assumed from our conversation over the luncheon table that the horse ought to be brought up." Her chin firmed, and she nodded. "That must be it."

They left the paddock and strode quickly back to the stable.

Neither spoke, but both scanned the fields as they went.

They reached the stable without sighting the horse.

Alerted by their heels ringing on the cobbles, the head stableman came out.

Adriana pounced, demanding to know if The Barbarian had been brought up to the yard.

It was instantly apparent that the head stableman knew no more than they. He called his men together, and questions flew, but not one of them had seen the horse since that morning, when Adriana and her groom had left the stallion cropping grass in his paddock.

When, plainly worried, Adriana turned to Nicholas, he met her gaze. "The horse couldn't have got out of that paddock unaided." He'd seen and approved of the latches on the gates. "He hasn't wandered off by himself."

She blinked, then resolution filled her eyes. "You're right." She swung to face the stablemen. "Someone has stolen The Barbarian. We need to mount a search."

When she glanced at him, Nicholas nodded encouragingly. "He's big and difficult to miss. Someone will have seen him, but you'll need to act quickly."

She drew breath and started issuing orders, which the men, Nicholas noted, were ready and willing to instantly obey. He supported her tack of covering all the estate's fields first. The estate's workers were most likely to have noted the big horse if they'd spotted him, and the paddock from which he'd been taken was more or less central within the large estate.

He shifted closer and, for her ears alone, murmured, "You need to cover all the compass points. Don't make any assumptions as to which way they might have gone. And you should put as many men as you can muster out there now. Once you have a sighting, you can narrow the search, but to begin with, cast your net wide."

She flung him a swift glance, then did as he'd suggested, sending a stable lad running to the house to summon every possible spare male and another to fetch the gardeners.

Nicholas didn't know the area well enough to help craft the search, but it was obvious that Adriana did and equally obvious that every man there was entirely amenable to following her dictates.

There was respect as well as a degree of protective loyalty in the faces turned her way.

Finally, with the men dispersing in every direction, she turned and, collecting him with a glance, strode briskly toward the house.

She looked at him as he fell in beside her. "I'm sorry."

He met her eyes. "Not your fault."

She faced forward and flung up her hands. "I can't believe that just as we're about to conclude the sale, someone steals the horse!"

He'd already considered that. "One other possibility did occur to me." He caught her gaze as she glanced at him. "Could the horse have been taken for a lark? Misguided, admittedly, but is it possible that your brothers and sister heard about the sale and thought to give you a shock?"

She halted at the bottom of the front steps and stared at him. "They heard me questioning Papa over the luncheon table. I asked about the papers and discussed various points regarding the sale." She frowned. "That said, I doubt they would have risked getting that close to The

Barbarian, but one can never tell with that horse. He might have gone along with it quite happily." Her chin firmed. "We should check."

He followed her up the steps. In the front hall, they came upon the butler.

Adriana halted. "Merriweather, did my brothers and sister leave the house after luncheon?"

"No, my lady. They spent the morning on the lake fishing, then retired to the old nursery to play soldiers. Waterloo again, I believe. They were so engrossed, I had to send a footman to fetch them to luncheon, and they scampered back upstairs as soon as they were freed from the table. Miss Tonkins came down later, saying the three were making so much noise she couldn't concentrate to write her letters, so it appears they remained there. Indeed, I suspect they're still there. Would you like me to fetch them?"

"No, thank you. I just needed to know that they've remained in the house." Adriana arched a brow at Nicholas. "So, no lark."

Grimly, he nodded. "Given that, we need to accept that The Barbarian has, indeed, been stolen. I heard a rumor that he was here. Others might well have heard the same rumor and been less scrupulous about getting their hands on such a magnificent horse."

She huffed. After a moment, she declared, "They won't get far. As you've already noted, The Barbarian is not usually the most placid of beasts."

"True. And in this instance, that will, very likely, be to our advantage."

Her eyes narrowed on his face. "*Our* advantage?"

He smiled, a predatory gesture of intent. "We were about to conclude the sale. As far as I'm concerned, at this moment, that horse is as much mine as yours—as much a Cynster asset as a Sommerville asset. Consequently, throughout the search, I'll be by your side every step of the way."

She stared at him for several silent seconds; what she saw in his face, he couldn't have said, but eventually, she nodded. "All right." Swinging around, she stalked down a corridor leading deeper into the house.

∾

Addie strode straight to the study. She needed to clear the desk. She picked up the bundle of papers on the end and realized they were the papers pertaining to The Barbarian.

She turned to Nicholas, who had followed her into the room. "You asked about The Barbarian's papers. These are what Papa had." She held out the bundle.

He came closer and, without taking the papers, glanced at several and nodded. "That looks correct." He met her gaze. "Do you have a safe?"

She tipped her head toward the wall behind the desk, which hosted a framed map of the estate.

"I suggest you put the papers there. After all"—his lips quirked—"I haven't paid for the horse yet."

She crossed to the wall, swung the framed map aside, opened the safe, and stuffed the papers inside. After shutting the heavy door and locking it, she pushed the frame into place, then bent to investigate the rolls of maps stacked on the shelves beneath.

A mixture of emotions roiled inside her; she felt as if she and her family had been about to close their hands on some promised treat, and at the last second, someone had snatched the prize away. A simplification, perhaps, but the feelings were the same; as a result, she was beyond determined to get The Barbarian back.

She found the map she wanted, drew it out, and turned with the roll in her hands. "Let's spread this out and see what we can make of things."

He helped her unroll the detailed map of the local area, and they anchored the corners with the inkpot and books.

Standing on either side of the desk, they were studying the map when Rogers, the head stableman, and Hicks, the chief groundsman, appeared in the open doorway. She saw them and beckoned. "Come in, and let's see where we are."

Nicholas shifted to one end of the desk, allowing Rogers and Hicks to line up along the front. Both men ran knowing eyes over the map.

"I was explaining to Hicks that The Barbarian was in his paddock here"—Rogers put his finger on the spot—"at around eleven o'clock this morning."

Addie nodded. "And we found him gone..." She glanced at Nicholas.

"A little before three o'clock," he supplied.

Rogers nodded. "So he was taken between, say, eleven and half past two."

"On a day like today," Addie pointed out, "with all the workers in the fields during that period, whichever way the blackguard went, someone is sure to have seen him."

Hicks humphed. "Not as if anyone could disguise that hulking beast." He tapped an area to the southeast of the house. "Me and the lads were spread out around here." His finger transcribed an arc. "None of us saw anything—not the horse nor anyone who shouldn't have been there, either."

"It's nearing four o'clock now," Nicholas observed. "Whoever took the horse wouldn't have wasted any time getting off the estate." He met Addie's eyes. "I think we can assume that the thief has quit the estate by now, but searching on the estate is still our best chance of learning in which direction he went." He gestured at the map. "Given the location of the estate, the thief could have gone in any direction."

"Hmm." She stared at the map. "If I was a horse thief with a horse to dispose of, I would make for Grantham or perhaps Lincoln. Any other useful town is farther away."

Nicholas shook his head. "That's assuming he's making for a town to sell the horse. If he's stolen it for someone specific, there's no saying in which direction he'll head."

He saw her take that in, then she grimaced and tilted her head in acquiescence.

A knock on the door had all four of them turning to look expectantly at the stable hand—the first of the searchers to return—who was hovering in the doorway.

The man saluted and reported, "No sighting anywhere south of the lake. We found the Tomkinses in their fields, and none of them had seen anyone riding by nor spotted The Barbarian."

Over the following half hour, that tale was repeated in various versions; people had been about, but no one had spotted the hard-to-miss horse or, indeed, anyone they hadn't expected to see.

The four gathered about the desk kept track of which areas had been cleared and which had yet to be vouched for. Gradually, the fields to the south, southeast, and east of the estate were deemed devoid of any sightings, and bit by bit, the northeast and northern areas were confirmed as being the same.

Nicholas watched Adriana deal with the older men as well as those returning from the search, many of whom had remained and now stood in groups, waiting for their next orders; without exception, the men treated her with unwavering respect. Not only was she patently a lady born to

command, she did so with instinctive tact. More, the men—all of them—
undeniably looked to her for leadership; they expected her to lead them,
and she did.

He hadn't before realized that such attributes would be attractive in a
lady, yet to him, in her, they most definitely were. Yet what captured his
attention and effortlessly held it was the conundrum she posed by being
the ton's most notorious flighty miss.

She is Miss Flibbertigibbet.

That was a truth almost impossible to accept, yet there she was,
before his very eyes, real, vibrantly alive, and in complete control of her
small army of helpers.

This was an undeniably stressful situation, ergo, equally undeniably,
what he was seeing was the real woman. But of the other, Miss Flibbertigibbet, what of her? He had no idea, but the lady before him was focusing
his interest in a way no lady ever had.

Indeed, he'd been taken aback by the strength of the impulse behind
his declaration in the hall. Nevertheless, that, too, was undeniably the
truth—his truth as it currently was.

Finally, a clatter of boots in the corridor outside heralded the news
they'd been waiting to hear.

"Spotted him, my lady!" Two of the younger stable hands rushed in,
their faces alight with excitement.

Adriana beckoned. "Show us where."

Eagerly, the pair approached the desk.

"It was the Denbys as saw him, my lady," one said as everyone else in
the room crowded around.

The other dutifully reported, "They saw The Barbarian being led off
by a dark-haired man riding a chestnut."

The first pored over the map and put his finger on a spot. "Just here.
On the lane to the village."

Nicholas saw that the village in question—there were three close by
—was Aisby.

"Right, then." Rogers straightened. "We'd better get after him."

Studying the map, Nicholas held up a staying hand. "From Aisby,
the thief could have gone in any of four directions." He glanced at
Adriana. "We've confirmed that the horse has been taken from this
property, ergo formally stolen. The most likely reason is for his worth
to breeders willing to deal with stolen animals. Such enterprises are the
dark side of the Thoroughbred breeding industry. I couldn't be a major

trainer without acknowledging they exist. However, illicit breeders are located throughout the country, not in a few specific regions as most legitimate breeders are. Our thief could be heading to any point of the compass." He held Adriana's gaze. "Therefore, we should send men to scout along all four lanes that the thief might have taken out of Aisby—north, south, east, and west—to determine in which direction our villain actually went. Then we can follow with a larger party to retrieve the horse."

She stared at him for a moment; behind her blank features, he sensed she was thinking, weighing...

Evenly, he added, "We need to act quickly, yes, but we also can't afford to make assumptions and head off in the wrong direction."

She wrinkled her nose; she was transparently impatient to get on the thief's trail. Nevertheless, she nodded. "You're right. We can't risk racing off willy-nilly."

Raising her head, she addressed the waiting men. Nicholas listened as, with Rogers's input, she organized four groups to ride out immediately and search for sightings of thief and horse along all four lanes leading out of Aisby. "Search for as long as you need to find someone who can tell you that the horse passed that way or, alternatively, that it didn't. If they're sure The Barbarian didn't pass them, ride back as fast as you can and report. For our purposes, a definite non-sighting will be as valuable as a sighting, at least in terms of determining the directions in which the thief didn't go."

The men nodded, and at her wave, they departed on their quest, eager and determined.

Hicks and his groundsmen, along with Rogers and the remaining stable hands, followed, leaving Nicholas and his unexpected hostess alone.

She looked down at the map and sighed. After a moment, she raised her gaze to his face. "Are you still intent on joining us on the search, or given it's obviously going to take some time, have you thought better of that?"

He studied her for a moment, then simply stated, "I meant what I said earlier. The Barbarian—acquiring him for my family's breeding stable—is important to me. Increasingly important, the more I learn about the horse. That someone has thought to steal him, more or less from under my nose... Not only does that confirm how important he might be to breeding stocks, but it also makes me even more determined to seize him back." He met her gaze. "I'll be pursuing the horse regardless of whether you and your men are with me."

She read the truth in his face and huffed. "Is The Barbarian really that important to the breeding stocks of England?"

"Yes, he is." He glanced at the framed map concealing the safe. "One thing puzzles me. No attempt has been made to steal the horse's papers."

When he cocked a brow at her, she confirmed, "There's been no hint of any break-in or incursion of that kind. Merriweather would have reported anything of the sort to me immediately."

So Nicholas had assumed. "In that case..." He frowned. "While I pointed to the illicit breeding trade, that no attempt has been made to lay hands on those papers—which any self-respecting thief acting on behalf of illicit breeders would know will add immense value to the horse—makes me wonder if, perhaps, whoever took the horse stole him not for breeding but to be someone's good-looking mount."

She laughed cynically. "If so, they'll soon learn their mistake."

"True. But if they think The Barbarian is just another horse and try to treat him accordingly—"

"They'll very quickly be in all sorts of bother." She tipped her head, a frown playing over her face. "Or not. One can never tell with that horse. Sometimes, he plays along, just to see what he might get or where he might get taken. He's canny, for a horse."

"Ultimately, however, his temper will out." Nicholas caught her gaze. "And we know what will happen then."

"Broken stalls. Terrified stable hands."

"Hmm. But whether that will benefit us by helping us locate him or only be worse for him, who can say?"

She pondered that, then her chin set, and she waved him to draw up a nearby chair. She pulled up and sank into the chair behind the desk, her gaze returning to the map on the desktop. "While the men are out picking up the trail, perhaps we should think about what we'll need to follow it and what strategy we should employ once we catch up with our thief."

Nicholas settled in the indicated chair and joined her in working out who and what they would need to most effectively pursue The Barbarian.

∽

The clock ticked inexorably on.

Addie fought not to stare at the small carriage clock perched on the corner of the desk as she and Nicholas discussed the likely next step and which people they should take with them. Given it was already after five o'clock and, consequently, their chase was likely to extend into the next day, the required supporters included her maid, Sally, in order to preserve the proprieties should they put up overnight at an inn.

Addie dispatched a footman to carry a message to the indomitable maid. "Luckily, Sally is accustomed to traveling with me." She paused, then added, "Although, this time, we won't be jaunting about in a carriage."

"Can Sally ride?" Nicholas asked.

"Yes, thank goodness. As long as we don't ask her to race anywhere, she'll probably enjoy the outing."

Nicholas requested the services of a stable lad and sent him to the Angel Inn in Grantham with a message for Nicholas's groom, whom Addie had seen earlier in the day. Nicholas instructed Young Gillies to pack both Nicholas's bag as well as his own and bring both to the Grange.

When she looked at Nicholas questioningly, he shrugged. "When we come up with the thief or thieves, the more men we have whom we can trust to handle a high-spirited, sometimes-difficult stallion, the better."

She couldn't argue with that.

And still the clock ticked on.

Nicholas's gaze rested on her. "Your men have to get out there, find and question people, then ride back. It'll probably be another hour before we hear from any of them."

She sighed. "I know." After a second, she added, "Patience is not my strong suit."

His lips twitched. "So I'd gathered."

Her fingertips were drumming a tattoo on the blotter when Merriweather appeared in the doorway.

When she arched her brows at him, he rather pointedly said, "I was wondering whether you had any orders for me, my lady."

She glanced at the clock. It was twenty minutes to six. Merriweather wanted to know if Nicholas was staying to dine.

Rapidly, she canvassed her options, but realistically, there were none. Yet every nerve in her body tensed at the thought that her father's "good day" might have waned, and thus, in the drawing room and over dinner, his mind might wander in impossible-to-conceal ways.

Still…no choice.

"Yes, of course." She glanced at Nicholas. "You will stay to dine, won't you? We usually sit down at six o'clock, and in this season, we don't stand on ceremony."

He, too, glanced at the clock, then returned his gaze to her face and inclined his head. "Thank you." Then his lips twitched again. "Aside from all else, enjoying a meal will fill in the time until the searchers return."

"Just so." She looked at Merriweather. "Mr. Cynster will dine with us. Please tell the earl and countess we'll join them in the drawing room shortly."

"Yes, my lady." Merriweather bowed and departed.

Addie focused on their unexpected and definitely-to-be-managed guest. It was on the tip of her tongue to inquire whether he was acquainted with her half brother, the wretched Phillip, but she couldn't decide if she truly wanted to know. If he said yes, what would she do? She could hardly withdraw the dinner invitation. Instead, she told him, "The last my parents knew, I was negotiating with you over the purchase of The Barbarian. They won't have heard that he's missing, presumed stolen."

Relaxed in the armchair, Nicholas studied her for a moment, reading her expression. Then, as she'd hoped, he gracefully inclined his head. "I'll leave explaining the current situation to you. I can imagine it might come as a shock to your parents."

"Indeed." She could use the excuse of shock to explain any random comments her father made. She pushed away from the desk and rose. By now, Merriweather would have warned her parents about their unexpected guest. With a wave, she indicated the open door. "Come. Let me introduce you."

She led the way to the front hall and on to the drawing room, with every step, intensely aware of the large male who prowled beside her.

Tamping down her hyperactive senses, she swept into the drawing room. As usual, her parents were seated on the long sofa set perpendicular to the massive ornate fireplace. Of her siblings, there was as yet no sign, but generally, the three joined the family about the dinner table.

As she drew near, she searched her mother's face and, in reply to her unvoiced question, received a small smile and an infinitesimal nod. Apparently, her father's "good day" was still in effect.

"Papa. Mama." Addie halted before them and, with a wave, indicated their guest. "Allow me to present Mr. Nicholas Cynster. As you know, he's here with a view to purchasing The Barbarian."

Her father, his hands folded atop his cane, smiled in ready welcome. "Cynster. Delighted to make your acquaintance, sir."

Nicholas bowed with ready grace. "The pleasure is mine, my lord." He bowed again to Addie's mother. "Countess. I'm honored by the invitation."

"Pshaw!" Her mother smiled approvingly and waved him to one of the armchairs facing the sofa. "You are very welcome, Mr. Cynster." She waited until he sat to say, "I'm acquainted with your mama, although I haven't seen her in some months. Not since we were last in town. Is she well?"

"Indeed. She and my father are in Ireland at the moment, visiting with my older sister."

"Ah, yes. The Countess of Glengarah. I believe I heard a whisper that she and that handsome husband of hers are expecting another child?"

"Yes, ma'am. Although I understand it will be some weeks yet before we hear any further news on that score."

"Well, then." The earl looked expectantly at Nicholas. "Have you viewed The Barbarian?"

"I have indeed, sir." Nicholas glanced at Addie. "As I've informed Lady Adriana, the Cynster Stable stands ready to make an offer."

Addie drew in a swift breath and leapt in to say, "As to that, Papa, there's been an unanticipated difficulty." She nearly winced and forced herself to baldly state, "In short, someone has made off with The Barbarian, but we're already on their trail." She rushed on, "We know the man who took the horse went by way of Aisby, and we have men out looking as we speak to determine which of the lanes the man subsequently took."

As if sensing the urgency she felt to impart the news quickly and completely, Nicholas added, "We're waiting at present, but once we have news of the man's direction, we'll set out in pursuit."

Addie held her breath as her parents blinked, then blinked again.

Eventually, as if clarifying a point he could barely believe, her father ventured, "Someone has stolen the horse?" He glanced at her mother. "I'm certain that wasn't a part of the plan."

"No, of course not," Addie hurried to reassure him. This was not the moment she would have picked for him to suddenly lose his mental way. "But you needn't worry. We'll have a sighting soon, and we'll be hot on his heels. We'll get The Barbarian back."

Her mother blinked again. "We?" Her gaze traveled to Nicholas. "Are we to take it you intend to assist, Mr. Cynster?"

"Indeed. I and my man will accompany Lady Adriana and her people. We've organized a group with all the necessary skills." Nicholas glanced at Adriana. "Lady Adriana's maid is included in the company. Along with the others chosen, she's holding herself ready to depart at a moment's notice, as are her ladyship and I."

Addie watched relief seep into her parents' expressions. No matter what she felt about Nicholas accompanying her, for that alone, she would accept his presence without the slightest quibble.

Besides, a sly voice murmured in her head, *this might be my chance to learn a thing or two about why I react to him as I do.*

A clearing of a throat drew all eyes to the doorway, where Merriweather stood. Majestically, he announced, "Dinner is served, my lord. My ladies."

"Thank you, Merriweather." Her mother rose, bringing the rest of them to their feet. She smiled at Nicholas and gestured for him to walk with her. "Shall we?"

Nicholas promptly offered his arm, and with an approving smile, her mother laid her hand on his sleeve and led him to the dining room. Addie smiled warmly and accepted her father's arm, and they fell in behind the other two.

As they crossed the hall, a clatter of feet on the stairs drew all attention to the three youngsters who came pelting down.

"Sorry!" Mortie sang. "We lost track of the time."

The latter statement was delivered with the charming smile that invariably got him off the hook for all minor misdemeanors.

Sure enough, her mother smiled on him, as well as on Angie and Benjamin. "Well, in this case, you missed out on talking to Mr. Cynster in the drawing room and hearing the latest rather shocking news, but I'm sure you'll catch up over the dinner table."

Addie nearly groaned. She did roll her eyes; as if her siblings needed any encouragement to interrogate a guest.

Her father noticed her reaction and chuckled and patted her hand. "Never mind, my dear. And it will help pass the time."

Apparently, she wasn't hiding her impatience to be off after The Barbarian as well as she'd thought.

With her siblings clustering around Nicholas, on a wave of almost unsettling domesticity, she and her father followed the group into the dining room.

Nicholas slipped easily into the persona he routinely used to charm his elders and his juniors. Given his family, he had plenty of experience on which to call.

As an honored guest, he was seated in pride of place at the earl's right hand, with Adriana opposite. Mortie sat beside Nicholas, while Benjamin, the youngest, sat beside Adriana, with Angela beside Benjamin, on her mother's right. Most of the leaves had been removed from the table, allowing for comfortable conversations that included everyone there.

Once the first course had been served and the curiosity of the three youngsters over what shocking event had recently occurred had been satisfied, Nicholas concentrated on interacting with the earl.

In that, he was aided by the earl himself, who, frowning lightly, said, "I had assumed...well, I had heard that your brother...Toby, is it? That he was the head of the Cynster breeding stable."

The countess looked up the table and caught Nicholas's eye. "That is the case, is it not?"

Nicholas inclined his head. "Normally, Toby would have been the one to respond to the rumor that reached us. He would have come here to assess and make an offer for The Barbarian." He smiled his most charming smile. "However, Toby is currently from home, so that task fell to me. While I routinely manage our racing stable, leaving the breeding stable to Toby's oversight, I am in overall charge of the entire enterprise —all that the Cynster Stable encompasses—so in Toby's absence, it fell to me to step in."

"Ah, I see." The earl nodded. "You're the senior partner, so to speak."

That was an odd yet accurate way to put it, and Nicholas inclined his head in agreement.

Glancing across the table, he noticed Adriana's eyes had widened, although her gaze wasn't on him but rather on her father.

Then the earl's gaze, which had, Nicholas noticed, grown somewhat vague, sharpened, and he glanced at Nicholas.

"So, sir, once you catch up to them, how do you plan to wrest the horse from the blackguards who took him, heh?"

"We think," Adriana rushed to say, "that it might well be that whoever took The Barbarian thinks he's simply a good-looking horse. A riding horse."

The earl looked confused, and Nicholas clarified, "There's been no attempt to steal the horse's papers, which Lady Adriana has shown me and which are safe and secure in your study. That the horse has been taken without those documents suggests that it's not one of the known gangs who prey on

Thoroughbred owners in order to supply illicit breeders. As I've explained to Lady Adriana, without his registration documents, The Barbarian is reduced to being simply a good-looking but temperamental stallion."

Adriana glanced down the table at her mother and siblings. "I've alerted the staff to the need to ensure the documents remain safe"—she returned her gaze to the earl—"so you need have no fear on that score."

The earl nodded in understanding, but then his face clouded with puzzlement. "What I don't understand is why the blighters thought to take the horse now. Just when we've got Mr. Cynster visiting."

Nicholas exchanged a glance with Adriana. "I think we can assume that whoever is behind the theft heard the same rumor that brought me here."

The earl's frown deepened. "Oh, I don't think that could be it." He looked down the table at the countess. "It doesn't seem likely, does it, my dear? That The Barbarian being here would be widely known?"

The countess patted her lips with her napkin, then replied, "I suspect we'll never know, my dear." With a gentle smile, she glanced up at Merriweather as the butler removed her plate. "Thank you, Merriweather. What have we for dessert this evening?"

The answer was a luscious raspberry charlotte russe that was so delicious that all conversation ceased while the company did it justice.

As he savored the sweet concoction, Nicholas decided that the earl's rather naive view of the degree of interest a rumor about a horse such as The Barbarian would generate in Thoroughbred circles was merely a reflection of the earl's lack of connection with that world. There was no real reason he would appreciate the avid attention that news of a horse like The Barbarian inevitably generated in such spheres.

The last mouthfuls of dessert were being consumed when a footman appeared in the doorway, all but quivering with eagerness as he paused on the threshold.

Addie saw and turned toward the doorway. "Yes, Phelps?"

The footman bowed. "A message from Rogers, my lady. They've a firm sighting of the rider leading The Barbarian out along the Grantham road."

"Excellent!" Addie looked across the table at Nicholas. She was beyond keen to get him away from her father, and this was the perfect excuse. She'd been on tenterhooks throughout the meal and felt they'd stretched their luck to the limit. She pushed back her chair and looked down the table, then back at her father. "Mama, Papa. Please excuse us. Nicholas and I must be off. Immediately."

Her father looked confused. "But... Surely, Mr. Cynster and Rogers can handle the business. No need for you to go, is there?"

Addie laid a comforting hand on her father's. "I have to go. I'm the only one who can ride The Barbarian, and if he decides he no longer wishes to be led, well, it might be difficult for anyone else to bring him back."

Her father's frown held more confusion than anything else; Addie prayed Nicholas wouldn't see that.

She glanced at him and caught his gaze, but continued speaking to her parents. "Given the hour, it's possible our company—you'll remember we mentioned taking several others—might be forced to spend the night at an inn, which is why Sally, my maid, will be accompanying me." She transferred her gaze to her father and patted his hand. "It'll all be perfectly above board. No reason to fret."

He was clearly fretting regardless, but her mother came to the rescue. "Of course, dear." She shifted her gaze to Nicholas. "And Mr. Cynster and his man will be with you as well. I'm quite sure everything will work out as it should."

Her mother's steady conviction sufficed to soothe and re-anchor her father. After studying her mother's serene expression, he looked at Addie, turned his hand to grip and lightly squeeze her fingers, then nodded. "Very well, my dear. You and Mr. Cynster have clearly got things under control." He looked at Nicholas and inclined his head. "We'll leave the matter in your capable hands."

Nicholas dipped his head as if accepting a commission. "Indeed, sir. You may rely on us." He glanced at Addie and rose.

She all but sprang to her feet. She swooped and kissed her father's cheek, then waved to her mother and siblings. "We'll send word!"

She whirled and led the way out. Behind her, she heard Nicholas murmur farewells, then he was striding after her.

Once in the hall, she slowed, a species of relief trickling through her veins. There'd been a few tense moments, but all in all, they—the family collectively—had survived the interlude in reasonable shape.

She halted and turned to Nicholas. "I need to change."

He nodded. "I'll go and assemble our party. Let's meet in the forecourt."

"I'll fetch Sally as well." She snatched up her skirts and started up the stairs.

On the landing, she paused and glanced back in time to see Nicholas stride out of the front door. Reassured that he was safely out of the house, she turned up the next flight and rushed on.

In the small sitting room at the top of the main stairs, the earl and countess stood at the window that overlooked the forecourt and surveyed the gathering below.

When the company formed up and rode out, with Addie and Nicholas Cynster leading the way down the drive, the earl shook his head. "I have to confess, my dear, that I'm no longer so sure...well, about anything. It was supposed to be the younger brother who came, and I really had no idea that the horse would be so very valuable that someone else might hear of it and steal him." Frowning worriedly, he glanced at his wife. "Did you?"

"No, indeed. But that fact might explain why old Wisthorpe never advertised his ownership of the horse." The countess watched the riders head into the shadows of the avenue and patted her husband's hand reassuringly. "Regardless, my dear, we have done our homework, and from all I've seen thus far of young Cynster... Well, he's not that young, is he? Which is a point to note, as that might prove to be a good thing. Indeed, I'm starting to wonder if Fate hasn't decided to lend our little project a helping hand."

The earl grunted. "Fate, I will remind you, is a fickle female. God help us if she's decided to dip her fingers into our pie, but if she has, then I expect we'll just have to trust in her wisdom and hope that everything works out all right."

The countess smiled in agreement, and by mutual accord, the pair turned away from the sight of their elder daughter riding away beside Nicholas Cynster.

CHAPTER 4

*A*stride Tamerlane, as the evening waned, Nicholas rode west beside Adriana, who was mounted on a fine chestnut. They were following the lane linking Aisby with the town of Grantham along which he had traveled back and forth over the past two days.

Suddenly frowning, Adriana turned to him. "If we're right and the thief took this road, he should have passed you while you were returning to the Grange after lunch."

Nicholas grimaced. "I didn't go back to Grantham. I stopped at the tavern in Aisby for a bite." The houses of Aisby village clustered a little way south of the crossroads. "He must have gone past while I was down there."

"Ah." Somewhat glumly, she faced forward, and they rode on.

The lane was bordered by dense hedgerows, with gently undulating fields stretching away to either side. They'd passed through two tiny hamlets, and the sightings they'd discovered—two farmworkers just outside Aisby and three laborers mending a gate in the last hamlet—had been clear and definite, keeping them trotting quickly along the Grantham lane.

Adriana grumbled, "While admittedly The Barbarian is eye-catching, it would have been helpful if even one of those workers had looked more closely at the man leading the horse."

Nicholas huffed in agreement. While the men had waxed lyrical about The Barbarian, all they'd been able to tell them of the rider was that he'd been neatly dressed—"a gentleman, most like"—dark-haired, wearing a hat, and had been riding a chestnut smaller than The Barbarian.

As most riding horses were smaller than The Barbarian, not even that point helped a great deal in identifying the rider.

They rounded a curve, and Nicholas glanced back along the line of their company. Young Gillies and Adriana's groom, Rory, were pacing their mounts on either side of the mare on whose back Sally, Adriana's redheaded maid, was perched. Behind that trio rode two not-so-young stablemen, Jed and Mike. Both had experience working with The Barbarian and knew the local lanes well.

Counting Adriana, that made six in their party who could help with handling the likely-to-be-difficult horse once they caught up with him. Facing forward and resettling in his saddle, Nicholas felt confident that their number and collective experience would be enough to meet any challenge the pursuit and retrieval of the stallion threw at them.

Acting on Nicholas's orders, Young Gillies had packed all their things, paid off the innkeeper at the Angel Inn, and brought their bags with him to Aisby Grange. With the leather bag lashed to his saddle providing a comforting weight at his back, Nicholas felt ready to ride wherever their pursuit of The Barbarian led them. He sensed the others in their group felt the same.

Ahead, a wooden bridge spanned a small river. As they approached the structure, Adriana called, "This is the river Witham."

They clattered across and, shortly thereafter, arrived at the spot where the lane met the larger road that, in that area, was the main route between Grantham, which lay to the south, and Lincoln, which was a good long way to the north.

They reined in at the edge of the road. Planted in the bank directly opposite was a signpost with two arms, the one to the left labeled "Grantham" and the one to the right labeled "Lincoln."

Their company halted, crowding behind them.

Nicholas looked left and right. "Which way?"

Adriana shook her head. "He could have gone in either direction, but if he'd intended to make for Lincoln, it would have been quicker and easier to take the lane north from the village."

"Beggin' your pardon, my lady," Rory put in from behind them. "But he couldn't be heading for Lincoln now, not with The Barbarian."

One of the stablemen—Jed—snorted. "Too right. The beast will expect to be fed and watered, and if he's not to be turned out into a nice paddock, to be put up in a nice, comfy stable, too."

Nicholas glanced at Adriana to find her nodding in agreement.

"That's true." She caught Nicholas's eye. "Sadly, The Barbarian is nothing if not spoilt. So"—she looked south—"given the time, that means the thief must have headed for Grantham."

"There's really nowhere else he would find a suitable place to stay," Rory said. "Leastways, nowhere he could reach before nightfall."

"And there'll be no moon tonight," Mike, the other stableman, put in. "I wouldn't want to be trying to lead a difficult and unfamiliar stallion over lanes I didn't know in the pitch dark."

Nicholas looked toward Lincoln. "Surely, where he might expect to reach will depend on what time he came through here."

"I don't think he can be all that far ahead of us." Adriana arched her brows consideringly. "A few hours at most. Definitely not enough time to reach anywhere else."

Nicholas didn't feel they could be sure of that. Although they'd questioned the workers who'd sighted the thief about how long ago the rider had passed, their answers had been vague, and outdoor workers were notoriously poor at estimating time. On top of that, he and the others hadn't thought to ask if the rider had been merely trotting or had been riding more rapidly along.

"Lincoln is more than a day away, but Grantham"—Addie pointed down the road—"is right there." She gathered her reins and turned Nickleby, her horse, that way. "The rider will have gone into Grantham." She tapped her heel to Nickleby's sleek side, and the horse obediently stepped out. "With any luck," she called over her shoulder, "we'll find the blackguard in Grantham and have The Barbarian back in our hands by nightfall."

A momentary hesitation followed, but no one argued, and the company fell in beside and behind her.

She pushed Nickleby into a canter, and soon, the roofs of Grantham rose before them.

"There's someone to ask." Young Gillies pointed to a workman trudging home along the verge.

The company slowed, and Young Gillies leaned from his saddle to hail the man and ask if he'd seen a rider on a chestnut leading a huge bay horse.

The worker shook his head. "But I've been trenching over there." He pointed to the west. "I only just got onto the road."

They thanked him and continued on. Once they entered the outskirts of Grantham, the grooms and stablemen stopped and asked every person they saw, but no one had seen the mounted thief and horse.

Given it was just past midsummer, it was still light when they reached the town's main square.

Rather grudgingly, Addie suggested, "We may as well stop at the Angel."

She was speaking of the same coaching inn that Nicholas and Young Gillies had patronized the previous night.

Nicholas rode beside her into the inn's cobbled yard. "We'd better see about getting rooms."

She grimaced, but nodded. "Just as well it isn't hunting season, or we'd have no hope. The Angel's one of the most popular inns in the district."

Their company drew up, and Young Gillies promptly hailed the ostlers in the manner of old friends. Still in her saddle, she listened as Young Gillies confirmed that the rider they were pursuing hadn't taken refuge—indeed, hadn't stopped even for just a bite—at the inn.

She sighed in disappointment and slid her boot free of the stirrup, then to her complete surprise, Nicholas, having already dismounted, appeared beside her, reached up, and lifted her down.

Her senses rioted, and she nearly swallowed her tongue.

For a finite second, she was weightless. She wouldn't have said she was a lightweight, but he made lifting her down seem both effortless and graceful.

He set her on her feet and steadied her.

Just as well, because she would have staggered.

Dazed and distinctly giddy, she blinked. Her senses surged, skittering and leaping; she hauled in a breath and held it, hoping to calm them, but they remained a very long way from settled.

Luckily, in the shadows of the yard, no one else seemed to notice.

Remembering the moment under the porte-cochere, she shot a sharp glance at Nicholas, but on releasing her, he'd turned to check that Young Gillies and Rory had the horses in hand.

With that confirmed, Nicholas turned back to her. His expression unreadable, he waved toward the inn's side door. "Shall we?"

She managed a nod—marshaling her tongue for coherent speech was still uncertain—and cast a last, lingering look around the yard. Disappointment pricked, and instead of making for the door, she baldly stated, "He's not here." She frowned. "I thought he would be. If he stopped in Grantham—"

"He might well have thought twice about putting up here." Nicholas glanced around, taking in a party of three riders—all obviously gentlemen—who had followed them into the yard. "If our thief has any inkling of The Barbarian's true worth, with him being such a noteworthy horse, it's likely our blackguard will take pains to avoid places where gentry congregate. Those of our class are much more likely to notice and remember a horse of The Barbarian's caliber."

She wrinkled her nose. "True."

"And that," Nicholas continued, "suggests we ought to scout out the other places in town where our thief might have sought a bed."

Addie brightened. Young Gillies, Rory, Jed, and Mike, having seen the horses stabled, chose that moment to join them, and she listened with approval as Nicholas instructed the four men to go around the town in pairs, checking all possible places at which the thief might have put up for the night.

"If by chance you find him, one of you stay and keep watch while the other returns to alert us."

"Aye, sir," the men chorused.

Nicholas nodded a dismissal, and the men left, eagerly vanishing into the encroaching darkness.

Grateful that, by then, her sense of balance had returned and her legs were once again steady, when Nicholas again gestured to the door, Addie walked beside him up the two steps to the inn's side porch, where Sally was waiting with everyone's bags piled at her feet.

Nicholas hefted his own bag and those of the two grooms. Addie claimed her traveling bag and Sally's as well, while the maid took Jed's and Mike's. Nicholas juggled the bags he held, opened the door, and sent it swinging wide. Addie walked through into the inn's side hall, and Sally and he followed.

By the time they fronted the reception counter, her head was once again clear, and she'd got a firm grip on her wayward wits.

She was acquainted with Melchett, the proprietor. His grizzled face lit when he saw her, and his expression brightened even more when he noticed Nicholas. "Mr. Cynster, sir! Didn't expect to see you so soon, but we're pleased to have you back regardless. Same room?" Melchett was already reaching for his register as his gaze returned, curiously, to Addie. "Lady Adriana." He bobbed his head respectfully. "Welcome, my lady. Will you be wanting to stay, too?"

Addie confirmed she did and, with Nicholas, organized rooms for their party.

Melchett laboriously completed the entries in his register. "Don't often have the pleasure of putting up any of the Sommervilles, what with Aisby Grange being so close, but today must be Sommerville day." With a wide smile, Melchett glanced at Addie. "What with your brother here and all."

Addie blinked, stared, then somewhat faintly asked, "Dickie's here?"

"Indeed, he is, my lady." Melchett's gaze went past her. "In fact, here he is now."

"Addie?"

She whirled to see her brother emerge from a corridor leading deeper into the inn.

Dark-haired, tallish, with a rangy build much like their father's, Dickie appeared the epitome of the well-bred young gentleman-about-town.

"I say." As he ambled toward her, he was grinning in a way Addie would have described as "distinctly mellow." His gaze went past her to Nicholas, then shifted to take in Sally, standing nearby in her cloak, and the bags piled about them. "What's up?" His lips still curved in that ridiculous grin, Dickie glanced Addie's way. "Are you running away from home?"

"No, you fool!" As he looped an arm about her and hugged her, she saw his gaze return to Nicholas, and even after Dickie eased his hold, he didn't let her go.

She prodded him in the ribs—sharply enough to break through his no-doubt-alcohol-induced absorption. He grunted and focused on her, and she waved at Nicholas. "This is Mr. Nicholas Cynster."

"Cynster?" Dickie's gaze snapped to Nicholas, and just like that, adulation replaced his suspicion. "I say, sir." Dickie released Addie and thrust out his hand. "It's a pleasure to meet you."

Obviously fighting a grin, Nicholas obligingly shook Dickie's hand, and Dickie blurted, "What brings you to this neck of the woods?" Then he colored and lamely amended, "Well, at this time of year."

Nicholas met Addie's gaze; she hoped he couldn't guess her thoughts. He'd asked earlier whether The Barbarian's disappearance might have been a lark perpetrated by her siblings. In answering, she hadn't thought of Dickie. As far as she'd known, he was still in London, although they'd been expecting him to arrive home at any time. She hadn't expected to find him in Grantham and couldn't imagine why he was, apparently, staying at the inn.

Before she could ask any of the questions burning her tongue, Nicholas returned his gaze to Dickie. "I've hired a private parlor. Perhaps we should retire there."

"Yes!" Addie seized Dickie's arm and gripped hard enough for him to feel her nails. "That's an excellent idea."

She dragged her brother toward the door that the bemused Melchett indicated. She paused before the door long enough to fling entirely redundant instructions to Sally, who was already gathering Addie's bag and her own and preparing to retreat to the room they would share, then Addie opened the door and hauled Dickie into the snug parlor.

She halted before the empty fireplace, released Dickie, and rounded on him. "What the devil are you doing here?"

At that moment, Nicholas stepped into the room and, thankfully, shut the door.

Dickie's eyes widened, and he rocked back on his heels—for a moment, Addie feared he would topple over backward—but then he blinked owlishly at her. "Came up with some friends. From Lunnon. London." He blinked again and vaguely frowned at her. "They're staying here, too. This was our final night together, as it were. They're off to Nottingham in the morning, and I'd planned to head home then." He peered at Addie, then glanced at Nicholas. "We called it a night a little while ago—the others are making an early start—and I came to the desk to get a fresh candle…"

Dickie glanced back and forth between Nicholas and Addie, and his blue gaze sharpened. "Here, what's going on?" He focused on Addie. "I know why *I'm* here, but why are *you* here?" He glanced sideways at Nicholas. "And with Mr. Cynster?"

Nicholas decided it was time to step in. "We're here because I called at your home with a view to buying one of your father's horses."

Dickie blinked at him. "The Barbarian?"

"Just so. We"—Nicholas glanced at Adriana—"were about to agree on the price when we discovered the horse had been stolen."

Dickie's eyes grew huge. "From his paddock at the Grange?" He looked at Adriana, and when, lips tight, she nodded, Dickie whistled, then said, "Well, that's a bit of a facer." He glanced at Nicholas. "Not many people knew the beast was there."

"Exactly!" Adriana caught her brother's eye; Nicholas saw the pointed look she bent on him. "We've learned that a dark-haired, well-dressed gentleman riding a chestnut led The Barbarian off the estate, and we've tracked him as far as Grantham."

Nicholas saw Dickie realize what his sister was endeavoring to convey to him. As dark-haired as she was fair and neatly yet elegantly dressed, he was the embodiment of a dark-haired, well-dressed gentleman, and Nicholas wouldn't mind wagering that Dickie rode a chestnut.

Sure enough, Dickie's expression darkened, and he scowled at his sister. "It wasn't me! Good Lord!" He flung up his hands. "What use would I have for a devil of a horse who won't let anyone but you ride him?"

Adriana studied her brother's face, reading it as only a sister could, then the tension that had wound her tight abruptly released, and she waved. "Sorry, sorry, but it had to be asked. You turning up here… It was a shock."

Dickie humphed, but appeared to accept her semi-apology with no further remonstrations. After a moment, he said, "So you followed the thief here…"

A tap on the door at Nicholas's back had him turning. He opened the door, saw Rory and Young Gillies, and pulled the door wide and waved them in. "What did you find?" Over the grooms' heads, Nicholas met Dickie's eyes. "Our grooms and two of the estate's stablemen have been searching through the town for any sign of the thief."

When Nicholas looked at Rory and Young Gillies, who had lined up facing their master, mistress, and Dickie, Young Gillies reported, "We couldn't find anyone who'd seen our thief or the horse."

"We tried all the other hostelries." Rory looked at Adriana. "We even woke the master of the jobbing stable to check if the blackguard had thought to stable the horse there, but no."

Dickie glanced back and forth. "Where was the last sighting?"

Adriana told him. She frowned. "Much as I can't see it, perhaps the thief went the other way. Toward Lincoln." She grimaced.

Rory shifted his feet. When the others looked at him, he colored, but doggedly offered, "If he was far enough ahead of us, he might have passed right through Grantham and headed straight on. If he'd timed it right—about dinnertime—it's a small enough town that, even leading The Barbarian, he might not have been noticed by anyone."

Dickie hummed in agreement and glanced at Adriana and Nicholas. "One thing I can vouch for is that no man leading The Barbarian passed us as we rode up on the London road. We only got here just over an hour ago, so if the thief had been that far ahead of you and had headed for London, he would have passed us, but I assure you, he didn't."

Nicholas nodded. "That's good to know. Our teeming metropolis is the last place we want the thief to take that horse."

The clocks about the inn started chiming. They all counted eleven chimes.

Nicholas glanced around the circle. "It's late, and there's nothing useful we can accomplish at this time. Let's get some sleep and meet again over breakfast in here." He met Adriana's blue eyes. "We can discuss the next stage of our search and how best to go about it."

Everyone agreed. Rory and Young Gillies bowed and departed, then Nicholas held the door for Adriana and her brother and followed the pair into the inn's foyer.

Dickie paused to get a candle from the sleepy-eyed youth now manning the counter, then the three of them turned toward the stairs.

Dickie pointed to the corridor running beside the stairs. "My room's down there." He saluted Adriana and Nicholas. "I'll see you in the morning."

They murmured goodnights, and Adriana settled the heavy train of her riding habit over her arm and started up the stairs.

Nicholas followed two steps behind, fighting to keep his eyes on the stair treads and away from the enticing hips, sheathed in teal velvet, swaying in front of his face. Their rooms were in the same wing, his closer to the stairs than hers.

She reached the last step and lowered her arm. As she stepped up to the floor of the gallery, her train slid free, and her bootheel snagged in the material, and she pitched forward.

In a family full of ladies who rode, Nicholas had seen the same thing happen so often that he reacted instinctively, leaping up the extra steps and looping one arm about the toppling figure's waist. He hauled her up against him as he straightened with his boots firmly planted on the gallery floor.

As usually occurred, they ended up breast to chest, pressed tightly together at the head of the stairs.

Not as usual, he wasn't holding one of his female relatives.

He was holding Miss Flibbertigibbet, whom a large part of him found utterly fascinating.

Her eyes, wide, met his, her gaze captivating.

She'd stopped breathing.

So had he.

Swathed in shadows, with no one else anywhere about—no one likely to interrupt—they stared at each other, transfixed, pulses pounding, while something undeniably primal stirred and swelled and filled the air around them, almost suffocating in its intensity, unspeakably alluring in its promise...

They teetered on that unforeseen, unexpected brink.

For long seconds, neither moved a muscle.

Then Nicholas drew in a slow breath and felt her breasts pressing even more provocatively against his swelling chest.

And in his mind, he heard his sister's voice. *Whatever you have to do, get that horse!*

This...wasn't one of the things he had to do.

Uncertainty prodded, and he eased his hold and took a small but definite step back.

She hauled in a breath; he tried not to stare at her breasts as they rose high.

Then she swallowed and, with commendable calmness, said, "Thank you."

He nodded.

Through the shadows, she briefly searched his face, then she regathered her train and inclined her head. "Goodnight."

He managed to murmur "Goodnight" in reply, although his voice sounded strange to his ears.

She turned and walked away.

Frozen, he stood and watched her glide through the shadows to a door some way beyond his own.

He waited, still watching, until she slipped inside. Only once he heard the door quietly close did the tension holding him ease.

He hauled in a deeper breath, then abruptly frowned, shook his head at himself, and stalked to his room.

He had more pressing things to do than appease his unexpected—unprecedented—fascination.

~

An hour later, Addie lay on her back in the bed in her room and listened to Sally snore.

Her thoughts rambled hither and yon, too often leading her into imagining possibilities that, in reality, were not at all realistic. Dwelling on such thoughts was certainly not helpful. Flirting with notions she should really not entertain, especially with the other half of the couple who featured in such scenarios being only down the hall, was akin to self-flagellation.

So she told herself.

It didn't really help.

When it came to Nicholas Cynster, she was, apparently, helpless to redirect her thoughts.

As for her dreams…

~

At eight o'clock the following morning, Nicholas sat at the breakfast table in the small parlor and waited, rather grumpily, for his compatriots to arrive.

He hadn't had the most restful night, which was odd. Usually, he slept like a log, and he wasn't at all happy with the notion that a female—no matter who she might be or how enticing having her in his arms had felt or how many lustful thoughts her luscious lips evoked—could so disrupt his sleep.

He chewed through a piece of bacon and ruthlessly smothered the thought of how, if they could see him, his sisters would laugh.

Eventually, Dickie opened the door, saw Nicholas, and looking a trifle bleary-eyed, came in. "Food. Good."

So saying, Adriana's brother drew out the chair opposite Nicholas, sat, and lifted the dome covering the scrambled eggs, sausages, and bacon.

Nicholas grunted a good morning, reached for his coffee cup, and saw Dickie's eyes fix on the mug.

"Oh, thank heaven. Ambrosia of the gods. Where?"

Hiding a grin, Nicholas pointed to the sideboard.

Dickie dragged himself out of the chair and over to the sideboard. After pouring himself a cup of the steaming brew, he closed his eyes and sipped, then sighed. "That's better." He opened his eyes and returned to the table with rather more energy.

After several moments of silent eating, because he was curious, Nicholas asked, "Who's the elder—you or Adriana?"

Dickie waved his fork. "Me. But only by a year." He paused, considering, then added, "That said, it's Addie who got all the serious and capable and practical traits, while I inherited a love for a wastrel-ish life."

Nicholas hid a frown. "That seems rather strange, given your sister is widely known as Miss Flibbertigibbet."

"I know!" Bemused, Dickie shook his head. "I have no idea how that happened. It seems nonsensical to me—as if the ton doesn't know her at all."

Nicholas tucked that insight away for later examination. After searching for a way to learn what he wanted to know about the siblings, he settled for asking, "Have you been in London since the start of the Season?"

"More or less. I went up as soon as the hunting wound down."

"Ah." Nicholas made a show of nodding wisely. "Doing the dutiful, squiring your mother and sister around."

"No, actually. At least not this Season." Dickie kept his gaze on the bacon he was slicing. "This year, Mama and Addie decided to give the whole circus a miss. I can't say I wasn't grateful!"

"So you've spent until now in London?"

Dickie nodded. "Always plenty to do there. M'friends and I generally head out to the ancestral acres about this time every year."

Meaning that for much of the time, he left his sister to shoulder the burden of managing the large household as well as, if Nicholas's guess was correct, dealing with all manner of estate matters, such as selling a valuable horse.

Recalling the vagueness he'd sensed in the ageing earl, Nicholas ventured, "Still, I suppose that, for the rest of the year, you'll be assisting your father, taking up the reins and learning the ropes, as it were."

Finally, Dickie shot Nicholas a glance. "I'm not my father's heir."

Genuinely surprised, Nicholas blinked. "You have an older brother?" *Whom no one has yet mentioned.*

Dickie's lips tightened. "Half brother. Lord Phillip Sommerville. I expect no one's mentioned him, and that's because he's estranged from Papa and all our family."

Nicholas regarded Dickie through newly opened eyes. "I see." And he did. Dickie's hedonistic lifestyle was the natural outcome of a young gentleman of wealth and position who lacked all purpose. He was drifting through life with no real aim.

Feeling rather more sympathetic, Nicholas caught Dickie's eye. "I made the acquaintance of your younger siblings when I called at Aisby Grange. They were investigating the utility of balloon bombs in the defense of their castle."

Dickie chuckled. "They're an entertaining lot."

From his expression, it was clear he was fond of the youngsters.

Nicholas smiled. "I also met your parents, of course."

Dickie's eyes widened. His "Oh?" sounded far less assured.

Before Nicholas could wonder at that, the door opened, and Adriana swept in.

Nicholas rose and drew out the chair between his and Dickie's.

She nodded in thanks and sat. As he resumed his seat, she surveyed the dishes. "Good. You left me some toast."

As she reached for the toast rack, a maid bustled in with a pot of tea. Nicholas watched as Adriana set about consuming a slice of toast and a cup of tea and wondered, as he frequently did, how young ladies managed to survive on such meager rations.

Dickie laid down his cutlery, pushed aside his empty plate, and took a healthy swallow of his coffee. Lowering the mug, he looked at Adriana. "As I'm here, I rather think I should join you in the hunt for The Barbarian and the villain who took him."

Adriana frowned, then swallowed and said, "I thought that you returning home would cover my absence."

"Yes, but," Dickie countered, "as you know, there's not much to be done in this season, and besides, all the staff know what they're doing. They don't need me hovering, and"—he cast an appealing look at Nicholas—"it seems to me that you could do with an extra pair of eyes and hands, let alone the whole question of propriety—and don't say you have Sally with you." Dickie rolled his eyes. "Regardless of Sally, if you stumble across any tonnish matron, there'll be gossip aplenty, while if I'm with you, no one will say boo."

Nicholas silently applauded Dickie's willingness to state that simple fact.

Predictably, Adriana frowned more definitely.

When she cut a glance Nicholas's way, he met it with rising brows, but was too wise in the ways of independent sisters to advance any opinion. In this situation, him siding with Dickie wouldn't be well received.

Dickie, too, was experienced enough not to push, and after heaving a put-upon sigh, Adriana picked up her cup, sipped, then lowered it and said, "If you're set on accompanying us, we'll need to send word to Mama and Papa. They're expecting you."

Dickie brightened and pushed back from the table. "I'll fetch pen and paper, and we can send off a note immediately."

He left in search of those items, leaving the door ajar.

Adriana sipped more tea and looked at Nicholas over the rim of the cup. After a second, she volunteered, "Dickie's actually quite a useful person to have along on an adventure." She set down the cup. "Despite any appearance to the contrary, he's observant and quick-witted."

Straight-faced, Nicholas nodded. "Good to know." It was also good to know that at least these two Sommerville siblings were the sort to have each other's back.

Dickie returned with paper, pen, and inkpot. He sat and wrote, more or less what Adriana dictated. With parental notification deemed appropriately dealt with, Dickie signed, sealed, and addressed the note, then held it out to the maid who came in to clear the dishes. "Melchett said he'd see to having this delivered."

The girl bobbed, took the letter, and bore it away.

"Now." Nicholas eyed the pair of Sommervilles. "We need to formulate a plan for our search, and you two know the area significantly better than I do."

Adriana frowned. "Plan? Given the thief isn't anywhere in town, he must have headed the other way." She arched her brows at Nicholas. "Surely we should take the road to Lincoln and with all speed?"

He'd already realized she was given to making impulsive and somewhat reckless decisions. He met her eyes and calmly asked, "What if the thief did come this way, but as Rory suggested, the blackguard managed to ride straight through Grantham without being seen? We know he didn't stop in the town, so presumably, he rode out along one of the other roads." He glanced at Dickie. "Your brother's observations confirm that the villain didn't leave town via the London road." He shifted his gaze between brother and sister. "From memory, that leaves the roads to Nottingham, Newark-on-Trent, and Melton Mowbray, plus the road east to Boston, although that seems less likely."

Dickie was nodding. "There's also a handful of lanes that lead off into the surrounding country between the London road and the road to Melton Mowbray. Our thief might have thought to evade any pursuit by taking more minor ways."

Nicholas nodded. "We'll need to check those as well."

A discussion ensued over how best to tackle the search. Having lived in the locality all their lives, both Sommervilles knew various people who lived around the town and also of places that would likely prove fruitful in terms of finding witnesses who might have spotted The Barbarian trotting past.

Given the number of roads to be covered and not, himself, having such insights, Nicholas was forced to agree to them splitting up into three teams. It was decided that Dickie would take Rory with him and seek sightings along the lanes between the London and Melton Mowbray roads and out along the latter road as well. Meanwhile, Young Gillies, Jed, and Mike would work their way through the local inns and stables again, in case they'd missed any information the previous evening, then assuming they found nothing, the three would check the easterly road that ultimately led to Boston, even though it was obvious to all that, had that been the thief's intended destination, he could have much more easily gone directly that way from the estate.

That left Nicholas to ride out with Adriana to check along the westerly road to Nottingham and also the northwesterly road to Newark-on-Trent.

Addie tamped down her impatience; despite her inclination to rush ahead, she could see the value in executing a comprehensive search. While the sense of time being wasted chafed, she agreed that if any of their teams discovered a definite sighting—a lead—one of the team would return to the Angel and wait to alert the rest of the company while the other member or members would continue tracking the thief and following his trail as fast as was possible.

With that decided, leaving Dickie and Nicholas to organize the grooms and stablemen, Addie went upstairs to explain their plan to Sally, who would be the only one of their party remaining at the inn through the day.

CHAPTER 5

*A*fter securing her riding hat and swiping up her gloves and quirt, Addie hurried down the stairs and emerged onto the inn's porch to see Nicholas waiting in the yard, beside her saddled mount.

The sight—and its implications—put a hitch in her stride. She disguised the near stumble as being caused by a crimp in her skirt. After needlessly resettling the train over her arm, she raised her head, went down the steps, and with every appearance of confidence, strode for her horse.

Nicholas straightened as she approached. When she halted beside Nickleby, Nicholas reached for her. "Allow me."

She steeled herself against the sensation of his hands closing about her waist and tightened her grip on her wits as he effortlessly lifted her to her side-saddle.

She didn't breathe—couldn't—until his hands left her. Surreptitiously drawing in a huge breath, she settled in the saddle and, willing her giddy senses to steady, inclined her head regally. "Thank you."

With a dip of his head, he reached for the reins of his big gray, a hunter the ostlers, accustomed though they were to such beasts, treated with awe and reverence. As she slid her boot into the stirrup, he swung up to the animal's back.

A quick glance around confirmed that the others had already left. Increasingly irritated by her continuing unhelpful reaction to Nicholas, when he waved her to the inn's arch, she was more than ready to ride out.

Nicholas allowed Adriana to lead, and she opted to head out of town along the westerly road to Nottingham. Not that they would be riding anywhere near that far, but only until they found sightings sufficient to determine whether the thief had gone that way.

Adriana paused beside two women carrying baskets of fruit into the town. The pair had been on the road since before dawn and hadn't seen The Barbarian.

She and Nicholas stopped to ask a farmer driving a cart into town, then Nicholas dismounted and strode into a field to speak with a group of workers, but no one had sighted the horse.

Farther along, several other groups of farmworkers likewise hadn't seen either thief or horse, yet none could definitively state that The Barbarian hadn't passed that way. Finally, on the outskirts of Saxondale, they came across a group of laborers digging out a culvert. They'd been working at the same spot for the past two days and could confirm beyond question that The Barbarian hadn't passed them.

"We're here from dawn to dark," the man in charge said. "Squire wants this done in a hurry, so we're here as long as we can see." He glanced along the road toward Grantham. "Don't reckon your man could have come along this way."

Nicholas agreed, and albeit reluctantly, Adriana did, too.

They thanked the laborers and wheeled their horses toward Grantham.

They rode quickly, eschewing all conversation. Not that Nicholas had anything he wished to discuss at that point, and Adriana, he'd realized, was not a needlessly talkative female.

Another point of stark contrast between her and her social façade. By all accounts, it was often difficult to get Miss Flibbertigibbet to cease chattering.

At Adriana's suggestion, they diverted south a little way to the hamlet of Barrowby, where she knew of an inn that served good food and ale. As the day was warm and, although not quite noon, breakfast was hours behind them, Nicholas readily supported the notion of taking a short break before they forged on.

The White Swan Inn had a pleasant garden to one side, and they elected to sit at a table there, beneath the spreading branches of old fruit trees. After they'd given a serving girl their orders, Nicholas left Adriana at the table and went to chat to the publican and any useful patron who might be in the taproom.

He was resigned to the news that no one had seen any sign of a large bay stallion, yet he gathered enough firm negatives to feel sure that the thief hadn't taken to the lanes in that direction.

He returned to the garden to see that the serving girl had delivered their meals and cider. Adriana was lowering her tankard after having taken a sip; he saw the tip of her tongue pass over her lips and paused for a second to tamp down his instinctive reaction before continuing across the lawn to join her.

Late blossoms bobbed all about her, a white-and-pink frame. She looked up as he approached, and the exquisite perfection of her features struck him anew. Her appearance was so utterly flawless, she looked like a Dresden figurine planted in the orchard.

When he saw her like this, the dichotomy between her two personas —Miss Flibbertigibbet and Lady Adriana Sommerville—was impossible to ignore. Patently, one was false, and one was real, and it was increasingly clear which that was. The need to learn why the other side of her existed had grown beyond mere curiosity and had burgeoned into compulsive fascination.

On reaching the table, he dropped onto the bench opposite her and forced his gaze to the slice of game pie waiting on his plate. "That looks —and smells—very good."

She nodded and forked up a bite of hers. "It is."

They ate in strangely companionable silence.

Somewhat to his surprise, it was he who broke it. "Your brother mentioned that you didn't grace London's ballrooms this Season."

He raised his gaze to her face, his expression nothing more than mildly inquisitive.

Addie read as much and lightly shrugged. "Papa's health wasn't as robust as Mama would have liked, and she didn't want to subject him to the demands of a Season or leave him at the Grange with just Angie and the staff. Admittedly, I could have gone down and swanned around under my aunt's aegis, but to be perfectly truthful, I've always found the rounds of balls and parties..." She paused, searching for the right word, and settled on "superficial."

Just like her alter ego.

Seeking to deflect further questions about herself, she fixed her gaze on his face. "Try as I might, I can't recall ever meeting you at any such ball or party."

His grin was swift and utterly charming. "As you might imagine, in my earlier years, I was pressured into attending, but even then, I only appeared at that sort of event when I couldn't get out of squiring my mother or sisters. Luckily for me, Toby is more inclined to see such entertainments as having some value, so these days, I hide in Newmarket as much as possible."

She softly snorted. "It seems we share a similar view on the usefulness of the Season."

They'd finished their meals. She drained her mug, and he did the same.

"Right, then." She set down the mug. "Back to our search."

Without further ado, they left the garden and made their way to where their mounts were waiting in the care of an ostler.

Addie set her jaw against the apparently inevitable sensory swoon that being lifted to her saddle by Nicholas provoked. She'd been counting on the impact fading, but it hadn't. Not at all.

If anything, the impulse to seek more of the dizzying sensations was growing, building, becoming a definite itch beneath her skin.

Determinedly ignoring the feeling, she led the way out of the hamlet and into the center of Grantham. They paused to check at the Angel to see if any of the other groups had picked up their quarry's trail, but no one was waiting with news.

Resolutely quashing her disappointment, with Nicholas beside her, she guided Nickleby onto the road to Newark-on-Trent.

Once clear of the town, she spotted a farmer's wife in a field and stopped to speak with her, but although the woman had been close by the road since dawn, she hadn't seen any big bay horse being led past. Addie thanked her and rode on, with Nicholas keeping pace alongside.

After two similar encounters, she grumbled to herself, "It would have been so much easier if the blackguard had stayed in Grantham overnight."

She'd thought she'd spoken too quietly to be heard, but Nicholas responded, "Given the timing, we have to find people who can be certain the horse didn't pass this way late yesterday as well as today."

She grimaced but nodded, and they rode on.

They reached Foston and spotted the curate, gardening in the grounds of St. Peter's Church. Nicholas dismounted and spoke with the clergyman, but while the jovial man could assure them no horse fitting the description of The Barbarian had passed the church the previous evening, he'd only just returned to his weeding, so couldn't speak for earlier that day.

After thanking the curate, Nicholas remounted, and they rode on.

At last, just before the village of Long Bennington, they came upon three workers baling hay in a field bordering the road.

This time, when Nicholas asked, he got a clear and definite if negative answer. The horse hadn't passed that way either that day or yesterday.

The men were so certain, once Nicholas remounted, Addie didn't hesitate to set Nickleby cantering back toward Grantham.

Nicholas drew level. She felt his gaze touch her face.

A minute later, he called across, "At least we know for certain the thief didn't bring the horse this way."

She swallowed a huff. "Let's hope the others have had better luck."

They rode steadily toward Grantham. By the time they reached the village of Great Gonerby, on a hill northwest of the town, the afternoon light was waning, and the horses were tiring. At least, her horse was.

Ahead, Nicholas spotted a small lookout beside the road and pointed to it. "Let's take a few minutes and give the horses a break."

Adriana nodded, and they slowed and turned off the road.

The lookout sported a water trough. They allowed the horses to drink, then let them graze the rough grass that pushed up between stones on the rocky ridge.

Several scattered boulders formed benches on which they could sit and admire the view over the town.

Nicholas settled on a boulder alongside the one Adriana had chosen and heard her sigh dispiritedly.

The compulsion to comfort her struck so strongly, so viscerally, he almost reached for her.

Reining in the impulse, he nevertheless cast about for some topic with which to distract her. Despite an inner resistance to admitting to even that much interest, as her dejected silence continued, he gave in and ventured, "I have to admit I've been dying to ask why you invented the façade of Miss Flibbertigibbet. Why it is that you assume that mask when in London or, at least, when moving in society there?"

She continued staring at the town. Her profile gave him no clue to her reaction.

When she didn't respond, he leaned forward, resting his forearms on his thighs, and with his gaze also on the distant roofs, said, "I assume you do so as a form of defense. A shield of sorts when waltzing through the Marriage Mart. What puzzles me is how on earth you pulled off such a pretense, not just once but consistently over a period of years"—he turned his head and looked at her—"given that you're nothing at all like Miss Flibbertigibbet is purported to be."

That elicited a huff overflowing with contempt and derision. "On the contrary, to the vast majority of the ton, Miss Flibbertigibbet and I are exactly alike." Abruptly, she met his gaze. "We look the same, and in the eyes of the bulk of society, appearance is what defines a lady."

Puzzled, he frowned. "I don't understand."

Again, she made a derisive sound and looked back at the view. "I spent most of my childhood in the country, at the Grange or visiting relatives or staying at one of my father's other houses. Few in the ton had seen me prior to my first Season. Then I made my come-out, and society saw this"—with a wave, she indicated her face and figure—"and instantly assumed that I was exactly as my image painted me. They were certain that I was Miss Flibbertigibbet before I uttered a word and, from the first, treated me accordingly. And before you ask, of course I tried to tactfully correct their misconception, but I soon discovered that the power of suggestion inherent in my appearance was simply too great to overcome. People insisted I was—that I had to be—the embodiment of what they saw."

Lips compressing, she paused, then somewhat grudgingly admitted, "I was younger, then, and feeling my way. When they refused to listen to me, I lost my temper, and instead of continuing to try to correct their mistake, I went in the opposite direction. In doing so, *I* made an assumption that proved to be incorrect. I thought that if I showed them how stupid, how impossibly vacuous, and how outrageously foolish their expectations of Miss Flibbertigibbet were, that would open their eyes, and they would realize it was all an act—all untrue. That their ideas of me simply couldn't be true."

Nicholas studied her face. Her expression suggested she considered all that to be water under the bridge. "But they never did realize."

"No." A second later, she met his eyes. "And then I realized the benefits of my disguise, the usefulness of the persona I had by then created and established in the eyes of the ton."

How anyone could miss the intelligence in her eyes, the gleam of the quick mind behind her periwinkle-blue gaze, was beyond him. Slowly, he nodded. "So now you use your fabricated façade to…"

"Screen people and keep the unworthy at bay." She arched a brow at him. "Some—not many but some—see straight through the mask, and several of those have become firm friends. As for the rest"—she shrugged

—"those who think the worst of me simply because of my appearance are not worthy of my notice."

Adriana hoped her firm delivery of that conclusion was sufficient to gloss over all the pain and hurt she'd endured before she'd reached that stage of self-comprehension. Of inner confidence.

Even as she thought that, the strangeness of the conversation registered. Normally, she would never have spoken about what had led to the construction of her Miss Flibbertigibbet persona, so why had she revealed all to him?

Perhaps because he's one of the few—indeed, the only personable male—who has ever asked.

The realization left her feeling just a touch vulnerable, but also set her wondering. She shifted on her rock. "Before, you intimated that you avoided the Season and all similar social events." She met his eyes, and when he made no move to deny that, simply asked, "Why?"

He blinked, then a faint smile edged his firm lips, and he looked out over the view. "Put simply, I'm far more interested in managing the Cynster racing stable than I am in anything the ton has to offer."

She snorted softly. "I imagine your mama would have something to say to that."

He grinned. "Mama and my aunts and various cousins and connections, but luckily, there are so many of us—of the wider Cynster family of my generation—that there's always some budding romance somewhere to keep them amused."

"So thus far, you've escaped?"

"Indeed. And that's left me free to concentrate on improving the Cynster Stable's standing and our results. Among other things, that means acquiring horses like The Barbarian." He paused, then added, "Having taken over the stables from my famous father, I feel a certain pressure to make my mark, and in reality, the only way to do that is to significantly improve our stock."

She grinned. "I have to admit that given you're the scion of a ducal dynasty, I was rather surprised to see you ride up, rather than sweep up the drive in a phaeton of the sort to make my brothers salivate."

His answering smile was full of amusement. "I leave that to others of the clan. I've always been more comfortable on horseback."

She bit her tongue on the observation that he cut a more dashing figure that way. She'd made enough unexpected revelations that day.

The horses were contentedly cropping, and the westering sun was still warm. Eager to keep the focus on him rather than allow it to swing back to her, she asked, "So how do you fill your days?" When he looked at her, she met his gaze. "Is it all watching races or...?"

"Mostly 'or.' Indeed, almost exclusively 'or.' Attending the major race meets takes up only a small portion of my time. The rest is spent mostly on Newmarket Heath, watching over training sessions. Beyond that, a lot of my time goes in learning what other trainers are up to, both in searching for ways to improve our methods as well as assessing the competition."

"I've run into Toby several times in London. You said he's also involved in running the stables."

Nicholas nodded. "My sister Pru used to manage the breeding stable, and Toby acted as her lieutenant. I was always in charge of the racing and training stable—that side of the business. When Pru married and went to live in Ireland, managing her new husband Glengarah's breeding stable instead of ours, Toby stepped into her shoes."

"So your siblings are as horse-mad as you?"

He laughed. "The older three of us could legitimately be labeled horse-mad, but the youngest, Meg, is entirely the opposite—she's determinedly uninterested in anything to do with horses. She routinely refers to them as 'smelly beasts.'"

She chuckled. "She sounds...willful."

Smiling fondly, he nodded. "She is."

Nicholas met Adriana's blue eyes and, once again, felt a visceral tug, a connection utterly unlike any he'd felt before.

Then again, how often had he sat with a gently bred female and discussed his life and his family, even in such a general way?

Before she could see any hint of the impulses rising within him, he glanced at the horses. "We should get on. One of the other teams might have had better luck and be waiting for us to return."

He got to his feet, and she rose with him.

They moved to reclaim their reins, but instead of waiting for him to lift her to her saddle, she used one of the boulders as a mounting block and scrambled up.

Somewhat cravenly grateful to be spared another jolt to his ever-increasing awareness of her, he swung up to his saddle and, when she tapped her heel to her horse's side, followed her out of the lookout and onto the road again.

They rode straight to the Angel, and he dismounted in the yard.

Walking to where, having slipped her boot free of her stirrup and swung around on her saddle, Adriana sat perched on her chestnut's back, Nicholas tightened his grip on his inner self's reins, lifted her down, and immediately released her and stepped back before any wayward impulse could prod him into doing anything more.

The sound of hooves clattering on cobbles drew their attention to the entrance to the yard. Dickie and Rory rode in. Their glum faces told their story even before they dismounted and confirmed that they'd discovered no sighting despite having found a goodly number of people to ask.

"The only thing I feel confident in stating," Dickie concluded, following his sister into their private parlor, "is that wherever our thief has taken The Barbarian, it isn't to the south or southwest."

Adriana slumped into an armchair. "And from our searching, it isn't to the west or northwest, either."

Nicholas followed the pair into the parlor and waved at Rory, who'd hung back, to join them. When Rory did and closed the door, Nicholas asked, "Have you seen Young Gillies and the others?"

Rory shook his head. "No, sir. Not since we all set out."

"That's odd." Dickie frowned. "They had the least distance to cover. They should have been back first."

Hurrying footsteps beyond the door preceded a sharp knock, then the door opened, and Young Gillies looked in. He saw them and grinned. "We think we know which way the blackguard went."

Needless to say, the announcement revived the rest of the company. Nicholas waved Young Gillies in, and everyone focused their attention on him. "The others?" Nicholas asked as Young Gillies shut the door.

"Settling the horses," Young Gillies replied. "We thought you'd want to hear what we found without delay."

"In that, you're correct," Nicholas informed him, glancing around at the keenly anticipatory expressions. He looked back at Young Gillies. "So tell us your news."

Young Gillies drew himself up. "Well, first off, he's not in town. We haven't caught up with him yet, but we did pick up his trail."

"Don't tell me he headed for Boston after all?" Dickie incredulously exclaimed.

"No, sir." Young Gillies shook his head. "After checking around town, we first rode out along the road to the east—toward Boston—and we quickly came across a road gang who were absolutely certain the horse hadn't been led past them yesterday nor today. It was hard to see how anyone could have got by without them seeing, and they said they were working until dark last night and were back at first light this morning."

Young Gillies glanced at Nicholas. "We decided that was good enough proof the blackguard hadn't gone that way, but learning that had taken us barely an hour, so we decided to backtrack toward Aisby and see if we could find any definite sighting to say that the villain had actually come all the way into Grantham. So we went back out along the northeast road."

"The road we came in on," Adriana clarified.

Young Gillies nodded. "Yes, that one. We started with the stall just on the edge of town, and the farmwife there said she hadn't seen The Barbarian go by. She's forever watching the road for customers, so it seemed she'd have seen if the thief had taken the horse past, but she only stayed until about six o'clock yesterday, so he could have gone past later."

Dickie was frowning. "That doesn't fit our thesis. He'd have had to go past her earlier than that."

"Aye." Young Gillies ducked his head. "We thought that, too, so we went on and found two other blokes, but although neither had seen the horse, they couldn't be certain about the times. That brought us to where the lane from Aisby joins the road. It was barely noon, so we thought we'd go on and see if we could find anyone farther up the road, just in case the villain had, after all, gone that way."

Young Gillies's round face lit. "And he had! We got as far as a little place called Manthorpe."

Leaning forward, Adriana nodded. "We know it."

"And we found two workers trimming a long hedge. They'd been at it these past days, and they—both of them—remembered the man leading the big bay horse going past, heading north."

"When?" Nicholas asked.

"Yesterday," Young Gillies replied. "Sometime late afternoon was the best time they could give us."

"Damn!" Dickie collapsed into a chair by the table. "Despite it making no sense, the blackguard was making for Lincoln all along."

Nicholas studied Adriana's, Dickie's, and Rory's flummoxed expressions. "You mentioned earlier that, from Aisby, if the thief was heading for Lincoln, it would have been quicker for him to go directly north from the village. How much quicker?"

Dickie's expression turned calculating. "Six, seven miles?" He glanced at Rory.

Rory nodded. "About that. Much faster to strike north from Aisby."

Adriana shook her head. "Why on earth did he take the route he did if all along he intended to head for Lincoln?"

Nicholas offered, "I can think of two possible reasons." When the others looked at him, he explained, "One, the thief isn't a local, so he didn't know of the local lanes or, alternatively, didn't want to risk striking north on lanes he wasn't sure led to where he wanted to go. That's one possibility."

Adriana grimaced. "I suppose that might have been so."

"The other possibility," Nicholas continued, "is that the thief used the roundabout route to throw us off the scent. Presumably, he hoped to make us think that he'd headed into Grantham. By doing so, he's gained an extra day as well as making tracking him that much harder."

Dickie softly swore, while Adriana's expression said she wished she could.

Feeling deeply annoyed at having fallen for the villain's ploy, Addie glanced out of the window. It might be nearly six o'clock, but there was plenty of light. "We've lost so much time! We should set off for Lincoln immediately."

She looked at the others to see all the men frowning.

"I don't think that's a good idea," Nicholas stated.

Dickie scoffed. "We won't even have any moonlight to help us, so we won't get far."

"Only get a few miles farther," Rory agreed, "and then we'd have to find someplace to stay. And there aren't that many decent inns along that road. Leastways not where we'd be come nightfall."

"Exactly." Dickie's tone suggested the matter was settled.

Frustration gnawing at her, Addie insisted, "Then we head out early. At first light."

To that, the others agreed, leaving her feeling faintly mollified.

A tap on the door heralded their host, who wanted to know if they were ready for their dinner.

The question reminded everyone of how hungry they were. Young Gillies and Rory departed to eat with Jed, Mike, and Sally in the taproom. Addie accepted the chair Nicholas held for her at the table, and they settled to address the plates of rabbit stew and crusty fresh bread the maids ferried in.

Nicholas had assumed that one of the reasons—possibly the most pressing reason—that Dickie had joined their company was to act as his sister's chaperon. Yet later that evening, after the dishes had been cleared away and they'd retreated to the armchairs before the small fireplace, apparently oblivious to any question of propriety, Dickie left to join the grooms and stablemen in the taproom.

It might have been that Dickie suspected his sister would gripe about them not racing after the thief immediately and chose to leave Nicholas to deal with that.

Instead, Nicholas had to contend with his escalating physical awareness of Adriana that seized on moments like this, when they were entirely alone, to well and make itself known.

Quashing the impulses that awareness spawned, he searched for some topic with which to distract them both and recalled Dickie's strange reaction on hearing that Nicholas had met the earl and countess. "Your parents," he ventured, "seem a devoted couple."

Adriana smiled fondly. "They are. They've been married for nearly thirty years. Mama dotes on Papa, and he adores her. These days, now that Papa no longer rides and Mama is—thank heaven—growing less fond of the social round, they spend much of their time together. Nowadays, I don't know what Papa would do without Mama."

He was watching her face closely and sensed her last sentence held some deeper, more nuanced meaning. What that might be... "From what Dickie said, I understand your mama is your father's second wife."

Adriana nodded. "His first countess died in childbirth. The tale goes that Mama was at the first ball Papa attended after he came out of mourning, and the instant he laid eyes on her, that was it. They were married some months later."

Nicholas felt there was something—some aspect—he should be delicately probing, but his sense of what that aspect might be was so vague, it was entirely unhelpful.

"What about your parents?" Adriana asked. "Are they devoted to each other, too?"

He softly snorted and met her eyes. "'Devoted' doesn't quite describe their relationship." He thought, then said, "You might have heard that Cynsters only marry for love."

"I have, actually. I assumed it was something along the lines of an old wives' tale."

He huffed a laugh. "No, it's not. To all intents and purposes, it's a statement of fact. So my parents are madly and utterly in love. Still, even after all these years." Thinking of them, he had to grin. "One outcome of that is that if you have any sense of self-preservation, you would never do anything that in any way might threaten Mama or Papa in the other's presence. They are ferociously protective of each other."

Adriana arched a brow, as if imagining that—or perhaps seeing his parents, whom he assumed she must have met at some point, in a different light.

After a moment, she mused, "Your father is known to be a superb rider. Is your mother interested in horses as well?"

"Indeed, she is. And between you and me, she's nearly as good a rider as Papa, and in certain circumstances, on certain horses, might even be more accomplished than he."

"Really? That's hard to imagine."

Nicholas laughed and launched into a tale of one long-ago summer picnic during which his mother's ability with a horse had shone.

Adriana countered with a story of a holiday at the seaside when her mother had demonstrated that she could drive a gig at a pace that, even now, purely in memory, made Dickie blanch.

To Nicholas's surprise, they whiled away an hour swapping family tales, some of which he hadn't thought about in years, and he suspected the same could be said for Adriana. A sense of rediscovery gripped them as they related and relived their memories. Although no experience of his was exactly the same as one of hers, he noted that, for both of them, their fondest childhood recollections were all of the country. London never featured, even though both had spent time there during their formative years.

Eventually, the chiming clocks drew their attention to the hour.

"Ten o'clock." Adriana met Nicholas's eyes, then pushed to her feet. "If we're going to make an early start, I believe we should retire."

He looked up at her. He could make some excuse—such as going to look for her brother—and let her go upstairs alone, but the thought of her tripping on her train and this time, without him there to catch her, falling down the stairs had him rising from the comfort of the chair. "Indeed." He straightened and waved to the door, then followed her from the room.

As they climbed the stairs, he steeled himself against the inevitable surge of expectation. No, he should name it for what it was—desire—stoked by an avid hope that she would stumble into his arms again...

She didn't.

He sensed that, even more than he, she watched her steps the entire way up the stairs; he thought he heard her utter a tiny sigh of relief as she successfully took the last step up into the gallery and the tension in her arm holding her train eased.

They continued along the corridor that led to their rooms.

He halted outside his door, and she paused beside him and, through the shadows, looked up at him.

His eyes found hers, and their gazes locked.

Temptation surged. Never in his life had he felt such a powerful compulsion to sweep a woman into his arms and kiss her witless.

He almost swayed, pushed by that invisible urge. Blindly, he searched for the doorknob and closed his hand about it as if clinging to some anchor in a raging, roiling sea.

Good Lord! He had to break free of the ruthless compulsion before he gave in to it and complicated everything.

Yet he couldn't drag his eyes from hers, couldn't haul his awareness from the interest—*the desire*—he sensed behind her perfect porcelain features.

Addie discovered she was breathless, rendered so by a flaring connection she'd had no idea could leap into being in such a forceful way. Her gaze locked with his, she fought to steady her whirling wits, but they wouldn't listen. Wouldn't respond any more than her clamorous senses.

Every element of her being was excited, eager, passionate, yearning, and willfully wanting, urging her to be even more reckless.

To take a step—a single step—into his arms.

To take the plunge and kiss him.

She stared, mesmerized, into his eyes, and the compulsion only grew.

So powerful was the incitement, so unrelenting, that she tensed to take that one small step.

The click of a door opening had her sucking in a desperate breath and looking down the corridor.

Sally emerged from Addie's room. The maid looked along the corridor and saw them—standing stock-still in the shadows—and smiled. "There you are, my lady. I was just coming to ask if you needed anything."

"No. I was just...on my way," Addie managed.

Without looking at Nicholas again—without risking falling under whatever spell had held her—she inclined her head his way. "Goodnight."

His answering "Goodnight" followed her as she walked the few yards to where Sally waited.

Behind her, she heard Nicholas's door open, then quietly shut.

As she preceded Sally into her room, Addie finally managed to fill her lungs again.

She allowed Sally to help her out of her riding habit and into her nightdress, then sat and let the maid brush out her hair.

The soothing strokes settled the last of her skittering nerves.

Only then did she allow herself to review those fraught moments in the corridor. It had felt as if some net, some force—some *thing*—had captured them and held them, urging them closer...

Recalling what, despite his impassivity, she'd been able to read in his face, she was fairly sure she hadn't been the only one feeling that pressure.

And that, indeed, was a point to ponder.

Twenty minutes later, as she lay in her bed and listened to Sally's not-so-soft snores, she had to admit that she honestly didn't know whether she felt grateful or annoyed over the maid's unwitting intervention.

Because increasingly, the question incessantly nagging at her was what kissing Nicholas Cynster—and being kissed by him—would be like.

CHAPTER 6

She had to keep her mind on the task at hand. That was the only way she was going to be able to stop herself from dwelling on that almost-kiss.

It was ridiculous. She'd woken with a sense of unrelieved longing dragging at her, and she was not at all amused at being prey to the sensation.

Resolved and determined to keep the pursuit of The Barbarian front and center in her mind, she hurried through an early breakfast, poking at Dickie—never an early riser—to hurry, and made a point of getting down to the inn yard before anyone else so she could use the mounting block and avoid having her senses unnecessarily scrambled.

She was perched on Nickleby's back, impatiently waiting, when Nicholas appeared, closely followed by a barely awake Dickie.

Sally was there and already mounted as well, and the grooms and stablemen were waiting with the horses. Within minutes, the company was mounted and ready, and nothing loath, Addie led the way out of the yard and turned to take the northbound road.

It was early, and there were few others about; they were able to go at a swift trot. Nicholas brought his gray up on her right, and eventually, Dickie appeared on her left.

"We may as well ride directly to Manthorpe." Dickie glanced across at Nicholas. "Given the sighting there was so definite, there seems little sense wasting time trying to track him until after there."

Nicholas nodded. "I agree."

With that decided and the outskirts of Grantham falling behind, Addie pushed Nickleby into a canter.

Nicholas and Dickie kept pace, as did the others behind them.

Soon, Addie felt happier, soothed by the sense of finally moving quickly on the thief's trail. Admittedly, they were more than a day behind him, but however irrational, the belief remained that they would soon catch up to him.

They passed through Manthorpe, and she took the lead in questioning people they found along the road, and they discovered two further definite sightings, first in the village of Belton and then just outside Barkston.

They were, finally, on the right track.

Increasingly confident, the company thundered along the road.

They reached the fork outside Honington where the road to Sleaford veered to the east. Addie and Dickie continued on along the Lincoln road, but Nicholas slowed. "Wait."

It took a moment for them all to draw rein. Addie and Dickie had to circle to return to where Nicholas sat his huge gray, staring toward Sleaford. When they reached him, he tipped his head in that direction. "How can we be sure he didn't take that road?"

"Well," Dickie said, "that leads to Sleaford, and even more so than Lincoln, if the blackguard had intended to go to Sleaford, it would have been so much faster going direct from Aisby."

"Actually," Addie put in, "it would have been faster still if he'd continued along that right of way from The Barbarian's paddock. Had he gone that way, he might not have been spotted by anyone, and we wouldn't have found any hint of him at all."

Nicholas saw that Rory and the stablemen and even Adriana's maid were all nodding.

"And if," Dickie continued, "we're leaning to the hypothesis that because there was no attempt made to get The Barbarian's papers, then our thief might simply have stolen the horse as a good-looking hack that will be easy to sell, then I really can't imagine why said thief would make for Sleaford."

Adriana explained, "There's nothing notable or useful about the town, and it's not the fastest way to anywhere else, either."

"Lincoln would be the best bet for selling a stolen horse," Jeb put in.

Everyone bar Nicholas and Young Gillies—the only non-locals— backed that assessment.

Nicholas knew he tended to err on the side of caution—Pru and Toby often told him so—and with time ticking inexorably by and everyone else being so convinced that the thief would have headed for Lincoln, he felt he had to set aside his innate inclination to insist on proof instead of assumptions. Accepting that, he turned Tamerlane's head toward Lincoln. "In that case, let's ride on."

They did, but it was slow going as they stopped and spoke with everyone they came across who might have seen horses passing along the road. Unfortunately, no one had seen The Barbarian, yet none of the non-sightings were definitive. Courtesy of the sighting at Barkston, they knew the thief had come that way on Wednesday afternoon, and it was possible he'd passed by either before or after their informants had been in position to see him.

Either that, or they hadn't been looking toward the road at that time.

Regardless, it was nearing noon when they approached Leadenham with nothing to show for their recent efforts. As breakfast had been so long ago, they stopped at the Three Feathers to assuage their hunger.

They ate at a long wooden table at the front of the inn. Seated on the end of one of the bench seats, Nicholas glanced at Adriana, sitting opposite. "Should we backtrack?" When she and the others looked blankly at him, he rephrased, "How likely is it that our thief turned down one of the minor lanes we passed?"

They'd ridden past the entrance to several country lanes, some leading east and some west.

All the locals in the company frowned and chewed, then Dickie swallowed and said, "I can't see why he would. Ultimately, all those minor lanes lead to either Sleaford to the east or Newark to the west, and I can't imagine why a horse thief would make for either town, not with Lincoln ahead of him."

That seemed to be the general consensus, one Rory summarized. "If our thief with a fabulous horse to sell didn't go to Grantham, then surely he'd go to Lincoln. He'd have a much better chance of finding a buyer there, even better than in Grantham."

Mike nodded. "It would have been risky trying to sell The Barbarian in Grantham, given the estate is so close. Someone might have recognized him."

Nicholas glanced at Adriana. "I thought few people knew the horse was at Aisby Grange."

She nodded. "But the thief wouldn't have known that."

"Really," Dickie said, pushing away his empty plate, "if we try to think like our thief, who finds himself at Aisby with a very noticeable horse in tow, one he wants to sell, most likely as soon as possible, and instead of heading east, which he could have easily done, he goes west until he hits a north-south road, and instead of turning south for Grantham or London, he heads north..." Dickie spread his hands. "Then, surely, he has to be making for Lincoln."

Despite a gut feeling that there were several caveats to that reasoning that, perhaps, should be considered, despite not being wholly convinced, faced with the certainty with which the others embraced Dickie's assertion, Nicholas swallowed his misgivings and agreed.

Minutes later, they were back on the road, riding toward Lincoln.

In light of the reluctance Addie sensed in Nicholas—his lack of conviction regarding their direction—she insisted they pause at every village and hamlet along the way, asking everyone they could find whether they'd spotted The Barbarian, either on Wednesday afternoon or Thursday morning.

Given the route the thief had taken and the distance between Aisby and Lincoln, it was virtually guaranteed that the blackguard would have been forced to find somewhere to spend Wednesday night.

They asked at every possible place as they rode north through Wellingore, Navenby, and Waddington, including several cottages and farms, but no one had seen the rider leading a huge bay stallion.

"Alternatively," Addie grimly said as they left the tiny tavern at Bracebridge Heath, "being a horse thief, the blackguard might have spent the night under some hedge."

Rory was starting to look unconvinced, too. "The Barbarian wouldn't have liked that."

Addie merely humphed, but the observation was accurate, and when he was displeased, The Barbarian had ways of making his feelings known. Then again, he was such an unpredictable horse, he might have decided that being in an unfamiliar place was a great adventure.

She grew increasingly frustrated when, even as they approached Lincoln and there were more people about to ask, not only had no one sighted The Barbarian but equally, no one could say that he hadn't, at some point, passed that way.

The answers they got were all negative, yet not one was definitive.

By the time they clattered into Lincoln proper, she was starting to worry that Nicholas had been right and, for some unfathomable reason, their quarry had turned off the road.

None of them knew Lincoln well, but she, Dickie, and Nicholas had all heard the Turk's Head mentioned as the place to stay. As the hostelry was famously located in the shadow of the castle, it was easy to find, and they clattered into the yard in midafternoon.

Of course, none of the inn's ostlers had set eyes on a huge bay stallion; that had been too much to hope for. Yet if their reception was anything to judge by, the inn was, indeed, the right one for them. Without so much as a blink, the proprietor arranged for a late luncheon to be served in a private parlor, and he promised their rooms would be ready immediately they quit the table.

Addie ate with Nicholas and Dickie in the parlor, while the others were served in the taproom. As the cleaned plates and emptied platters were being removed, Rory looked around the parlor door and raised his brows in question.

Nicholas waved him in. "Bring the others. We need to work out some sort of plan."

Addie had been doing her best to keep her dejection to herself. She was determined to remain positive and encouraging, and hearing Nicholas speak of a plan helped in the sense it gave her something definite to focus on, namely a way forward.

Rory ducked his head and went to fetch the others.

Nicholas pushed back his chair and rose. "I'll ask the innkeeper for a map of the area. That'll give us some idea of what we face."

By the time he returned, map in hand, the rest of their company had arrived.

Nicholas spread the map over the table, and they all gathered around.

It was instantly apparent that Lincoln was even more of a hub for roads leading in every direction than Grantham had been.

Young Gillies glanced at the small clock on the mantel. "It's nearly five o'clock." He met Nicholas's eyes. "By the time we get out there, most workers—those we'll be wanting to question—will already be heading home for their supper."

Nicholas nodded and looked down at the map. "At this hour, there's not much point trying to find the right people to ask. But perhaps we can make use of the time by investigating how far we might have to go out along each of these roads"—with a finger, he indicated the roads fanning out from the town's center—"before we encounter either fields or those businesses where we might reasonably expect to find people keeping an eye on who passes along each road."

There were ten—*ten!*—roads they had to cover.

Addie inwardly shook her head at the enormity of the task, but undaunted, Nicholas divided the roads between the members of the group. As before, Sally would remain at the inn while the other seven rode out, this time each going alone to scout the way, except for Addie, who after Nicholas shared a look with Dickie, Nicholas stated he would accompany.

In reality, she was accompanying him, but regardless, that meant she wouldn't be sitting at the inn twiddling her thumbs and feeling utterly useless.

"And," Nicholas said, straightening from the table, "we need to remember that tomorrow is Saturday and many workers will only be at their workplace for half the day."

Dickie nodded. "So doing what we're doing now—assessing where along each road we'll be able to ask our questions—will allow us to act more quickly tomorrow and hopefully get the answers we need."

"Exactly," Nicholas said.

On that quietly rousing note, they headed out to reclaim their mounts.

Addie rushed to use the mounting block; she remained wary of the way her senses betrayed her whenever Nicholas got too close, and him placing his hands about her waist and lifting her to her saddle definitely qualified.

The others quickly mounted, and in a group, they clattered out of the yard, then separated, each heading for the road they were to assess.

Most headed south or east, but Nicholas turned his horse northward, and she followed suit.

Nicholas led the way up the road, following signs to Riseholme, but they didn't need to go as far as the village before they were in open country again. Although the businesses they passed were closing or already shut, they noted a jobbing stable and a blacksmith's, both fronting the road, and beyond the last cottages on the town's outskirts, they found evidence that suggested a culvert was in the process of being repaired.

Nicholas dismounted and scrambled down the bank bordering the road to take a closer look at the site. After assessing progress, he climbed back. "It looks like the workers will return tomorrow."

Adriana nodded. "And no rider could come this way without them noticing."

"Indeed." Nicholas swung up and settled in his saddle. "As far as this road goes, that gives us enough places to ask tomorrow and be certain of getting a definitive answer." He stood in his stirrups and scanned the area ahead, then sank back to his saddle and pointed up the road and to the left. "One of the ostlers told me that lane will take us across to the Burton road. If we ride across and go back into town along that route, we can investigate it as well."

Adriana dipped her head in agreement, and together, they rode on.

The sun was sliding down the western sky when they reached the road to Burton and turned southward, riding toward Lincoln once more.

A cattle yard and two competing carters' yards located on opposite sides of the road looked to be their best chances of securing information the next morning, and closer to the center of the town, they found another jobbing stable.

As they walked their horses along the street toward the Turk's Head, Nicholas said, "Given tomorrow is a half day for most, we'll likely do better to ride this route in reverse." He glanced at Adriana. "Out via the road to Burton, then across via the lane and back to the inn via the Rise-holme road."

She nodded. "That will give us the best chance of finding the right people to ask."

They turned in under the inn's archway and saw Jed and Young Gillies already back and waiting.

Nicholas dismounted and handed Tamerlane's reins to Young Gillies, then went to Adriana's side and, when she realized and quickly freed her boot from the stirrup, he closed his hands about her slender waist and lifted her down.

Her boots met the ground, and he told himself to release her. It still took an appreciable length of time between his mind issuing the directive and his hands obeying. That moment of fraught tension on the previous night rushed into his mind; it was something neither he nor she had moved to address in any way, but now was neither the place nor the time.

As his hands fell from her and they stepped apart, Dickie came trotting into the yard, followed by Rory and Mike.

With everyone back, Nicholas suggested they convene about the map in the parlor and share their news, then plan for the next morning before settling to their dinners.

Everyone agreed, and they were soon in the parlor, gathered about the table and poring over the map. They took turns noting the businesses or work sites they'd identified along each road at which, on the morrow, they hoped to find people who could tell them whether The Barbarian had passed by.

Nicholas straightened. "Either way—a definite yes or a definite no—will get us farther."

Of the ten roads fanning outward from the town's center, not even the one along which they'd ridden into town could be deemed clear. He studied the map. "We've lost too much time not to be thorough." He glanced around, meeting the others' eyes. "Unless we get a definite answer—yes or no—we'll need to continue along each road until we can definitively state that the thief took it or that he didn't."

The others nodded their understanding.

"As for the road we assumed he used to reach the town"—Nicholas glanced at Dickie and Rory, who, tomorrow, were slated to cover that road—"we need proof positive that he did, indeed, arrive in Lincoln."

Everyone grimaced, realizing that, if that proof did not eventuate, then all their searching would be the equivalent of a wild-goose chase.

"That said," Nicholas went on, "there's no sense in the rest of us wasting the day." He glanced at the others. "We'll search the roads out while Dickie and Rory cover the road in. That will be the best use of our hours."

They discussed times and agreed to leave as soon as businesses opened in the morning, then reconvene at the inn after one o'clock, when most businesses would be closed and the workers heading home.

"We can share what we learn over luncheon," Nicholas concluded. "With any luck, we'll have a positive sighting to follow, but regardless, we'll need to plan our next steps."

He tried to make the declaration encouraging; he'd noted that both Sommerville siblings were growing dispirited. He was starting to understand their characters, Adriana's especially. She was impulsive and inclined to be reckless, and Impatient was her middle name.

As he rolled up the map, the maid looked in to see if they were ready for the evening meal. As usual, the stablemen and grooms retreated to the taproom, where they could be comfortable and lower their guards out of the presence of their betters. The maid quickly came in and set the table for Nicholas, Adriana, and Dickie. They took their seats, and two other serving girls ferried in a soup tureen and two platters—one of roast lamb and mutton and the other piled high with roasted vegetables. Bread and butter appeared next, and they set to. After their day, Nicholas, for one, was hungry, and Dickie clearly was, too; between them, they made rapid inroads into the soup and bread and butter, followed by the roasted fare.

In contrast, Adriana consumed a mere cupful of soup and a small portion of the roasted meat and turnips and made no more attempt at conversation than Nicholas or Dickie.

The silence struck Nicholas as strange. While he was accustomed to such gustatorily induced lack of conversation when eating with other males, he hadn't previously encountered a female who ate in silence. He couldn't decide if such a happening was good or a portent of which to be wary; he kept glancing at Adriana, waiting to find out.

Finally, when the tureen and the main course were removed and a plain bread pudding placed before them, she straightened in her chair, and her lips parted as if she was about to speak, but then she only sighed.

No, Nicholas thought. *This really won't do.*

He cast about for some topic that might engage his companions. While he didn't have much hope that the subject would do the trick, he ventured, "Do you spend much time hunting around Aisby?"

Both Sommervilles looked up. From the light kindling in their eyes, he'd struck conversational gold.

"Of course!" Dickie replied. "We regularly ride with the Belvoir when it rides out of Grantham, and there's various local hunts nearby."

"As you might imagine," Adriana put in, "given the countryside, the riding is superb! Lots of long runs, which, of course, is why the Belvoir come up to Grantham so often during the season. Our country is more challenging than theirs."

"Definitely," Dickie averred.

Nicholas leaned his forearms on the table. "What hunters do you have?"

They disposed of the bread pudding with barely a pause for breath. When the serving girls came to clear the table, Nicholas ordered brandies for himself and Dickie, and with Adriana, who declined a digestive, they retreated to the armchairs before the unlit fire.

The summer days had continued warm, and the evening was rather balmy.

To Nicholas's relief, the conversation rolled on unabated as they sat savoring the brandy and happily describing horses, both those they owned and those they'd seen in action and admired.

"Your Tamerlane must be a sight in the chase," Dickie said. "Lots of power there."

Nicholas dipped his head. "It took me some time to convince him of the need to run with other horses close about him. He loves to run, but likes space. He doesn't approve of being crowded."

"With a stride like his," Adriana shrewdly observed, "I doubt many horses could pace him."

Dickie cocked a brow at Nicholas. "I daresay The Barbarian would, if he was at all inclined to run in a hunt."

Adriana looked at Nicholas. "Is that why you want him for your breeding stable? For hunters?"

Nicholas shook his head. "For racers initially. Stayers. His stamina and strength as well as his action suggest his offspring could be magnificent on the track. That said, we're also likely to pair him with the sort of mares that will bear heavy hunters."

"Hmm." Adriana eyed him calculatingly. "You mentioned us getting offspring as part of your offer for The Barbarian. Can we stipulate that those should be hunters rather than horses more suitable for racing?"

He grinned. "Of course."

"Oh, but I might want a racehorse—just one." Dickie took a sip of his brandy. "I could leave it with the Cynster Stable for training, couldn't I?" When, laughing, Nicholas inclined his head in assent, Dickie went on, "I rather fancy being a racehorse owner, you know."

Adriana laughed, too, and the siblings settled to ribbing each other about their prospects regarding The Barbarian's offspring.

Smiling, Nicholas listened, entirely content for, of course, such talk was predicated on the horse being sold to the Cynster Stable.

By the time they rose to retire, Addie could view their present predicament and look forward to the coming day with some degree of equanimity if not positivity. Her natural optimism, which had been quashed by their failure to find any hint of the thief, had re-emerged, due in large part to Nicholas and his attempts to distract them.

As they started up the stairs, she felt very much in charity with him.

They reached the head of the stairs, and all three of them turned left. Dickie's room proved to be nearest the stairs, and he bade her and Nicholas goodnight and, smothering a yawn, waved them on and retreated into his room.

She and Nicholas strolled on along the dimly lit corridor, which ended in an alcove, presently curtained, with two other corridors stretching to left and right. "Sally said my room was around the corner."

Nicholas nodded. "Yours is to the left. Mine's along on the right."

They neared the end of the corridor, where they would part, and their steps slowed.

At least, Addie's did, and Nicholas matched her pace.

Her mind was suddenly awash in memories—of the sensations, feelings, and impulses that had assailed her the previous night, during those moments when she'd stood in the shadows with him, separated only by inches and the pressures of social constraint.

She remembered. In detail.

Curiosity welled. And as anyone who knew her would have said, more than any other impulse, curiosity was her besetting sin.

Instead of turning toward her room, she continued to the alcove. "I wonder what's behind the curtain?"

That wasn't what she was curious about, but the alcove was there, holding out the promise of privacy, which she suddenly craved.

With quick fingers, she found the gap between the curtain's halves and slipped through, and after a second's hesitation, Nicholas followed.

"Oh," Addie breathed as she stopped and stared.

Nicholas came to stand by her side; judging by his silence, he was equally enchanted.

In daylight, the alcove would merely be a bow window overlooking the town. At night, that night, the same view, illuminated by starlight, was transformed into a fairytale vista.

Rising above the silver ripple of roofs, the nearby castle loomed on the horizon, a dense, dark shape black against the midnight velvet of the sky. The moon was barely a crescent suspended in the firmament; together with the stars, it cast just enough light to etch the keep in glinting silver.

"This is simply lovely," she breathed.

After a moment, his voice low, he rumbled, "Indeed."

She glanced at him and saw that, rather than looking at the scene outside, his gaze was locked on her.

Their eyes met, and doubting she'd ever get a better opening, she seized it and ran.

"I wanted to thank you." She turned to face him. Courtesy of the alcove's dimensions, the movement put her directly before him, with only inches between her breasts and his chest.

His face was all angles and shadows. "For what?"

"For doing what you did to cheer us up." She tipped her head, her eyes still on his. "You did that deliberately."

He didn't deny it, and his lips curved fractionally.

The slight movement sent a rush of unexpected, unprecedented need surging through her.

She didn't think. She simply reacted.

One small step brought her flush against him. Boldly, she reached up, twined her arms about his neck, and whispered, "So thank you." Then she stretched upward and kissed him.

Even as her lips touched his, she realized she'd been wanting to do that for days.

Ever since she'd first set eyes on him in the Grange forecourt.

Then his lips moved beneath hers, and who was kissing whom became an entirely redundant question.

She kissed him, and he kissed her, and sensation surged and sparked and built, and a cloud of desire, sweet and pure, spread and swirled about them.

His arms rose and locked about her, holding her to him, cinching her against him as he bent his head and changed the angle of the kiss.

Changed the tenor of the exchange from sweet and alluring to hot and demanding.

To passionate and exciting.

She parted her lips in blatant invitation, and he instantly accepted. His tongue swept over her lower lip, almost reverently tasting, then he plunged into her mouth and claimed.

Her senses swooned, but then, avid and greedy, focused on the sensations. Her wits were enthralled, and she savored and rejoiced.

Every touch, every caress, reeked of power carefully controlled. Just like him.

If a kiss could testify to the man, his did.

She felt as if she was waltzing even though her feet were planted on the ground.

She'd wanted to know. Now, she wanted to know even more.

She tightened her hold about his neck and pressed even more deliberately tempting—indeed, deliberately more inciting and challenging—kisses to his firm, too-knowing lips.

Show me.

That was her message, her demand.

And the male in him responded.

Between one heartbeat and the next, heat flared.

Passion erupted, a hot wave rising through them both to clash and fuse and claim them.

Need and hunger rolled in a heady wave through her and weakened her knees.

Good Lord!

She'd never felt the like, never dreamed of the power behind the compulsion to seize and be seized.

For a second, she teetered, and she sensed he did, too.

With a wrench, they broke the kiss.

They'd done it together. Even as she realized they were both panting as if they'd been running some race, even as she registered the frantic thud of her heart and sensed the echo of his, through the shadows she took in his wide eyes, dark in the night, and knew her own were equally large.

Shocked. Surprised.

They were both stunned by what they'd unleashed.

And unleashed was what it was, for she could still sense that power in the air, an almost-living, sentient hunger.

A compulsion, and they both knew to what end.

He blinked, and his gaze lowered to her lips.

He moistened his, then managed, "You should go. To your room."

His voice was like gravel, deep and dark and edged with wickedness held at bay.

She swallowed and forced her head to nod. It was the best she could do. Speech was beyond her.

Slowly—reluctantly; she had to force herself to do it—she drew her arms from about his neck.

His hands gripped her waist, almost in spasm, but then he held her steady and, as her arms fell from him, anchored her in place as he stepped back. Instantly, she felt a chill all down the front of her where his warmth had been withdrawn.

She hauled in a breath, the first she'd taken in too long.

There was nothing she could think of to say or that she wanted him to say to her.

With a dip of her head, she turned, slipped through the curtain, and walked the few paces to her door.

She opened the door, heard Sally's snores, and knew she was in the right room.

Fighting not to look back, she went inside and shut the door quietly behind her, then she leaned back against the panel and, eyes still huge, stared into the dimness as, determined anew, she looked inside.

For several seconds, she examined the cauldron of roiling emotions surging within her.

She raised her fingertips to her lips and traced the swollen curves, amazed that such a potent mix of feelings could be brought to life by just a kiss.

A kiss between her and Nicholas Cynster.

For long moments, she considered that truth and wondered just what Pandora's box her curiosity had opened.

CHAPTER 7

$\mathcal{T}$he following morning, Addie rose with the dawn and, with Sally's help, prepared to ride out, asking questions and scouting about for any hint of their thief, as they had planned the previous evening.

Alongside Nicholas.

As far as she could see, the only way to carry on was to hide every iota of awareness that kiss had stirred and, essentially, pretend it had never happened.

She wasn't sure how successful she would be in that endeavor, but when she encountered Nicholas over the breakfast table, she quickly realized that he was attempting to pull off the same sleight of hand.

Beyond a grunt in response to her airy good morning, he barely glanced in her direction.

Certainly, as she settled at the table between Dickie and Nicholas and helped herself to toast, from Nicholas's behavior, no one would have guessed that anything at all had occurred between them.

In the quiet of the night, in the alcove at the end of the corridor, with their lips pressed to each other's—

Stop it!

She shifted on her seat and sternly quelled the impulse to verbally prod him.

Luckily, Dickie was not a morning person. She doubted her brother even noticed the silence at the table.

As soon as they'd cleared their plates and drained their mugs, they quit the parlor and found the others of their company—all except Sally—waiting in the foyer. In a group, they went out to the yard and reclaimed their mounts.

Addie failed to head for the mounting block in time.

Nicholas appeared before her. He met her gaze, then his hands closed about her waist, and he hoisted her up to her saddle.

For one second, as she looked down at him, her hands resting on his wrists, their gazes held, and she felt the connection between them, scintillating and undeniable, then he looked down and released her and moved to mount his gray.

She drew in a breath and raised her head and, as soon as he was in his saddle, led the way out of the yard.

As they'd discussed, they started out of town along the road to Burton.

Their first stop was the two competing carters' yards. After they'd tied their horses' reins to the railing fence of the yard on the right and, without quite meeting her eyes, Nicholas had lifted Addie down, he pointed across the road at the lad manning the yard gates opposite. "I'll go and see what he has to say." He tipped his head toward the woman who sat in a small office beside the gate in the railing fence. The office door stood wide, and the doorway and the desk beyond faced the roadway. "Why don't you try her?"

Addie looked at the woman and nodded. "I will." Refusing to allow herself to watch Nicholas cross the street, she raised her chin and advanced on the office.

The woman looked up as Addie darkened her doorway, and smiled. She was a jovial-looking woman, neatly dressed. "Yes? Can I help you?"

Addie returned her smile. "I hope so. We"—she waved vaguely across the road—"are trying to trace a stolen horse."

"Are you?" The woman's eyes widened. "My goodness, but that's intrepid of you, miss. Do you often do that sort of thing?"

Addie blinked. "No. But this horse was stolen from my father's property, so I'm helping to look for him."

"Oh, I see." The woman looked past Addie. "You're helping that very handsome gentleman over there, are you?" The woman grinned knowingly and winked at Addie. "Nice work if you can get it, I say!"

"Yes, well." Addie hauled in a quick breath and told herself not to get distracted. "He's rather striking—a very large, powerful bay stallion."

The woman stared across the road, and her grin grew wider, then she

glanced at Addie and blinked. "Oh. You mean the horse? I thought you
meant…" Again, her gaze went past Addie. "But then, he's more of a
chestnut, isn't he? Not a bay."

Addie gritted her teeth and hung onto her temper. "The horse—have
you seen it?"

"Big powerful bay stallion? No. But"—the woman folded her arms
and leaned forward to whisper—"I can tell you what I have seen these
past weeks. Councilor Phelps, riding his big black out toward Burton
every Thursday. Now"—the woman sat back—"what do you think of
that, heh? Given his house, along with his missus, is out Greetwell way?
The goings-on I do see, you'd never guess the like."

"I daresay." Addie eased back. "Thank you very much—"

Quick as a snake, the woman reached out and grasped Addie's sleeve.
"Oh, but you'll want to hear about Mr. Moffat."

"No, actually—"

"Trust me, you will. He's got a bay horse, but it's a gelding. P'raps it
was the one you're looking for, but he got…you know? Snipped."

"Our horse has only just been stolen, so—"

"Well, then, perhaps it was Old Man Smiggins as took him. Everyone
knows that man will deal in any sort of stolen goods."

Addie tried to twist her sleeve free of the clutching fingers.

"Out by the river, he is, but you'll need to be careful if you go out that
way. Can't trust that old codger. He's forever waving around his fowling
piece and making threats."

Addie managed to free her mangled sleeve and quickly stepped back.
"Thank you for your help."

"Oh! Oh! Wait!" The woman reached for Addie again, but she
skipped backward, out of reach. "But"—the woman came out of her
chair, hands outstretched—"you'll want to know about…" The woman's
gaze flicked past Addie, and in a blink, her anxious expression transformed into a beaming smile. "Oh, hello there, sir. Can I help you?"

Addie glanced at Nicholas and wondered how to warn him not to
accept.

"Thank you"—his face was set in an utterly bland and bored expression—"but I'm merely here to fetch Lady Adriana." He looked at Addie
and offered his arm. "If you're finished here, my lady?"

"Thank you, yes." Addie grasped his arm and, without actually
looking at the woman, risked a last nod in her direction. "Again, thank
you for your help, ma'am."

Nicholas drew her away, and they started walking toward the horses.

From behind came a plaintive "Oh, wait! I might know something more..."

"Thank you," Addie breathed. "I've never had that happen before. I couldn't get away."

"I imagine she's bored, just like the lad over there." He tipped his head toward the other carter's yard. "I take it she hadn't seen The Barbarian."

"No. Just a big bay gelding ridden by a Mr. Moffat." She glanced across the road. "Did you learn anything from the lad?"

Nicholas nodded. "As I said, he's bored and keeps himself amused by noting all the horses and carriages that pass. He, too, mentioned Mr. Moffat's bay. However, he's quite certain that The Barbarian hasn't passed along this road, certainly not over the past days."

"Hmm." Addie glanced at Nicholas's face. "That sounds rather definite, doesn't it? If both are sure?"

"Indeed." They reached the horses, and Nicholas steeled himself and lifted Adriana to her saddle, released her, then met her gaze. "I think we can skip the cattle yard and, on the testimony of our two carters' gatekeepers, declare that The Barbarian didn't travel this road."

She sighed. "In that case, we can ride straight on to the lane and across to the Riseholme road."

He nodded, untied his reins, swung up to the saddle, and together, they rode on along the road to Burton.

They made good time to the lane, then had to slow for a large flock of sheep to clear out of the way before they could canter on and, eventually, turn south on the Riseholme road.

Luckily, as they'd started out early, the men working on repairing the culvert were still laboring away.

A cleric stood on the verge above the culvert, looking down on the men.

As they slowed their horses, Nicholas glanced at Adriana. "Do you want to question the priest?"

She frowned slightly and shook her head. "He'll just try my temper, and it's already been tried enough this morning."

He laughed softly. "All right. You take the men. I'll tackle the priest."

They drew rein a little way away, dismounted, and walked their horses to the edge of the culvert.

Nicholas hailed the priest. "Reverend?" When the man swung to face him, Nicholas smiled with ready charm. "If I might have a quick word?"

"Of course, sir." The man stiffened his already rigid posture. He was thin and weedy, and the dull black of his cassock did his complexion no favors. "Although I should correct you there. I'm merely a curate attached to St. Mary's in the town." In turning to Nicholas, the curate had stepped away from the culvert. Now he glanced back and, with a deepening frown, watched Adriana as she approached the men. "As some of these workers are doing penance for their sins, I thought to come and make sure they perform as required."

"I see." Judging by the curate's pursing lips, Nicholas deemed it wise to add, "Lady Adriana will not"—*distract*—"keep them from their work. She'll merely ask the same questions I thought to put to you."

"Lady Adriana?" The curate looked at Adriana with immediate respect. "Are you sure she doesn't need help?"

"Quite sure. She's accustomed to dealing with staff, after all." That observation, uttered in a drawl that suggested the curate had called Adriana's abilities into question, brought the man up short.

"Oh yes. Of course." After a second, he refocused his rather beady eyes on Nicholas. "What did you wish to ask, sir?"

"Were you here yesterday, watching over the men?"

"I was. I'm very conscientious, you know."

"I see. And when did they start their excavations?"

"On Thursday morning, bright and early. I walked out with them, so I can be certain about that."

"Excellent." That meant the curate was standing on the verge for the entire period during which the thief might have passed along the road. Having gained the man's complete attention, Nicholas explained, "We're trying to track the movements of a Thoroughbred horse—a very large, powerful bay stallion. I don't suppose you've seen such a beast being led along the road?"

The curate frowned. "Thoroughbred stallion?" His eyes narrowed on Nicholas's face. "Why, exactly, are you seeking this horse, sir?"

Nicholas inwardly sighed, but from his manner, the curate might actually know something. "The horse belongs to the Earl of Aisby. I was in the process of buying the horse from the earl when the beast was stolen. Consequently, the earl's family and I are trying to find the horse. Once we do and reclaim him and subsequently finalize our deal, the horse is destined for the Cynster Stable at Newmarket."

Usually, when he mentioned Newmarket and the Cynster name, men were only too willing to help.

Not the curate.

His eyes blazed with a zeal so bright that Nicholas blinked.

"Horse racing!" The curate uttered the words in the same tone he might employ to denounce calamitous blasphemy. "The work of the devil, sir! Why, if I'd seen that horse, I would certainly not tell you! I want no part in assisting in such corruption and sin. Such—such—"

The sputtering cut off as Adriana approached. She didn't walk; she prowled, hips swaying.

Nicholas caught only the briefest of warning glances before she linked her arm in his and tugged him down to place a kiss on his lips. Then she looked at the curate and smiled like a cat anticipating savoring an entire dishful of cream. "Thank you for your help, sir, but clearly, it's time I reclaimed my lover."

So saying—and leaving the scandalized priest literally gasping—she drew Nicholas to where her mount waited, and paused so he could lift her to her saddle.

Without looking at the goggling curate or the gang of workmen who had watched the entire performance with huge grins splitting their faces, he obliged, then he drew in Tamerlane's reins, swung up to the saddle, and nodded at Adriana. "After you, my lady."

She battled to swallow a laugh and, smiling widely, tapped her heel to her horse's side and, with a regal wave for the laughing men, led the way down the road, back toward Lincoln.

Grinning himself, Nicholas waited until they were out of the curate's sight to draw alongside his savior. "Thank you. I had no idea he would react like that."

"Obviously." She was still grinning.

"Your...performance was rather outrageous."

She chuckled. "You just witnessed Miss Flibbertigibbet in action."

"Ah—I see." He replayed the curate's words, then offered, "From what the curate let fall, I suspect The Barbarian hasn't passed this way."

"He hasn't. The men were adamant, and they most certainly would have noticed. They struck me as the sort to grasp any excuse to pause in their work."

Nicholas didn't sigh, but he sensed she did, inside at least. "Let's head back to the inn. Perhaps one of the others has had better luck."

As they rode on in companionable accord, he reflected that their adventures of the morning in pursuit of The Barbarian had got them past the awkwardness of rediscovering how to interact in the wake of that star-tling—amazing, searing, mind-numbing—kiss.

He hadn't forgotten it and doubted she had, either, but they hadn't had time to dwell on it; the succession of events had kept them moving forward, and any tension between them had dissipated.

They reached the Turk's Head to find that none of the others had returned as yet. Given the time, those having to venture farther afield would likely have stopped for a bite to eat somewhere.

Accepting that, they called for a late luncheon, which they consumed in the private parlor.

Addie reined in her impatience and told herself she had to eat, to keep up her strength for what was plainly going to be a far longer and more wearying chase than she'd anticipated.

She tried to look on the bright side—or to find a bright side to look upon—but in that, she wasn't all that successful.

Beside her, Nicholas ate calmly, methodically working his way through the platters.

She viewed his stoicism with mixed feelings; one part of her resented the way he could remain so steady and steadfast and not fall prey to incip-ient despondency as she did, while another increasingly larger part of her was grateful for his rocklike solidity. He was fast becoming the anchor for their entire company and for her in particular.

The serving girls were clearing the last of the empty plates when a stir outside the door was followed by Rory, Jed, and Mike looking in.

Addie beckoned. "Come and share your news."

Rory led the other two into the room. "Not much to share. None of us found anyone who'd seen The Barbarian being led past."

"Nor us, either." Dickie came through the open door, followed by Young Gillies.

As Young Gillies held the door for the last of the serving girls, then shut it behind her, Dickie sighed and came forward to claim one of the chairs at the table.

Addie glanced at the clock. It was already after three.

Dickie looked across the table at Nicholas. "So we've wasted another day with nothing to show for it."

Nicholas held her brother's gaze and arched a brow. "Not quite." He rose and fetched the map they'd used the previous evening for their plan-ning session. He unrolled it over the table, and Addie and Dickie weighed down the corners with the various pots of condiments the serving girls had left.

The grooms and stablemen gathered around as, still standing, Nicholas looked down at the map. "Let's see what we've learned."

He pointed to the Burton road. "At the carters' yards, we found two independent witnesses who are certain The Barbarian did not pass that way. So he wasn't taken out of town on that road." His finger shifted to the Riseholme road leading directly north from the town. "And here, we found a work gang with a cleric supervising, and no one in the group had seen any such horse go past, and as they were digging out a culvert right by the road, they would have noticed."

Nicholas straightened. "So now we know that the horse was definitely not taken out of town along those two roads, either by the thief or anyone else." He glanced at the others and arched a brow. "What did you learn along the other roads?" He pointed to the road that led southwest. "What about this one—the Tritton road? Jed, that was you, wasn't it?"

Jed bobbed his head and reported that he'd found a livestock yard out along the road with lads manning the gates. "They was perched on the gateposts, watching everyone go back and forth. They said they're there every workday, and they haven't seen any horse like The Barbarian."

Nicholas shifted focus to the roads heading east, then northeast. One by one, each road was reported on and accounted for by one or other of their party.

Finally, they came to the road on which their party had ridden into town. Dickie, who, with Rory, had searched along there, said, "We retraced our steps via Melville Street and across the bridge over the Witham, then followed the road around the common. Beside the road there, we came across a team of woodcutters, cutting and trimming felled trees. They were absolutely certain The Barbarian hadn't passed them, and they'd been in that spot since Thursday morning."

"But they weren't there when we rode past yesterday afternoon," Rory said, "else we would have asked them then, but apparently, they were on the road itself, delivering some of the wood they'd cut and dressed to a depot along the road closer to the town. Long story short, when we put everything together, they were somewhere along that road— either beside it where they were cutting the trees, or on the road itself in their dray, or at the depot, which is right by the roadside—since Thursday morning until now."

"And," Dickie concluded, "they hadn't seen The Barbarian at any time, going into or out of town. It seems certain that if he had passed them, they would have noticed."

Adriana pulled a face. "That sounds definite enough."

Rory glanced at the others. "A bit farther along, that road forks, one arm being the road we came up on and the other heading down to Sleaford." He looked at Nicholas. "Seems the thief didn't go either way, up or down. Not if he didn't pass those woodcutters."

That left them facing an undeniable conclusion.

Her tone suggesting that her disgust at the situation was vying with despondency, Adriana put the inescapable into words. "The wretched thief didn't come to Lincoln after all."

Shaking his head in a puzzled way, as if he still couldn't quite believe it, Dickie said, "The blackguard must have gone to Sleaford, never mind that that makes no sense."

Adriana glanced out of the window. "There's still plenty of light. If we take the road to Sleaford—"

"No." When the siblings and everyone else looked his way, Nicholas calmly stated, "Yes, we've clearly overshot, but we did that because we made assumptions. Ones that didn't turn out to be correct. We're now three days behind our thief. We can't afford to make yet more assumptions that might lead us even farther astray."

Everyone was watching him. Evenly, he continued, "We would do well to pause and think of our thief. He hasn't got the horse's papers. If he'd been acting as an agent, stealing the horse for some underhanded breeder, then he would have made some effort to get hold of those documents. Given he didn't and hasn't got them, the only thing he can do with The Barbarian is to sell him, not as a Thoroughbred stallion but as an ordinary riding horse. And we all know what trouble he's going to have when he tries to ride him or allows someone else to try. I suspect that once we find the town to which the thief has gone, locating him isn't going to be difficult. Someone will have heard of his problems. Consequently, I'm less concerned about our speed in catching up with him than that we do, in fact, track him down."

By now, Nicholas had a firm grip on his role in their company. Specifically, he had to steer it without appearing to exercise control. Given the Sommervilles' mercurial temperaments, he had to rein in their impulsiveness and moderate their enthusiasms, while at other times, he needed to counter their disappointment and dejection with subtle encouragement and by stoking hope.

"What we need to do," he rolled on, "is to stop making assumptions and start plotting the thief's course based on established fact. On sure and certain sightings." He glanced around the company. "By my reckoning, the last such sighting we had of The Barbarian was on the road north of Grantham, before the road forked between Lincoln and Sleaford."

"Exactly." Addie sat straighter. "And as he didn't come to Lincoln, he must have gone to Sleaford, and we should follow with all speed."

Nicholas met and held her gaze. "But what if he didn't?" He glanced at Dickie and the others. "What if he didn't head to Sleaford at all but took the road toward Lincoln and turned off it at some point?"

The others all frowned, and Nicholas met her eyes again. "What if we rush down to Sleaford, then find no sign of him there? What then?"

She didn't have an answer, and none of the others did, either. She sighed and fought not to slump in dejection. "So what should we do?" At least she managed not to wail.

Along with everyone else, she looked to Nicholas for an answer.

With a dip of his head, he obliged. "What I think we have to do is backtrack to our last certain sighting and come forward again, this time more carefully so that we pick up the true trail." He paused, clearly considering, then suggested, "As we've come this far north, I suggest we ride directly back along the road we came in on as far as Leadenham. We were more careful after that. We asked many more people between Leadenham and Lincoln than we had on the earlier stretch, between Barkston and Leadenham." He glanced at Addie and Dickie. "We can start questioning people south of Leadenham. If he did turn off the road somewhere along there, then we might pick up his trail again without having to go all the way back to Barkston."

Addie recognized a sop to her pride when she was offered one and knew it behooved her to accept his suggestion with grace and some degree of humility. She remembered her nagging concern as they'd ridden into Lincoln that they had, in fact, lost the trail; it seemed she'd been right.

Slowly, she nodded. "That sounds the best—most sensible—plan." She tried not to sound too glum. She looked at Dickie, and he nodded in agreement, rather more readily than she.

With that decided, they agreed to have an early dinner and leave at first light. Given it was high summer, first light was very early, but all were eager to get going again, to ride south and find the dastardly thief's trail.

To varying degrees, each of them felt they'd been made a fool of—by the thief and, at least in Addie's case, also by her own impetuousness. That rankled.

The grooms and stablemen went out to have their dinner in the taproom. Addie left her brother and Nicholas in the parlor and went upstairs to find Sally and tell the maid their news while changing out of her riding habit. By the time Addie came down again, the table was being laid and the serving girls were streaming in with steaming dishes to set before them.

The Turk's Head was a renowned hostelry, and the food was excellent. The succulent meal went some way toward alleviating Addie's mood.

But she was still rather glum when, as soon as evening closed in, they left the parlor and climbed the stairs to their rooms.

She and Nicholas parted from Dickie at his door, and they continued along the corridor, pacing side by side.

Nicholas couldn't see Adriana's expression as they ambled along; she kept her gaze firmly fixed on the worn red runner muffling their footsteps.

He sensed that she was not as cast down as she had been earlier, yet...

The compulsion to cheer her up was a living thing inside him.

He looked ahead—at the alcove that featured prominently in his memories.

Distinctly fond memories that pricked and prodded and nudged, insisting that he needed to follow up and explore further.

That he needed to confirm that the fireworks of the previous night hadn't been just his imagination.

That his incendiary reaction to her kiss and her equally startling reaction to his would occur again.

If they kissed again.

The itching insistence twined with the compulsion to, at the very least, distract her from her glumness. Both seemed to be excellent moves on his part.

They neared the end of the corridor, and their footsteps slowed.

He looked at the curtains, once again drawn against the night. "I wonder if it's cloudy tonight." He glanced her way and, when she looked at him, caught her gaze and arched a brow. "Shall we see?"

Amusement touched her lips, and a gleam—possibly of excitement—shone in her eyes. "Indeed. Let's."

She stepped forward and pushed between the curtains.

He followed, tucking the curtains closed behind him.

She'd gone to peer out of the bow window. Looking up, she said, "No moon. No stars."

He didn't wait to hear more, just curled an arm about her waist and turned her to him.

She came, unquestionably eagerly, her head rising as she looked into his face.

He had no idea what she saw there and didn't wait for her to comment. He raised a hand and framed her jaw, tipping her face up as he bent his head and set his lips to hers.

And the magic was there again, from the first touch, the first gentle brush of their lips.

They both froze for a split second, as if they'd each been waiting for just that confirmation.

Then they dove into the kiss.

Hungrily, greedily, their lips met—in clear demand, in blatant wanting.

Provocatively, she parted hers, and he plunged in, needing to taste her again, to savor the delights of her and glory in the heady surge of desire that rose through them both.

Compelling, heated, that combined desire was a lure like no other, enticing, inciting...

Her mouth was a lush haven, a cornucopia of pleasure at which he wantonly supped. Her hands, which had fallen to his chest, clenched, her fingers curling in the lapels of his hunting jacket.

Then using her grip on his coat, she brazenly stepped into him, breast to chest, and pressed an intense, even more incendiary kiss on him.

Sparks flared, and flames leapt. Then a conflagration roared into being.

Like the surge of a good hunter to the huntsman's horn, their passions rose and seized them. Owned them.

Drove them on, into a searing exchange of unrelenting hunger and deepening need that left them mentally reeling.

Addie clung to Nicholas and gloried in the moment, in the heat, and most of all, in their exuberant passions. Amazed at the way her senses whirled and spun, immersed in the flames that raged and burned yet only left her hungering for more, she drank in every last iota of sensation.

And she wanted more. *More.*

With flagrant intent, she kissed him ever more fervently, astonished at her reaction, at the need that bubbled and surged inside her. Giddily pleased at all she felt, she pressed closer yet, eager, demanding, and wanting to know what came next.

One of his hands rose to cup her breast, and she gasped through the kiss and rejoiced.

Then she put her mind—what remained of her wits—to crafting a way to encourage him further, to make it clear what she wanted.

More.

Blessed man, without further prompting, he gave her what she desired.

His hand closed, and despite the fabric of her riding jacket, his clever fingers sought and found her nipple and gently squeezed.

She nearly swooned at the sharp pleasure that speared through her.

She laced her fingers at his nape and drew him deeper into the kiss, then, driven to communicate how much she approved, she opened her hands, speared her fingers through his thick, silky hair, and clutched tight.

Tight.

For a second, his breathing hitched, but he obliged and continued his attentions, concentrating first on one breast, then, when that was swollen, aching, and heavy, shifting his ministrations to the other.

She was riding the crest of a sensual wave when footsteps, beyond the curtain and nearing, broke through the haze and jerked her—and him—back to the world.

Their lips parted a fraction, and they both froze, listening, waiting.

The footsteps—two pairs—moved past, then a door nearby opened. A second later, they heard a heavy sigh, and Sally said, "I don't know where she is, but I daresay she'll be along shortly."

"All right, then," Rory replied. "I'll see you in the morning."

The pair exchanged goodnights, then the door to Addie's room closed, and Rory's footsteps continued along the corridor until they heard him climbing the stairs to the next floor.

Addie exhaled and focused on Nicholas's face. His expression, what she could see of it in the dimness, was unreadable, all hard angles and etched planes, but his lips were faintly swollen; hers, she felt sure, were more so.

Freeing a hand from his hair, she traced his lower lip with one fingertip. "That was…" *Wonderful. Glorious.* "Amazing."

His eyes held hers, then he parted his lips, caught her finger between his white teeth, and nipped the tip. Then he soothed the tiny hurt with a soft, gentle, lingering kiss. He released her finger and, in a voice impossibly deep, murmured, "Try 'eye-opening.'"

She managed a breathless nod. "That, too."

Her head was still whirling, her senses giddily spinning.

He lowered his arms and eased back from her. "You'd better go. Before Sally decides to come searching."

She studied his eyes for a second more, then dipped her head and turned. He held the curtain for her, and she ducked through.

On legs that were not quite steady, she walked to her door.

She grasped the knob and looked back. Nicholas was standing outside the curtain, watching her.

She smiled—a smile reflecting all the effervescent joy surging through her—then she opened the door, went inside, and quietly shut the door behind her.

CHAPTER 8

*N*icholas could only be grateful that they'd planned to leave the Turk's Head at dawn and ride directly to Leadenham. Consequently, since they'd come downstairs, he and Adriana had spent no time alone, and the pace they adopted the instant they passed Lincoln's outskirts, a canter alternating with a rapid trot, was an effective barrier to conversation.

After their encounter last night...

He was too well acquainted with the female mind to assume he could make accurate predictions, so he couldn't be sure where their interaction was heading, yet of one thing he was certain. He wanted to find out.

Given their earlier inquiries along the road, they'd agreed that it was most likely The Barbarian had not been brought north of Leadenham. Once they reached that village, Nicholas insisted on slowing and searching for sightings—doggedly and thoroughly—along every minor lane that gave off the road.

The siblings grumbled under their breath and patently chafed at the bit, but he held firm in insisting that every lane had to be investigated before they rode farther south. He soon realized that, as long as he didn't waver, the pair would—albeit grudgingly—acquiesce, but if left to their own devices, they would encourage each other to unwisely rush ahead.

Addie curbed her impatience and fell in with Nicholas's decree, yet as they plodded along the minor lanes, searching for people to ask about The Barbarian, her frustration steadily mounted.

As it was Sunday, there were not so many workers in the fields or around the lanes to ask, so they had to resort to visiting cottages and politely inquiring, often having to chat a little to elicit people's cooperation, and all those efforts took time!

Nevertheless, mile by mile, they worked their way south past Fulbeck, Caythorpe, Frieston, and Normanton.

With the sun long past its zenith and the afternoon well-advanced, with everyone in their company hungry and rather crotchety with it, by mutual agreement, they halted at the Coach and Horses Inn in the hamlet of Carlton Scroop.

Addie left Nicholas, Dickie, and the grooms and stablemen to deal with the horses and question the inn's ostlers. She entered the low-ceilinged taproom, with its huge, heavy beams running across the ceiling and horse brasses tacked here and there. The innkeeper stood behind a bar counter that ran the length of the side wall opposite the huge fireplace, which was presently empty. All around the rectangular room, square-paned windows had been set open to let in the summer breeze, which was just as well as, it being Sunday afternoon, the taproom was crowded. Most of the wooden tables were occupied, and a steady hum of conversation blanketed the space.

Inevitably, glances were directed her way. She exchanged nods with three farmers; Aisby Grange wasn't far away, and she and Dickie were well-known in the area.

The innkeeper, McGrath, saw her and, from his position behind the bar, nodded respectfully.

After directing Sally, who had followed at her heels, to claim a large unoccupied table set to one side of the fireplace, Addie headed toward the bar and McGrath.

She could barely drum up sufficient enthusiasm to ask McGrath and his serving girls the now-standard questions, and as she'd expected, they returned the now-standard answers. No one had seen any massive bay stallion. No horse of that description had been stabled at the inn over recent days or, indeed, ever.

With that established, she confirmed that Mrs. McGrath was still manning the kitchen and would be delighted to serve their company of eight with suitable and sustaining fare. The others came in, crowding in the doorway. Addie waved to where Sally sat waiting and, with one of the serving girls in attendance, followed the group to the table.

They sat and gave their orders for food and drink, which the serving girl cheerily informed them would be delivered as soon as maybe and whisked off to see to it.

Seated at one end of the table, with Sally beside her and Nicholas and Dickie opposite, Addie shifted on the wooden bench. She'd been doing rather a lot of riding over the past days, far more than she was accustomed to, and her thighs had started to protest.

The drinks arrived and provided a momentary distraction. She took a long swallow of her cider; riding the roads in summer was thirsty work.

"I suppose," Dickie said, staring at his ale, "that if we find no sign of The Barbarian over the next few miles, we'll end up all the way back at Barkston." He glanced at Nicholas. "What then?"

Nicholas grimaced. "Then, we come north again, but we'll have to stop at every cottage and farm. There has to be someone who saw the horse being led along the road."

The serving girls appeared with their meals. As their group settled to eat, Addie considered the possible directions a man leading a horse could take from Barkston or, more specifically, from the last known sighting of the horse by a farmer harrowing his field. "Our last sighting was just north of Barkston, meaning past the lane heading west toward Marston and also past the lane going north to Brownlow. The next intersection on that road is where it forks." She looked at Nicholas. "We took the road to Lincoln, so our thief—for whatever incomprehensible reason—must have gone to Sleaford."

Nicholas met her gaze and arched a brow. "Once past the fork and heading toward Sleaford, aren't there lanes leading off the road?"

"Well, yes," she admitted. "But those going south lead more or less to Aisby and the estate."

"Except for the road through Ancaster," Dickie put in. "But you're right. Why would he turn south along that when he's already crossed it farther south while on his way toward Grantham?" Dickie frowned. "That would truly be leading us in circles, and surely he's done enough of that already."

"What about lanes going north?" Nicholas asked.

Addie grimaced.

Dickie did, too, and admitted, "There are several. The lane through Ancaster to Byards Leap, and farther along, there are several lanes that lead to Rauceby."

Addie wanted to ride directly to Sleaford. "Are we all agreed that, from where the thief was last seen in Barkston, then given we've found not a single sighting of him all the way along the Lincoln road, then at the fork, he must have gone to Sleaford?"

Most of the company nodded, but imperturbably, Nicholas amended, "*Toward* Sleaford. We can all agree that he took that turn and continued along the road that leads, ultimately, to Sleaford." He caught Addie's gaze. "But we can't afford to lose his trail again. While I agree that in the circumstances, it's unlikely he took any of the lanes leading south, we need to ask all along the way and, by finding sightings, ensure we remain on his trail."

Addie sighed and looked at her brother. "You would think that being so close to the estate, and in a locality where the Sommervilles are well-known, if anyone had seen The Barbarian go past, they would have sent word."

Dickie brightened. "How do we know they haven't?" Then his enthusiastic expression almost comically collapsed. "But no. That couldn't have happened." He glanced at Nicholas. "People around about know us by sight, but they don't know The Barbarian at all or that he's ours. Papa wanted the horse's presence at Aisby kept quiet, and we all agreed."

Rory, Jed, and Mike were nodding. Rory added, "Everyone thought it a good idea. Anyone who knows horses can see he's valuable. Seemed sensible not to let it get around that he spent a lot of his time alone in a paddock."

Nicholas inclined his head. "That was wise."

They finished their meals, and the serving girls came to clear the table.

As the girls departed, ferrying away the empty plates and promising to return with jugs of ale to refill the men's tankards, Addie noticed a neatly dressed man tentatively waving in an effort to draw her attention. She smiled in reply and, to Dickie, said, "Farmer Conran's over there, and he's seen us. We'd better go over and say hello."

To Nicholas, she explained, "Conran owns and runs a farm near Honington, which you might recall was the hamlet we passed, close to the junction with the Sleaford road. He's a neighbor of sorts."

Dickie got to his feet, turned, spotted Conran, and raised a hand in greeting. Addie rose and followed her brother to where the middle-aged farmer sat at a table by the door.

Conran rose as they approached, and he nodded in greeting.

"Good afternoon, Conran." Dickie offered his hand.

A tall, heavily built widower, Conran smiled, clasped Dickie's hand,

and shook it. "Mr. Sommerville." Conran's gaze shifted to Addie, and his smile deepened. He bowed his head. "Lady Adriana. It's good to see you both."

"Indeed." With an easy smile, Addie sank into the chair Dickie held for her, and at her wave, Conran resumed his seat.

Dickie settled in the chair beside her. "How's things?"

"Can't complain," Conran replied. "The weather's been excellent for our animals, and the grain is growing well."

All three knew it was Addie who was best acquainted with how the estate's fields were faring, and she responded in similar vein.

Conran dipped his head, acknowledging that the niceties had been observed. "I can see that you're busy, but McGrath mentioned you were looking for a horse some thief led off—a big bay stallion?"

Addie sat up. "Yes, we are. Have you seen him? Or them? The horse and thief?"

His gaze on her face, Conran solemnly nodded. "It seems that I did."

"When?" Dickie asked.

"It would have been Wednesday, latish. I was in my lower field, the one that borders the Sleaford road just past the turn to Lincoln."

Addie nodded. "We know it."

"Aye, well," Conran went on, "I was watching my men baling the hay we'd just cut. I was on my old mare, so I could see over the hedge, and the sun striking the horse's coat caught my eye. Beautifully glossy, he was, and looked to be a damned fine horse. If I'd been closer, I'd have been tempted to ask the fellow leading the beast where he was taking him. If he was for sale. But I was up the side of the field, too far away to hail him."

Addie hauled in a breath and held it. "Just to be sure, can you describe the horse?"

"Well," Conran hedged, "I couldn't see much about his gait—I only saw him barrel up, so to speak—but he was a rich bay in color, with a darker mane and tail. Very tall and powerful looking. He made the horse the man was riding look small, although I don't think it was."

"The man." Dickie looked to be restraining himself from leaping in excitement. "Did you get a good look at him?"

Conran wrinkled his nose. "Not as good a look as I got of the horse. Naturally, my eye was drawn to the beast. What I saw of the man... Well, he was dark-haired. A gentleman, I'd say. Rode well. Decent cut to his coat, and that was dark, too. He was riding a chestnut, a nice enough mount, but not in the same league as the bay."

Not many horses were in the same league as The Barbarian.

Conran was looking back and forth between Addie and Dickie. "Is that any help?"

Addie refocused on Conran and beamed. "Yes! Thank you for thinking to tell us. That's exactly the news we've been searching for."

Dickie pressed, "And the man was definitely riding toward Sleaford?"

"Aye." Conran nodded. "He wasn't looking around. You know how it is—he was riding with his gaze fixed far ahead, set on getting along."

"The time." Addie caught Conran's eye. "Would the man have reached Sleaford before dark, do you think?"

Conran nodded. "Easily, I'd have said. Perhaps not in time for dinner at the usual hour but well before nightfall."

By the "usual hour," Conran meant six o'clock.

"Thank you!" Addie and Dickie chorused as they rose.

Conran lumbered to his feet, and Dickie shook hands again.

Addie beamed. "We must get back and tell the others. We've been chasing the thief for days."

Conran dipped his head. "Glad I could be of help."

Still beaming her gratitude, Addie turned and, with Dickie on her heels, rushed back to the table where the others sat waiting.

As she and Dickie slid onto on the ends of the benches, she declared, "You'll never guess what we've just learned!"

Between them, she and Dickie related the gist of what Conran had told them.

"So!" Ready to be off, Addie fixed her gaze on Nicholas. "You wanted a firm sighting, and now, we have one. Are we off to Honington, then?"

Nicholas studied her for a second, then looked at Dickie. "Honington is only about a mile or so down the road, isn't it?"

To Addie's eyes, her brother didn't look as eager as she was to be up and doing. He nodded. "That's right. And it's a hamlet. There's nowhere to stay—there or anywhere near."

"There's nowhere to stop farther along, either," Rory put in. "Not until we get to Sleaford, and if you want to check all the lanes along the way, especially about Ancaster, well, then, we're not going to get to Sleaford tonight, not with it being Sunday evening by then and so few people about whom we can ask."

Jed was nodding. "We'll have to stop and ask at every farm and cottage. It'll be slow going for sure, if we set off now."

"So I was thinking." Nicholas met Addie's eyes. "And while we are, I assume, within reach of Aisby Grange, it's some miles away, and returning there for the night will simply mean we have to ride all the way back to Honington in the morning."

The prospect of returning home for the night didn't appeal to Addie, not on any front. That her father would be enjoying another "good day" wasn't a risk she wanted to take.

When she said nothing, Nicholas continued, "As I see it, our most efficient way forward is to remain here overnight and start off again in the morning, riding straight down to Honington and Conran's lower field and starting our search from there."

She fought back a scowl and saw his lips twitch.

"At least," he offered, "we'll know we are, once more, on the right track. On the right road, heading in the right direction." He glanced around the table. "We need to make sure that we stay on the right road from now on."

Determinedly, Rory added, "Even if that means checking every lane the blackguard could have gone down."

Nicholas—and everyone else in their party bar Addie—nodded in agreement.

Addie swallowed a sigh along with her disappointment. After a few fraught seconds of wrestling her impatience into submission, she stated, "In that case, we should speak with McGrath about hiring some rooms."

Feeling thoroughly stymied—crimped and caged—in the matter of chasing the thief, perhaps not surprisingly, Addie found her mind turning to the possibilities of making headway on the other front she was increasingly determined to pursue.

She had no idea what Nicholas thought of what was developing between them and where—if anywhere—it might lead.

She certainly didn't know, and it was that lack of knowledge that she was set on rectifying. At least as a first step.

There might be further steps after that—steps she might wish to take once she understood what might be—but as of that moment, the question uppermost in her mind was defining the nature and extent of the attraction that had flared to such powerful life between them.

How to accomplish that...

Once they'd arranged for rooms for their party, she retreated to her chamber and changed out of her riding habit into a simple summer gown of pale-green cambric. Suitably garbed, she went downstairs determined to forge ahead.

Nicholas's and Dickie's rooms were along the corridor from hers. Although the pair had followed her upstairs, while she'd been changing, she'd heard their footsteps passing her door and returning downstairs.

A quick glance into the taproom confirmed that Nicholas hadn't taken refuge there, although Dickie, Rory, Jed, and Mike were gathered about a table by the window.

So where was Nicholas?

Given his passion for horses, she opted to check the stable first.

Sure enough, as she was crossing the cobbled yard at the rear of the inn with the open stable door her goal, Young Gillies strode out of the barn, making for the inn's back door. Grinning cheerfully, he saluted her. "If you're looking for Mr. Cynster, my lady, he's in with Tamerlane."

She smiled back. "Thank you." And confidently, she walked on.

It was late on a summer's afternoon, and few people were about. With no guests arriving at the inn or likely to over the next hours, the three stable lads were engaged in a rowdy game of marbles on the tack room floor. Unobserved by the three thoroughly absorbed players, Addie grinned and started down the aisle of horse stalls.

The light was dim, and the air, sweetened by the scent of fresh hay, was faintly dusty. Horses occupied several of the stalls. Some glanced at her curiously, but most didn't bother. The single long aisle was empty, but as she walked farther along, a horse whinnied, and Nicholas stepped out of the last stall in the row and closed the gate behind him.

He saw her approaching and, strolling to meet her, arched a brow.

Serenely, she smiled. "Having spent so many hours in the saddle, I thought I'd stretch my legs in a walk."

His gaze rested on her for a moment, then he asked, "Where were you thinking of going?"

"Through the orchard to the brook. It'll be pleasant in the shade." There was a lovely little spot she and Dickie had discovered years ago in which one could sit and listen to the brook babbling past.

She was perfectly certain that Nicholas suspected her of having some ulterior motive—quite obviously, she'd come to find him rather than requesting her brother's company—but equally, she judged that he was not the sort to allow a lady to wander alone in such a setting, bucolically peaceful or not.

Sure enough, he stated, "I'll go with you."

Hiding a spontaneous smile, she turned to the door. "By all means." She waved at the bright day outside. "Shall we?"

In silence, he paced beside her as she led the way to a corner of the yard, through the gate there, and on along a path that wended beneath the bright-green branches of the orchard's trees, many still sporting blossoms here and there.

They were out of sight and hearing of anyone from the inn. She seized the chance to probe an issue pertinent to her aim. "I gathered that, by choice, you spend little time in London, yet you've been on the town for what? A decade?" Eyes innocently wide, she glanced at him.

He met her gaze briefly. "I'm thirty-two, so longer than that."

He was a trifle older than she'd thought, not that that made any difference. "And in all those years, you haven't developed a"—airily, she waved—"tendre for any lady?"

"No." A flat, definite negative.

Her heart leapt, but immediately, he countered, "What of you? You've had… Is it four Seasons? Given your family's wealth and standing, I find it difficult to believe you've had no offers."

"Ah, but it's Miss Flibbertigibbet who goes to London and gallivants about during the Season, and she's never going to receive an offer from any eligible parti."

"You aren't Miss Flibbertigibbet." The words were a declaration of incontrovertible fact.

She conceded the point with a dip of her head. "But most in our world don't know that. Few outside the family do"—she met his gaze—"and now, you."

They'd reached the end of the orchard, and she looked ahead and led the way on, between the larger trees and into the denser shade that bordered the brook. Some yards farther along, the path ended at a grassy spot on the bank. She was pleased to find it much as she remembered it, enclosed by trees and bushes. In that season, the brook ran too low to support any fishing, so the spot was as close to being private as any place she could think of.

She halted with her boots sinking into the lush grass.

Nicholas halted beside her. After taking in the scene, he glanced at her. "If your previous question was by way of learning if I'm in the habit of dallying with ladies, the answer is no. Frankly, I don't have time for inconsequential dalliances—I have better things..." He paused, then amended, "More important things to do."

"I was serious about Miss Flibbertigibbet being me in London. The whole point of creating her was to shield me from the overwrought attentions of the so-called gentlemen who are attracted by this"—she waved at her face and figure—"and my birth, dowry, and connections."

His gaze on the rippling water, he huffed. "I can imagine." After a moment, his voice lower, his gaze still on the babbling brook, he went on, "If I'm following your train of thought correctly, that means that both of us are free of all entanglements and, therefore, free to pursue..."

She swung to face him, stepped into him, and raising her arms and winding them about his neck, pinned him with her blue, blue gaze. "This."

She pressed her lips to his in a deliberately challenging and provocative caress, and a fire of need smoldering inside him ignited.

As if sensing that, she pushed nearer still, the curves of her body a blatant incitement as they pressed into his harder muscled frame, then she murmured something incoherent and, in the next instant, dove even deeper into the kiss.

Into the conflagration created by his need and her desire. By his passion and her wanting.

There was really no question in either of their minds over what they sought in that moment.

More.

More of this, whatever this was. More of the tastes that sated their mutual hunger.

More of the heat and the spiraling pleasure.

He supped at her lips, at her luscious mouth, then wrested control of the kiss from her.

Predictably, she tried to regain the ascendancy, but he held her off— held her back. In this sphere, experience counted.

Yet inexperience and a blatant disregard for social restraint were a heady mix, an incitement she turned into a weapon aimed directly at him. At the greedy, hungry need she enticed and provoked.

She was insistent and pushy, her busy hands divesting him of his jacket and flinging it to the grass before she spread her palms and questing fingers across the fine linen of his shirt and wantonly traced.

Instinctively, his hands had spanned her waist; he responded to her flagrant provocation by using one arm to cinch her to him so he could send his other hand roaming.

First over her pert breasts, already straining beneath the bodice of her gown. He paid due homage, then sent his palm skating down, tracing the indentation of her waist before swooping lower to caress the lush curves of her derriere.

Her hands closed, clutching, clinging, while her lips burned with encouragement and a species of reckless abandon that lured like a siren's call and laid waste to any thought of stepping back.

Unable to do so, incapable of resisting her demands, he closed his hand about one ripe globe and kneaded.

She rose on her toes, her hips pushing against his thighs, and using both hands, he cupped her bottom and lifted her, drawing her even tighter against him.

Through the kiss, she made a choking sound, then she leaned into him, so insistently that he had no choice but to sink to the grass and sprawl full length; it was that or topple backward.

With their legs tangling, she propped on his chest and continued to kiss him with such ravenous need and oh-so-deliberate provocation that his head spun.

He speared his fingers into her hair, drawn back in the bun she usually wore, and held her head steady as he ravaged her mouth—and she kissed him back with equal fervor.

Then she reached up, caught one of his wrists, tugged his hand from her head, and guided it down until his palm touched her breast.

He'd never been slow to interpret such signals and readily devoted himself—and his hands and fingers—to giving her what she wanted.

And then, she wanted still more.

"Adriana." Her name on his lips was an outright plea, but for what, he wasn't certain.

In response, she dragged him into another searing kiss, then rolled to her back and hauled him with her, partly over her. Then she drew back from the all-consuming kiss to breathe across his lips, "Show me. Now. I need to know."

Despite her breathlessness, determination rang in her words.

He raised his head enough to look into her porcelain-doll face and saw her eyes—bright, blazing blue—glinting from beneath her heavy lashes.

Her lush lips were swollen and gleaming from their kisses, but the set of those lips and her chin left him in no doubt that she was hell-bent on exploring further. And that called to him—to the Cynster part of him—and drew it to the fore more forcefully than any other lady ever had.

She blinked up at him, then those gorgeous lips parted, and the tip of her tongue slid along her lower lip. Then she whispered, "Please."

He closed his eyes on an inward groan, then opened them, and before she could utter another word, he swooped and covered her lips with his.

And with the same deliberation she'd been demonstrating, he waltzed them into passion's flames.

The bodice of her gown sported a front placket with a row of small ivory buttons. He slipped them free, and when he pushed half of the bodice aside and slid his hand beneath, she murmured in outright encouragement.

He proceeded to sate their senses, to submerge them in a panoply of sensations. Educating her senses and judging her reactions and her heightening desire via all the little murmurs and gasps she uttered became a game, one of unalloyed delight.

Then his fingers tightened about one pert nipple, and she moaned, and the sound went straight to his head—and his groin—and he found a new goal, an even more desirable reward to seek and work toward.

And neither of them wished to stop there.

Between them, the flames of desire steadily rose, fed by the tactile sensations he pressed on her as he explored her breasts, the delicate, sensitive skin a delight to him as well as a source of pleasure to her.

When he bent his head and took one tightly furled nipple into his mouth, she gasped. He artfully played, his tongue lapping, then curling about the taut peak, before his teeth tightened about the distended bud, and she made an incoherent sound and her fingernails sank into his shoulders, deeply enough to mark.

He inwardly grinned and released her now surely throbbing nipple on a sigh of satisfaction.

Then he turned his attention to her other breast.

But all too soon, she grew even more demanding.

Addie had never engaged in such wanton conduct before, but now that she'd taken the plunge, she wanted to dive even deeper into desire's sea, wanted to bathe her senses in the glorious, heady, scintillating pleasures.

Her nerves had never felt so tight—so tense with expectation and so apt to spark with a species of intense delight she'd never experienced before.

All she could think of was rushing ahead and learning about everything that might be and savoring every last pleasure.

It was she who, not content with his attentions to her breasts, with a not-so-subtle shifting of her hips and legs, encouraged him to reach beneath her skirts.

When he did, the first trailing touch of his fingertips up the swell of her calf utterly captured her attention. Her entire being—certainly every iota of her conscious mind—locked on the tantalizing drift of his fingers as they steadily rose, tracing her knee before lazily, slowly, sweeping higher, up her inner thigh.

Then excruciatingly lightly, he touched the fine down covering her most private place, and some elemental prompting pushed her to tip her hips, wantonly inviting his exploration.

He obliged, and something inside her flashed and soared, and she held her breath as every sense focused on his touch, on the delicate strokes of his fingers, on the slickness he drew forth, and on the ever-expanding need that gripped her.

His knowing fingers found the tight little nubbin shielded within her folds, circled, then pressed, and she gasped and shivered and immediately wanted more.

More of that scintillatingly delicious pleasure.

He gave it to her, and her need rode the escalating waves that rippled through her, welling and swelling with every caress until that relentless, driving, compulsive need filled her to bursting and pushed her on.

Her hands had fallen to his shoulders. She clutched, sinking her fingertips into the solid muscle in desperate entreaty, and finally, he ceased exploring, and one long finger pressed in, in, then deeper, and she knew beyond question exactly what she wanted.

Through the kiss she still held him to, she told him as plainly, as fervently as she could, and thank heaven, he understood and obliged, with a mastery that stole the last of her breath and captured her senses and, with every knowing thrust of his finger, wound her nerves tighter.

Tighter.

She made a strangled sound, and he thrust a second digit in alongside the first, and her hips lifted of their own accord, or so it seemed.

A pool of molten passion simmered at her core, stoked by every solid intrusion of his fingers. Heat spread beneath her skin, fueling a deeper, elemental need laced with a strange yearning.

Her body felt alive in a way it never had before as her nerves ratcheted ever tighter, like a spring being wound to the breaking point.

Need escalated, and passion burned, and her body and mind, in concert, as one, seemed poised on some cusp, waiting, waiting, even as the tension gripping her grew to utterly desperate heights.

Then on a last, sure, deliberate thrust, the spring shattered.

She drew back from the kiss on a breathless gasp. Her senses flew, and she moaned as lightning streaked along her nerves and intense pleasure sizzled down every vein.

For a long moment, her senses overwhelmed, she hovered on a plane of rapturous delight.

A pleasurable warmth flooded her mind, and she felt like she was floating.

Yet even as every muscle in her body released and relaxed, she felt him tense.

He seemed in the throes of some internal battle.

Surprised, she struggled to raise her heavy lids. As she did, he drew away and, on a half-smothered groan, rolled to his back on the grass beside her.

Her senses returned in a rush, the sudden reawakening to their surroundings informing her of just how completely suspended her awareness of the world had been. That over the past however many minutes, she'd been deaf and blind to anything beyond him and her and how he'd made her feel.

For a long moment, they lay side by side on their backs on the grass. Above them, beyond the leafy branches of the encircling trees, the sky was still a summer blue.

The brook babbled on just past their feet.

Her wits, she realized, had been in abeyance, too. As they settled and the ability to think returned, she frowned. Then she glanced sidelong at Nicholas. At his rather stony profile. "I was born and raised in the country," she informed him. "Technically, I might be an innocent, but I know what should come next."

She'd found—or rather, he'd given her—her release, but he'd yet to attain his.

Without looking at her, he cleared his throat and, his voice all gravel, grated, "Not this time."

He sounded as if he was speaking through clenched teeth.

She turned her head so she could study his face. With her gaze, she traced his jaw, confirming it was rigidly set. She debated, but had to know. "Why? I was—am—perfectly willing."

"I know."

There was both tension and meaning in those words, but she couldn't fathom the latter. And doing so was suddenly extremely important. "So"—airily, she waved a hand—"why pull back? Why stop halfway through the act?"

His lips tightened. Several fraught seconds passed, then he stated, "Because we've reached the point of no return. There is no going further." He glanced sidelong at her and met her eyes; his eyes were darker, his gaze more intense. "Not unless you're willing to consider marrying me."

Genuinely flabbergasted, she opened her eyes wide. "*Marrying* you?" She added the first words that popped into her head. "I'm Miss Flibbertigibbet, remember. No sane gentleman should want to marry me."

His jaw tightened, and his gaze held hers.

Nicholas bit back the words: *If that's so, then I must be insane. Or at the very least, I've lost my mind.*

Adriana Sommerville was not the type of lady to whom it was safe to hand such a revealing confession.

She'd driven him to distraction, to the point where he'd been putty in her hands—or rather to where he'd been so blindsided by lust and longing and need that he'd fallen in with her direction. He'd been on the cusp of surrendering—to her, to instinct, passion, and a well-nigh overwhelming need—and claiming her, in the grass by a babbling brook no less, when sledgehammer-like, reality had hit him.

If they became lovers without any stated understanding between them, when they found The Barbarian and completed the sale and he rode away…he had no guarantee that she wouldn't blithely wave him off, let him go, and he would never see her again.

The realization that had fallen like a ton weight on him was that such an outcome would be…something he couldn't easily live with.

When it came to it, he had no idea what she was thinking—*if* she'd even been thinking when she'd initiated this interlude by coming to find him in the stable. He had no real insight into how she saw him. If she had any vision of them beyond them being just incidental lovers.

Looking into her big blue eyes, all he could see was genuine surprise tinged with disbelief.

He shifted his gaze back to the sky. "I'm not like the gentlemen you met in London. I can promise you I'm not interested in your birth, dowry, or connections."

"No?"

"Not in the slightest. As for the rest, however..."

"My face and...the rest of me?"

He nodded. "Those definitely have appeal."

She huffed out a laugh.

After a moment, she turned her head and looked upward as well. "Is it normal to feel so relaxed?"

Speak for yourself. "For you—the female in this pairing—yes."

"Hmm. I wish to put on the record that the circumstance of you not feeling equally relaxed is due to your own decision."

He grunted.

"Still..." With a sinuous movement, she wriggled in the grass. "I suppose that explains this...languid feeling." She spread her arms, holding them up to either side, wrists limp, one hanging over him. "Boneless. I feel boneless."

She was killing him. He shut his lips on several revealing retorts and clung to silence. Waiting; when it came to her, he'd discovered that he needed an abundance of patience.

Sure enough, eventually, she murmured, "'Consider marrying you.' What, precisely, do you mean by that?"

His heart leapt. He couldn't remember it ever doing so before. *Good Lord! I need to be careful.*

"I mean," he replied, "that given who we are—you a Sommerville, me a Cynster—becoming lovers is not an option. A short-lived dalliance —or even a long-lived one—is not in our cards."

She turned her head his way, and he felt her frowning gaze.

After a moment of studying his unrevealing profile, Addie clarified, "So it's marriage or nothing?"

Several seconds passed before he replied, "It's going forward as friends or becoming lovers with the understanding that marriage is our ultimate destination." He turned his head and met her gaze. "Your choice."

For a long moment, she looked into his caramel-brown eyes and wondered if, given what they'd already shared and the intensity—the power—of what had flared to life between them, she would ever be content with retreating to being just friends.

I simply can't see it.

But marriage?

He's asked for an understanding, not a cast-iron commitment.

She had so much to think about. To think through.

My choice—but I don't have to decide this instant. Or even today.

As if reading her mind, he said, "Think about it. Carefully. As I said, the decision is yours."

He shut his lips on the rest, but she grasped the implication regardless —once you make that decision, there'll be no going back.

She nodded—as much to herself as to him—just as the clanging of a bell shattered the bucolic peace.

They both sat up and looked around. The sound had come from the inn.

"It must be dinnertime." He got to his feet and held out his hand to her.

She gripped his fingers and rose, then released his hand, swiftly redid the buttons of her bodice, and shook out her skirts.

She raised her head, and he reached out and tucked an errant lock of hair behind her ear.

Their gazes held for an instant, then they turned and, side by side, made their way back to the inn.

CHAPTER 9

Their company rode out of Carlton Scroop at first light.

Accustomed to being up before dawn to watch his horses training on Newmarket Heath, Nicholas had no trouble with the early hour. Nor, apparently, did Adriana. From the instant she'd come downstairs that morning, she'd been focused on one thing—finding The Barbarian.

Dickie, however, was not an early riser. He'd dropped back to ride with Rory and Young Gillies, where he wouldn't be expected to converse beyond grunts, leaving Nicholas to lead their small troop with Adriana beside him.

He'd spent a restless night, plagued by dreams interwoven with and inspired by recent memories. To say his rest had been "disturbed" would be an understatement.

He glanced sideways at the female who had featured so prominently in those disturbing dreams; she was riding alongside with her gaze fixed unwaveringly ahead. After considering the sight for several seconds, he faced forward and wondered—not for the first time—what it was about her that so captivated him.

Yes, she was beautiful, but many ladies were. Her personality, on the other hand, was certainly unique.

The previous afternoon, when she'd come to find him in the stable, he hadn't had any idea matters would progress to the point where, with full knowledge of what he was saying and doing, he would make the declaration he had, much less issue such a stipulation.

Regardless, he'd meant every word. And still did.

What was making him decidedly uneasy was that he'd reached that point—the point of making deliberate and definite statements regarding him, her, and a joint future—without engaging in any notable degree of rational, logical thought.

He was known as a cautious man, yet she, reckless, impulsive, and impatient, effortlessly drew forth his streak of Cynster wildness.

He'd always been aware the hedonistic propensity to throw himself into a situation was there, deep inside him. All the Cynsters had to it to some degree. In his immediate family, Prudence had indulged that side of herself for most of her life, while in Toby, the same inclination showed in his addiction to the excitement of the missions he undertook for Drake Varisey. The streak was weakest, if it was there at all, in their younger sister, Meg, but in virtually all his cousins, male or female, that susceptibility to the thrill of danger—in whatever shape danger manifested—was very much a character trait.

From an early age, he'd learned to hold against the temptation of that side of his nature, to rein in his natural impulsiveness and think before acting.

Yet when it came to Adriana, the conditioning of years had comprehensively failed.

He hadn't thought—not at all. He'd simply known.

Known to his bones that she was the lady he wanted as his wife—more, whom he *needed* as his wife.

Where that certainty sprang from, what had given it birth, he couldn't say, but it was there, a rock-solid and unshakeable conviction that would not be denied.

Now, he simply had to make it happen.

As far as he could see, steering her to the complementary conclusion —that he was the one for her—was his surest path to his goal. Hence his stipulation of an understanding that any liaison would, ultimately, lead them to front an altar somewhere.

She raised a gloved hand and pointed ahead at a cluster of roofs to the left of the road. "That's Honington. We don't need to stop. Conran's lower field is around the corner and farther along the Sleaford road."

Nicholas nodded. "Let's pause for a moment when we reach that spot."

The previous evening, they'd debated which road they should take—to continue down the road they'd been following to Honington, the fork to Sleaford, and Conran's field or, once again, to make a leap of faith and, from the inn, take the lane that, while being a shortcut via Sudbrook village to the road to Sleaford, met the Sleaford road well past Honington. Adriana and Dickie had maintained that there were no major lanes between Conran's field and the Sudbrook lane intersection, but when questioned more closely, they'd admitted there were several minor lanes along that stretch.

Nicholas had put his foot down. Backed by Young Gillies, the stablemen, and even Rory, he'd pointed out that making assumptions had cost them days. More, the difference between the two routes was a matter of a mile or so. There really was no benefit in rushing ahead and, potentially, once again missing the thief's trail.

Adriana had grumbled but, a moment later, had acknowledged that, as their thief wasn't behaving in any predictable way, not as any of them had expected a horse thief would, perhaps it would be as well to pick up the trail at the last sighting.

Nicholas had uttered a silent hallelujah and said nothing more. As long as they stuck to the thief's trail and religiously verified which way the villain went, he was perfectly content to let Adriana lead the way.

As they neared the fork and the turn toward Sleaford, he glanced at her face.

Her expression suggested that she was fully focused on their pursuit, leaving him still wondering what direction she would take regarding the matter between them.

Addie slowed and, at a trot, went around the turn into the Sleaford road. Beside her, Nicholas wheeled his big gray, and the rest of their company streamed in their wake.

It was a constant battle to keep her gaze forward and not allow it to slip sideways to dwell on Nicholas. There was no point in her trying to study, analyze, or calculate; she'd always relied on her instincts to guide her, and in this case, they'd spoken clearly. Consequently, her decision regarding Nicholas was a foregone conclusion, but she'd decided that, for today, she should keep her mind focused entirely on tracking their thief.

They were only miles north of the Grange. She knew the road well, as did Dickie, Rory, Jed, and Mike.

When Farmer Conran's lower field came into view, she slowed Nickleby to a walk and tipped her head toward the stubbled expanse. "That's where Conran was when he saw The Barbarian." She met Nicholas's gaze. "So the thief rode along here with The Barbarian in tow."

Nicholas nodded and scanned the way ahead. "According to the signpost at the fork, Sleaford is twelve miles ahead." He looked at her. "The Sudbrook lane is the next major intersection. Between here and there, where might we find another person who saw our quarry ride past?"

She frowned. "It was Wednesday afternoon when he rode along here. Wednesday is market day in Sleaford. That being so"—she glanced back at Rory—"old Mrs. Milford might have been on her way back home in her cart."

Rory nodded encouragingly. "She might have passed him."

Addie felt anticipation surge. "Depending on when she left Sleaford, she might even have seen him close to the town."

Enthused, she tapped her heel to Nickleby's side and increased their pace to a canter. When Nicholas ranged alongside, she flung an eager glance his way. "Old Mrs. Milford lives in a cottage just up the Sudbrook lane."

In short order, they reached the cottage. While the others waited with the horses in the lane, Addie, accompanied by Nicholas and Dickie, walked up the neat paved path to the cottage and jangled the bell that hung beside the front door.

No one appeared.

"She'll be out in her garden," Dickie said. "It's at the back."

"She sells vegetables she grows at the market," Addie explained as she and Nicholas followed Dickie around the cottage.

The rear plot was long and narrow and divided into neat rows. In that season, each strip of ground was covered in profuse growth. They peered and hunted, but couldn't see anyone.

Eventually, Nicholas cupped his hands about his mouth and, facing down the garden, called, "Mrs. Milford?" and a gray head popped up at the rear corner of the garden.

Mrs. Milford's eyes were better than her hearing. She saw them and waved. "Good morning, your ladyship. Sirs." She straightened and started to make her way toward them.

Reminded by the old lady's rolling gait that she had a bad leg, Addie hurried down the central path to meet her. "Good morning to you, too, Mrs. Milford." Addie flashed a bright smile and halted at the opening to the side path the other woman was on.

Short and stocky and wreathed in smiles, Mrs. Milford joined her. The old woman's gaze went to Dickie and Nicholas as they came up, and she nodded politely. "Gentlemen." She returned her gaze to Addie's face. "What can I help you with, my lady?"

"We were wondering if, on your way home from the Sleaford market last Wednesday, you might have seen a man—a rider on a chestnut horse —leading a big bay stallion."

"Heading toward Sleaford, most likely," Dickie added.

Mrs. Milford's eyes widened. "Why, yes, indeed. I remember seeing him. Well, the horse is what I took note of. Hard not to, he was so large. I swear the beast turned his head and watched me as I drove past."

Addie could well imagine. "He is a very curious horse."

"He was stolen from the Grange," Dickie explained, "and we're trying to track him."

Before Mrs. Milford could comment on that, Addie, unable to keep the excitement from her face or voice, asked, "Where did you see them?"

Mrs. Milford blinked, then replied, "As Mr. Sommerville said, it was on the Sleaford road, between here and the Ancaster turnoff."

Addie's shoulders slumped. That was only a short distance farther on. But… She frowned. "By my reckoning, you would have had to leave the market early to get almost home before you passed them." She fixed Mrs. Milford with a hopeful look. "Are you sure it wasn't closer to Sleaford that you saw them? Perhaps the other side of the Ancaster turnoff?"

Mrs. Milford smiled. "You're right, of course."

Addie's heart leapt.

"I did leave the market early. There was a rush on my produce, and everything went in just a few hours. So I had a bite of lunch at the inn and headed home. That's why I was on the last stretch when I passed them— the rider and the horse."

With her hopes plummeting back to earth, Addie summoned a weak smile. "Thank you. That's got us a little farther." Sadly, only a few hundred yards.

Behind Addie, Nicholas shifted, drawing Mrs. Milford's gaze. "Did you get a good look at the rider?" he asked.

Mrs. Milford shook her head. "I'm sorry, sir. I didn't really focus on the rider. He had his head down, almost to his chest, as I recall."

Nicholas nodded and tendered his thanks, as did Dickie.

The three of them took their leave and walked back up the long garden, around the cottage, and out to the lane.

"Anything?" Rory asked hopefully.

Addie left it to Dickie to relay the information. She went straight to Nickleby's side, and Nicholas followed to lift her up to her saddle. His hands closed about her waist, and he hoisted her up. She nodded her thanks, and he released her and turned to accept his reins from Young Gillies, leaving Addie to ponder why it was that, rather than sending her nerves leaping and skittering as had happened previously, the simple contact somehow reassured and, in some strange way, comforted her.

With a mental "Huh," she wheeled Nickleby and set off down the lane to the Sleaford road.

Sadly, even though they called at every farm and cottage along the way, Mrs. Milford's sighting proved to be the last before they reached the lane to Ancaster. The lane led north to Ancaster village and continued on to Byards Leap, which was on a larger east-west road, but before that, there were numerous smaller lanes leading in various directions.

Luckily, there were a lot more cottages along the lane leading to Ancaster as well as in the village itself.

They split up into three groups—Nicholas and Addie, Dickie and Young Gillies, and Rory, Sally, Jed, and Mike—and went door-to-door, searching for anyone who had seen The Barbarian. Addie even led Nicholas to the door of Ancaster Hall, but although the squire had attended the market in Sleaford, he hadn't returned until late and hadn't seen rider or horse.

Unfortunately, the news that a valuable horse had been stolen from Aisby Grange meant that it took more than half an hour for Addie to satisfy the squire's curiosity and politely extricate herself and Nicholas.

By the time they caught up with the others, who, predictably, had paused outside the village inn, it was nearly midday.

"Nothing," Dickie reported as she and Nicholas rode up. "Quite a few were at the market in Sleaford, but they all stayed for a meal and came back latish and didn't pass thief or horse on the road."

Rory added, "We also asked everyone whether they'd seen the rider and horse going north up this way, and no one did, but none could say that the thief didn't slip past them, either."

Dickie tipped his head toward the inn. "Why don't we get a bite to eat and ask Gallagher, the publican, and anyone else who's there if they spotted The Barbarian?"

Nicholas nodded. "An excellent idea."

They dismounted and led their horses around the side of the building into the yard where two young lads leapt to their feet, eyes growing wide at the quality of horses they were to care for. Young Gillies and Rory dallied to ensure the horses behaved, while the others headed into the inn.

Gallagher recognized Addie and Dickie and readily listened to their tale and their questions, but ultimately, shook his head. "I didn't see any such horse meself, and more to the point, I haven't heard anyone else who's come in here mention seeing the beast, either." He made a wry face at Addie and Dickie. "And you know what people 'round here are like. They would've noticed a horse like that and been eager to share what they saw over a pint."

Addie managed a weak smile and thanked Gallagher, while Dickie asked if he minded them questioning those currently in the taproom anyway.

Gallagher waved them on. "Can't hurt. No one likes horse thieves."

They gave Gallagher their orders, then proceeded to make their way around the room, asking if any of the seven patrons had seen The Barbarian.

None had been on the Sleaford road during the critical afternoon, but two farmworkers had been repairing a fence beside the Ancaster lane just north of the village.

The older man shook his head in definite fashion. "Sure as I'm sitting here, no such horse passed us that afternoon."

The other nodded. "And there's no way we would've missed seeing such a beast."

Nicholas asked, "You're sure it was Wednesday last that you were repairing that section of fence? Not any other day?"

"Nope." The older man sounded certain. "Had to be last Wednesday because Squire—it's his field—rode up to check with us midmorning and told us he was off to Sleaford market."

"And as we all know," the other man said, "that means it was Wednesday."

Dickie clarified, "And the stretch of fence you were repairing was just north of the village, before any of the smaller lanes go off this road?"

"S'right," the older man said. "So unless the thief went into one of our cottages or houses along here, he didn't pass this way."

Addie and Dickie were hugely relieved. Even Nicholas brightened.

The three of them returned to the table where the rest of their company had gathered and were accepting the plates the serving girls had brought out.

Leaving it to Dickie to explain what they'd just learned, Addie slid onto one end of the bench seat and drew her plate toward her. She picked up the mug of cider Dickie, after completing his explanation, slid her way. She sipped, then said, "Well, at least we can now go back to the Sleaford road and continue along." Over the rim of her glass, she met Nicholas's eyes. "And between here and the town, there's only really the lanes to Rauceby that we need to check."

Nicholas met her gaze, read the challenge within it, and carefully nodded. The last thing he wanted her to do was, once again, rush ahead. He picked up his fork and considered the large slice of pie before him. "We'll still need to ask everyone we can find. We need to be certain he went into Sleaford proper and didn't stop somewhere on the outskirts."

She and Dickie mumbled that it would be difficult for anyone to hide The Barbarian in that area without someone catching sight of him.

Nicholas acknowledged that with a dip of his head. "Just so, and until we actually locate our thief and The Barbarian, we need to remain thorough and vigilant in our search."

The siblings cast him identical looks of suppressed frustration, which made him inwardly smile, but which, otherwise, he ignored.

After finishing their meals, they quit the inn and rode south to, once again, turn onto the Sleaford road.

As they continued along, time and again, Nicholas had to rein in the siblings' impatience to push ahead. He quickly realized the best way of doing that was to send the pair to the farmhouses and cottages to ask the inhabitants if they'd seen their quarry. Given that, of their company, they were the two whom locals would recognize and most wish to accommodate with information, that was easily justified.

After the next positive sighting they uncovered—on the outskirts of the hamlet of Wilsford, sufficient to confirm that the thief hadn't turned south but continued toward Sleaford—both Adriana and Dickie ceased their mutterings against Nicholas's enforced thoroughness and threw themselves into finding another sighting. Their efforts soon engendered the usual sibling rivalry, something Nicholas recognized and subtly encouraged, given that kept the pair engaged with the search rather than fighting against his yoke and wanting to race ahead.

When they reached the turn north to Rauceby, Addie and Dickie insisted on first pursuing any possible sightings along the next stretch of the Sleaford road. Nicholas could see their point—that if they found such a sighting they could ignore the minor lane—and when Addie almost immediately found a farmworker's wife who had been overseeing her children playing in their front garden when "a massive bay horse went prancing past, led by a man on a chestnut horse," everyone felt vindicated.

They forged on with even greater determination.

Increasingly, the siblings and, indeed, the entire company, saw the value in Nicholas's approach and, when they hit the outskirts of Sleaford, threw themselves into the endeavor. Although still not plentiful, the sightings were sufficient to, step by sure step, lead them into the town.

Carefully and methodically, they tracked horse and rider, confirming that, late on Wednesday afternoon, the thief had brazenly led The Barbarian up Southgate, the main street running south to north through the center of the town. Along the way, he'd passed the lane leading to the London Road, as well as a road leading southeastward, known as Mareham Lane, which ultimately led to Threekingham. They'd also established, somewhat painstakingly, that their quarry had ignored the major eastward road to Boston, the town most of their number had assumed the villain had been making for.

Instead, the rider had continued north along Southgate to the point where that road became Northgate, at the southwest corner of the marketplace in the very middle of the town.

They cast about, but as it was Monday, there were far fewer people about the market square, and those they found were hurrying home from being elsewhere or after shutting up their shops.

While the others dismounted and quartered the surrounding area, Nicholas remained on Tamerlane's back, holding the other horses' reins while he studied the signpost that stood at the corner of the market square.

According to the arms on the post, a well-used road appropriately labeled Eastgate led to Ruskington, which lay some way to the northeast. In the opposite direction, Westgate led to the causeway of Sleaford Castle. They'd seen the ruins, looming over the road to their left as they'd entered the town. That was one lane Nicholas doubted the thief had taken.

The highest arm on the post pointed up Northgate, which was marked as the way to Holdingham.

By Nicholas's reckoning, that meant the most likely—but not certain —route the thief had taken from that spot was via Northgate to Holdingham or via Eastgate to Ruskington. However, it was possible that he'd come this far into the town to see someone and, subsequently, later on Wednesday evening or night when there were fewer people around, had left again by one of the other roads—to London, Threekingham, or Boston.

Nicholas weighed the latter possibility. While the chance was there, it was far more likely that the rider had continued up Northgate or ventured out on Eastgate. Unless the others found any other sightings, those two roads should be their primary focus on the morrow.

However, the information on the signpost that Nicholas found most interesting was the distance to the other towns. Judging by the time of the last sighting they'd already found, close by where Nicholas currently sat, the thief wouldn't have been able to reach any of those other towns before nightfall.

Nicholas was pondering what that meant when the others returned. One glance at their faces as they neared was enough to inform him that their recent inquiries had proved fruitless.

"Nothing," Dickie confirmed. He paused to lift Adriana to her saddle, then accepted his reins from Nicholas, as did the others.

While they resettled in their saddles, Nicholas glanced at Adriana. "Do the Sommervilles have any acquaintances who live in Sleaford?"

"No." Puzzled, she blinked at him. "Why?"

He looked at Dickie. "You mentioned that your father had endeavored to keep the fact The Barbarian was on the estate, if not exactly secret, then not widely known. An acquaintance, however, might have visited or caught some reference in passing, and The Barbarian's paddock was bordered by a right of way. The horse's presence in that paddock might have been more widely known among locals than your father realized."

Both siblings grimaced. After a second, Adriana shook her head. "Obviously, circling around as he did, the thief went out of his way to put us off his trail. Yet I really can't understand why he came this way. There's no one connected with the family who lives in this direction. No close acquaintance, no one to whom Papa is likely to have mentioned The Barbarian or who visited the Grange in recent times."

Nicholas nodded. "That supports the notion that our thief may simply be an opportunistic horse thief with no real idea of The Barbarian's worth."

Adriana huffed. "And, therefore, also no idea that we might pursue him so doggedly."

Nicholas tipped his head in agreement. "Indeed."

After a moment, with their horses growing restive, Dickie asked, "What now?"

Nicholas glanced around. "It's dusk—the shadows are not just lengthening but darkening. We're unlikely to find the sort of people we need to ask about our thief still abroad." He met Adriana's eyes. "I suggest it's time that we look for a place to lay our heads for the night. We can resume our search tomorrow."

Addie grimaced. It was disappointing not to be able to forge on, especially when the sightings they'd found in the town had been so definite and also so frequent. People had noticed the massive bay horse and, despite the several days that had elapsed, hadn't forgotten. "I suppose if people have remembered The Barbarian so well to this point, they'll still remember seeing him tomorrow."

Everyone agreed.

Dickie pointed up Northgate. "The Packhorse Inn is just along there. It's generally spoken of as the best inn in Sleaford."

They turned their horses' heads that way and were soon riding beneath the archway into the inn's cobbled yard. The innkeeper was glad to welcome them—all eight of them. As well as larger rooms for well-born guests, the inn boasted a dormitory above the stables and rooms in the attic for accompanying staff.

Jed, Mike, Rory, and Young Gillies opted for beds in the dormitory above the horses; it was plain the four preferred to remain near their charges.

Addie wondered if the thief was being equally careful with The Barbarian.

Dickie asked their host, Quilley, if he'd seen or heard any mention of a big bay stallion being led through the town. Quilley hadn't, but he'd returned from a week-long visit to Boston only that day and promised to ask among his staff.

Having put up with Sally's snoring for more nights than she liked, Addie grasped the chance to secure the maid her own room in the attic. Although pleased with the arrangement, when a housemaid showed Addie to her chamber, Sally trailed behind and lingered to help Addie out of her riding ensemble and into a gown of magenta twill suitable for dining at a country inn.

"I did hear Mr. Cynster bespeak a private parlor, my lady, so it's not as if you'll be dining with the hoi-polloi." Sally shooed Addie to the dressing-table stool, foraged in Addie's bag and found a brush, and proceeded to undo and redo Addie's hair.

Imagining dining with Nicholas and Dickie, Addie permitted Sally's fussing. Looking her best—or the best that circumstances allowed—seemed like a good idea. If Dickie did as he had in Lincoln and, later, left Nicholas and her alone...

She stared blankly—blindly—at the mirror as all the thoughts she'd held back throughout the day came rushing forward, swirling chaotically through her mind.

"There!" Sally put the final touch on her creation—a twisted chignon —then swooped and picked up Addie's riding clothes. "I'll give these a good dusting and bring them back later."

"Thank you." On impulse, Addie added, "I can manage on my own tonight. No need for you to wait on me. You've been a brick putting up with all our riding. You can take the evening off—you deserve it."

In the mirror, she watched Sally beam and bob before collecting her own bag and bustling to the door. She opened the door, swished through, and closed it behind her.

Addie refocused on the mirror. On her face, on her eyes. She looked into the bright blue and let her thoughts claim her.

That she would respond to Nicholas's ultimatum wasn't in question. Metaphorically, he'd thrown down a gauntlet; of course she would pick it up.

She appreciated why he'd phrased the matter as he had, as an "understanding that marriage is our ultimate destination." Among their class, dalliance between him, a scion of a ducal dynasty, and her, a still-young lady of impeccable birth and high station, would be the stuff of scandal, but in society's eyes, an impending betrothal afforded them the license to explore intimacy, at least to a degree.

Exactly what degree was never specified, but the assumption that marriage was their intended destination gave them a great deal of leeway.

For several years, deep inside, she'd felt jealous of other young ladies who, courtesy of such social license, had been able to explore physical liaisons with their beaux. For years, she'd felt shut out, locked out and doomed to forever be on the outside looking in when it came to such experiences.

That hadn't been solely a function of being Miss Flibbertigibbet, although undoubtedly her social persona had contributed to some extent, but even as Adriana Sommerville, until meeting Nicholas, she'd never met a man, gentleman or otherwise, whom in even her wildest moments she would have contemplated taking as a lover.

She'd almost resigned herself to dying an old maid and never knowing what lying with a man was like.

And then she'd set eyes on Nicholas Cynster, and in all candor, ever since, some part of her mind had dwelled on nothing else.

Imagining...

She had an excellent imagination, yet even so, she hadn't foreseen just how...*compelling* the physical act, even just the prelude to it, would be.

Every part of her had wanted to rush on and embrace the entirety of intimacy, of being intimate with Nicholas.

And that was the point, wasn't it? She could and would do so only with him.

Yet being intimate with a man and marrying him were two separate and quite different things, a point Nicholas's "understanding" recognized and acknowledged. If they embarked on an intimate liaison with the intention of progressing to a wedding, despite society's expectations, it was still possible to mutually cry off. To step back from the altar, providing they both agreed.

If only one of them wished to back away...that would be difficult. But even after several months of indulging as their understanding permitted, if they both concluded that a marriage between them would not work, albeit reluctantly and grudgingly, society would allow them to part.

Essentially with a "least said, soonest mended" attitude.

Despite most of her wanting to rush ahead—to pick up Nicholas's gauntlet and run with it—some small part of her questioned what would happen if one of them wanted to dissolve their understanding while the other remained firmly set on fronting an altar.

What then?

As far as she could see, that was the only potential problem with Nicholas's proposition.

For herself, she was more than willing to risk it. Nicholas fascinated her in ways she didn't understand, in ways she wanted to understand, and doing so would undoubtedly take years. She was fairly certain that love—abiding love—could grow from just such a fascination, and even if it didn't, she already felt sufficiently fond of him to feel confident in her ability to craft a comfortable marriage with him.

She had never set her mind or heart against marriage. She'd simply seen it as an unlikely outcome for her. If married to the right man, she was only too ready to admit the relationship could be wonderful. Life-altering in so many ways. She only had to look at her parents to see and appreciate the succor and support that a sound, love-based marriage could bring to both parties.

On her own account, she had no qualms about tossing her cap over the proverbial windmill and forging on regardless.

But what if? What if, after she and Nicholas indulged—after he'd initiated her into the pleasures of the flesh—he found her, found continuing to be with her, less than enthralling and, in all honesty, was no longer keen to marry her?

Of course, being Nicholas Cynster and a rigidly honorable gentleman, he would hide his reluctance and, outwardly complacent, put his ring on her finger.

But she would know, wouldn't she?

Could she live with that? With a marriage in which the husband she loved didn't actually love her?

She stared at her reflection and wished she had some way of peering into the future.

There has to be some way of creating an honorable caveat that will allow him to back out of our understanding.

She narrowed her eyes on her reflection and drummed her fingertips on the dressing table.

Uncounted minutes later, a deep *bong* reverberated through the inn. Apparently, they used a large gong to summon travelers to the dining room.

With the barest inkling of an idea fermenting in her brain, Addie rose, shook out her skirts, and went downstairs.

She walked into the private parlor Nicholas had organized to find him and Dickie already there. Two serving girls followed her into the room, bearing a tureen and a plate of crispy bread.

Nicholas held a chair for her at the square table, and she sat and, once the tureen had been placed before her, served them portions of chicken-and-vegetable soup.

She bided her time as they worked their way through the ensuing courses. As they ate, they discussed their plans for the next day. They agreed that, immediately after breakfast, together with Rory, Young Gillies, Jed, and Mike, Addie and Dickie would venture forth to search around the town for anyone who could point them in the direction the thief had taken after he'd left the marketplace. Meanwhile, Nicholas would remain at the inn and act as coordinator of their efforts, directing the various pairs this way and that.

"There's really only two roads he could have taken," Dickie pointed out. "He either went east on Eastgate or continued along Northgate."

Nicholas swallowed. "Unless he's a local and turned west or even came to the marketplace to meet with someone and turned south again." After a moment of apparently imagining that, he grunted and returned his gaze to his plate. "In reality, he could have gone in any direction. All we can be sure about is that he was in the road alongside the marketplace, and according to our last sighting, he was heading north."

Addie let their comments and arguments flow past her, which earned her puzzled looks from them both, but she had other things to think about. Namely, how to explain to Nicholas what, exactly, her response to his ultimatum was.

Finally, with dinner dispensed with and the dishes removed, they retreated to the chairs by the fireplace. Conversation lagged, and soon, they were all smothering yawns.

After another jaw-cracking yawn, Dickie announced, "Today was yet another long day in the saddle. I'm for bed, the better to throw myself into our search bright and early tomorrow." He met her eyes and grinned. He wasn't an early riser.

"In that case"—she rose as he did, and Nicholas followed suit —"we'll expect to see you at the breakfast table, shall we say at six o'clock?"

Dickie groaned. "Seven. There's no sense in going out *too* early—the people we need to speak with won't appear before eight."

As he was correct, Addie dipped her head in regal agreement. "Seven o'clock, then. But not a minute later."

Dickie grumbled and led the way upstairs. At the head of the stairs, they parted, with Dickie going into a room close by.

With Nicholas ambling beside her, Addie walked down the corridor that, on that level, bisected the inn. Nicholas's room lay to their left, while hers was one door farther down on the right.

Luckily for Addie's plans, tonight, there was no Sally sharing her room. No one to know where she spent the night.

They drew level with Nicholas's door, and he paused.

Addie gripped his sleeve, stepped across him, and opened his door. She sent it swinging wide and barged inside, tugging at him to follow her. "There's something I need to tell you."

CHAPTER 10

To Addie's relief, after an initial hesitation, Nicholas glanced swiftly back along the corridor—no doubt confirming that her brother had gone into his room, closed his door, and hadn't seen her performance—before looking back at her. After a second of studying her, he consented to step into the room, and quietly shut the door.

She released his sleeve, took two steps, and whirled to face him. She drew in a huge breath and let it out in a rush of words. "You said I had a choice to make between continuing as merely friends or becoming lovers."

He halted before her, his gaze locked with hers. "Provided that, if you opt to become lovers, it's on the understanding that you'll accept an offer from me in due course."

She managed a reasonably decisive nod. "I've made my choice."

He searched her face. "And?"

She stepped into him, breast to chest, gripped his shoulders, stretched up, and pressed her lips to his.

The connection—one of heat and need and wanting—leapt instantly to the fore. If she'd needed any reassurance that the mutual hunger she'd encountered before was still there, on both their parts, that immediate reaction—him to her and her to him—was impossible to mistake. As if underscoring that he was equally affected—equally susceptible—his hands closed around her waist and gripped tight, seizing and holding.

Confidence solidifying, she drew back enough to open her eyes.

When his lids rose, she met and held his gaze. "Becoming your lover—lying with you—is what I want. However, while I'm not in any way set against marrying you, I do not wish you to feel that I'm trapping you into marriage by pressuring you to..."

When she foundered, one dark brow arched. "Initiate you into the pleasures of the flesh?"

"Yes!" She fought down a blush. "Exactly. That." She drew in a tight breath and forged on, "To me, lying with you and marrying you are two completely separate things. I want to—I need to—know what lying with a man is like, and you, it seems, are my only hope of learning all I wish. Given our circumstances, nobody will know that I've spent the night in your bed. If—not after, not tomorrow, but at some later time, after we come to the end of this adventure—you still wish to offer marriage, I'm willing to promise I will definitely consider it." She searched his eyes. "But I don't want you to offer because you feel you should. That you must."

She tipped up her chin. "If and when you make an offer, you will need to convince me that you really mean it—that your wish to marry me is genuine, real and true, and not an action prompted by honor or some such notion." Her gaze locked with his, she declared, "That's what I want and what I'm willing to agree to."

He studied her for several long moments, then said, "You spoke of spending the night in my bed. That, in the circumstances, there's no reason anyone would know." He arched a brow. "What about tomorrow night and the night after?"

She frowned and, scrutinizing his features, bit her lower lip. His gaze remained steady, unwavering, giving her no clue as to his thoughts. After a moment, she released her lip and offered, "Perhaps we should start with just one night." She tipped up her chin again and challengingly stated, "I want you to seduce me with, for you, no strings attached."

Nicholas continued to cling to his libido with a white-knuckled grip. He flicked a glance at the door, then returned his gaze to her face. "I believe most would see this"—he gestured between them—"as you seducing me."

She stared at him, then wildly waved both hands. "I don't care who is said to be seducing whom. Can we just get on with it?"

She gave him no chance to reply, but framed his face, hauled his lips to hers, and plunged them both into the unrestrained conflagration of an out-of-control kiss.

The reins slithered through his fingers before he'd found his mental feet, and then he was kissing her back with equal ardor, with equal wildness, with equally unfettered desire.

She tugged, and he obliged and waltzed them toward the bed.

As, with a glorious disregard for even the slightest self-preservation, she flung herself into the exchange and, progressively and comprehensively, razed his every defense, what little remained of his rational mind noted that here, now, in this sphere, he was dealing with the lady whose alter ego was Miss Flibbertigibbet.

She was reckless in her eager willingness, in the blatant encouragement she pressed on him. Encouragement that verged on the edge of outright taunting, an unvoiced challenge.

She flirted outrageously—with her lips, with her scorching kisses, with her greedy hands and evocative fingers. He gave as good as he got; with her, it was impossible to hold back, to exercise any meaningful control. She wanted, and he gave. He hungered, and she fulfilled his every craving.

As for her impulsiveness, that knew no bounds.

Like a steam locomotive barreling along the tracks toward its predetermined destination, she raced on.

And drew him with her.

Impossible to resist; freed of all social restraint, she was a force of nature that called to him on some primal plane.

She divested him of his jacket. He countered by stripping her bodice away, revealing the fine lawn blouse beneath. Tiny buttons demanded a degree of dexterity he hadn't been sure he possessed, but by the time she'd undone the buttons closing the placket of his shirt, he was dragging the halves of her blouse from the waist of her skirt and sliding his hands between the gaping halves to palm and cup her pert breasts.

He closed his hands, and both of them stilled—just for a second, for a heartbeat. Despite the muting shield of her light corset, reaction to that first suggestive touch struck them both and ratcheted the tension building within them one notch tighter.

Then her lips firmed beneath his, and he—they—dove back into their blatantly inciting kiss.

Hunger burned in their blood and laced fire over their lips and tongues. Appeasing that avid need became the be-all of their existence. Nothing else mattered.

How they had progressed so effortlessly to that point—one well beyond any notion of return—he neither knew nor cared. As he released the laces securing her skirt and, helped by his hands, the fabric slithered down her long legs to puddle on the floor, all he could think about was having her. Joining with her in the age-old dance. Showing her the way to intimacy.

Just how focused, how devoted all of him was to that aim was a revelation, in and of itself.

The laces of her corset, which thankfully closed up the front, challenged the patience of both of them, but then the restricting garment came free, and he flung it aside.

Before he could haul her against him, she wriggled and squirmed, then stepped back and hauled her fine chemise up and off, over her head.

For a heartbeat, with the fine silk dangling from an extended finger, she stood poised, nymphlike, bathed in the soft moonlight beaming through the uncurtained window.

He stared. Salivated. *Hungered.*

He reached for her as she reached for him, and their lips met again in a scorching kiss that was all fire and heat and passion and raging, out-of-control desire.

In a jumble of limbs, they fell on the comforter covering the bed.

She reached for him, trying to tug him over her, but he ducked out of her hold and swung to sit on the side of the bed. "Wait," he commanded, his voice little more than a gravelly growl. He bent and tugged and pulled off his boots.

From the corner of his eye, he saw her lie back on the pillows. Knowing that, on several counts, it would be unwise to keep her waiting, he stood, undid his belt and the flap of his breeches, then pushed the buckskin down, stepped free, and was back on the bed, stretching out beside her, before her wide eyes got more than a glimpse of his rampant erection.

But he'd forgotten—temporarily—that this was Miss Flibbertigibbet's alter ego. Her gaze rose to his face, and her lips formed a perfect O. Then her hands reached and found his throbbing member.

He sucked in a breath and closed his eyes.

Her fingers traced, then encircled his girth, then she palmed him and closed her hand…

For long, torturous moments, she played—and he felt compelled to let her.

This was her first time, and despite her forwardness and utter lack of modesty, educating her mind and her senses was his ultimate goal.

Gradually, even beneath the sensual torment of her ministrations, his wits realigned. He nudged her face up and claimed her lips and mouth again, put his hands on her breasts, and set about restoking their fire.

He let her explore and seized the same rights, the same license to pleasure.

For uncounted minutes in the heated dark, they communed on that sensual plane open only to lovers.

He showed her the ways, taught her to experience, enjoy, and savor the most delicious of intimate delights.

In return, she eagerly followed his lead and proved herself an avid student.

Step by step, through scalding caresses and tantalizing touches and demands laced with a desire so hot it burned, he sank deeper, more profoundly under the sway of the compulsion to please her. To give her all—everything—she desired and more. To reveal the totality of the landscape that passion could paint. To thrill her with fresh experiences and new insights—into him as much as herself.

Under his steady, experienced guidance, he pushed her to know herself sexually. To revel in that understanding. And in so doing, he opened himself to her in a new and very different way to any previous lover.

This, with her, was so very different. He'd wondered if it would be— had heard and suspected that it might be so—and so it was proving. His devotion to her pleasure—to this depth, this intensity—was something novel and new.

It was almost frightening, so complete was that compulsion's hold on him.

Of course, she wanted to rush ahead, but on that point, he was adamant. He wanted her beyond heated and ready when he entered her. He wanted her so desperate she wouldn't care about the inevitable pain.

It had been a long time since he'd last lain with a virgin. With her, he wasn't willing to take any chances.

That fleeting thought brought another to mind. In an effort to distract her and himself, he pulled back from the searing exchange enough to ask, "Why just one night?"

From under his heavy lids, he scanned her features. Lips swollen, eyes closed, head tipped back, she was so gloriously lost to passion, he felt he stood a decent chance of gaining an honest, unshielded answer.

When she didn't reply, he stilled his hands.

A faint frown tangled her fine brows. "Because...I want to know. I'm curious. And once—tonight—will answer my questions. Satisfy my curiosity." She raised her lids enough to look at him. "Won't it?"

He stared at her for a second—at the blue glint of her eyes beneath her lashes—then he ducked his head to hide his grin. "That's my aim—to satisfy you." He illustrated by pressing an open-mouthed kiss to her bare stomach.

Her lids fell, and on a smothered moan, she arched lightly beneath him.

He refocused on the task before him, rekindling their passions and fanning the flames, while some small part of his brain turned over her words, and the Cynster in him recognized and gleefully accepted her challenge.

That of ensuring that this one night would not be enough. That the pleasure he lavished on her would sink to her bones and bring her back, tomorrow and the next day and the next, eager and hungry for more.

He fell to with alacrity, with a devotion that was absolute.

And as she writhed beneath his hands, her body rising helplessly beneath his ministrations, and the pressure to seize the moment and join with her built, he gloried in her open, unrestrained responses and drank in her delight.

The time was right, the moment upon them. She was frantically eager as he parted her thighs and settled between. The tip of his engorged erection unerringly found her scalding slickness, but before he could press gently in, she tipped her hips in flagrant invitation, and he reacted and thrust deep.

She gasped, but not in pain. Her eyes flew open, and her luscious lips once again formed a perfect soundless O.

Her nails sank into his arms as he set his jaw and, lids falling, nudged deeper still, pushing farther into the scalding haven of her body, then with one last, almost involuntary thrust, he seated himself fully within her body's embrace.

He refocused on her face, and the stars in her eyes almost undid him.

Her expression was a combination of amazed, astonished, and utterly delighted.

And he hadn't even moved.

A vague notion explaining her lack of pain floated through his mind. She'd ridden a great deal throughout her life. While he'd definitely felt the resistance as he'd entered her, the pressure had been slight, barely there.

"Oh." The shiver of sound escaped her lips, laden with joyful wonder. Then she clamped about him—hard—and it was he who saw stars.

He hung his head and groaned. "Adriana..."

"It feels so strange." She experimented, relaxing, then tightening.

He reacted in the only way he could. He waited until she released him, drew back, thrust in again, and reseized the reins.

For once, she didn't protest. Instead, within two thrusts, she joined him, rising to the rhythm he set, eagerly following his lead, then, increasingly desperately, urging him on.

Addie wasn't sure she hadn't gone blind. She couldn't seem to focus any of her senses on anything but the pounding beat of Nicholas's body coupling with hers. In those moments, nothing existed beyond the utterly thrilling dance of thrust and retreat. The movement, the impact on her glorying senses, commanded every iota of her awareness. The compelling reality seized her wits, her entire awareness—held her very soul captive —all trapped in a web created by the elemental, striving, driving beat.

Passion, need, hunger, and desire swirled in a vortex through them.

The feel of him inside her was simply rapturous. She'd never imagined that part correctly, never had any true sense of just how deliciously delightful the act could be.

Yes, it was intimate, in a way and to an extent she instinctively felt she should be wary of, yet with Nicholas—the only gentleman she'd ever trusted—the experience was nothing short of amazing.

And unbelievably pleasurable.

She'd wanted him to show her the ways, the pathways of intimate pleasure, and he had.

Comprehensively.

She reached up and, framing his face between her palms, drew his lips to hers, and dove into a kiss and, with her lips and tongue, told him just how very grateful she was.

He groaned into the kiss, then the tempo escalated, and a wave of passion rose and swamped them.

They rode on, now clinging in desperation, clutching and holding, needing and wanting, overwhelmed by an inescapable urgency to reach the inevitable culmination.

Inside her, inside him, tension wound and gripped. Need and desire scaled new heights.

Deep in their landscape of fiery hunger, a peak of sensation beckoned, and metaphorically hand in hand, they raced toward it.

Her skin felt afire, her every sense locked on reaching the pinnacle. And then they were there, and a last powerful thrust sent her soaring.

The tension inside her shattered, and glory rained down upon her as shards of brilliant sensation streaked down her nerves and fractured her perceptions.

Pleasure, deep and profound, flooded her as, with a groan, he followed her over the precipice and into ecstasy.

Gradually, her senses returned, and she discovered she was floating on a sea of satiation. Oblivion bloomed on her horizon. It beckoned, and she surrendered and sank into glorious peace.

Propped on his elbows above her, her head caged between his forearms, with his head hanging and every muscle quivering in the aftermath of what, when all was said and done, had been a long-drawn-out engagement—admittedly, his choice, not hers—Nicholas discovered he couldn't think.

At all.

Giving up the attempt of mustering even a single coherent thought, from under heavy lids, he examined her face.

Peace infused every perfect line. In the waning moonlight, her complexion—already perfect—seemed to glow.

He'd done his best. Indeed, in his estimation, he'd transcended all his previous efforts in this sphere.

He hoped it would be enough to ignite in her the same flame that burned so steadily within him.

The need to cleave to one woman was a new development for him, but he was too well-versed in the ways of Fate to fight it.

That she'd admitted, however obliquely, that he was the only one she'd ever considered for the honor of introducing her to passion went some way to alleviating his natural feelings of vulnerability.

How could any man not feel vulnerable when faced with the reality that his entire future happiness rested on the willingness of one specific woman to join her life with his?

He now understood far more accurately how his male relatives felt. That each continued to survive and successfully enjoy their happy marriage was reassuring.

Sufficient minutes had elapsed for him to have regained the required strength to ease from the luscious clasp of her body and lift from her.

She mumbled something and tried to hold on to him.

He was too heavy and would crush her. He ignored her wordless directive and, instead, brushed a kiss across her forehead, then slumped into the mattress beside her.

He laid his head beside hers, then exhaled long and deep.

On a grumble, she turned and snuggled against him.

He smiled into the dark, raised an arm, and draped it about her, holding her close.

Then he closed his eyes and tumbled headlong into the abyss of sleep.

Nicholas woke with the dawn to an empty bed.

That didn't surprise him. He suspected—hoped—that Adriana would be thinking over all that had occurred over the hours of the night and—again, he hoped—reaching the conclusion that one night hadn't entirely quenched her curiosity.

Lying on his back with his hands behind his head, he gazed at the ceiling as the interlude scrolled through his mind. He felt fairly confident he'd done enough to whet her appetite.

While their interactions during the day were slowly evolving into a partnership, he felt certain that building a solid intimate connection with her would be crucial to gaining her wholehearted agreement to marry him. That was his ultimate goal and, to his mind, his surest route to attaining it was to gain her trust.

As Miss Flibbertigibbet and even as Lady Adriana Sommerville, she was undoubtedly wary of trusting gentlemen. In that respect, intimacy was key, because for a lady, especially one like her, intimacy depended on trust.

Knowing that he was the only partner she'd ever trusted to that extent left him feeling smugly pleased. Reassured by the thought, he rose, washed, dressed, and went downstairs.

He reached the private parlor to find both Sommerville siblings in attendance, although how much of Dickie's wits were functioning was open to debate. He looked up, vaguely waved, then smothered a yawn and went back to consuming a plate of scrambled eggs and bacon.

Entirely wide awake, Adriana studied Nicholas with a slightly wary, speculative gaze. Clearly, she was waiting to see what tack he would take after their night spent in his bed.

He smiled—he hoped reassuringly—and dipped his head to her, then went to serve himself from the dishes laid out on the sideboard. After piling his plate, he returned to claim the seat on her right, opposite Dickie, who remained wholly focused on his meal.

A tap on the door heralded a serving girl bearing a tray holding a coffeepot and a teapot. Both Sommervilles perked up, and Nicholas, too, eagerly accepted a steaming cup of coffee.

After savoring a mouthful, Dickie opened his eyes and attacked his plate with renewed vigor.

Adriana sipped her tea and, gradually, relaxed.

Noting that, Nicholas judged it safe to speak. "I suggest that, as soon as we're finished here, we get started on our search." He glanced at the clock on the mantelpiece. "It'll be eight o'clock by then, and all the likely people will be out and about."

Perhaps unsurprisingly, the siblings looked eager.

As soon as they'd all finished their meals, Adriana rang for the maid, and Nicholas went to ask Quilley for a map.

He returned with a plan of the town and spread it over the now-cleared table.

Adriana and Dickie leaned forward, peering at the web of streets and lanes.

Nicholas tapped a spot just south of the inn. "We know he reached here. What we don't know and need to learn is where he went next."

Footsteps approaching the door Nicholas had left open had the three of them looking that way. Rory and Young Gillies appeared, with Jed and Mike behind them.

Nicholas waved the four closer. "Perfect timing. Let's divide up the roads along which we need to search."

As they'd agreed the previous evening, Nicholas remained at the inn while the other six ventured forth in pairs—Adriana with Rory, Dickie with Young Gillies, and Jed with Mike—to painstakingly track the rider of the chestnut horse and The Barbarian.

"And," Nicholas instructed, "when you find someone who saw them, try to get some firm idea of the time, then bring the information back to me. Ditto if you find anyone who can categorically state that the blighter didn't pass them at any time last Wednesday evening."

Young Gillies, Rory, and the two stablemen saluted.

Addie nodded, as did Dickie, and they all trooped out to start trawling their allotted routes for any useful sighting. As the roads and lanes of interest radiated outward from the corner of the marketplace, quite close to the inn, this time, they essayed forth on foot.

With Rory, Addie visited all the shops and stalls around the marketplace, those that were permanent fixtures and not there only for the markets on Wednesdays. As it was Tuesday and she found no one with any useful information, as she and Rory walked back to the inn to report their comprehensive failure, she mused, "We might have to wait until tomorrow and ask again, once all the market stallholders are here."

She didn't—truly didn't—want to waste another day. Another night, however...

Rory's reply jerked her back to the here and now. "Perhaps," he offered, "the others have found something. Stands to reason one of us will. The villain came here, so where did he go?" Jaw setting, Rory nodded. "Someone has to know."

"Hmm." Addie saw no reason to argue. "The challenge is to find that someone."

On Addie's and Rory's heels, Jed and Mike trailed into the inn. At Addie's questioning look, they grimaced. "Nothing," Mike reported.

"Not a whisper," Jed confirmed. "You?"

Addie shook her head and led the way to the parlor.

She walked through the open doorway to see Dickie and Young Gillies looking as pleased as punch. Her heart leapt. "You found him?"

Nicholas, too, was smiling. "Not quite. We've been waiting for you to come in to put it all together." He waved them to the table on which the map of the town lay spread and anchored at the corners.

Drawing nearer, Addie saw that he'd been busy. He'd got wagering counters, presumably from Quilley, and used the small discs to mark the sightings they'd found while on their way into town. The red discs denoted their positive sightings, and black discs indicated those places where they'd had solid confirmation that the thief hadn't passed that way.

The line of red discs traced the progress of the thief and The Barbarian into and through the town.

"As of this morning, we'd traced the thief to this point." Nicholas tapped the red counter that sat at the corner of the marketplace. He glanced at Addie, Rory, Jed, and Mike. "Given where you were searching, I trust none of you discovered any positive sightings of our quarry?"

They all shook their heads.

"That's to be expected." Nicholas glanced at Dickie and Young Gillies. "Courtesy of our latest information, this is where our thief went." Addie watched him place a red counter over the front of the inn.

Nicholas elaborated, "Quilley did as he'd promised and asked his staff. One of the serving girls works only on Tuesdays and Wednesdays, and when, this morning, he asked her about the horse and rider, she said she saw the rider on the chestnut horse leading The Barbarian up Northgate, heading north past the inn. She was leaving to walk to her home, which is out along the Boston road, but she paused and stared at the horse—even she recognized that The Barbarian was noteworthy. Then, however, she turned south, so she didn't see where the rider went, only that he was heading north past the inn."

Along with the others, Addie waited as Nicholas picked up another red counter. "Next." He placed the disc a little farther along Northgate; Addie leaned closer and saw the counter lay on top of the manor house, just up the street. Nicholas went on, "While Dickie collared the squire, Young Gillies spoke with his stable lads. Three of them were dallying in the yard, kicking a ball about, when one spotted The Barbarian trotting past. As you might imagine, they stopped and stared, and despite the distance from the road, they gave an excellent description of the horse."

Young Gillies nodded. "No doubt at all that it was The Barbarian they saw."

"The shadows were lengthening by then," Nicholas went on. "We don't have another positive sighting, but Dickie and Young Gillies persevered and found a group of laborers repairing a drystone wall here." He placed a black counter farther up Northgate, beyond the edge of the town itself. "This"—he tapped the line that, at that point, led west from the road—"is a lane called The Drove. The four laborers were at the corner last Wednesday and are sure the rider and The Barbarian never passed them."

"They are absolutely sure." His eyes bright, Dickie added, "And they were there until full dark and back again at first light the next day. They're being paid on completion, so they were—still are—pushing every day to get it done."

"So"—Nicholas straightened, although his gaze remained on the map —"the question before us now is where did the thief go after he passed the manor?" He shook his head. "There's not much of the town left and no lanes leading into the country at all."

"Only this lane." Addie tapped a line leading east from about a hundred yards beyond the manor. It was labeled Church Lane and, predictably, led to the church before curving south again, eventually joining Eastgate. "He could have taken that, but it simply curves and leads back into the town."

They all stared at the map, then Nicholas said, "Either way—whether he took Church Lane through the backstreets or found shelter somewhere beyond the manor but before The Drove—given the hour, he must have stayed with someone in the town."

Dickie looked up. "We should check with the other inns and taverns. Perhaps he stayed at one of those."

"If he had," Nicholas said, "I expect we would have already heard of it." He glanced at Addie. "I doubt The Barbarian would have been easily housed or, at least, not without some fuss."

She humphed. "One can never be sure with that horse. He might have decided to play meek and mild, just to see what happened."

"But he wouldn't have liked being closed into a typically small inn's stall or, worse, a tavern's stall, would he?" Nicholas's gaze remained on her face.

"No," she admitted. "Besides, if the thief had stayed overnight some-where around there"—she waved at the area on the map—"then on Thursday morning taken Church Lane back into the town, most likely he would have headed out along Eastgate. Otherwise, he would have passed right through the town again, which makes no sense. Regardless, we still should have found someone who saw him that morning. Heaven knows we asked enough people throughout the town."

Rory and Dickie agreed.

"The Barbarian's not a horse people miss," Young Gillies pointed out. "We've proved that again and again."

For a silent minute, they all stared at the map and the counters.

"It's as if," Dickie said, "the thief rode past the manor and...vanished."

Nicholas raised his head, stared at Dickie, then looked at Young Gillies. "Those stable lads at the manor. Did you ask if they recognized the rider or the chestnut horse?"

Young Gillies blinked, then shook his head. "Didn't think of it." His expression lit. "I'll go and do that right now."

Nicholas waved at Dickie. "Take Mr. Sommerville with you. If the lads have a name, it might mean more to him than you."

Fired with renewed purpose, Dickie eagerly joined Young Gillies, and they strode from the parlor.

Nicholas glanced at Addie, then suggested that Jed, Mike, and Rory might like to get a drink in the taproom. "You'll see Mr. Sommerville and Young Gillies return. Come back then."

Jed and Mike gratefully accepted the dismissal and retreated through the doorway, but Rory hovered.

When Nicholas glanced questioningly at him, Rory said, "If you don't mind, I'll stay. I can't imagine they'll be that long."

"By all means." Nicholas returned his attention to the table and the map.

Addie resumed her position beside him and stared at the map as well.

Several seconds later, Nicholas tapped the map at a spot past the manor, a little farther up Northgate and on the opposite side of the road. "As far as I can make out from this map, other than the manor, this"—he traced the small estate bounded by Church Lane on the north and east and by Northgate on the west—"is the only house and grounds of any size in this part of town." He glanced at Addie and Rory. "Do either of you have any idea who lives there? At the very least, they might have a groundsman who saw which way the thief went last Wednesday."

Addie peered at the map, then shook her head.

Rory looked, too, then shrugged. "No clue."

Just then, a serving girl, apple-cheeked and with her hair piled in an untidy knot, looked into the parlor. "Will you be wanting anything to drink, sir? My lady?" The girl flapped a hand toward the taproom. "We saw your men drinking and wondered."

Addie brightened. "Nothing to drink, thank you, but perhaps you can help us." She beckoned the girl to the table and pointed to the map, at the house in question. "Do you know who lives there?"

The girl dutifully approached the table and bent over it to peer at the map.

"The inn's here." Nicholas pointed. "And that's the manor."

"Oh." The girl straightened, a smile on her face. "That's Styles Place, then." The girl glanced at Addie, and at her encouraging look, the girl lowered her voice to a conspiratorial whisper. "The master, Mr. Styles, died some months ago. Down in London, it was." The girl's eyes grew round. "Beaten to death, he were, over some floozy he'd been visiting, or so they say." The girl glanced at the map. "It's his widder-lady there now, Mrs. Styles. She's a nice one. Ask any of us, and we'll say she didn't deserve a cur the likes of Mr. Styles for a husband. For her sake alone, all the town's glad he's gone."

Addie glanced at Nicholas, then thanked the girl for her help.

The girl bobbed. "Pleased to be of assistance, my lady."

At Addie's smiling nod, the girl bobbed again and took herself off.

Addie looked at Nicholas, then at Rory. "Perhaps our widow-lady's groundsman might know something."

On the words, the thunder of boots heralded the return of Dickie and Young Gillies, both looking triumphant. They were followed by Jed and Mike, who'd seen the pair rushing for the parlor and had come to share in the excitement.

One look at Dickie's and Young Gillies's faces was enough to assure everyone that there was, indeed, cause for joy.

Nicholas gestured at Mike to shut the door. The instant he did, Nicholas fixed Dickie and Young Gillies with a commanding look. "What did you find?"

Instead of answering, Dickie swung his gaze to Addie. "You'll never guess who took The Barbarian!"

Her eyes widened. "The thief's someone we know?"

Before Dickie could respond, Young Gillies, looking at Nicholas, said, "I told Mr. Sommerville we should come straight back here and tell you what we learned *before* going off to see, but he had to go and look." Young Gillies bent a censorious frown on Dickie. "Luckily, we weren't spotted."

"Look at what?" Addie demanded. "And spotted by whom?"

"Phillip, that's whom." Dickie's jaw set pugnaciously. "He's our thief, the one who took the horse."

"What?" Addie was stunned.

Grimly, Dickie nodded. "I know—who would have thought it of pompous Phil? But the stable lads at the manor recognized him as the gentleman who's been staying here—at the inn, would you believe it?— and hanging around at Styles Place. That's a small estate just up the road, a little beyond the manor on the opposite side."

"Yes, we know." Addie glanced at Nicholas, then looked back at Dickie. "One of the serving girls told us a widow owns the property now, a Mrs. Styles. Her husband was beaten to death in London some months ago. He sounds to have been an unsavory sort, and his passing isn't much mourned by the town."

Dickie snorted. "He's certainly not mourned by our dear Phillip. Or by the widow, it seems." Dickie looked at Nicholas. "When the stable lads identified the gentleman as staying at the inn and spending his time at Styles Place, given we know The Barbarian isn't stabled here, I wanted to check if the horse was in the stable at Styles Place." Dickie glanced at Addie. "I didn't know who the gentleman was at that point." He shrugged. "It was easy enough to climb over the wall and creep up to the stable."

Nicholas moved to the table and tapped his finger on the map. "This is Styles Place."

Dickie looked, then put his finger on a spot within the estate. "The stables are here. Young Gillies and I went over the wall about here"—he indicated a point along Church Lane—"and sneaked up behind the stable. We could look through gaps around the rear doors and shutters, and sure enough, we found The Barbarian."

"He's in a large stall," Young Gillies reported, "and looking well enough, but he seemed restless, like he's waiting for someone to take him for a run and is getting frustrated that no one has come."

Addie nodded. "He expects a run every few days and gets annoyed if no one obliges."

Nicholas looked at her. "And you're the only one he'll allow on his back?"

"For my sins."

"The chestnut was in the stable there, too," Young Gillies said. "A few stalls away. He's a nice-looking horse as well."

Addie frowned. "I've seen Phillip riding a good-looking chestnut in town."

She glanced at Dickie, who immediately answered the question she hadn't asked.

"Once we knew the horses were there, we thought to scout about a bit, get the lie of the land, so to speak, so when we visit, we'll have some idea of the place. We were skulking about the rear garden when we saw two people—Phillip and the widow—strolling the lawns. That's when it struck me that Phillip, of all people, is our thief. He fits the description perfectly, and there he was"—Dickie gestured—"right in front of me, with The Barbarian and the chestnut in the stable nearby. You could have knocked me down with a feather."

He paused, then went on, "They were talking, so as soon as I stopped gaping, I tried to get close enough to overhear."

Young Gillies snorted. "Gave me a heart attack, he did, edging so close. I thought sure as hell they'd see him."

"Yes, well, they weren't expecting anyone to be there," Dickie explained, "so they weren't looking. And I overheard enough to know that Phillip and the widow are decidedly chummy, and the widow invited Phillip to stay to dine, and he accepted." Dickie drew in a breath. "So that's where he is, and that's where he'll be for the rest of the day into the evening."

Nicholas pinned Adriana with his gaze. "This is Phillip, your half brother?"

She nodded. "Phillip Sommerville, our father's heir. He's eleven years older than Dickie, and the only child of our father's first marriage. His mother died when he was nine. Papa married again just over a year later, and Phillip has never forgiven him for that. Phillip and the family have been estranged"—Adriana shrugged—"ever since." She looked at Dickie. "Certainly for all of our lives."

"I see." Nicholas juggled all that they'd learned in the past hour. "Why do you think Phillip took The Barbarian?"

"No idea," Dickie avowed.

Adriana frowned. "I can't even imagine how he came to know the horse was at the Grange." She met Nicholas's gaze. "Phillip gives the place a wide berth. I can't remember the last time he visited." She glanced at her brother. "Truly, Phillip is the last man I would have imagined as our thief."

Rory was nodding. From their expressions, it was clear he, Jed, and Mike all agreed with Adriana's assessment.

Nicholas thought, then glanced at Young Gillies. "The horse looked well cared for?"

Young Gillies nodded. "The beast seemed fine, and the stable was well-kept, neat and tidy with plenty of clean straw about. Smelled right, too."

"Good. So at this moment, we know where The Barbarian is and that he's in no immediate danger." Nicholas looked at Dickie. "The stable lads said your half brother was staying here."

Dickie nodded. "I was thinking about that. If Phillip's been spending his days with the widow, he wouldn't have been around here to see us going in and out."

"Quilley doesn't know us." Adriana turned to Nicholas. "And you organized the rooms, so the Sommerville name isn't in the register."

Nicholas tipped his head her way. "Wait here while I check with Quilley." He strode for the door, then paused and looked back. "Lord Phillip Sommerville?"

Adriana and Dickie nodded. Nicholas opened the door, stepped out, and closed it, then made his way to the reception desk.

It was just after midday, and Quilley was there, going over his accounts. When Nicholas explained that he'd thought he'd seen an acquaintance who might be staying at the inn, the innkeeper was entirely willing to allow him to scan the register.

Sure enough, the name of Lord Phillip Sommerville was scrawled in the book, indicating he'd been residing at the inn for the past nine days.

Nicholas tapped the entry with obvious satisfaction. "I was right. I take it Sommerville is still here?"

"Yes, indeed, sir," Quilley replied. "He often stays for weeks at a time, or at least, he has over the past year. Not quite so much before that." Quilley caught Nicholas's eye. "Very friendly with Mrs. Styles, he is. He spends most of his days at Styles Place."

"I see. But he returns here at night?"

Quilley nodded. "Oh yes. Every night. He usually comes in just after ten o'clock."

"Excellent." Nicholas closed the register. "If you happen to see him before then, I'd appreciate it if you didn't mention I'd been asking after him. I hope to surprise him when he comes in."

Quilley smiled. "Of course, sir. Will you and your company be wanting your luncheon, then? I can have the girls bring it through."

Nicholas agreed and returned to the parlor.

He was greeted with wide eyes and expectant looks. After closing the door, he related what he'd learned.

Dickie looked distinctly bellicose. "Why do we have to wait until tonight? Ten o'clock, no less. Why not go over and storm Styles Place right now?" He paused, then amended, "Or at least after luncheon."

"Because," Nicholas patiently explained, "we don't know what part your half brother plays in this. We don't know why he took the horse, and we don't know what part, if any, Mrs. Styles plays, either. The smart way to proceed is to allow your half brother to come to us and learn his role in this directly from him. The Barbarian is safe and well for the moment." He glanced at Rory, Young Gillies, Jed, and Mike. "That said, it won't hurt for us to keep a watch on Styles Place to make sure the beast isn't moved elsewhere."

Addie humphed. "Given what we've gone through to find him, I second that."

She listened as Nicholas arranged with Rory, Young Gillies, Jed, and Mike that they would take their luncheon in the taproom, then divide up the watch on Styles Place through the afternoon and into the evening.

Nicholas instructed, "You can come back for dinner. If Sommerville is going to dine with Mrs. Styles, he won't be moving the horse then."

The four agreed and departed for the taproom as two serving girls arrived bearing platters of cold meats, cheeses, and bread, and jugs of ale and cider.

Addie settled with Nicholas and Dickie about the table. While they ate, she considered the implications of what they'd learned. Eventually, she said, "Obviously, Phillip took The Barbarian from his paddock at the Grange. Although he hasn't visited for years, he grew up at the Grange and would know all the byways about the estate and in the area very well."

Dickie grunted. "He knew we would follow, so he went by a round-about route, heading first toward Grantham, then around past the Lincoln Road."

Nibbling on a piece of cheese, Addie nodded. "He deliberately laid a false trail, but what I still can't fathom is how he knew The Barbarian was at the Grange." She met Dickie's eyes, then looked at Nicholas. "I'm absolutely certain no one on the estate would have told him. No one there is in his pocket."

Nicholas studied her for a moment, then asked, "How can you be so sure of that?"

She inwardly sighed and tipped her head Dickie's way. "Dickie labeled him 'Pompous Phil.' Phillip is that and more. He's an arrogant prig, officious, sanctimonious, and often contemptuous and not only to members of the family. He's standoffish and looks down his nose at everyone, as if he's better and somehow more worthy than anyone else. He's perennially starchy, stuck-up, and top-lofty to an extreme degree. At his best, he's chillingly polite." She met Nicholas's gaze. "None of the staff like him, and I will eat Miss Flibbertigibbet's most frippery bonnet if anyone on the estate is in league with him."

Nicholas exhaled. "I see." After a moment apparently spent considering the word picture she'd painted, he inclined his head. "That's quite a character reference."

"Indeed," she replied. "And it leaves us with the unanswered question of how Phillip learned The Barbarian was at the Grange."

"And our next question," Dickie put in, "is what the devil he thinks he's going to do with the horse."

Nicholas frowned. "Given he came prepared to lead The Barbarian, presumably, he knows the horse can't readily be ridden."

"Even more to the point"—Addie pushed away her plate—"is why he's simply keeping the horse here." She looked from Dickie to Nicholas. "It seems he's had The Barbarian at Styles Place for almost a week. Why?" She spread her hands. "Why steal a horse, then just keep him in a stable for six days?"

They pondered the point, but none of them could think of an answer.

Addie sighed, then looked somewhat bleakly at Nicholas. "So we have an entire afternoon to just sit and wait?"

He met her eyes, and his lips twitched. "Sadly, that's correct. Wait, have dinner, then wait some more. Until ten o'clock."

Addie groaned, and Dickie joined her.

CHAPTER 11

*A*fter some argument, when, that evening, the clocks about the inn chimed for ten o'clock, Nicholas was alone in the inn's foyer, waiting for Lord Phillip Sommerville to show his face.

Nicholas had succeeded in convincing the younger Sommerville siblings that any confrontation with their half brother would be better conducted in private. He'd left Adriana and Dickie pacing before the unlit fireplace in the parlor. Despite the siblings' assurances that Phillip wouldn't recognize Rory, Jed, or Mike, the three were tucked away with Young Gillies in the taproom, safely out of sight.

With one shoulder propped against the wall beside the open doorway to the noisy taproom, with his arms crossed over his chest, Nicholas was calculating how long it would take for a gentleman to walk from Styles Place to the inn when the door opened and Phillip Sommerville strolled in.

If Nicholas hadn't been so well acquainted with Dickie, he wouldn't have seen any resemblance in Phillip; the half brothers shared the same mid-to-dark-brown hair and had eyes of a similar blue, but their features differed, with Phillip's being much more chiseled and harsh, more stony, with little sign that the man laughed much, if at all.

And just the way Phillip carried himself testified to his haughty nature.

With several cousins who, when it suited them, could appear haughty in the extreme, Nicholas wasn't intimidated. When Phillip drew level, as if just noticing him, Nicholas unfolded his arms and straightened away from the wall. "Sommerville, isn't it?"

Phillip swung Nicholas's way. For a fleeting instant, Nicholas saw something like alarm flash through Phillip's eyes, but in the next instant, his heavy lids lowered, and he regarded Nicholas with wary distance. "Yes." Phillip faintly frowned. "Are we acquainted?"

Nicholas smiled with easy confidence. "Not that I'm aware of." He extended his hand. "Nicholas Cynster."

Phillip's eyes flared, and Nicholas sensed spiking alarm.

Phillip swallowed and, with increasing wariness, shook Nicholas's hand. "Ah..." Phillip glanced at the reception counter. "Are you staying here, at the inn?"

"I am." Smoothly, Nicholas waved toward the short corridor that led to the private parlor. "Along with two friends, who are known to you and would dearly like a word."

"Oh." Phillip's eyes remained wide. "I...see."

Inwardly, Nicholas frowned. Why the devil was the man so nervous? Not to say jumpy.

Then again, if he was a horse thief, meeting an unexpected Cynster might be rather unsettling.

Plainly unsure what to do, Phillip hadn't moved.

With every appearance of bonhomie, Nicholas clapped him on the shoulder. "I really think you should speak with our mutual friends."

Obviously reluctant, yet ultimately unresisting, Phillip Sommerville allowed Nicholas to usher him to the parlor door. Nicholas received the distinct impression that Sommerville felt helpless, like a condemned man being led to the gallows.

Nicholas reached past Phillip, set the parlor door swinging, and waved him through.

Phillip crossed the threshold and, scanning the room, took two cautious paces forward. Following and closing the door, Nicholas wondered who Phillip thought was waiting to speak with him.

Then Phillip's gaze landed on his half siblings, who were standing, waiting, before the hearth. Instantly, Phillip stiffened, and his head rose. After several seconds of mutual staring, Phillip stiffly inclined his head. "Richard. Adriana."

Phillip's voice was every bit as haughtily aloof as Adriana had intimated.

A fraught second passed, then Phillip glanced sidelong at Nicholas before looking back at Adriana and Dickie. "Mr. Cynster gave me to understand that you wished to speak with me."

"Indeed." Her eyes lighting with temper, Adriana advanced. Her face a mask of contained fury, she halted two paces from her half brother. "What I"—she glanced at Dickie as he came to stand beside her, then looked back, even more belligerently, at Phillip—"we"—she gestured at Nicholas, including him—"*all* of us want to know is what the devil you think you're doing, stealing The Barbarian from Papa."

Nicholas shifted so that he could see Phillip's face. There was something beyond the obvious going on, but Nicholas couldn't guess what.

In response to Adriana's accusation, Phillip's expression remained inscrutable, his features granite hard, but neither Adriana nor Dickie gave any indication of softening, much less retreating.

Eventually, Phillip's lips parted. "I—"

Adriana flung up a hand. "Don't think to deny it. We tracked you here and have any number of people who saw you leading The Barbarian this way."

"We know," Dickie said, his voice challenging, his tone condemnatory, "that at this very moment, The Barbarian is in the Styles Place stable, along with your horse."

"Perhaps," Adriana acidly suggested, "we should summon the constable, and all of us can go to Styles Place and take a look in the stable."

"No—please!" Phillip's façade crumpled. His features sagged. Every vestige of rigidity went out of his frame. His shoulders slumped, and suddenly, he looked like a man burdened by and buckling under some horrendous weight.

Adriana and Dickie stared at Phillip in surprise tinged with alarm.

Phillip didn't—wouldn't—look at them. Instead, his gaze angled downward, he drew in a wavering breath and swallowed. Several seconds ticked past, then he drew a deeper breath and raised his gaze to Adriana's and Dickie's faces. "Please, let me explain."

That such a plea was entirely unexpected was obvious. Both Adriana's and Dickie's eyes widened in shock, their expressions telegraphing just how taken aback they were.

In the interests of steering matters onward, Nicholas caught Adriana's eye and waved toward the armchairs before the fireplace. "Why don't we sit and hear what your half brother has to say?"

Much like players on a stage who had lost their scripts, the three allowed him to guide them to the chairs. There were only three, which suited Nicholas. He got the Sommervilles to sit, then took up a commanding stance beside Adriana's chair, with one arm stretched along the mantelpiece.

Now looking older and more worn than his thirty-five years would account for, Phillip looked up at Nicholas, then glanced at his half siblings. Bleakly, he asked, "What do you want to know?"

"Start at the beginning," Nicholas advised.

Adriana nodded. "If you don't, we'll never understand."

Phillip heard the warning in her tone. He took a moment to gather his thoughts, then, his gaze on the empty hearth, said, "Several years ago, I met a lady—Mrs. Styles. Viola. In London. We...became friends. I saw her whenever she was in town, for the Season or when she was visiting friends. We...grew close." He paused, then, his voice lower, went on, "Eventually, we became lovers."

Adriana stirred. "This was while her husband was still alive?"

Phillip nodded. "Her marriage had been one of convenience. She's the daughter of a wealthy merchant, and Styles needed the funds. It was never a happy marriage and...well, it happened. Whether Styles knew or not, I—we—don't know, but he wouldn't have cared. He never...bothered Viola and hadn't for years."

Phillip seemed to be following his own story in his head. "Then last year, Styles died. Or more accurately, was killed. In some dark alley in town, when he was leaving one of his doxies. He had certain tastes and preferred their company." Phillip dragged in a shuddering breath. "Viola and I...we thought that, after she observed the usual period of mourning, finally, we would be able to marry. We'd started talking of it, planning..."

His features hardening, Phillip bluntly stated, "But then it all came crashing down about our ears."

Before any of them could ask how, he rushed on, "About two months ago, I got a note from a man I didn't know. He signed himself 'A Well-wisher.'" Phillip snorted. "Of course, he was anything but. He wrote that he had something of mine—a letter he thought I would want back—and told me to meet him in a tavern off Fleet Street that evening." Phillip's shoulders slumped even more. "The only letters I could imagine not wanting him to have were my letters to Viola. I couldn't understand how anyone could have got hold of one of them, but of course, I went to the meeting to find out what was going on."

He paused, then grimly continued, "Sure enough, the man—I don't know his name—handed me one of my letters to Viola. Until then, I hadn't known she'd kept them. He said he had more. Lots of them, in fact." Phillip closed his eyes. "Including ones I had written to her before Styles was killed."

"Before?" Nicholas repeated.

Phillip opened his eyes. "Yes, and you can see how it might appear. Me writing…such things to Styles's wife, including how I wished we could find some way out of her marriage so we could be together, and then Styles being murdered." He stared bleakly up at Nicholas. "Based on the letters, it would be easy for the authorities to make a case that I had had the man killed." Phillip glanced at Adriana. "Can you imagine the scandal?"

"All too clearly," she grimly replied.

Dickie leaned forward, his gaze locked on Phillip's face. "So what did you do?"

Phillip blew out a breath. "Unsurprisingly, the man offered me a deal. He would hand back all the letters if I brought him something in return. Something my family owned."

Incredulous, Addie stared at her half brother. "The Barbarian?" When Phillip nodded, she exclaimed, "But how did he even know The Barbarian was at the Grange?"

Phillip shook his head. "I have no idea, but he knew. He told me about the horse, described him. He told me Papa had the horse and that he was keeping him somewhere on the Grange estate. I had to scout around and find the beast, but knowing he was a stallion, that wasn't hard. As soon as I saw him, I knew it would be easier to lead him, so that's what I did."

Phillip looked at Dickie. "I expected that you and the stablemen would try to track the horse, so I took a roundabout route." Phillip frowned slightly. "I thought we would have the horse at Styles Place for only a few days, but it took longer than I anticipated for the man to send me instructions about what to do next."

"Take a step back," Nicholas said. "The man who contacted you and told you to take the horse. Do you know who he is?"

Phillip shook his head. "I've thought and thought, but no."

"Was he a gentleman?" Nicholas asked.

"Yes, he was. But I'm certain I've never seen him before, and when I met him at the tavern, the light was poor, and he was sitting in shadow. I never got a clear look at his face."

Addie frowned. "So how did he get your letters to Viola? Does she have any idea? Was there a break-in, and someone stole them?"

Phillip shook his head. "She's as flummoxed as I am. The whole household is sure there has been no break-in, and as you might suppose, she's been living very quietly since Styles's death. She didn't even go up to London for the Season this year, so the house was never left empty." Looking thoroughly lost, Phillip shook his head again. "We simply don't know how he got the letters, and we've no idea who he is."

"It occurs to me," Nicholas said, "that there's nothing to say the man who met you isn't a go-between, and whoever got the letters and is wanting to trade them for the horse is someone quite different." When Addie glanced up at him, he met her eyes. "Using agents is common in the horse trade, especially if there's anything less than perfectly legal about the sale."

Slowly, Phillip nodded. "You're right. Looking back on our discussion... Well, the man didn't seem to have any personal interest in the exchange." He looked at Nicholas. "His attitude was more that of a man acting as an agent."

A short silence fell, then Dickie, his gaze fixed on Phillip, said, "You mentioned you were waiting for instructions regarding what to do with the horse."

Phillip nodded; Addie had noticed that the longer they spoke, her half brother's interaction with her and Dickie was becoming less stiff, more normal. "The man told me to bring The Barbarian here—to Styles Place —and once the horse was safely in the stable, to run the flag up the flagpole at the top of the house." Phillip glanced at Nicholas. "You can see that pole from miles away, all the way across the fens."

Looking at Dickie, Phillip went on, "So I did all that, and we waited. And waited. Then yesterday morning, Shaw, Viola's butler, found a note pushed under the front door. It was addressed to me in the same hand and, once again, was signed from 'A Well-wisher.' The letter said that tomorrow evening, I should take The Barbarian to The Drove—it's a lane just north of here—and hand him over to the man who will be waiting there and receive the bundle of letters in return."

Nicholas was frowning. "That—all of that—strongly suggests that your well-wisher is someone who knows the area. He certainly knows the house."

Phillip inclined his head. "I agree." He paused, his gaze shifting to Dickie then to Addie before he looked back at Nicholas. "I'm worried there'll be some twist in this, but I have no choice. I have to get those letters back. If they're ever made public..." He let out a shaky breath, but

Barbarian is worth a great deal to the Sommervilles and, ultimately, even more to the Cynsters."

Puzzled, Phillip glanced from Nicholas to Adriana, then looked at Dickie before returning his gaze to Nicholas. "I'm sorry. I don't follow. How is The Barbarian connected with the Cynsters?"

Between them, Nicholas and Adriana explained.

"So, you see," Adriana concluded, "Papa has already agreed to sell the horse to the Cynster Stable."

"And," Nicholas added, "from the perspective of a breeder and trainer of racehorses, The Barbarian's bloodlines are such that the world of English racing truly needs him to go to one of the top stables and not vanish into the underworld of less-than-reputable breeders."

Phillip cocked his head. "Could that be who is ultimately behind this? Another breeder, possibly one of the less-than-reputable ones?"

"It's possible," Nicholas conceded, "but at this point, I'm less inclined to that notion." He explained about the importance of the horse's papers.

"Hmm." Phillip frowned. "I'm not sure the man who contacted me was the sort who would have known to ask about such papers. To demand them for his client." He met Nicholas's gaze. "He didn't seem the horsey type, although I admit that's a conclusion based on superficial observation."

Nicholas nodded. "I'll have a better idea when I see the man in The Drove, when he comes to keep his appointment with you." He looked at Adriana and Dickie. "What we need to decide is how best to proceed to successfully retrieve the letters in question and learn who is ultimately behind this—which, as the future owner of The Barbarian and a member of the English racing world, I have a vested interest in knowing—while keeping The Barbarian in our hands."

Unsurprisingly, Adriana and Dickie launched into a discussion of their options. As the pair best knew the area and also the horse, Nicholas let them lead the way, as did Phillip.

Nicholas seized the moment to study the three Sommervilles. He accepted that Phillip, in acting as he had and, subsequently, owning to his fears, hopes, and dreams, had sacrificed considerably—his pride, for a start. Despite his staunchly upright character, he'd been prepared to stoop to being a thief, stealing from his own family no less, to protect Viola Styles.

Not having met Mrs. Styles, Nicholas had no way of knowing if she truly deserved such devotion, but he knew the value of what Phillip, through his actions, had already offered up for her. In order to protect her. Nicholas respected that.

He'd also seen the shift—a seismic shift—in Adriana's and Dickie's attitude to Phillip. He understood their change of heart and could only applaud their readiness to jettison their previous antagonistic stance and embrace Phillip's cause. That was what family did—what family should do.

Of that, he wholeheartedly approved.

On top of all that, although he didn't know why, he sensed that forging a better relationship with Phillip and embracing Viola was important to Adriana especially. And what was important to her was, by definition, now important to Nicholas.

That was the way love worked, and he was no longer in any doubt that connection now existed between him and her.

Eventually, with her expression resigned and not a little troubled, Adriana declared, "Phillip will need to follow the instructions and take The Barbarian to The Drove tomorrow evening—" She broke off as the little carriage clock's tinny chimes were echoed by the distant pealing of the town bell. She huffed. "Make that *this* evening." She looked at Phillip. "You'll need to hand over The Barbarian and get the letters in return."

"You should count them to make sure they're all there," Dickie put in. "Do you know how many there were?"

Phillip blinked. "Most likely, Viola will know. I'll ask."

Adriana narrowed her eyes on Phillip. "We can all ask, because you're going to introduce us to Viola later this morning." Before a startled Phillip could comment, much less protest, she waved. "But back to the handover in The Drove. The rest of us will need to be there, to seize the man and take back The Barbarian."

Her gaze shifted to Nicholas in a look he interpreted as hopeful—hoping he would support her idea. He inclined his head. "That seems the most straightforward plan."

The relief in her eyes told him that she understood how important The Barbarian was to him and appreciated that he was willing to risk the horse even in such a minor way.

Phillip had been looking from one of them to the other. "But... You've found The Barbarian. You could simply reclaim the horse—I can hardly complain when you do—and return to the Grange and complete your purchase." He shifted his gaze from Nicholas to Adriana then to Dickie. "I can't ask you to take such a risk. I…don't have the right."

Dickie screwed up his face. "Don't be daft. This isn't about you asking us—"

Adriana cut in, "It's about us helping you deal with a blackmailer, which, of course, we'll do!"

Phillip's gaze rested on his half siblings, his expression one of honest humility and dawning hope, then he looked at Nicholas. Adriana and Dickie did, too.

Nicholas met Phillip's gaze. "They're right. This is not about you asking. This is about us offering. And for us and you, what Adriana has suggested is the right thing to do."

Phillip's features wavered, and he blinked rapidly, then his gaze raked them all. "Thank you." Looking down, he paused, then more quietly said, "After the past years, I'm not sure I deserve your help, but"—he glanced at Adriana—"I know we—Viola and I—need it. So…thank you. I don't know if I'll ever be able to say that enough."

Dickie grinned devilishly, reached out, and cuffed Phillip on the shoulder. "Don't worry. We'll think of suitable ways for you to pay us back."

The insouciant comment broke the tension and made everyone smile.

Nicholas stirred. "It's late." He glanced at the carriage clock, then looked at the three Sommervilles. "I suggest we turn in and reconvene over breakfast." He tipped his head toward the table across the room. "If you'll join us, Sommerville, we can thrash out the details of a plan for the evening."

Phillip agreed. He still seemed dazed, hardly daring to believe the change in his situation.

They all rose and headed for the door.

Adriana led the way, reiterating to Phillip that he would be introducing them to his ladylove later in the morning.

Nicholas brought up the rear. Considering the three before him, he couldn't help but smile. They might have started the day estranged, but they'd fallen into a style of interaction that was very familiar to him.

Family was a remarkably powerful thing.

∾

Fifteen minutes later, Nicholas was lying on his back in his bed, staring at the moonbeams traversing the ceiling and wondering if he'd won the challenge Adriana—possibly unwittingly—had laid before him the previous night, when the doorknob turned.

An instant's pause followed, as if a silent debate was being waged on the other side, then the door opened, and Adriana walked in.

Nicholas smothered a triumphant grin. After closing the door, she started across the room, and the moonlight caressed features set in a rather pensive expression—pensive enough to make him wary.

She halted by the side of the bed and imperiously waved at him to move over, then she shrugged out of her light robe, let it slither down, and clad only in a whisper-fine nightgown, climbed beneath the sheets and settled on her back beside him.

He blinked into the dimness, unsure what she expected of him.

She huffed. "I thought you might come to my room."

"I wouldn't presume." And that would definitely have been a presumption. "Not after you were so sure that one night would be enough for you."

"Yes, well, that was before. Now..." She turned on her side, facing him.

He felt her gaze on his face, turned his head, and through the soft shadows, met her eyes.

She studied his expression for a moment, then said, "I really don't know what more I don't know, so to speak—what more there is for me to explore—but I don't want to spend the night thinking about Phillip or his Viola or even The Barbarian, and I suspect that, between us, you and I can create an effective distraction."

He fought to keep his lips straight. "So I'm just a distraction?"

Entirely seriously, she replied, "It's something you excel at." She held his gaze, and again, her features reflected an inner uncertainty that was more about her than him. "As for the rest," she softly said, "I can honestly say that I just don't know."

She leaned close and kissed him, and he accepted the kiss and sued for more, and when she granted his petition, he swooped and claimed and parted her lips.

He'd never seen her as a lady who could be easily steered; she had to be tempted. He had to lure her to see and appreciate the full gamut of what, together, they might have—a cornucopia of sensual delights. If she would take his hand.

If she would be his.

Granted the opportunity he had hoped to gain, with single-minded determination, he set about advancing his cause, namely that of seducing her into becoming his wife.

Whatever it took. Whatever she needed to convince her to be his. To take his hand and walk forward beside him into a future that, together, they would shape.

He knew that was how, for them, a marriage would work, and he rather thought she knew it, too.

As the moon waned and the shadows wrapped about them, and they wrestled and gloried amid the tangled sheets, he devoted himself to wooing her with passion.

With the depth and intensity of feeling she and only she evoked.

Addie had returned to him determined to learn more. Instinct assured her there was a wealth of experience she'd yet to gain. That she'd barely scratched the surface of the intimate domain. What she'd imagined as a pond had turned out to be an ocean. As his hands roved her body and his lips and fingers teased her flesh and pleasure rose in a wave and crested and washed through her, she was increasingly certain that instinct was correct.

Correct in driving her into this man's arms.

Correct in urging her to remain there. To seize him and let him seize her.

To embrace all that might grow between them.

The physical experience was only a part of it. There was so much more she sensed, elusive and enticing, in the background. The elements of the power that seemed to well and grow and infuse them as they writhed and joined. That filled them to bursting as they rode hard for the peak and straight into the nova of ecstasy that hovered beyond.

The explosion of pleasure shattered them, fragmented them, then filled them anew with a passion-drenched glory.

She wanted it all, not just to know but to claim as hers.

Deep inside, she sensed that, in this, she saw his truth, his ultimate destiny, and in her heart, she knew it was, indeed, her destiny, too.

As they slumped together, wrung out and so deeply sated neither could move, Nicholas knew he'd done his very best to open her eyes to the reality of what was growing between them. And in so doing, he'd done the same to himself; he'd ripped away the veils and would never be able to deny what he'd seen. Not to himself.

This, then, was what happened when a Cynster fell in love.

There was no going back.

It was just as well that he didn't want to.

That he was determined to seize Adriana Sommerville and never, ever, let go.

Sometime later, after they'd disengaged and Addie had settled alongside Nicholas with his arm snug about her, knowing from his breathing that he was not quite asleep, she murmured, "I never thought to feel...*compelled* to help Phillip, but I do." She shifted her head to gaze at Nicholas's face; his eyes were closed, his features relaxed. Somehow, that made it easier to explain, "He's not like he used to be—so much so that I have to wonder if everything we've seen of him over the past two decades and more was a façade. Always a façade. I cannot imagine—indeed, I cannot believe—that had our previous view been his true nature that he could have transformed into the man we spoke with last night, a man willing to go against what I accept are his strong principles to shield a lady he admits he loves. If you'd told me before that Lord Phillip Sommerville would ever do such a thing, I would have laughed in your face."

"Hmm" came from Nicholas. After a second, he added, "Men—especially men of our class—have a habit of hiding their feelings behind a mask."

She nodded. "And I'm convinced now that what we saw as Phillip before was the mask, and what we're seeing now is the real man."

Nicholas shifted, settling more comfortably beside her. "I'm sure you're right."

Addie thought at length, comparing the Phillip of then to the Phillip of now. "I cannot stress how much he's changed. It's nothing short of astounding."

A deep, rather reluctant chuckle greeted that. "Love will do that to a man."

Truer words, Nicholas thought, *have never passed my lips.*

After several silent moments, she stroked his chest and whispered, "I want you to know that Dickie and I, indeed, the whole family, truly appreciate that you're willing to accept the risk of handing over The Barbarian. While we all will be doing our utmost to ensure nothing goes awry and we reclaim him immediately, there's always a chance something will go wrong." He felt her gaze trace his face. "You came with me to find and secure the horse, and we've accomplished that. Given how important the horse is for you and your family, you could simply take The Barbarian back to Papa, conclude the deal, and ride off with the horse in tow. You could insist on doing that."

He said nothing.

Then she asked the question he'd hoped she wouldn't. "Why haven't you?"

This was Adriana Sommerville; she wouldn't let him duck the question. He cast about for a way to answer that would satisfy her. "Two reasons. First, despite The Barbarian's superior attributes, breeding-wise, at least for racing, he's not the last stallion in England. Second, your father still holds his papers, so as long as we don't lose track of him, we'll be able to claim him back easily enough. That last point, however, is crucial. I don't want to—we absolutely must not—lose track of that horse."

All of that was true. It just wasn't what had been in his mind when he'd agreed with their plan to hand over the horse.

"So," she murmured, "as long as we don't lose sight of The Barbarian, you'll be content."

"Yes."

"Good."

That last word was uttered on a soft sigh, and he felt her limbs relax.

He waited, savoring the moments as she slid into slumber while held securely in his arms.

His mind wandered to their plan and all it encompassed.

Including that he, the head of the Cynster Stable, was indeed acquiescing to an endeavor that would put at risk the most magnificent stayer he'd ever set eyes on.

Love will do that to a man.

Those earlier words echoed in his brain.

Being the most powerful of forces on earth, love was more than capable of dictating his actions. And he was willing to accept that.

That he looked on that conclusion with utter equanimity surely ranked as one of the biggest revelations of the night.

CHAPTER 12

$\mathcal{T}$he chatter about the breakfast table that morning was noisy and vigorous. Addie was determined to keep her wits from wandering off, to meander in delicious aimlessness through her memories of the night. And the early morning. A very large part of her mind was enthralled and wanted to examine and scrutinize each and every aspect of the remarkably heated engagements, but she couldn't afford to allow such absentmindedness to show. Not before Dickie. Or Phillip, either!

Or even Nicholas.

He was the only one likely to guess the source of her distraction, but she wasn't at all sure she wanted him to know how deeply he and the pleasures he'd wrought had ensnared her.

Her safest way forward was to keep her mind unrelentingly focused on all they needed to accomplish that day.

After revisiting and confirming the bare bones of their plan of how to manage the handover and the retrieval of the letters, Addie turned her mind to their immediate next step. She pointed her butter knife at Phillip. "You need to go across to the Place as soon as we've finished breakfast. I'm sure Viola will be expecting you, and you need to explain about us and prepare her to meet us." Raising her piece of toast and marmalade, she added, "We'll follow half an hour later."

Phillip's resistance was etched on his face. "I'm not sure—"

"We can't simply turn up on her doorstep, Phillip. Not if she knows—

as I'm sure she does—how matters stood between you and the family before. She'll need to be warned that things have changed." Inspired, Addie added, "It's the first step you have to take so that we can welcome her into the family. Far better she meets Dickie and me first so she can see with her own eyes that we're not ogres and that we're not going to cut her." She beamed at Phillip. "The best way to convince her that—once we deal with this matter—all will be well going forward is for her to meet and get to know us. Besides, she's as involved in this situation as anyone —indeed, she's the one most under threat. She deserves to know what's going on." Addie tipped her head. "She might even have some insights that we lack and would be happy to have."

With the matter couched in such terms, Phillip had no real choice but to agree.

After cleaning his plate, he patted his lips with his napkin, then fastidiously laid it aside. He nodded to Addie, Dickie, and Nicholas and rose. "In half an hour, then."

Addie watched him leave with a firm and steady stride, smiled contentedly, and crunched her toast.

～

Half an hour later, Addie stood on the path leading to the front door of Styles Place and surveyed the house. Two stories, built in dressed limestone with a leaded roof and tall chimneys, the residence exuded an aura of quiet prosperity, respectability, and gentility.

The many-paned windows gleamed, especially those in the three bay-windowed turrets that decorated the first floor, one jutting above the wide front door and one in the middle of each wing to either side. All the stonework was in pristine condition, as were the roof and chimneys. The garden beds flanking the path and stretching to either side along the front façade were full of roses and other flowering bushes, kept neat and trim, but not overly manicured.

Viewing the house and garden, the appearance of which suggested that Viola Styles was a competent and careful mistress, Addie felt reassured. All she could see augured well for the future of Aisby Grange.

Eagerness mounting, she stepped briskly down the path. With Nicholas at her back and Dickie ranging beside her, she walked to the wide front door and waited while Dickie pulled the bell chain.

A distant clanging ensued, and a moment later, footsteps approached on the other side of the door.

The door opened to reveal a stately yet not-at-all-condescending butler. He smiled pleasantly. "Can I help you?"

"Good morning," Addie replied. "I am Lady Adriana Sommerville. This"—she flicked a hand toward Dickie—"is my brother, Richard Sommerville, and this"—she waved her hand over her shoulder—"is Mr. Nicholas Cynster. We're here to meet with Mrs. Styles and our brother, Lord Phillip Sommerville."

The butler looked quietly delighted. "Indeed, my lady." He bowed. "If you will come this way, the mistress and Lord Phillip are in the drawing room."

With a graceful inclination of her head, Addie walked into a cool tiled hall, not overly flowery but with definite feminine touches to soften the hunting scenes hanging on the pale-lemon walls. Dickie and Nicholas followed her inside.

After closing the front door, the butler led them to an open double doorway on the left. Curiosity welling, Addie consented to being ushered into the drawing room, a pleasant, rectangular room with windows over-looking the front garden and a large fireplace in the center of the wall opposite the door.

Phillip was standing before the hearth. As they appeared, a lady rose from a nearby settee to stand beside him.

The butler announced them, but Addie's attention was all for the lady. On the shorter side of average and just a touch plump, Viola Styles looked to be about thirty years old. Her hair was a pretty brown, drawn back, anchored in a bun, and puffed out to form a frame about her face. That face belonged to someone with a sweet nature, yet there was an air of character, of quiet resolve, in the steadiness of the lady's soft blue gaze.

Indeed, with respect to Viola Styles, the word "soft" rang in Addie's mind, but even more notable, at least to her, was the resemblance to her own mother—the lady Phillip had been so furious with his father for marrying.

The observation only made her more inclined to welcome Viola Styles with open arms.

With a genuinely delighted smile lighting her face, Addie went forward. She held out her hands. "Mrs. Styles. It's a pleasure to meet you."

Viola blinked. Instinctively, she reached for Addie's hands, taking them in a gentle clasp. "I'm delighted to make your acquaintance, Lady Adriana." Viola's eyes scanned Addie's features. "Welcome to Styles Place."

Viola would have curtsied, but Addie tightened her grip on Viola's hands. "Please"—she smiled encouragingly—"just Addie." She glanced at Phillip. "And I hope you will permit me to call you Viola. As I understand it, we will, God willing, soon be family."

Phillip was staring at her as if he wasn't sure that what he was seeing was real.

Addie smothered a snort. "Phillip." She tipped her head meaningfully at Dickie and Nicholas, both of whom had come strolling up in her wake.

"Oh. Yes." Phillip leapt to introduce Viola to Dickie and Nicholas.

Addie released Viola's hands to allow her to greet the pair.

That accomplished, Viola waved them to seats.

Addie sat on the other end of the settee, while Nicholas and Dickie sank into armchairs opposite, and Phillip resumed his position before the empty hearth.

Addie decided that more reassurance wouldn't go astray. "I hope," she said, addressing Viola, "that Phillip has explained that we are here to help and, indeed, that we're determined to retrieve these letters of his, even though that means handing over The Barbarian."

Nicholas added, "We believe it will be possible to complete the exchange, after which we'll reclaim the horse."

"We also," Dickie determinedly put in, "want to unmask whoever is behind this—whoever is blackmailing you and Phillip."

"Indeed," Addie replied. "We can't allow anyone to imagine they can blackmail a Sommerville and get away with it." She was very aware that Phillip's weren't the only secrets the family was harboring. "So"—she looked up at Phillip—"it's time to make plans. All of us, together."

Phillip glanced at Viola and somewhat tentatively said, "It seems the best way."

To Addie's relief, Viola nodded firmly. "I'm sure it is." She looked at Nicholas and Dickie. "We need help, and I would be grateful and honored to accept help from such quarters."

Her gaze shifting to rest on Addie, Viola drew in a breath and, looking openly puzzled, ventured, "Lady—" She broke off and amended, "Addie, I admit I'm confused. I had thought"—she glanced fleetingly at Phillip, and her befuddlement was plain—"that you were Miss Flibbertigibbet."

Viola returned her gaze to Addie and lightly frowned. "But that plainly isn't so."

Addie parted her lips on a brief explanation, but Phillip spoke first.

His gaze on her, he huffed and said, "I fear, my dear, that my sister has a temper. Miss Flibbertigibbet was her response to...the importunings of immature gentlemen." When, surprised that he'd known that, Addie blinked at him, he arched a dark brow as if asking "Am I right?"

She opened her mouth, then closed it. Glancing at Dickie, she saw he was grinning and nodding, while Nicholas, elegantly relaxed in the armchair, was regarding her with a fond expression that suggested he understood her reaction to Phillip's unexpected insight.

Yes, she'd been angry, but had it been that obvious that Miss Flibbertigibbet had arisen from that?

The idea threatened to derail her thoughts. She shoved it aside for later examination and refocused on Viola. "That might be correct, but regardless of how Miss Flibbertigibbet came to be, she's not here now."

The firm declaration had Viola smiling. "So I see, and I must admit I'm glad of that. I was exceedingly trepidatious over how our first meeting would go."

Addie felt her cheeks warm, and the others all smiled. "Enough of me. I'm sure I don't need to remind anyone that we're here to discuss how best to deal with this dastardly blackmailer."

Viola glanced at Phillip. "I take it Phillip has explained the pertinent details of our situation."

Addie, Dickie, and Nicholas nodded.

"Well, then." Viola pressed her palms together in her lap. "What are we going to do?"

Nicholas sat back and let Adriana, Dickie, and Phillip explore the possibilities, interrupting only to clarify critical points, such as confirming that The Barbarian truly would allow only Adriana to ride him.

"He's broken to the saddle and bridle, of course," she said, "but he's simply a willfully stubborn and picky horse."

"I gather he allowed Papa's old friend, Wisthorpe, to ride him," Dickie said. "He seems an only-one-person-at-a-time horse."

The discussion shifted to the details of how to actually make the handover in The Drove.

Phillip looked at Adriana. "Perhaps you might take a look at The Barbarian this afternoon. The grooms say he's restless. A decent gallop might take the edge off and leave him more inclined to be docile during the handover and whatever eventuates after that."

Adriana agreed. "To be candid, I'm amazed he allowed you to lead him even as far as here without him deciding to create a ruckus, simply because he could."

Phillip met her gaze. "I admit I was on tenterhooks several times, especially leading him through Sleaford. Until I had him on the rein and was leading him off the estate, I hadn't truly appreciated how strong and powerful he is."

Dickie offered, "The grooms have always said he's an unusually curious horse. I don't think he's ever been this way before, so perhaps the new scenery and sights and sounds were enough to entertain him."

That led the group to wondering whether, like Phillip, the blackmailer hadn't truly appreciated what manner of beast he was bargaining for.

After several minutes of speculation, Nicholas was about to interrupt and redirect the group's attention to the actual handover, but Viola, clearly less given to idle imaginings than the Sommervilles, beat him to it.

He continued to observe and was heartened by what he saw. It was plain that, having responded to the threat against Phillip by jettisoning their previous opinion of him and leaping to his defense, Adriana and Dickie were also intent on embracing Viola, including as a future member of their family; they were already openly treating her as such.

Adriana's acceptance of Viola was marked and unwavering. To Nicholas's eyes, it was plain that Adriana viewed Viola as a good influence on Phillip, which, indeed, was likely the case. The differences between the arrogantly priggish nobleman Dickie and Adriana had described and the man standing before the fireplace were beyond striking, and Nicholas saw, time and again, Phillip look to Viola for confirmation of his direction.

Whether Phillip knew it or not, Viola was already his behavioral and emotional lodestone.

For his part, Nicholas was a great deal more comfortable dealing with a family all cleaving together in opposition to a mutual foe. As a Cynster, leaping to the defense of family members was an ingrained trait, and seeing the same clear-eyed intent in Adriana and Dickie, and Phillip and Viola's acceptance of their help, was reassuring on a fundamental level.

These were people he understood. People he could work with.

The group finally agreed on the essential elements they felt would be needed to complete the handover, retrieve the letters, then reclaim The Barbarian.

With the three Sommervilles pondering how and where to conceal themselves as well as the necessary grooms and stablemen, Viola looked at the clock on the mantelpiece and broke the temporary silence. "It's nearly noon. As we're all going to be involved in our plan, might I suggest that it would be appropriate and useful for your company— including your grooms, stablemen, and maid—to remove from the inn and put up here?" She appealed to the group. "Aside from all else, there's a chance the blackmailer might call at the inn and, by some quirk of fate, learn of your presence and take flight before the handover is made."

Adriana wrinkled her nose. "True." She glanced questioningly at Dickie and Nicholas. "We could go and gather our things and perhaps ask Quilley not to mention to anyone that we'd been there."

Viola nodded decisively. "If you go now, you can do that and settle in here before luncheon." She rose and looked at the others as they got to their feet. "I'll have rooms prepared and tell Cook you'll be here for luncheon and dinner, too."

"And meanwhile," Adriana said, exchanging a conspiratorial smile with Viola, "we'll be off to the inn and fetch our bags."

In complete accord, the two ladies led the way.

Smiling to himself, Nicholas followed, with Dickie and Phillip bringing up the rear.

Later that afternoon, after they'd enjoyed a genial luncheon during which they'd thrashed out the finer details of their plan, Nicholas was once again on Tamerlane, cantering alongside Adriana perched on The Barbarian's back.

The horse definitely needed the exercise and kept tossing his head, tugging at the reins and wanting to run.

Nicholas could only admire Adriana's steady hands as she held the huge horse in, without apparent effort enforcing her will on the stallion.

His gaze passed appreciatively over her, then dropped to the horse. Again, he was struck by The Barbarian's powerful stride, his massive and proudly held head, and the remarkable fluidity of his gait.

Nicholas kept his mind focused on the horse, manfully resisting the inclination to contemplate the activities of the previous night and the question of whether Adriana had yet come around to his way of thinking.

She would in time.

He clung to that conviction, yet was grateful when, sighting a suitable stretch ahead, she tapped her heel to The Barbarian's flank and called "Come on!" and together, they allowed their horses to lengthen their strides into a flat-out gallop.

They flew over the grass.

Nicholas had to push Tamerlane to keep up with the flying bay, which said a great deal about The Barbarian's caliber. Admittedly, Adriana rode much lighter than Nicholas. Nevertheless, The Barbarian's style, strength, and speed were undeniably impressive.

The gallop wasn't short and ended only when they reached the edge of the escarpment overlooking the western edge of the fens.

Exhilaration singing in her veins, Addie drew up just short of the escarpment's lip, and Nicholas halted his big gray beside her. In perfect accord, as they had been throughout the gallop, while their breathing slowed, they sat and looked out over the fields to the far horizon. Below them, the land, green and lush in that season under a wide pale-blue sky streaked with wispy white, stretched to the distant shore of The Wash.

Since The Barbarian had arrived on the estate earlier that year, Addie had ridden him every few days. Although Rory always accompanied her, in reality, he never rode *with* her; she and The Barbarian always forged far ahead. As soon as they hit a gallop, they were all but impossible to keep up with.

Nicholas on his Tamerlane had accomplished that; the thrill of riding with someone else for company was a feeling she'd missed.

She'd noticed the assessing—indeed, covetous—glances Nicholas had thrown The Barbarian. She turned her head and met Nicholas's gaze. "You've fallen in love with this horse, haven't you?"

His brows rose, then he replied, "Speaking as a breeder, yes. He's a remarkable find, and I want him standing at the Cynster Stud without delay."

That confirmed her reading of just how much he now wanted—lusted after—the bay stallion. "Thank you for being willing to risk him in the handover. No matter how much care we take, there will be a risk—an outside chance, perhaps, yet still a chance—that we might lose him to the blackmailer. I truly appreciate your readiness to go along with our plan."

He shrugged and looked out over the fens. "Our plan holds the promise of exposing whoever is behind this, and that, I assure you, is also important to me."

She slid her boot from the stirrup and swung around, but before she could attempt to slide down from her high perch on The Barbarian's back, Nicholas had dismounted and was there to lift her down.

They tied their reins to the branches of two low-growing, windswept trees, then walked to stand a yard from the escarpment's edge.

The vista was truly mesmerizing.

After several moments of drinking in the view and the peace that surrounded them, without glancing his way, she murmured, "Given Papa agreed to sell The Barbarian to you, you could have objected to the plan, but you didn't, and for that"—she swung to face him, looped her arms about his neck, and smiled in blatant appreciation—"I most sincerely thank you."

His hands closed about her waist, and his brows rose in patent hope, and she laughed, stretched up, and kissed him.

She'd intended the kiss to be playful and light, but within seconds, the exchange had plunged deeper into passion's sea. Hunger rose between them, his as well as hers; she had assumed the night's activities—bolstered by those of the morning—would have assuaged their appetites, but apparently not.

Too soon, curiosity transformed into need—a burning desire to explore the arena of alfresco lovemaking—and she couldn't resist the compulsion, the need to know, to experience everything possible with him.

She made her wishes known and gloried when he obliged. His muttered "There's no one for miles. It's safe enough" answered the question she no longer had breath enough to ask.

Together, they sank to the thick grass, and soon, she discovered the extra-special thrill of making love in the open air, where the breeze caressed her heated skin and the albeit-distant threat of someone possibly coming across them heightened her senses to a phenomenal degree, simultaneously increasing her awareness of every tactile delight and escalating the pleasure.

The illicit pleasure.

She came apart in his arms, and he quickly followed, and as passion ebbed and their desire cooled, the moment seemed almost innocent. Touched by simplicity.

On a groan, he turned onto his back, taking her with him. She settled slumped upon him and allowed her mind free rein to absorb all that had invested the engagement—the pleasures, yes, but also the emotions.

She could almost envision the connection between them like a twining rope growing stronger—more resilient and less likely to break or to be easily cut—with every bout of physical sharing. She wasn't at all sure how that happened; she only knew it did.

Glorying in the soft weight of her draped over him, Nicholas lay on his back, his muscles lax, his brain working furiously. It was time, he judged, to speak more definitely of marriage.

He shifted his head and brushed a kiss to her temple. "Once we marry, we'll be able to do this any time we feel so inclined."

She stilled; he felt it to his bones. He held his breath and waited, unsure how she would respond.

Eventually, she murmured, "Is that a proposal?"

If he said yes, she might take offense and stubbornly refuse, and then...

He drew in a slow breath and carefully replied, "It's more an observation on what might be. Not a formal proposal as such."

"I see."

Unable to interpret her tone and, surprisingly, touched on the raw, he acerbically added, "Trust me when I say that when I propose—and yes, I very much intend to do so formally—you'll be left in no doubt whatsoever that I am, indeed, proposing."

Addie raised her head and drew back enough to study his eyes. Obviously, his desire to marry her hadn't waned. She'd thought it might after several intimate encounters; indeed, she had assumed it would. Instead...what she saw in the warm brown of his eyes assured her that, in the same way her own fascination with him and their connection had grown with each excursion into intimacy, so, too, had his hunger for her.

A shiver of responsive need tracked down her spine. She quelled it, along with the frighteningly powerful compulsion to pursue his comment, to probe and prod and see where it led...

She drew in a quick breath and, searching his eyes, said, "I agreed that I would consider marrying you, and I will. When the time comes."

He nodded. "And when that time does come, as it will"—his arms tightened about her possessively, then eased—"trust me, you'll know how you want to respond."

She saw the confidence in his gaze, but also glimpsed a deeper, hidden vulnerability. The latter gave her a strange jolt. She'd never been important to any man before.

It was a strange feeling, a realization that, for her, opened up a completely novel aspect of their situation. As comprehension sank into her consciousness, she owned to feeling a touch rattled by how far matters between them had progressed—how deep the connection between them had reached.

Into my soul. And into his.

She would have shaken aside the idea as silly, only it wasn't.

In embarking on her journey of discovery with Nicholas, she'd never imagined it would come to this.

That it could.

The sound of a dove in the nearby trees jerked her back to the here and now, and she remembered they were still entangled.

She pushed up. "We should head back."

She was cravenly grateful that he agreed without a word.

Once they'd straightened their clothing and Nicholas had lifted Adriana to her saddle, he swung up to Tamerlane's back, and side by side once more, they set off to return to the Place.

As they cantered, Nicholas kept his gaze forward and counseled himself to patience.

If her silence as, with the glow of aftermath still rosy in her cheeks, she'd gazed at him was any indication, he was slowly and surely succeeding and steadily advancing toward his goal.

But he couldn't push or press.

She was Lady Adriana Sommerville, Miss Flibbertigibbet, and he had to allow her to make up her own mind.

That evening, Addie gathered with the rest of the company about the dinner table, and they went over the details of their plan one last time.

While a rhubarb pudding was being placed before them, Nicholas looked at Phillip. "We're assuming the man who contacted you will be the one who meets you in The Drove. I know you didn't see his face clearly, but from your meeting in the tavern, what do you remember of him?"

Phillip thought, then offered, "He was solidly built. Burly. I never saw him standing, but I got the impression he was tall."

"So a large man," Nicholas said. "What color hair?"

Phillip tipped his head, his gaze distant as he thought back. "Brown, I think. Mid brown, not dark, with a touch of gray at the temples."

"Straight or curly hair?" Addie asked, getting into the spirit of the interrogation.

"Lightly curly."

"What shape was his face?" Nicholas asked.

"Squarish. Quite fleshy." After a moment, Phillip added, "He had large hands. Thick fingers. And"—he screwed up his face in thought—"I think he was wearing a coat with a light check. Tweed, maybe." He refocused on the others. "I'm quite sure I'd never met him before."

Nicholas looked at Addie and Dickie. "Does that description suggest anyone to you?"

Both thought, but eventually, shook their heads.

"He's not a neighbor," Addie offered.

Dickie added, "I don't know anyone like that, but I can't say I've never crossed paths with him, either." He met Nicholas's eyes. "At a race meet or boxing match or someplace like that."

Nicholas nodded. "At this point, he could be anyone. If he's an agent acting for someone else, he might not even have been in this area before."

With dessert dispensed with, at Viola's suggestion, they rose and retreated to the drawing room.

Addie was increasingly delighted with Viola and the effect she'd had on Phillip. Indeed, Addie was increasingly in charity with her previously detested half brother, given he'd had the good sense to fall in love with Viola.

That Phillip was in love with Viola and she with him was utterly beyond question. The way they looked at each other said it all.

Phillip's conversion from arrogant prig to halfway-reasonable gentleman had Addie hoping that, now, Phillip might understand what had moved their father to marry again.

Time, no doubt, would tell, but at that moment, they had a blackmailer to deal with.

As the company settled on the settee and in the armchairs, Addie returned to a point that had been nagging at her. She looked around the company. "One thing I don't understand—how did the blackmailer get hold of Phillip's letters?" She turned to Viola. "I assume you'd kept them. Were they here? In this house?"

Viola colored faintly and nodded. "Yes." She glanced at Nicholas and

Dickie. "I kept them in a drawer in my bedroom." She looked back at Addie. "I've thought and thought, but I can't imagine how any thief might have found them."

Dickie huffed. "And why would any old thief take letters like that, but nothing else?" He caught Viola's eyes. "I assume nothing else went missing."

"No," Viola replied. "And you're right. It's the most puzzling thing. I know the letters were there several months ago, shortly after my husband died and I added Phillip's last letter to the bundle." She glanced at Phillip. "But after that, of course, Phillip had greater freedom to call, so there were no more letters." She looked at the others. "I only searched for them when Phillip returned to London with news of the blackmailer. That was when I realized they were gone."

"I hesitate to ask," Addie said, "but are you sure none of your staff were involved?"

"Quite sure." Viola's nod was decisive. "All the staff here have been with me for years and…well, they've always been a great support."

Phillip added, "They're protective of Viola and highly unlikely to do anything that might harm her."

"And, of course," Viola went on, "being in mourning means I haven't been entertaining at all, not even at the relatively restricted level I did when Styles was alive." She thought, then added, "Since Styles's death, the only visitors to the house have been family members, and I can't see why any of them should have felt the need to search my room, for letters or anything else."

Addie grimaced. "So how the blackmailer got the letters remains a mystery. As, indeed, does how he knew to search—or send someone to search—for them."

She noticed that, while everyone nodded in sober agreement, Nicholas's gaze was somewhat distant. She caught his eye. "What?"

He held her gaze for an instant, then said, "I keep tripping over the fact that the blackmailer knew enough to find the letters. He knew The Barbarian was in your father's possession. Knew the horse was on the estate. He knew all that, yet he didn't know enough to get Phillip to steal the horse's papers as well." When Viola looked puzzled, Nicholas explained, "Without the papers, which establish The Barbarian's pedigree and provenance, his value is hugely diminished."

He looked at Phillip. "If the blackmailer's purpose is to sell the horse —if his aim is to make money—then he's going about this in a deucedly strange way. Any horse thief worth his salt—the sort who might know enough to target a horse of the caliber of The Barbarian—would know about a Thoroughbred's papers."

Frowning, Viola asked, "Can the blackmailer sell the horse without his papers?"

Nicholas nodded. "But not for anything like the horse is worth. Without the papers, he's just a good-looking horse."

"He's also an unrideable horse," Phillip put in, "so it's not as if just anyone would buy him."

Nicholas nodded. "Exactly. Which brings us back to the notion that it's an illicit breeder who the blackmailer is hoping to sell the horse to, but—"

Dickie flung up his hands. "But any illicit breeder would know about the papers, and he'd want them as well."

"More," Nicholas said, "without the papers, any illicit breeder would know that buying the horse would be a significant financial risk." He glanced at Addie and Dickie. "As long as your father can produce the papers and we can locate the horse, the earl will be able legally to reclaim the beast." Nicholas shook his head. "It really makes very little sense."

Addie was frowning as well. "Even if everything goes according to the blackmailer's plan, presumably, whoever he sells the horse to will know from whom they bought the beast, and once we turn up and reclaim The Barbarian, that buyer will promptly want his money back and set the authorities on the blackmailer's trail."

"So one would think." Along with everyone else, Nicholas imagined that scenario. Finally, he glanced at Adriana. "Originally, I wondered if, perhaps, I had led the thief to Aisby Grange and The Barbarian, or rather that the thief had followed me there, spotted The Barbarian, and whisked him away." Lips twisting, he glanced around the circle. "That sometimes happens. I'm known to rarely leave the Cynster Stable, at least not to travel into the country. Other major breeders have spotters in Newmarket to advise them of any unusual occurrences in the horse-breeding world, and one might have been curious enough to follow me into Lincolnshire, especially as it's not hunting season."

"But the thief turned out to be Phillip," Viola said, "not some unknown spotter."

Nicholas nodded. "And in reality, a spotter would have reported back regarding The Barbarian's existence and location, not simply taken him. Anyone working for a major breeder would know about registration papers and the need to have them as well." Frustrated, he shook his head. "Without those papers, The Barbarian is of limited value to anyone, even an illicit breeder willing to trade in stolen horses. Buying The Barbarian —a virtually unrideable stallion—without his registration papers makes no real sense."

He looked around the circle of faces. "So what is the blackmailer's plan? Why target this particular horse?"

Phillip was nodding. "And was it, in fact, the horse itself or some connection with us"—he glanced at Viola—"some link with either Viola or myself, that brought The Barbarian to the blackmailer's notice?"

"You mean," Dickie said, "that the blackmailer knew he had something he could use to force the pair of you to give him something in return, and he looked around and settled on The Barbarian?"

Phillip inclined his head. "To me, at least, that seems plausible."

Silence fell as everyone pondered that prospect and whether it got them any further.

Eventually, Nicholas shifted focus. "Another question is whether the man who met Phillip in the tavern is the blackmailer—meaning the person who wants the horse—or merely an agent acting on orders."

Adriana nodded. "If he is a go-between, then even if he hands over the letters, us then seizing him might not lead us to the blackmailer— meaning the one actually behind this."

The others murmured reluctant agreement.

"Another point that's been bothering me," Phillip said, "is how did the man I met in the tavern—or if he's merely a go-between, then the ulti- mate blackmailer—know about The Barbarian in the first place?" He looked at Adriana. "From what I've gathered, Papa didn't advertise that he had the horse."

Nicholas tipped his head Phillip's way. "That's another excellent question."

Viola looked from one of them to the other. "We seem to have a lot of questions to which we have no answers."

Adriana sighed. "Indeed."

"Given it seems unlikely that it's another breeder, illicit or otherwise, behind this," Nicholas said, "then learning why the blackmailer wants The Barbarian in particular will almost certainly give us a clue as to who the blackmailer is."

Everyone agreed, but as that still got them no further, by mutual accord, they set aside all unanswered questions and speculations and returned to reviewing their arrangements for the handover.

Phillip observed, "I expect he'll be waiting farther along The Drove, where it's open fields on either side."

"Most likely," Nicholas concurred. "He won't want to risk being seen by some cottager."

"So," Adriana said, "when, leading The Barbarian, Phillip rides his chestnut along The Drove to meet the man, we'll already be in position behind the hedges."

"Us and the grooms and stablemen," Nicholas confirmed. Viola had added two of her stablemen to their group. Nicholas went on, "All told, we'll have nine on watch, stationed around the likely handover site and along the lane in both directions, ready to follow regardless of which way the blackguard goes."

Dickie nodded. "And whichever route he takes, we'll follow."

Viola frowned. "But as the meeting is at ten o'clock, in the very last of the light, surely he won't be able to go far tonight."

Nicholas shrugged. "Most likely, he'll head north to Holdingham. That would be within reach."

Phillip nodded. "If he stays there overnight, he'll be able to head north, east, or west, or even south, bypassing Sleaford, in the morning."

"That does seem his most likely move." Adriana looked at Phillip and Viola. "Are you sure about the number of letters there should be?"

"I'm sure." Viola looked at Phillip. "There should be seventeen in all."

He gave her a weak smile. "I'll make sure to count them before handing over The Barbarian's reins."

"Once you do," Nicholas continued, "you'll come straight back here and wait to hear from us as to which way he's gone." He looked at Adriana and Dickie. "Meanwhile, we three and the others will wait in The Drove and on the lanes and follow the man when he leaves. After we know where he's gone to ground for the night, we'll return here as well and make plans for following him when he continues on tomorrow."

They sat and imagined how that would play out.

Adriana mused, "We do need to follow him, don't we? We can't just stop him in The Drove and take back the horse, because that won't necessarily tell us what this is all about."

"What the man does with the horse will tell us whether he himself is the blackmailer or if he's working for someone else," Nicholas said.

"If he's just a go-between, working for the blackmailer," Dickie said, "we'll need to follow long enough to learn who the blackmailer is, then expose the pair of them." He sounded quite bloodthirsty.

Silence ensued as they pondered that.

Eventually, Viola stirred. When the others looked at her, she said, "In reality, how easy will it be to reclaim the horse?"

Along with the others, she looked at Nicholas.

He smiled reassuringly. "Given the earl holds The Barbarian's registration papers, which includes a detailed description of the horse, then that together with my standing in the Thoroughbred breeding industry will ensure that laying claim to the horse will be a mere formality." He glanced at Phillip, Adriana, and Dickie. "Having three Sommervilles, including the earl's heir, present will make the outcome a foregone conclusion."

Adriana, whose position afforded her a clear view of the clock on the mantelpiece, rose. The three men started to stand, but she waved them back. "It's not quite time, but I need to change into my riding habit." She glanced again at the clock. "I'll meet you in the hall at nine-thirty on the dot."

With that, she turned and strode purposely from the room.

Nicholas watched her go.

At nine-thirty, they gathered in the hall, then leaving Viola to hold the fort, with her good wishes for success in their ears, they headed out to the stable to claim their mounts and ride out to the meeting place along The Drove.

They parted from Phillip at the stable. He would wait until just short of ten o'clock, then lead The Barbarian to the appointed spot. The huge stallion was openly curious about what was going on.

Nicholas, Adriana, and Dickie, together with Young Gillies, Rory, Jed, Mike, and Harold and Oscar—Viola's stablemen—mounted and headed out from the Place via the rear drive to circle around and get into their designated positions from which to watch where their mystery man took The Barbarian.

CHAPTER 13

*N*ight was creeping across the landscape, cloaking lanes, hedges, and fields in steadily deepening shadow.

Nicholas hunkered behind the thick hedge that bordered the narrow lane known as The Drove. Thankfully, the hedge was so high that, even perched on a horse, no one in the lane would be able to see him or Adriana, who was crouching beside him.

Dickie was on the other side of the lane, similarly concealed. The rest of their party were scattered, with Harold and Oscar stationed along The Drove to the west, just in case the man went that way. The others were hidden around the intersection where The Drove met the Holdingham road running north out of Sleaford.

Everyone expected the man—be he the blackmailer or his agent—to head for Holdingham to seek shelter for the night. All of them had their horses hidden in copses well back from the lane, yet close enough to reach so they could follow their quarry.

Nicholas tugged out his fob watch and angled it to catch what starlight there was. It was the dark of the moon, and near-blackness engulfed them, but he managed to make out the hands. Tucking the watch back, he leaned close to Adriana and whispered, "A minute to go. Phillip should be arriving soon."

She nodded. Tense and expectant, she reminded him of a tightly wound spring about to explosively release.

Several silent seconds later, hoofbeats slowly approached from the west. The man—their quarry—was arriving.

In the shadows, Nicholas and Adriana shared an expectant glance.

As the man obligingly halted his horse almost level with where they crouched, the double *clop* from Phillip's horse and The Barbarian reached them.

They held still and silent as Phillip reined in. After a second, he said, "As you can see, I have the horse." They heard a jingle; presumably, Phillip had gestured with The Barbarian's reins. Phillip asked, "Do you have the letters? All of them?"

"As promised." The man's voice was deep, solid-sounding, the voice of a heavily built man.

Nicholas heard a creak as the man shifted in his saddle.

"Here. It seems they're yours again."

Several creaks and the rustle of paper were followed by Phillip's terse "You'll understand if I count them, just to be sure."

"Be my guest." A hint of amusement colored the man's tone.

Nicholas and Adriana waited, not exactly patiently, as, presumably, Phillip counted the letters.

He grunted. "Sixteen. With the one you gave me earlier, that makes seventeen."

"Which," the man said, entirely unperturbed, "was all there was."

Phillip must have nodded. They heard him shift, no doubt tucking the letters safely away, then came the jingle of a bridle. "Here. He's all yours. May he bring you the joy you deserve."

"Aye, well. We'll see about that." After a second, the man said, "He's certainly a good-looking horse."

Nicholas caught Adriana's gaze as, alert, she looked wide-eyed at him. He nodded. The man's tone made it crystal clear that he hadn't known much about The Barbarian until that moment.

Given that, it seemed unlikely he was the one interested in acquiring the stallion.

The man, or rather the agent—Nicholas felt confident in labeling him that—must have been studying the horse. Then he said to Phillip, "You can leave now."

The command in his voice left them in no doubt the agent wasn't a man to be taken lightly.

Phillip's tack jingled, and hooves clopped as he turned his chestnut. "I can't say it's been any sort of pleasure doing business with you." His tone acid, he added, "And it will suit me perfectly should I never again lay eyes on you."

The agent chuckled. "We have the same wish, then. Off you go."

The drum of hooves informed them that Phillip had obeyed and quit the scene.

Crouching behind the hedge, Nicholas and Adriana remained unmoving, all but holding their breaths. The agent waited until Phillip had gone. In the nighttime stillness, Phillip's horse's hoofbeats could easily be heard as he left The Drove and headed back into Sleaford.

Once the black's hoofbeats had faded, the agent grunted. Then he edged his horse forward. "All right. Let's see about getting you stabled for the night."

A short interval of shifting hooves and horsey snorts suggested that the man's horse didn't appreciate being forced into close proximity with the massive stallion, who was, no doubt, ready to be difficult. But eventually, the agent got both horses facing the same way and set off eastward.

Nicholas exchanged a look of vindication with Adriana. They'd thought the man would go that way.

As soon as their quarry was far enough down the lane to risk it, they raced across the field for their horses.

Nicholas tossed Adriana up to her saddle, then swung up to his. They rode to where a gate allowed them access to The Drove. Dickie, having retrieved his horse, was waiting, and as quietly as they could, the three of them trotted slowly in the agent's wake.

He was far enough ahead that he'd already turned out of The Drove and disappeared from sight before they reached the intersection.

There, they received their first surprise.

Holding the reins of his horse, but not mounted, Young Gillies was waiting in the middle of the Holdingham road, facing south toward Sleaford.

Frowning, Nicholas drew rein. "Which way did he go?"

Young Gillies nodded southward. "Bold as brass, he headed into Sleaford."

"Really?" Adriana stared down the road, then glanced at Nicholas. "Surely going through Sleaford is taking a huge risk."

Nicholas shrugged. "Apparently, our agent likes to live dangerously."

"Agent?" Young Gillies turned to mount his horse. "Do we know that now?"

"I think so." Nicholas met Adriana's gaze. "From his tone, he didn't know anything about The Barbarian until he set eyes on the horse in the lane."

Dickie murmured, "It certainly seemed that way. I was watching through the hedge, and after Phillip left, the agent circled The Barbarian, staring in that wide-eyed way that says he'd had no idea what sort of horse he was picking up until then."

Adriana urged her horse into a slow walk toward Sleaford. "Let's see where he's gone."

Young Gillies brought his horse up to walk alongside Dickie's, behind Nicholas and Adriana. "Rory, Jed, and Mike followed him into the town. One of them will be waiting to show us which road he took."

They reached the wall surrounding Styles Place. By then, Harold and Oscar had trotted up behind them. Nicholas waved at the pair to return to the Place for the moment, then the rest of the group continued on, past the manor, in which lights still shone.

Their second surprise of the night came when, just north of the Pack-horse Inn, Rory, on foot, pushed away from the wall where he'd been hidden in shadow and signaled, somewhat frantically, for them to stop.

They reined in, and Rory hurried up.

"You'll never guess," he whispered, "but the blackguard's gone into the inn."

"The Packhorse?" Dickie was incredulous.

Rory nodded. "Far as we could tell, he handed over the horses—his and The Barbarian—to be stabled for the night, then took himself into the inn."

Nicholas stared at the inn's archway. "Those ostlers know we're looking for that horse. We asked them about him."

Rory nodded earnestly. "We remembered. Jed and Mike went into the yard as soon as the gent was inside and asked the ostlers to keep seeing the horse under their hats. They were happy to. As Jed and Mike know The Barbarian, and he knows them, they stayed in the stable to make sure he's all right and settled for the night."

They all stared at the inn, then Nicholas shook his head. "I can barely believe it, but all we can do is keep watch and wait until he leaves."

Between them, they devised a schedule of watchers to cover the night.

Eventually, leaving Rory and Young Gillies with Jed and Mike, who had yet to return from the inn's stable, to spell each other in pairs through the night, and promising to send Harold and Oscar down as well,

Nicholas turned Tamerlane and, with Adriana and Dickie, trotted quietly back to Styles Place.

～

On being informed of where the agent had chosen to spend the night, Phillip and Viola were as incredulous as the others. But after a moment's thought, Viola pointed out that there was no reason the agent would have known Nicholas, Adriana, and Dickie had been asking about the horse, and he would have felt confident that neither Viola and her staff nor Phillip would have advertised their interest in The Barbarian.

"Given that we tend to keep to ourselves behind the walls of Styles Place," she concluded, "he might have felt that spending the night in Sleaford wasn't any great risk."

That seemed to be self-evident, and in a state of some disorientation —all but Viola had expected to spend the night on the road somewhere and had packed accordingly—they retreated to their rooms and spent what, for them all, for various reasons, proved a restless night.

Nicholas rose early and slipped out of the house to check with the men on watch at that time. Rory and Young Gilles had, apparently, just relieved Harold and Oscar, who had returned to Styles Place.

"Anything?" Nicholas asked as he joined the pair in a deeply shaded alley opposite the inn.

"He hasn't moved yet," Young Gillies replied.

Rory added, "Harold asked the ostlers to give us a wave when they got the order to ready his horse."

Nicholas nodded. He stared at the inn for a few more minutes, then left the two grooms to their vigil.

He returned to Styles Place to find breakfast laid out on the sideboard in the drawing room, with Shaw, the butler, standing ready to supply coffee as required.

Nicholas was glad to accept a steaming cup of the dark and fragrant brew. He sat at the table and addressed himself to a plate piled with samples of every dish. If they were to spend the rest of the day following the agent, he wanted sustenance to see him through.

One by one, the others appeared and joined him. Dickie was the last, seemingly barely awake.

"I'm definitely not a morning person." He set down a piled plate and dropped into a chair. Bleary-eyed, he looked across the table at Nicholas. "Has he stirred at all?"

"Apparently not."

With a grunt, Dickie fell to eating.

Nicholas glanced at Phillip and Viola. Judging by their relaxed expressions, both were hugely relieved to have got all the letters back.

Viola caught Nicholas's eye and smiled. "We've decided to burn the letters." She glanced at Phillip, seated beside her. "It'll be safer that way."

Phillip grunted, sounding exceedingly like his younger brother. "Less chance of anyone misinterpreting and accusing me of having Styles beaten to death."

"Indeed." Rather cheerily, Viola patted his hand.

Nicholas studied Phillip's reaction, the softening of his austere features whenever he looked at Viola, and the happiness shining in her eyes. After a moment, he looked down at his plate.

Several seconds later, unable to stop himself, he glanced at Adriana, who had chosen to sit opposite him. Admittedly, he had his back to the windows overlooking the garden and she might have wanted to contemplate the view, yet he had to wonder.

She hadn't come to his room last night.

He didn't know how to interpret that, whether her no-show spoke more about how she felt being under Viola's roof, which, in Adriana's mind, in a convoluted way, might also be considered to be Phillip's, or if, as she'd originally intimated, once—or as was the case, several times— had proved enough to satisfy her sexual curiosity.

She was keeping her attention on her plate. Indeed, given the slight line between her brows, it seemed her mind was distant, her thoughts on something else entirely.

Her attention certainly wasn't on him, and he honestly didn't know where they now stood vis-à-vis each other.

He returned his gaze to his plate and told himself to wait. Not to push, not to prod, but to give her the time and space to make up her own mind. Regardless of what he did, she would anyway, and if he pressed, she might resist, more or less instinctively, which would not advance his cause.

His goal remained unwaveringly clear, front and center in his mind. He was determined to secure her as his wife.

Not pushing would, in reality, be a small price to pay, but it was proving harder than he'd thought. His focus on her was so all-absorbing that the temptation to stretch out a leg and brush her ankle with his boot was well-nigh overwhelming.

While he polished off the last of his sausages and eggs, he reminded himself that, her current uncharacteristic unresponsiveness notwithstanding, the interaction between them had been going well. The connection between them continued to grow and strengthen, or so he thought.

But what does she think?

How did she view what had developed—was still developing—between them?

Did she see a future for them yet? Or for her, had the novelty worn off?

He was staring at his empty plate and contemplating those questions when Rory appeared in the doorway.

One look at the groom's face was enough to tell them all that he was the bearer of portentous news.

Adriana swiveled to face the doorway. "What is it?"

His eyes alight, Rory stepped into the dining room. "Well, first off, you don't need to hurry. Only just come down to breakfast, our man has." He looked at Nicholas. "Young Gillies, Jed, and Mike are still there, keeping watch, but we thought I should come and report that we've learned the man's name."

"You have?" came from several throats.

"How?" Dickie asked.

"Well, Young Gillies got along well with Quilley before, so he slipped in and asked Quilley who the gent was. Made out like he'd seen him before somewhere, and Quilley obliged and told Young Gillies the man was a Mr. Wesley Kirkwood."

"What?"

Along with everyone else, Nicholas looked at Viola.

She'd paled to a remarkable degree, and her hand shook as she set down her knife. She stared, horrified, at Rory, then swallowed and asked, "Wesley Kirkwood—you're sure that was the name?"

Rory bobbed his head. "Yes, ma'am. That's what Quilley told Young Gillies."

Phillip reached out and closed his hand about Viola's. When she looked at him, still plainly stunned, he gently asked, "Who is Wesley Kirkwood?"

Viola blinked, then swallowed and said, "He's a cousin of Styles. He was here for the funeral and came to the house for the wake. Before that, I hadn't seen him for years. Oh—" She broke off, pressed her fingers to her lips, and turned shocked eyes to Nicholas, Adriana, and Dickie. A second later, she lowered her hand. "Wesley called about a month ago. He said he was traveling north and begged room for the night, and of course, I agreed."

Viola's featured hardened as did her gaze. "He was late down to breakfast the next morning. I'd been up and about downstairs for some time. He said he'd slept late, but"—she looked at Phillip—"he must have searched my room and taken the letters then."

Various comments colored the air.

Viola's expression was outraged. "I thought his visit odd at the time, but from Styles, I'd understood that the family considered Wesley a law unto himself."

"If he's acting as the agent of a blackmailer..." Nicholas broke off and frowned. "But it sounds as if Wesley was the one who stole the letters."

Adriana was also frowning. "How did this Kirkwood know about the letters? Or at least, know there was a possibility they might exist?"

Phillip grimaced and gently squeezed Viola's hand. "No matter how careful one is, there are always rumors." He met Viola's eyes. "Kirkwood must have guessed he might find something...useful in an incriminating way in your bedroom."

Adriana fixed Viola with a questioning gaze. "What can you tell us of Wesley Kirkwood?"

Viola readily replied, "My understanding is that he leads the life of a bachelor gentleman, knocking about London." She shrugged. "He's in his latter thirties and, apparently, has funds enough. When he called, he was dressed well, and as far as I've ever heard, he's never asked anyone in the family for money."

Nicholas asked, "When he called, either after the funeral or more recently, did he make any comment that could have suggested he resented you inheriting the estate and all your husband owned?"

Viola clearly thought back, but eventually, she shook her head. "No. I can't remember him ever mentioning anything to do with the estate or funds."

"Have you ever got the impression that he was particularly interested in horses?" Nicholas asked.

"He drove himself when he visited, but other than that, I've never heard anything to suggest he was any more horse-mad than Styles." She met Nicholas's eyes and weakly smiled. "Which is to say not at all. Unlike you"—she glanced at the three Sommervilles, including them —"all of you, to Styles and, I feel certain, to Wesley as well, horses are merely a means of conveyance, nothing more."

Adriana snorted and looked at Nicholas. "Despite Kirkwood being the one to steal the letters, him not being particularly interested in horses fits our hypothesis that he's working for someone else."

Nicholas nodded. "He still sounds more like a go-between."

A thunder of boots had Rory stepping clear of the doorway. A second later, Young Gillies appeared. "The ostlers just signaled that Kirkwood is getting ready to leave."

That had everyone pushing back their chairs.

As he stood, Nicholas glanced at Viola. She, too, had got to her feet.

She met his eyes with an expression stating she was incensed and also determined. "I'm coming, too." She looked at Phillip. "We can take your curricle and follow the others."

When Phillip opened his lips, no doubt on a protest, Viola silenced him with a raised hand and a steely look. "We need to follow Wesley to whomever he's delivering the horse—and being a delivery agent sounds just like him—but when we do eventually make ourselves known to Wesley Kirkwood, I very much intend to be there."

So saying, she whisked away from the table and led the way from the room.

Fifteen minutes later, Jed and Mike rode out of Sleaford, heading north in Kirkwood's wake, keeping their eyes on The Barbarian's glossy hide at a distance sufficient to raise no suspicions.

Farther back still, the stablemen were followed by Nicholas, Adriana, Dickie, Young Gillies, Rory, Harold, and Oscar, all mounted and ambling along, with Phillip and Viola in Phillip's curricle, with Sally perched on the seat behind, rolling slowly in the others' wake.

~

Addie was soon exceedingly bored.

She, Nicholas, and Dickie trotted steadily along, as they had since leaving Sleaford that morning. It was hardly her idea of riding, but Kirkwood was clearly in no huge hurry and, some way ahead, was keeping to a trot, and they, perforce, had to match his pace.

Stifling a sigh, she looked ahead along the road and spotted Jed and Mike, who had dropped back to be the next up in the line. The company was strung out, with two of the six grooms and stablemen following Kirkwood closely enough to be sure of seeing which way he went. The three pairs rotated every few miles in case Kirkwood thought to look back and check for pursuers. Thus far, apparently obliviously, he'd trotted sedately on.

"He's like an old woman," she grumbled. "Can't he shake the reins and go for a nice little gallop?"

From the corner of her eye, she saw Nicholas's lips—his highly talented lips as she could now attest—curve in an understanding smile.

She swallowed a humph. At least he understood.

From Sleaford, Kirkwood had traveled north through Holdingham and set out along the Lincoln road, but soon after, he'd turned west along a minor lane. Subsequently, he'd stuck as far as possible to minor lanes, meandering about, tacking back and forth but, overall, steadily heading in a northwesterly direction. He'd been forced to dip a few miles south to cross the river Trent just north of Newark-on-Trent.

Not long after, as they were ambling northwest along the Ollerton road, Jed came riding back with the news that Kirkwood had stopped at an inn, presumably for lunch.

Courtesy of Viola's cook, their party had been supplied with two large picnic hampers stuffed with food. They pulled off the road and halted by a stream and settled to consume the repast provided.

The stablemen continued to operate in shifts, keeping watch on Kirkwood and The Barbarian, while spelling each other so they could eat.

Eventually, Young Gillies came riding back with the news that their quarry was on the move. They quickly packed the detritus of their meal into the hampers and set off again.

Soon, Kirkwood turned north, although he continued to cling to minor lanes.

"Why," Addie grumbled, "is he insisting on taking the long way to anywhere? Wherever he's going, the main roads would get him there faster."

With annoying calm, Nicholas replied, "True, but I suspect it's more important to him to avoid the others who would also be using the main roads. For instance, members of the ton who would notice The Barbarian, pay particular attention, and be unlikely to forget."

Dickie huffed. "He's trying not to leave a trail of sightings of a very notable horse."

"Exactly." After a moment, Nicholas added, "He might also be thinking to go easy on the horse or, at least, avoid instances where managing The Barbarian might prove problematic."

Addie snorted. "The Barbarian doesn't need to be babied. In fact, quite the opposite. He could push all day and not raise a sweat. He has enormous stamina."

"We know that," Nicholas replied. "It's the primary reason I want him for breeding. But it sounds as if Kirkwood has little experience of high-powered Thoroughbreds. Despite The Barbarian's looks, Kirkwood might think the horse needs to be treated gently—that he's delicate."

Dickie laughed. "The words 'delicate' and 'The Barbarian' don't belong in the same sentence."

Addie and Nicholas wordlessly agreed.

They trotted on, and a little while later, she ventured, "I take it we're assuming that Kirkwood, in the role of agent, is taking The Barbarian to deliver the horse to his master. Where do you think his master might be?"

They bandied guesses about, but other than "somewhere to the north," they really had no idea.

Once their speculating had run its course, they fell silent again.

And continued on.

Addie was hugely relieved when, in the late afternoon, Rory and Young Gillies dropped back to report that Kirkwood had stopped at a small tavern on the outskirts of Epworth, the next small town along the road.

They halted, gathered, and debated their options, and Young Gillies mentioned seeing a sign for a coaching inn that was, apparently, located in the center of Epworth.

"Jed and Mike are watching the tavern," Young Gillies said, "and the blackguard was already settled, with the horses snug in the tavern's barn, before we left to bring word to you."

Nicholas asked, "If we drive straight past the tavern and on into the town, how likely is he to spot us, in particular, Lord Phillip and Mrs. Styles in the curricle?"

Rory and Young Gillies exchanged a look, then Young Gillies offered, "The tavern faces south, rather than looking onto the street. Reckon we'd be safe enough just rolling through like any other travelers."

"He hasn't shown any sign he's aware of being followed," Rory added.

With no alternative apparent, they agreed to accept the risk and trot straight past the tavern and on to the coaching inn.

With everyone ready, Nicholas broke the party up so that he, Addie, and Dickie, in a group, led the way, with the curricle following sufficiently far behind to appear to be unconnected, with Rory and Young Gillies riding along beside the carriage, screening its occupants from anyone looking out from the tavern. Harold and Oscar would bring up the rear, ambling along before stopping to relieve Jed and Mike, sending them on to the coaching inn.

The plan proceeded smoothly, and they reached the inn without raising any alarm. Nicholas and Phillip organized rooms for everyone; in that season, there weren't that many people traveling along that road, and other than two traveling salesmen, they had the place to themselves.

When, after having left Harold and Oscar on watch, Jed and Mike reached the inn, they assured everyone that their quarry had, to all appearances, remained entirely oblivious of their passing.

"He never so much as looked out," Mike said. "Only interested in his dinner, it seemed. We left him to it, with Harold and Oscar in one corner, having a pint and keeping an eye on him. We found a spot outside, comfy enough and out of the breeze, and we'll set up there to keep watch overnight."

Nicholas commended them, as did Phillip and Adriana, then the company split up, heading for their rooms to settle in.

They reconvened in the inn's parlor, then repaired to the dining room to consume a surprisingly tasty meal.

When Adriana and Viola commented favorably on the quality and variety of dishes, the innkeeper confessed that his wife, the cook, was delighted to have more-discerning palates on which to practice her culinary skills. "From London, she is, and she misses the challenge."

After paying appropriate homage to a delicious lemon tart, their party retreated to the parlor, which was empty save for them. They drew the comfortable armchairs into a group before a window overlooking the street and settled to pass the time.

Twilight was fading to night when the conversation turned to where Kirkwood was heading.

Dickie suggested, "Perhaps the tavern is his place to meet with whomever he's fetched the horse for."

"Or perhaps that person lives nearby." Adriana frowned. "Is there any chance he'll hand over the horse tonight?"

Nicholas considered that; it wasn't a thought that had previously occurred to him but... "What would be the point? If someone arrives to fetch the horse tonight"—he leaned closer to the window and looked out at the sky—"on what is a virtually moonless night, they won't be able to travel anywhere. Unless they're a local and live very close, they'd have to remain at the tavern, too."

"In which case," Phillip concluded, "we'll be able to confront both of them—Kirkwood and his master—tomorrow, before they have a chance to leave."

"Our men will warn us if anyone arrives and seeks out Wesley," Viola stated with a calm certainty that dampened the restlessness affecting the others.

Nicholas had had reservations about the wisdom of Viola joining their company, but she'd remained remarkably steady and steadfast throughout the long day, and he'd grown to be grateful for her calm, anchoring good sense. Her presence helped to counter the mercurial temperaments of the Sommervilles; in terms of drama, all three had had their moments.

Young Gillies and Rory appeared in the parlor doorway.

Nicholas beckoned them in.

The pair approached, and Young Gillies reported, "He's settled in for the night, it seems. Harold and Oscar are still on watch, and Jed and Mike are in the kitchen having their supper."

"We need to keep watch through the night." Nicholas looked around their group. With input from Phillip, Dickie, and the two grooms, he worked out a schedule of two-hourly watches to span the night. Phillip and Dickie were both night owls and were happy to take the midnight to two period. Jed and Mike were volunteered for the two to four o'clock slot, while Rory and Young Gillies, both accustomed to very early mornings, were happy to take the four to six o'clock spot.

After glancing at the clock on the parlor wall, Nicholas said, "So I'm on first watch." He got to his feet. "I'll amble down there now and send Harold and Oscar back."

He left the others commenting on the lack of nighttime traffic on the road. Rory and Young Gillies followed him into the hall, then went in search of their supper.

Before the front door, Nicholas paused. It was summer, but they'd traveled a fair way north, and the night would likely be chilly. He detoured to his room for his greatcoat. After donning the caped coat, he descended the stairs, strode out of the inn's front door, and made for the tavern at a pace that suggested he was a gentleman indulging in a post-prandial stroll.

He located Harold and Oscar in the shaded doorway of a small warehouse opposite the tavern. The spot afforded an unobstructed view of the tavern's front door, the yard, and the doors of the stable that stood to one side.

Nicholas explained the arrangements for the night's watches and dispatched the stablemen to the coaching inn. Then he propped one shoulder against the warehouse's door frame and, safely wreathed in shadow, settled to keep watch.

Twenty uneventful minutes later, he heard light footsteps approaching. The footsteps halted just before the recessed doorway, then Adriana peered around the edge and saw him. She smiled and, stepping past him, slipped into the shadows, turning to stand beside him and look out at the tavern.

After a moment, Nicholas inquired, "Bored?"

She chuckled. "Yes. Dickie went off—I suspect to find Rory and Young Gillies and inveigle them to play cards to keep him occupied. And while I'm very pleased that Phillip has had the good sense to find a lady like Viola, there are only so many meaningful looks and wordless exchanges that I can bear. At least in any one sitting."

He laughed softly. Folding his arms across his chest, he thought, then admitted, "Given your and Dickie's descriptions of Phillip, while initially I saw some hints of such a character, the longer he's in Viola's company, the less I see of that man."

"Hmm." After several moments, she confided, "I can see Papa in him now. I never could before."

Nicholas waited, but she said no more.

After several minutes of silence, he ventured, "If you were bored at the inn, I greatly fear you'll be even more bored here." He shifted his gaze to her face, to what he could see of her profile as she stared across at the tavern. "But you would have known that would be the case, so why are you here?"

She tipped up her chin. "Because I wanted to talk to you in private, and this seemed the perfect opportunity." She met his gaze. "Not least because it will put paid to my boredom, killing two birds with one stone."

He refused to be diverted and arched his brows. "What did you want to speak with me about?" He told himself not to get his hopes up; for all he knew, she might want to talk about London.

She returned her gaze to the tavern and plainly took a moment to organize her thoughts. "I wanted to ask just how serious you were about us marrying."

He blinked, but didn't have to think. "Entirely serious." He paused, then clarified, "Absolutely, definitely serious." She briefly glanced his way and, jaw firming, he added, "I won't change my mind."

She looked back at the tavern and vaguely waved. "I had to ask. Just to be sure..."

That he wasn't teasing?

It dawned on him that her years as Miss Flibbertigibbet might have left her vulnerable in ways he hadn't foreseen. "I want to marry you." The words came easily. "I'm perfectly, unswervingly clear about that."

I'm waiting for you to realize you want to marry me.

She drew in a breath, then nodded and said, "In that case, I... wondered how you imagine a marriage between us would work. For instance, where would we live?"

"Newmarket." That hadn't required any thought, either. "The farmhouse there is essentially mine. It's the family home and is close to the stable, which is where I spend and will continue to spend most of my days."

"Your parents and siblings don't live there?"

He shook his head. "These days, my parents live primarily in their London house, and my younger, unmarried sister lives with them. My brother, Toby, is occasionally at home, at the farmhouse, but he's a gadabout and spends a lot of time away." He had to be vague about Toby, given his time away was mostly on missions for Drake Varisey.

"How long does it take to travel from your house in Newmarket to Aisby Grange?"

"It's roughly seventy miles, so a long day in a curricle."

Her gaze on the tavern, Addie nodded. "And what do you imagine I would do as your wife?" She glanced at him and briefly met his eyes. "What would my role be?"

Her alter ego might be Miss Flibbertigibbet and her character invariably impulsive, but in this, she was determined to be sensible and look before she leapt.

"To manage our household—and, I suppose, manage me, at least socially." He softly snorted. "I'm sure my mother, aunts, sisters, and female cousins will definitely expect you to do that." He shifted, and she felt his gaze touch her face. "I would hope to have a family as well, and you and your contributions will be central in that."

The sudden surge of emotion—of yearning need—that welled and spilled through her shocked her. She hadn't thought of having children before—she'd never had reason to dwell on the issue—but now he'd opened that door...oh, *how* she wanted.

In an effort to conceal just how powerfully affected she was by that prospect, she wrenched her mind back to her list of questions. "Would I have any role to play in your business?"

Again, she felt his gaze touch her face.

"If you wished to, yes. I would welcome your insights. As you've been riding hunters all your life, you'll have a good feel for the other side of our breeding business."

"Other side?"

She listened, not just with curiosity but with burgeoning interest as he explained that the Cynster breeding stable also produced riding horses—including hunters and lady's mounts—as well as carriage horses. That said, the racing stable was clearly his passion; without her having to prompt, he painted a reassuringly clear picture of how he ran the place. In so doing, he gave her enough detail to allow her to imagine a place for herself within the enterprise.

Nicholas wasn't surprised when she had yet more questions. He was entirely happy to answer them. He'd realized that, in her own inimitable way, she was answering his questions of the morning.

She *was* considering marrying him. Genuinely and sincerely.

The knowledge buoyed him, and he fought to rein in his eagerness as he did his best to encourage her to envisage a future by his side.

While they talked, they kept their gazes trained on the tavern. Other than several no-longer-sober farmhands who staggered out a little before the tavern owner decided to put out the lamp burning beside the front door and bar the door for the night, no one went in or came out.

Adriana reached the end of her questions and fell silent.

He told himself that the course of wisdom was to leave her to cogitate and not press or prod by asking her what she thought.

Then quiet footsteps—two pairs—approached from the center of the town, and a few seconds later, Phillip and Dickie arrived.

There was no one about to see as Nicholas and Adriana stepped out of the entryway, yielding the space to the other two.

"I wondered where you'd got to," Dickie said as he moved past, into the shadows.

The other three shushed him, and he grinned and, lips shut, lounged in the recessed doorway.

Phillip exchanged nods with Nicholas and Adriana, and they started walking back to the inn.

Nicholas paced beside Adriana and waited, but it seemed she'd exhausted her questions. Or, as she kept her gaze on the path before them, she was busy digesting his answers.

Either way, he told himself that he should be pleased.

Indeed, perhaps for the rest of the night, he wouldn't sleep alone.

His mind was engrossed with fond memories and hopes of what might be when they reached the coaching inn, mounted the steps, and walked around to the side door, left unlocked for patrons returning late.

He followed Adriana inside, and together, they climbed the stairs.

They stepped into the gallery, and she halted.

Through the dimness, she met his eyes, smiled, then stepped closer, stretched up, and planted a soft kiss on his lips.

She retreated before he could react, slipping out of the curve of the arm that had instinctively risen to hold her to him. "Thank you for bearing with my inquisition and being so forthcoming." She again met his eyes as she stepped away. "Goodnight."

He managed a croaked "Goodnight" in reply.

He stood in the shadows and watched her walk quickly down the corridor, then she opened a door and stepped into her room.

A second later, he heard the soft click as she shut the door.

Still, he stood and stared, taking stock of his raging libido and absorbing the fact that, at least for tonight, there was no relief in sight.

CHAPTER 14

$\mathcal{T}$he next morning, Nicholas came down to breakfast in an uncharacteristic grump. He was normally a sound sleeper and didn't appreciate restless nights.

Adriana was already seated at the large table set up for their group, along with Viola and a sleepy Phillip. To Nicholas's jaundiced eye, Adriana seemed bright-eyed and in good spirits. He nodded in the group's general direction and endeavored not to scowl as he made for the sideboard.

After loading a plate with the selections on offer, he approached the table and determinedly claimed the place beside Adriana.

She shot him a careful, questioning look as, his gaze on his plate, he sank onto the chair. "Good morning," she said.

"Morning," he replied, including Viola and Phillip with a glance.

Busy eating, they nodded back.

Adriana continued to study him. He could almost hear her unvoiced *And...?*

He cast her a dark glance and lied. "I was wondering what Kirkwood is up to." He looked at Phillip. "Have you heard?"

Phillip shook his head. "Rory and Young Gillies returned at six o'clock. Viola met them on the stairs."

Viola picked up her teacup. "They reported they'd seen no sign of Wesley. Harold and Oscar relieved them and are currently on watch."

Nicholas nodded and applied himself to the food on his plate. He steadily worked his way through the eggs, sausages, and bacon, and gradually, bit by bit, his mood improved.

Eventually, Dickie joined them, but he was no more inclined to conversation than the rest of them.

It was after eight o'clock, and they'd finished their breakfasts, with Adriana and Viola sipping tea and the three men drinking the last of the coffee, when Harold, along with Young Gillies and Rory, appeared in the dining room's doorway.

Nicholas and Phillip saw, but after taking stock of the pair of traveling salesmen seated at another table, instead of coming forward, the trio drew back into the inn's front hall and, expectation in their faces, waited.

"It looks like Kirkwood's on the move," Nicholas quietly said and pushed back his chair. Adriana started to rise, and he drew out her chair for her. On the opposite side of the table, Phillip did the same for Viola. Dickie reluctantly rose, and as a group, the five of them quickly and quietly left the room.

They joined the grooms and stableman in the hall.

"Harold just brought word." Young Gillies tipped his head toward the stableman. "Seems our man's finally ready to go on."

The pronouncement resulted in a flurry of activity. Nicholas and Phillip went to settle with the innkeeper, while Adriana and Viola rushed upstairs to finish their packing and Dickie and the grooms went to ready the horses and Harold went to round up Jed and Mike.

Five minutes later, everyone met in the inn's parlor. They reasoned that, having come from the south, Kirkwood would continue northward along the road leading past the inn. Consequently, they gathered in the front parlor and, in a group, stood back from the parlor window and watched.

Several minutes later, Kirkwood appeared, mounted on his nondescript chestnut and leading The Barbarian on a long rein.

As Kirkwood clopped past the inn, The Barbarian turned his huge head and stared at the parlor window.

Addie stared back. "Can he see me, do you think?"

"I sincerely hope not," Dickie murmured. "The last thing we need is for him to kick up a fuss and insist on coming to you for you to take him for a gallop."

The huge horse continued to stare their way in an unnervingly determined manner, but to their collective relief, didn't pull back on the rein.

Eventually, The Barbarian faced forward and followed Kirkwood out of the town, and Addie breathed again.

Mere minutes later, their company pulled out of the inn's yard.

Rory and Young Gillies, the first pair delegated to keep Kirkwood in sight, went ahead. Nicholas, Adriana, and Dickie followed, dawdling until they were far enough behind the grooms to appear unassociated. Jed and Mike came next, followed by Phillip and Viola in the curricle fifty yards or so behind, with Harold and Oscar bringing up the rear.

Addie tried to keep her mind on their pursuit as, just as they'd done the previous day, they trotted, walked, then trotted again in Kirkwood's wake. As they'd expected, he continued northward out of the town, but very soon after, he started veering west again.

Overall, his direction remained northwesterly, and as he had the day before, he consistently kept to minor lanes and byways. The stablemen and grooms rotated in the same fashion as the day before, with two always keeping their quarry in sight. Luckily, the country through which they were traveling made hanging back easy enough, but by all accounts, Kirkwood remained oblivious to even the notion of being followed.

Those delegated to shadow him were amazed by the man's over-weening arrogance.

Young Gillies shook his head. "He never looks around or checks to see if anyone's taking notice. You'd never guess he was leading a stolen horse."

Addie forbore from pointing out that merely meant that Kirkwood was wily enough to understand how to project the right appearance. As Miss Flibbertigibbet, she knew how easily people's beliefs could be manipulated by how someone behaved.

There was little conversation as they faithfully followed Kirkwood's path. With nothing to distract her, she couldn't stop her thoughts from sliding to consideration of the man riding beside her and the distractingly enthralling prospect of what life as his wife might be like.

She'd spent a long and largely wakeful night going over his revelations, weighing, considering, and assessing how and in exactly what way she might carve a place for herself in his life, and while she still had several questions on that score, none were of the sort where the answer would change her mind.

Indeed, as she'd realized in the wee hours of the morning, her decision was already made. The possibilities of a life at Nicholas Cynster's side called to her in a more powerful way than she'd ever imagined they might. In fact, they lured and enticed.

She felt increasingly impatient to have done with Kirkwood and the entire blackmail plot so that she could focus entirely on Nicholas, on his pending offer, and on the question of how her response should be phrased.

So she could concentrate on the notion of marriage, specifically marrying him.

Until the exchange of the previous evening, she hadn't been sure that prospect had truly been real.

Until he'd assured her that he remained intent on marrying her, she'd more than half expected him to have lost interest or at least to have started to. Yet the absolute unwavering sincerity and rock-solid honesty with which he'd responded to her queries regarding the firmness of his intentions, not once but twice—last night and two days before—had pulled her over the hurdle of her hesitation. The hurdle of her past.

As Miss Flibbertigibbet, she'd learned not to trust in the glib words of gentlemen.

Yes, there'd been some who'd been earnest and true, and she'd done her best to discourage them gently. She'd never been drawn to any of them as she was to Nicholas.

Indeed, she'd never been drawn to any man as she was to him... which, in reality, was her answer. Her response to his offer, when he eventually made it.

She shifted in her saddle. Her gaze fixed on the never-ending road ahead, she forced herself to face the truth that, deep down, one last niggling uncertainty remained.

One last Miss Flibbertigibbet-induced vulnerability.

How strong was what he felt for her?

The love that linked her parents had lasted for decades, apparently since they'd first set eyes on each other; if anything, it had grown stronger with the years. In a marriage within their class, it was that—the power of the link, the soundness and resilience of the connection—that counted most, that gave a marriage its strength. That encouraged a marriage to grow and evolve through the years and allowed a couple to weather the storms of a shared lifetime.

She knew what she felt for Nicholas, a fascination that had only grown more powerful with each passing hour, a potent connection that already surpassed anything she felt for anyone else at all.

With Dickie riding alongside them, she couldn't question Nicholas, but regardless, how did one ask another person about that? How did one assess the strength of another's feelings?

I might have to take that on trust. Simply trust that he truly feels for me as I feel for him.

Neither Lady Adriana Sommerville nor Miss Flibbertigibbet could easily approach that gate.

Nicholas rode beside Adriana and tried to limit the number of times he glanced sidelong at her.

He told himself—constantly—that the tiny line between her brows meant she was thinking. And given that she wasn't looking around but staring, unseeing, into the distance, very likely she was absorbed with precisely those considerations he wanted her to dwell on.

From her questions of the previous evening—and that she'd followed him to seize the chance to ask them—surely meant that she was, as he wished, giving serious thought to accepting his proposal and becoming his wife.

Time and again, he told himself that such behavior on her part was precisely what he wanted, yet he was loweringly aware that beneath a certain impatience lurked a particular anxiety.

What if she said no?

What if, after all her questions and cogitations, she decided against his offer?

What then?

His mind stalled, balked, unable to even approach that possibility.

Is this what love makes men feel?

So helpless, so dependent?

So consumed by a yearning only another can slake?

In posing those mental questions, silently acknowledging his own uncertainty, he realized that her questions most likely sprang from a similar source.

A similar vulnerability.

No lady who could create Miss Flibbertigibbet and loose her upon the ton could be considered a tentative, timid soul.

Adriana was anything but that, yet she, too, felt unsure enough to question and interrogate…

He sat straighter in his saddle. He shot her another sidelong glance; drinking in her pensive expression, he no longer felt quite so exposed.

Looking ahead, he continued to hold his position beside her as they faithfully trotted in their quarry's wake.

Kirkwood paused at an inn northwest of Selby, roughly midway between Selby and Tadcaster. While he enjoyed a decent luncheon and took his ease at the larger establishment, their party had to make do with a hurried meal at a small tavern off the main lane.

Among the group, impatience was rising, hand in hand with frustration at Kirkwood's ambling progress. Nicholas did his best to maintain an unflappable air, but even he was susceptible to the building tension.

Kirkwood quit the inn and, as ever keeping to the minor lanes, continued past Tadcaster and on toward Wetherby, maintaining his northwesterly heading. As the afternoon dragged on, after skirting Wetherby, he struck more northward, picking up a road to Knaresborough.

"Please don't let it be that we have to spend another night on the road," Dickie moaned.

"And another day following at this pace." Adriana shifted in her saddle. "We're crossing into Yorkshire as it is. How far north does he intend to go?"

"Not Scotland," Dickie said, in a tone suggesting that would be one step too far. "Surely he can't be heading into Scotland."

Nicholas decided the question was rhetorical and didn't answer.

Then Adriana glanced his way. "Are there any major horse breeders in Scotland?"

Grimly, Nicholas replied, "A few."

Dickie swore in a manner that, no doubt, reflected the company's feelings.

As the houses of Knaresborough came into view, Kirkwood veered away from the town, once again taking a small lane and still heading in a northwesterly direction.

As their company took the turn and fell in in Kirkwood's wake, Adriana glanced westward and frowned. "The sun's setting." She looked down the lane in the direction in which Kirkwood was heading. "He's going to have to find shelter soon, but why not in Knaresborough? It's not such a large town, and from memory, the next town in this direction is… Ripon." She glanced at Nicholas. "Is that correct?"

"I think so." Nicholas finished her thought. "But Ripon's too far away for him to reach before twilight deepens."

"Perhaps he knows this area," Dickie said, "and knows of a nice little inn that will suit him."

"Or perhaps," Adriana said, her tone lightening in hope, "he's close enough to his destination—to where he intends to hand over the horse—to simply carry on."

Nicholas met the questioning look she threw him and nodded. He turned in his saddle and signaled to Young Gillies and Rory, who were riding between the three of them and the curricle. When the grooms trotted up, Nicholas waved them on. "Catch up with Mike and Jed. Tell them to close the distance and be especially alert for any turns. We think Kirkwood might be approaching the handover point."

The grooms' expressions lit, and they nodded and urged their horses past and on down the lane.

When Adriana looked at Nicholas hopefully, he shrugged. "It won't hurt to take extra precautions."

Predictably, she and Dickie trotted on a little faster.

As it transpired, Adriana's postulation proved correct. Kirkwood continued along the lane until he came to the tiny village of Scriven.

Rory was waiting for the rest of the company in the lane before the village. He explained that Scriven was little more than a hamlet consisting of a church, several cottages, and a small inn clustered around a sloping triangular village green. After some discussion, they circled the village on local tracks and gathered at the rear of the church, where there were hitching posts and rails to which to tie the horses. With their mounts and the carriage horses secured, on foot, they quickly made their way through the graveyard toward the front of the church, which stood on higher ground at the apex of the green. Keeping to the cover of the trees and the hedge bordering the churchyard, they crept to where Jed, Mike, and Young Gillies waited and joined them in peering down the slope.

In the middle of the green, some fifty yards away, Kirkwood paced back and forth. He'd left his horse tied to a tree by a distant corner of the green and continued to hold The Barbarian on the long leading rein.

The Barbarian was calmly cropping the thick grass and ignoring Kirkwood.

Nicholas dragged his gaze from the stallion and studied Kirkwood. The man was pacing, not impatiently, but from the way he glanced every so often to the west, it seemed plain he was waiting for someone to arrive from that direction.

Beside Nicholas, her gaze locked on Kirkwood, Adriana whispered, "He's waiting to hand over the horse to whoever he's working for."

Nicholas added, "And he's expecting that person at any minute."

"Finally," Adriana breathed, and there was steel in her tone, "we're going to get some answers."

Watching Kirkwood, Nicholas thought, *On the blackmail front at least.*

~

Minutes ticked by as they continued to watch. Everyone was alert and tense, yet with the end of their campaign in sight, no one broke ranks; they waited patiently and silently while Kirkwood paced.

The church's position at the top of the downward-sloping green gave them an excellent view of the entire expanse.

Then the clop of hooves reached them, and two men rode up along the lower edge of the green, arriving from the direction in which Kirkwood had been glancing.

Relief and expectation suffusing his expression, Kirkwood swung to face the newcomers.

The pair saw him and dismounted. After tying their horses to a nearby tree, they trudged up the green toward him.

Anchored by The Barbarian, Kirkwood was closer to the church than the lower edge of the green. The huge horse had his head down, nibbling grass, although Nicholas knew the stallion would be well aware of all around him. When Kirkwood tried to draw the horse to him, presumably to meet the approaching men, the beast ignored the tug on the rein, refusing to even acknowledge it.

Then the newcomers drew close enough for Nicholas to make out their faces.

"Damn!" In disbelief, he studied the features of the taller of the men, a well-built dark-haired man wearing a caped greatcoat much like Nicholas's. "That's Nigel Devenish."

Adriana glanced at Nicholas. "Who's he?"

Nicholas looked from Devenish to Kirkwood and back again. "He's another major breeder. Come on!" He pushed through a gap in the hedge. "They're about to sell the horse!"

With his greatcoat flapping about his booted calves, Nicholas strode determinedly down the green. Adriana was right behind him, and Dickie quickly joined her. Phillip and Viola followed, and the grooms and stablemen spread out behind them, circling to ensure that none of the three men in the center of the green made a break for their tethered mounts.

As they neared, Kirkwood, with his back to them and unaware of their approach, offered The Barbarian's leading rein to the man who had arrived with Devenish.

"Here you are." Kirkwood released the rein into the other man's grasp. "As promised."

Just then, Devenish, facing upslope, heard their footfalls, glanced up, and saw them. A second later, he recognized Nicholas.

Devenish's head rose, and Nicholas saw him stiffen. The instant Nicholas was close enough, Devenish called, "Cynster!" He glanced sideways at the other two men, who whirled to face the descending company. Suspicion filling his expression, Devenish looked back at Nicholas. "What the devil are you doing here?"

Grim-faced, Nicholas tipped his head toward The Barbarian. "Helping the rightful owners reclaim that stallion."

Devenish swung to face Kirkwood and the man with whom Devenish had arrived. He addressed the latter, a shorter, slighter, more nattily dressed gentleman. "Wisthorpe? What is this?" Devenish glanced at Nicholas, but continued to speak to the other man. "You can't seriously be thinking of staging some kind of auction, not after I paid the deposit."

Nicholas halted two paces from Devenish and, with Devenish, studied the other man. "Wisthorpe?" He'd heard the name before, but where?

Adriana, Phillip, and Viola halted to Nicholas's left, while Dickie, his expression pugnacious, came to stand on Nicholas's right.

Eyeing Viola and Phillip, Kirkwood edged uneasily back.

Her eyes narrowing on Wisthorpe, Adriana said, "If you're the current Viscount Wisthorpe, I presume you were heir to the late viscount, Henry Wisthorpe."

Wisthorpe's gaze had been shifting from face to face. He knew Devenish and Kirkwood, but patently had no clue as to who any of the rest of them were. He looked at Adriana, then raised his head and straightened to his full if unimpressive height; all the other men there were distinctly taller than he. "Yes, indeed. I am Viscount Wisthorpe. I inherited the title and estate from my father's cousin." His pale gaze shifted to The Barbarian, still cropping grass at the end of his rein. "Along with that horse."

"Actually," Adriana crisply informed him, "Henry Wisthorpe bequeathed The Barbarian to his very old friend, the Earl of Aisby. The horse now belongs to the earl."

Wisthorpe attempted to look down his nose at them all, but couldn't quite pull it off. "I beg to differ. The horse was part of the estate and should, by all that's holy, have come to me." He tipped his chin even higher. "He's mine to dispose of, and that's all there is to it."

Nicholas inwardly sighed. "As Lady Adriana informed you, in reality, that's not the case." He caught Devenish's eye. "Ask him for the papers."

Devenish promptly looked at Wisthorpe and tipped his head toward The Barbarian. "I can see that's the horse you described to me. If he truly is yours to dispose of, I assume you can produce his papers."

Wisthorpe frowned and darted a look at Kirkwood, who returned it with a blank, plainly uncomprehending stare. Wisthorpe brought his now-wary gaze back to Devenish. "What papers?"

Devenish's jaw set, then in a clipped tone, he replied, "The papers that attest to the horse's Thoroughbred pedigree via registration with the Jockey Club and which also, incidentally, act as proof of your right to sell him as the Thoroughbred he is."

Wisthorpe's widening eyes testified that he'd had no notion of the existence of any such papers. The glance he sent Kirkwood was panicked and accusing.

Nicholas helpfully added, "Without those papers, The Barbarian is merely a good-looking horse."

"A very nice-looking horse," Devenish put in, "but essentially useless to any breeding stable, or at least, any legitimate enterprise. Consequently, he's worth very much less. Indeed, he's not even worth as much as the deposit I've already paid you."

Nicholas nodded. "Wisthorpe might not have mentioned this, but the horse is not only a stallion and exceedingly powerful and strong, but he's also temperamental and all but unrideable."

Devenish snorted. "His value is diminishing by the moment." He fixed Wisthorpe with a cold, invincible stare. "I want my money back."

Thoroughly panicked, Wisthorpe waved his free hand. "Wait. No. There must be some way…" Patently flummoxed, he looked at Kirkwood.

Kirkwood held up both hands, palms outward, and took a step back. "You told me you wanted the horse. You never said anything about needing any papers as well."

Addie had been watching closely. She felt Phillip, beside her, step forward.

"No, indeed." Phillip's tone would have cut glass. He dipped his head fractionally to Wisthorpe. "Lord Phillip Sommerville." Superiority dripped from the words.

Addie shared a quick grin with Dickie; never had she imagined being grateful for Phillip's ability to project sanctimonious arrogance.

Phillip waved a languid hand, indicating the others of their party. "I'm here with these others to reclaim my father's horse." His gaze passed on to Kirkwood. "And to have a word with you. Wesley Kirkwood, I gather. It seems you blackmailed me and your cousin's widow for nothing. Or at least"—Phillip tipped his head toward The Barbarian—"for nothing more than a good-looking nag."

Wisthorpe had paled. His gaze fixed on Phillip, Wisthorpe looked faintly green. "Lord Sommerville," he whispered.

Then he whirled on Kirkwood. "What have you done, you dolt?" Wisthorpe raised both hands, shaking them in a fury. "What have you involved me in?" His voice rose. "Blackmail? Of a peer? Of a member of the nobility?" Fists clenched, he glanced at the sky and shrieked, "What use is the beast to me if I can't sell him and clear my debts and join society in a manner to which my birth and station entitles me?"

Devenish blinked. "Debts?

"Argh!" Wisthorpe dropped the leading rein and flung himself at Kirkwood.

"No!" Addie darted forward, trying to dodge the wrestling men. "Catch the rein!"

Too late. With a soft snort, The Barbarian took off.

"Damn it!" Addie straightened and watched the bay stallion race up the green. "He was waiting for that to happen."

Nicholas halted beside her, and Nigel Devenish came to stand on her other side.

Devenish stared after The Barbarian. As the horse showed them a clean pair of heels as he took the hedge beside the church in style, Devenish murmured, "Damn, indeed. What a fabulous gait."

"Come on." Nicholas started up the green. "We'll have to chase him." He glanced back at Devenish. "There's nowhere near here that the horse would know." He tipped his head toward the church. "Our mounts are behind the church."

Sobering, Devenish nodded. "I'll get my horse and meet you there."

Addie was already hurrying to the hedge. Reaching it, she scanned the views to either side of the church.

The land there, on the edge of the Yorkshire Dales, was deceptive; it looked like gently undulating fields, but there were steep gullies here and there. Perfect places in which a runaway horse might hide.

Nicholas and Dickie joined her, then Phillip and Viola arrived.

"I can't see him anywhere," Addie said. "Can any of you?"

Everyone searched, but no one saw any sign of a glossy bay hide.

Addie sighed. "This is just like him. He'll think this is a great joke. He'll run a bit, then find somewhere that suits him to hide."

Nicholas asked, "Will he wait for us there—wherever he stops?"

She nodded. "Most likely. He likes to run and is inordinately curious, but he's not actually a wanderer."

Dickie nodded. "He'll be out there somewhere."

"Waiting for us to come and fetch him and take him home." Hearing others approaching, Addie turned to see Devenish, mounted on a very nice black, leading Kirkwood's and Wisthorpe's horses and acting as rear guard for the grooms and stablemen who, stern faced, were shepherding Kirkwood and Wisthorpe up the slope.

Wisthorpe was still glowering and shooting daggers at Kirkwood, who looked rather rumpled, having fought Wisthorpe off.

Both men appeared somewhat cowed, but also gave the impression they were each, independently, looking for ways in which to escape any further retribution.

Nicholas regarded the pair, then lifted his gaze and swept the rest of the company. All, including Devenish, were looking to him for direction. He spread his arms and waved. "At this point, The Barbarian could be anywhere. We'll have to spread out."

From his perch on his horse's back, Devenish had also been surveying the ground. "I assume we'll have to go on foot?" He looked at the Sommervilles.

Dickie grimaced, and Addie nodded. "If we go mounted, he'll run and expect us to chase him. To him, this is all a game."

She repeated her assessment that The Barbarian would have run for a short distance, then found a place that suited him to wait.

Nicholas had been studying Kirkwood and Wisthorpe. They didn't have enough men to leave any guarding the pair. "We've an hour, possibly two, of decent light left. We need everyone out searching." He pointed to Wisthorpe and Kirkwood. "That includes the pair of you. You'll search with the rest of us, but if you find The Barbarian, don't think to make off with him. Not unless you want to find the authorities on your trail."

"Indeed," Phillip said, ice in his voice. "We haven't yet finished with you. There are several matters we need to discuss, but we need to find the horse first."

"And," Devenish put in, "there's the not-so-little matter of my deposit. We'll need to discuss repayment." He swung down from his saddle and fixed Wisthorpe with a pleasant look that was nevertheless openly intimidatory. "I'll expect to see you back here, by the church, once we have the horse again in hand. As Cynster and Sommerville intimated, don't even think of slipping away. If you attempt to do so, I will be only too happy to join with the others in helping the authorities hunt you down."

Nicholas hid a smile. Devenish, while normally an entirely amenable man, had a reputation for being able to turn on the aggression and menace when it suited him.

Both Kirkwood and Wisthorpe looked suitably cowed, at least for the moment.

"Right, then." Nicholas turned and pushed through the hedge. "Let's get to where we left our horses. We'll be able to see the lie of the land better from the other side of the church."

Once they were gathered behind the church, Nicholas divided the area spreading outward from the churchyard into pie-like slices and delegated a searcher to each sector. "Make sure you're thorough and pay particular attention to any dips and hollows. This is a horse that likes to hide. If you find The Barbarian, given he'll be trailing a rein—or at least we hope he still is—if you feel confident you can catch him, do so and lead him back here. If you don't like your chances, call for help. None of us should be out of hearing of someone else."

He looked around the group. "All right. You each have your areas." He turned to take one last look at the wider view. "After you've searched your area, return here. Hopefully, by then"—he glanced around the faces —"one of us will have the horse."

With determined nods from most, they set out, spreading in every direction. Nicholas helped Adriana over the low stone wall, then she went toward his right, while he walked straight ahead. Dickie headed off on Adriana's other side, and in concert, they started to scour the fields.

CHAPTER 15

*A*ddie had volunteered to search this particular sector because she'd glimpsed the distant canopies of an old orchard. The Barbarian was partial to apples. If he'd sensed the orchard and its bounty, he might have gone that way.

Then again, he could just as easily have gone in the opposite direction. His equine brain was impossible to predict.

She strode over the open fields, scanning to either side as she went. Nicholas was tramping through the fields to her left, while Dickie was rambling on her right.

The farther they went from the churchyard, the wider the area they each had to search and the more separated they became. She duly zigzagged, left to right and back again, making sure she covered every possible dip and fold in the terrain. This was very definitely not flat country. Soon, she'd lost sight of both Nicholas and Dickie.

She came to a stone wall, located and clambered over a stile, and dropped into the next field, only then realizing it was occupied by a flock of black-faced sheep. "At least the livestock around here aren't cattle."

After wading through the curious flock, she reached the next wall and the next stile and, once on the other side, found herself among the first trees of the old orchard.

About ten yards from the stone wall, the ground dropped away quite steeply, angling down into a narrow valley. A small stream burbled along the valley's bottom; as the valley floor was cloaked in deepening shadow, she heard the stream rather than saw it. She peered through the twisted branches of the old trees clinging to the rock-strewn downward slope, trying to see the upper reaches of the valley, which lay some way to her left.

She frowned. "It's more like a cleft at the end."

Luckily, the wider opening of the valley lay not far away on her right. By walking in that direction, she was able to reach the valley floor without having to scramble over rocks.

If The Barbarian had taken refuge in the valley, he would have had to come via the same route. As she followed the small stream deeper into the shadows, she scanned the earth, less sunbaked and a bit softer there, for any impression of hooves.

She was about halfway along the valley, a little past where she'd climbed over the fence above, when she spotted a likely indentation. She crouched, traced the mark, and measured it against her palm, then she smiled, straightened, and looked up the valley. She squinted into the shadows. "I know you're there."

The hoofprint wasn't old, and few horses had such large shoes.

With renewed enthusiasm, she strode forward.

Twenty yards on, in a small clearing just before the valley narrowed to an impassable cleft, she found The Barbarian. His glossy bay hide stood out in the gloom cast by two old trees. He had his head down, cropping the lush grass beside the stream.

"There you are!" Knowing better than to rush toward him, she walked calmly forward, then spotted the long leading rein trailing across the grass. She diverted to it, bent and picked it up, then gathering and looping the leather strap in her hands, she followed it to the horse, crooning in the way she usually did when she fetched him for a ride.

The Barbarian raised his huge head and watched her close in. When she stopped beside him, he bobbed his head at her, exactly as he always did, almost as if inviting her to climb on his back.

She patted his glossy neck. "Unfortunately, I have no saddle, so I'll have to walk you out." Smiling, she met his horsey gaze, then with one last pat, she turned. "Come along."

She walked forward, but The Barbarian didn't budge.

She tugged just a little. When he moved not an inch, she turned back and fixed him with an exasperated look. "I can't ride you."

The horse stared implacably back.

Stubborn met stubborn, and the horse won.

Addie let out a frustrated groan and looked around. "I need a mounting block."

Nearby, a boulder jutted from the valley wall, which was approaching vertical at that point.

She played out the leading rein, which proved long enough to allow her to scramble up and stand atop the boulder. Balancing there, she looked at the horse, then drew the rein taut and tugged. "If you want me to ride you, you'll have to come closer and stand over here."

As if he understood every word, The Barbarian consented to amble across. She nudged his head around, and he obligingly lined up beside the outcrop.

She regarded him with a great deal of suspicion. "Now hold still while I get on."

She had to hike up her riding skirt and, still holding the leading rein and with the heavy train over one elbow, balance on one leg, throw her other leg over, and more or less jump on.

"Oh!" She caught herself with both hands spread on the horse's back. After confirming that she was safely astride the broad expanse, she shook her head. "I'm amazed I didn't go right over." His glossy hide was decidedly slippery.

Taking stock, she arranged her skirts as best she could, tucking the train beneath her, then settled. When Phillip had taken the horse from his paddock at the Grange, he'd used a simple rope halter to which to attach the leading rein, correctly guessing that The Barbarian was choosy over whom he would allow to bridle him. Consequently, when they'd taken the horse to be collected by Kirkwood in The Drove, knowing he might be leading the horse on, they'd once again fitted The Barbarian with the rope halter and leading rein.

From her perch on the huge horse's back, she stared at his head as a twinge of fear wormed down her spine. With the halter and leading rein, she had only one rein and no bit with which to manage a massively powerful, unpredictable horse.

But she was on his back already, so...

"You had better behave yourself," she muttered and tapped her heels to his sides.

He obligingly fell into an easy walk, and she breathed again. She was familiar with his stride and swayed to his rhythm well enough. But it had been a long, long time since she'd ridden astride, and she'd never before ridden without a saddle and a proper bridle. Luckily, The

Barbarian's girth was so massive, settled on his back, she felt reasonably safe.

As for the absence of bridle and reins and the consequent lack of control, she tried not to think too hard about what might go wrong.

"All we have to do is walk out of this valley and make our way back to the church." She continued talking, babbling about the countryside, knowing the horse was listening and that the sound of her voice would calm him and, she hoped, distract him from thinking of what else he might do.

They came to the end of the valley, and using the leading rein, she directed The Barbarian in a slow upward arc, climbing steadily and not too sharply to reach the level of the fields above.

She skirted the old orchard, avoiding the trees and their low-hanging branches. "You're doing well," she assured the horse. "It's mostly flattish from here."

She'd got used to the oddness of the familiar gait without a saddle and was starting to relax when the wall at the end of the orchard came into view. Eyes widening, she quickly said, "There's a gate near the corner."

Even as she said the words, she knew it would be no use. The Barbarian didn't like gates. Instead, he loved fences and walls, delighting in clearing them with a powerful leap. He had to have jumped several walls to reach the orchard and the valley below.

Sure enough, beneath her, his muscles bunched and fluidly stretched as he picked up speed, and she panicked. "No! *Stop!*"

She hauled on the single rein, but the horse had the wall in his sights. She would have as much chance of stopping a runaway locomotive with a ribbon.

Then she felt the horse gather himself, and with a desperate shriek, she wound her fingers in his thick mane and clutched tight.

For the first time in years, she squeezed her eyes shut as they soared.

The Barbarian came down smoothly.

She didn't.

With no stirrups to anchor her, she rose free of his back and came down off-center with jarring force. Despite her frantic grip on his mane, she went sliding sideways, and then she was flying over his shoulder.

The ground rushed toward her far faster than she'd expected, then the whole world turned black.

Nicholas trudged out of the treed dip he'd just finished searching to no avail. Stepping up to level ground, facing the now-distant church, he scanned the sky. Twilight had arrived, and the shadows were deepening into the dark of encroaching night. He estimated there was less than an hour to full dark.

Grimacing, he accepted that, empty-handed—or rather, horseless—though he was, he needed to return to the church. The others would be gathering there. He'd heard no calls for help and had heard and seen nothing to suggest that the horse had been found.

Looking to his left, he surveyed the fields through which Adriana and Dickie had been searching. In the distance, he spotted Dickie heading toward the church, also with no horse.

Nicholas studied the nearer fields, the ones Adriana had been quartering. Field by field, he scanned all the way to the church, but found no sign of her.

Perhaps she'd already gone back? He could see people milling near the church wall, but at this distance, couldn't make out who they were. Yet if anyone was going to be the last to return, to be the one who searched most diligently for as long as she possibly could, he would wager it would be Adriana. She wouldn't have given up yet.

She hadn't called out—or rather, he hadn't heard her call. While he'd been searching in the dip, he'd realized his ability to hear the bleating of the sheep in the pasture above had diminished to almost zero.

If Adriana had called, would he have heard?

He had no option but to look for her. He wouldn't be able to think of anything else—of what they might try next—until he knew she was safe.

Telling himself that she was simply searching until the last possible minute, he clambered over a wall and, after confirming she wasn't anywhere between where he now was and the church, he turned and started walking in what he hoped was the direction she'd taken.

He crossed one field, scanning as he went, then clambered over a stile and dropped into the next field, only to find a flock of black-faced sheep clustering in the nearest corner.

Puzzled, he studied them. The group was pushing close together, as sheep did when spooked.

He wondered what had frightened them. Slowly, eyes narrowed the better to pierce the gloom, he scanned the gently sloping field—and saw The Barbarian.

The stallion was standing with his head down a little way inside the gate in the far corner of the field.

Relieved on one score, still concerned on the other, Nicholas walked toward the horse. He had no idea if the stallion would remember him well enough not to bolt.

He was still twenty yards away when he realized the horse was nudging at something on the ground...

His eyes focused on a crumpled mass of teal velvet. Of their own accord, his feet slowed.

"No!" The denial burst from him, and then he was racing, uncaring of whether he spooked the horse or not.

He fell to his knees beside the velvet mound. "Adriana!" The anguish pouring through him filled the single word.

Frantically, he searched at her throat for a pulse and found her heart beating steadily and strongly. The beat echoed inside him, a fundamental reassurance.

He reminded himself he'd seen countless men thrown from horses, yet none had died.

She was lying partially on her side, her arms lax, her legs tangled in her skirts. Her riding hat was still on her head.

His panic edged down a notch, and he started checking for injuries, for broken bones or twisted limbs. After carefully shifting her to lie on her back, he tested each leg and arm, relieved to find all unbroken. He spread his hands over her rib cage and gently assessed, but could find no hint of broken ribs, and her breathing, now he was focusing on it, was even and unhindered.

She might not be badly injured.

His heart was slowing to a more normal pounding. Her riding hat would have helped cushion her head. Infinitely gently, he shifted her again and started on the slow process of checking her spine, from her nape to her hips. Nothing seemed out of place.

The relief that hit him was immense. With the tips of his fingers, he traced the line of her jaw, shaken anew by the tumult of emotions roiling through him. He drew back his hand and rocked onto his haunches. For a moment, he simply let his eyes roam over her, reassuring that deeply shaken part of him that she was, it seemed, merely knocked senseless.

Not seriously injured.

That conclusion brought him back to the here and now.

He glanced around, confirming that the last of the light was rapidly fading. He pushed upright and looked in the direction of the church. He could make out the spire, outlined against the sky, but little else.

Cupping his hands about his mouth, he yelled, "To me! Here!"

He waited, but heard no cry in response. He hadn't really expected one; the others should all be back at the church by now.

A horsey harrumph had him turning to see the huge stallion—whom he'd completely forgotten about—gently nudging Adriana with his nose.

Nicholas studied the horse. He could carry Adriana and, simultaneously, lead the beast back to the church, but that would take a very long time, especially in the deepening dark.

Would The Barbarian consent to carry him while he carried Adriana?

He was accustomed to riding highly strung Thoroughbreds. He knew that if The Barbarian obliged, he could rely on the horse to pick his way safely across the fields.

That was more than he trusted himself to do while carrying Adriana on foot.

"What have I to lose?" he murmured.

When the big horse raised his head and, across Adriana's still form, looked at him as if asking what he was going to do, Nicholas grasped the nettle. He walked to where the leading rein lay in the coarse grass, bent, and picked up the strap.

"We need to get her back to the church. To the curricle. She can't ride you at the moment, but I can, and I can hold her on your back. Not the same as her riding you, and there will be no galloping—not yet—but she needs help, your help, now."

While he'd talked, keeping his tone even, he'd gathered the long rein and slowly walked closer. He halted beside the massive horse. The Barbarian had raised his head, watching him. Nicholas met the horse's eye. "If you're willing to help, you'll need to allow me on your back."

He'd never been certain how much the more intelligent horses understood, but from what he'd seen and heard of the big bay stallion, he was willing to wager that The Barbarian grasped at least something of what he was endeavoring to convey.

"First," he went on, "we need to find some way for me to get astride while carrying her in my arms."

He scanned the wall and focused on the corner where the gatepost met the side wall. The wall was built of stacked stones, with obvious gaps between. "That might be a possibility." He looked at The Barbarian. "Shall we see?"

After several seconds assessing the logistics, he bent and eased Adriana into his arms. He stood and hefted her into a more secure hold, and the horse nudged her face with his nose.

"Yes, well," Nicholas said. "Let's see how far your affection takes us."

With the horse following tamely enough, Nicholas walked to the corner of the field. It took a little maneuvering, but by using the rails of the gate as well as the gaps between the stones in the wall, he managed to climb to the top of the wall with Adriana still in his arms.

Finally, he stood on the wall and looked toward the church, but although he thought he saw movement in the churchyard, he couldn't distinguish individual people, and there was no one crossing the fields toward them.

Resigned, he studied The Barbarian. The top of the wall placed Nicholas at a reasonable height to be able to mount the beast while holding Adriana. He met the horse's eye. "Are you going to cooperate?"

The horse whinnied and waggled his great head.

Nicholas inwardly sighed and tugged on the rein.

After several adjustments, The Barbarian stood aligned beside the wall.

"All right, then. Let's see." Nicholas held his breath and, balancing on one bent leg with Adriana clasped awkwardly against his chest, swung his other leg over The Barbarian's back and, all in one motion, lowered, then half fell, onto the stallion's broad back.

The horse shifted only fractionally.

Nicholas waited, fearing some unhelpful reaction, but after a moment, the horse glanced sideways and around, then thrust his head forward, tugging on the rein.

Nicholas exhaled, loosened the rein a trifle more, and gently tapped his heels to The Barbarian's glossy sides.

The horse obediently set off, walking with his long-legged gait toward the fence at the top of the slope.

From midway across the field, Nicholas saw the next gate, set as the other had been, close by the corner formed by the walls, and realized why Adriana had been thrown. "You decided to jump that other wall, didn't you? And she wasn't strong enough or didn't have time to rein you in."

Managing this horse with a single rein wouldn't have been easy, even for Nicholas.

He tightened his grip on the rein, just in case the horse decided to try jumping again. But how was he going to manage the gate? He didn't like his chances of leaning sideways, not while juggling Adriana. The last thing he wanted to do was drop her on the ground.

As they approached the gate, he reluctantly concluded that, given the wall across the field wasn't as thick as the wall on the side, he would have to take the risk and lean down to the latch. It was that or lay Adriana down on the top of the side wall, open the gate, come back for her, go through the gate, leave her on the top of the wall on the gate's other side, then close the gate against the flock of sheep who were following, clearly hoping for escape, before picking Adriana up again.

"And hoping all the while that you"—he addressed the horse—will behave."

He really didn't like his chances.

They were almost to the gate when Dickie strode up to it, looked over, and saw them. "Thank God!"

"Indeed," Nicholas feelingly replied.

"I was almost back to the churchyard when I thought I heard you call. As I couldn't see you in the group there, I came back to search." Concern etched Dickie's face as he took in his sister's limp form. "What happened?" His gaze flicked to The Barbarian. "I can barely credit that the beast is letting you ride him."

While Dickie opened the gate, let them through, then shut the sheep in again, Nicholas told him what he assumed must have happened. "I'm suitably grateful that The Barbarian consented to carry us both."

Dickie huffed and, as Nicholas set The Barbarian walking again, fell to pacing alongside. "All of that sounds very like Addie and this beast, too. He's quite devoted to her, but he can be entirely unpredictable when he kicks up his heels."

They walked steadily across the fields toward the church.

"The others must all be back by now," Dickie said.

From The Barbarian's back, Nicholas could see the cluster of figures gathered near the horses and curricle. Although twilight had fallen, there was sufficient illumination to be able to count heads and see faces once they were close enough.

Even though sounds carried easily in the country quiet, none of those waiting noticed them as they plodded across the darkened field. The grooms, stablemen, and Sally were too engrossed watching Phillip, Viola, and Nigel Devenish tearing strips off Kirkwood and Wisthorpe.

Nicholas battled back a grin at one of Nigel's more colorful threats, then his gaze fell to Adriana's face, and all tendency to levity fled. She hadn't stirred. While he was fairly certain she'd been simply knocked unconscious, he needed to see her open her eyes and hear her speak again before the vise clamped about his chest would unlock.

Finally, Viola saw them. A hand flew to her lips, then she tugged forcefully on Phillip's sleeve and, when he glanced at her, pointed at the small group in the field. Phillip and Nigel stopped their haranguing and looked.

As everyone took in the sight—and its implications—even from a distance, Nicholas sensed the geysering, intensifying fury that erupted within the group's members, directed at Kirkwood and Wisthorpe.

Nigel swung to face the pair and stabbed a finger at them. "You'd better pray Lady Adriana recovers soon and has taken no lasting hurt."

The furious menace in his voice had Kirkwood and Wisthorpe freezing.

With everyone's gazes returning to the figure in Nicholas's arms, Viola and Phillip rushed to open the nearest gate.

Sally hurried to join them as The Barbarian walked out of the field and into the churchyard and obediently halted. In a distant part of his brain, Nicholas could barely believe how obligingly docile the temperamental horse had been.

With his senses relocking on Adriana, he managed to maneuver and hand her down into Phillip's and Dickie's arms. As Nicholas's hands slid from her, she stirred, and his heart leapt—in hope, in earnest fervent yearning.

He slid down from The Barbarian's back. Experience had him pausing to stroke the horse's long nose in appreciation and thanks. Only then did he realize how rigid his features were; they literally felt carved from stone, as if they might never soften.

He gave The Barbarian's rein to Dickie, then ducked around the horse to where Phillip had laid Adriana down on a patch of thick grass. Viola and Sally were crouched beside her. Sally had removed Adriana's hat and now flapped it at her face while Viola waved smelling salts under Adriana's nose.

As Nicholas watched, with her eyes still closed, Adriana raised a hand and batted away the small bottle. "Eh! I hate that stuff."

Her voice was surprisingly strong.

And the vise about Nicholas's chest released, and he could, at last, breathe. He did, deeply, and found Nigel halting beside him, his gaze on Adriana.

"I finally remembered who she is." Brows arching, Nigel glanced at Nicholas. "Miss Flibbertigibbet. Really, Nicholas? That's who you've finally decided to wed?"

Nicholas debated questioning how Nigel had guessed how he felt, then decided against it and, instead, pointed to The Barbarian; the huge stallion had shifted closer to Adriana and was clearly keeping an eye on her. "Regardless of ownership, that horse considers himself hers."

Nigel looked at The Barbarian, then nodded. "Good point."

Having opened her eyes, Adriana grasped Viola's proffered hand and allowed Viola and Sally to help her sit up. Her color was returning, and judging by the questions she immediately posed, her wits were already back.

Reassured, Nicholas turned to regard Wisthorpe and Kirkwood, who were standing together a few paces away with the grooms and stablemen keeping a close eye on the pair.

Following his gaze, Nigel tipped his head their way. "What do you want to do with them?"

"We have the horse back, and it seems Adriana wasn't hurt." The latter realization allowed Nicholas to think again. He could already foresee several pitfalls if they didn't resolve the situation in the correct manner.

He glanced at the group around Adriana and, with a tip of his head, summoned Phillip. When Adriana's half brother joined him and Nigel, his voice low, Nicholas explained, "We need to decide how to handle this." He bent an uncompromisingly warning look on Wisthorpe and Kirkwood; both looked thoroughly uncomfortable but too unsure of themselves to make a move.

Nicholas met Phillip's eyes, then glanced at Nigel. "For several excellent reasons, it would be best for all concerned if nothing about this affair becomes widely known."

Chief amongst those reasons was the existence of Phillip's letters to Viola prior to her husband's violent demise, let alone Phillip consequently becoming a horse thief. That Miss Flibbertigibbet had been involved in chasing halfway up England after a stolen horse was also not a story the ton needed to hear. Assuming that Nigel knew no details of the blackmail and Phillip's actions, Nicholas was hoping that the excuse of protecting Adriana would prove sufficient to gain Nigel's support.

To Nicholas's considerable relief, Nigel grimaced and said, "I agree. The Devenishes would infinitely prefer that the news that we were, however unwittingly, drawn into the sale of a stolen Thoroughbred never becomes public. Aside from all else, we don't want to seem like a gullible bunch." Nigel looked at Nicholas. "You know the sort of approaches we'd get."

Nicholas nodded, then caught Phillip's eye and arched his brows.

His lips thin, Phillip fractionally inclined his head. "Despite their actions, both Kirkwood and Wisthorpe are gentlemen, and both, it seems, wish to better their standing in our world. Given their scheme has come to naught, I suspect they won't be any more eager than us to bruit the details to said world."

Nigel huffed. "That would hardly recommend them to those they are hoping to impress."

Nicholas nodded. "Exactly."

Dickie joined them. "Addie seems entirely recovered and is being her usual bossy self." His happy grin gave everyone to understand that he viewed the latter happening with relief. He looked from one to the other. "So what are you plotting?"

"How best to punish Kirkwood and Wisthorpe without punishing ourselves in the process," Nigel replied.

"I believe I have an unquestionable right to be involved in that endeavor." Adriana arrived with Viola, and the pair joined the group.

Addie inserted herself between Nicholas and Devenish and leaned—just slightly—against Nicholas, using him as a prop as unobtrusively as she could. Although her head had steadied, it still ached, and her bones felt rattled, the connections a trifle wobbly. She'd fallen off horses often enough to recognize the signs and feel confident they would soon pass. But they had to deal with Kirkwood and Wisthorpe now. They couldn't put that off.

She eyed the pair, who were whispering to each other. "Might I suggest that we interview them and make sure they fully comprehend exactly where they stand?"

"I also think," Viola said, her tone determined, "that we should make sure we have the entire story straight. I, for one, am not at all sure just who, of the two of them, was the instigator here."

"An excellent notion." Devenish turned to regard the pair. "It would be prudent of us to be certain on that point." He exchanged a look with Nicholas. "It's always good to know your potential enemies."

Nicholas nodded, and as a group, they went to confront the errant pair.

Addie moved with Nicholas, grateful when she felt his arm slide supportively around her.

They halted in an arc, trapping Kirkwood and Wisthorpe against the churchyard's waist-high wall.

Addie opened the proceedings. "First, allow me to say, on behalf of the Sommervilles, that your roles in this drama will not be forgotten." She let her gaze rest first on Kirkwood then even more weightily on Wisthorpe. "Not tomorrow. Not ever."

"Speaking of your roles," Viola said, "please enlighten us as to which of you thought that stealing private correspondence from me to blackmail Lord Sommerville into delivering the horse to Kirkwood was a reasonable idea."

Her tone made both men squirm.

Inside, Addie smiled. Viola was going to make an excellent countess.

"It was him." Wisthorpe pointed at Kirkwood. "All him. I had no idea that was what he was planning." He looked at Kirkwood as if only just realizing the manner of man with whom he'd chosen to associate. "It was entirely his idea."

Kirkwood glowered at Wisthorpe. "And that's the thanks I get? It was *you* who came looking for *me* and asked if I knew of any way of getting the Sommervilles to give up the horse. It's you who wants the beast, not me!" Kirkwood endeavored to look down his nose at Wisthorpe. "And you said you didn't care how I did it, just as long as you could get your hands on the horse." Pugnaciously, he demanded, "And I delivered, didn't I? Just as you asked."

"But blackmail?" Wisthorpe looked genuinely upset. "Surely you knew I didn't expect you to stoop so low."

"Actually," Viola said, "that raises another point that is not at all clear." She fixed her gaze on Kirkwood. "We know what Wisthorpe sought to gain through this scheme, but what did you expect to gain, Wesley?"

If Kirkwood had looked uncomfortable before, he looked downright shifty now. He didn't reply, but his eyes tracked sideways to Wisthorpe.

And Phillip laughed. "Ah, I see." When the others looked questioningly his way, he succinctly explained, "Future blackmail. Information he could later hold over Wisthorpe."

"What?" Horrified, Wisthorpe stared at Kirkwood, sputtered, then stepped away.

For his part, Kirkwood continued to look belligerent.

Disgusted, Addie shook her head. "A nice pair of immoral dunderheads you've proven to be. You truly deserve each other."

"Indeed." Nicholas continued. "But it won't do your families any good to have your exploits spread about the ton, will it?"

Both men blinked. Their expressions blanked.

"Just think of how such a story will be received in the drawing rooms of London. And elsewhere." Devenish's expression suggested he was imagining that. "Quite a juicy tidbit. The hostesses will be deliciously horrified, and the clubs will be all a-hum."

The company fell silent, contemplating that vision.

Then Nicholas said, "Perhaps, if you both agree to make suitable amends, we might—I say *might*—agree to overlook your falls from grace."

"First," Addie said, crossing her arms before her and fixing her most censorious gaze on Kirkwood, "you need to make restitution to Mrs. Styles. You went into her home and stole personal belongings. You disrupted her household and dishonored your status as a guest, let alone a relative. You should have been protecting her, but instead, you attacked her. It's hard to imagine more dastardly behavior among our class."

Her words hit Kirkwood like a slap. He blinked, then blinked again.

Then he looked at Viola and, after what was plainly an inner struggle, dipped his head to her. "My sincere apologies." He looked at Addie. "I don't know what more I can do."

Addie arched a brow at Viola. "Is an apology enough?"

Viola thought for a moment, then her jaw firmed, and her gaze hardened. "No." She looked at Kirkwood. "Your mother, Amelia Kirkwood, is in her declining years. You are her only son, and she's forever complaining that you never visit her." Viola's gaze grew intent. "What I want from you in recompense for your appalling behavior is a solemn promise, witnessed by all here, that you will visit your mother at least once a month and, on each visit, stay for a minimum of one full day. Further, that you will ensure that she has every possible assistance and luxury in the years ahead." Viola held Kirkwood's gaze. "And you know I will hear from the family if you don't perform as required."

Kirkwood looked stunned, but when they all stared at him, patently waiting for his agreement, he finally nodded. "All right."

"Swear to that on your honor as a gentleman," Devenish demanded, and reluctantly, Kirkwood obliged.

Addie nodded. "Very well. Next comes your debt to the Sommervilles."

"And the Cynsters," Nicholas put in. "Having a horse we've negotiated to buy stolen from under our noses is not the sort of behavior of which the family approves."

For the first time, Kirkwood looked alarmed.

Addie glanced at Phillip and Dickie. "Do you have any ideas? Any demands?"

"First," Phillip said, his gaze condemnatory, "that you will never again set foot on the Styles Place estate, nor approach Viola at any time, in any place whatsoever. If you see her walking along Bond Street, you will cross to the other side. If she arrives at a ball you are attending, without uttering a single word as to the reason why, you will immediately leave."

Dickie was nodding. "As for the Sommervilles in general"—he darted a glance at Addie—"I believe we require your oath that you will never, ever, set foot on any Sommerville estate, nor will you ever, under any circumstances, approach a Sommerville. The same restrictions that apply to Mrs. Styles will also extend to us. All of us. Anyone who is a Sommerville." Dickie looked at Kirkwood contemptuously. "We never want to encounter or hear from you again—not in our clubs, not at Tattersalls, not in any drawing room nor at any ball."

It was banishment of a sort, limited to some extent, yet a definite curtailment of Kirkwood's social activities.

As the reality of the restrictions facing him dawned on Kirkwood, he appeared to mentally reel.

His voice harsh, Phillip demanded, "Do we have your oath?"

Somewhat dazedly, Kirkwood gave it. Almost fearfully, his gaze shifted to Nicholas. Kirkwood swallowed, then asked, "What of the Cynsters?"

"As to that"—Nicholas looked from Kirkwood to Wisthorpe—"by my reckoning, you both owe my family a debt. You, Wisthorpe, were the one who sought to take possession of a valuable Thoroughbred that wasn't yours." Nicholas shifted his gaze to Kirkwood. "And you, Kirkwood, were the one who solicited and facilitated the theft. In my eyes, you are both equally guilty."

Devenish was nodding. "Indeed. And, I believe, we'll all feel more comfortable if the social restrictions the Sommervilles have imposed on Kirkwood also apply to you, Wisthorpe. No setting foot on Sommerville land or social interactions of any sort with members of the Sommerville family." Devenish grinned, all teeth. "And I would suggest it's appropriate that we extend that prohibition to the Cynster and Devenish clans as well." Devenish arched a brow at Nicholas. "What do you think?"

Nicholas inclined his head. "An excellent suggestion."

Addie fought to mute her delighted smile. By ton standards, the Sommervilles were a small family. In contrast, the Cynster and Devenish families were extensive, more like the clans Devenish had labeled them.

All in all, she was feeling much better about Kirkwood's and Wisthorpe's punishments.

"In addition," Nicholas went on, "while I considered the notion of banning you from all race meets and racecourses in England and Ireland —noting that I have the connections to enforce such a ban—it occurs to me that you are both the sort of slightly shady characters who might be of use to both me and my connections at the Jockey Club."

"Ah." Devenish's expression was one of dawning appreciation. "A strikingly apt idea."

"Consequently," Nicholas said, "I will make arrangements and inform you both of when you will be expected to present yourselves at the Jockey Club in Newmarket to volunteer your services as agents of the club, to be their eyes and ears in patrolling the meets at some of the smaller courses with a view to learning of any proposed underhanded practices."

"Yes." Devenish beamed. "That will be a fitting use for your questionable talents and an appropriate recompense for the attempted theft of a Thoroughbred horse."

"Furthermore," Nicholas continued, "your selfless service to the club will last for a period of five years. During that time, you will perform as requested without fail or risk the wrath of the Cynsters and Devenishes."

Both Kirkwood and Wisthorpe looked thoroughly defeated, and when Nicholas pressed for their word that they would respond immediately to any summons from the Jockey Club, they obliged, albeit in hangdog fashion.

With Nicholas and Devenish looking pleased with themselves, it was left to Addie to remind everyone, "Lastly, I believe, Wisthorpe, that you owe Mr. Devenish a sum of money."

That resulted in Wisthorpe being forced to own to his parlous financial state, which, indeed, had been the motive for their entire sorry plan. After Wisthorpe had, distinctly shamefacedly, negotiated a repayment schedule with Devenish, there was no more starch, let alone fight, in either of their would-be villains.

Their company—Nicholas, Addie, Phillip, Viola, Dickie, and Devenish—regarded the now-quite-miserable miscreants. Under their censorious scrutiny, the pair hung their heads and shifted uncomfortably.

Finally, Nicholas glanced at Addie. "Is that enough, do you think?"

She studied Kirkwood and Wisthorpe for a moment more, then nodded. "Yes." With a swish of her skirts, she turned her back on the pair and started walking toward their horses. "We have The Barbarian back, and that's the most important thing."

Also, courtesy of the stupid plot and their determination to unravel it, she and Dickie had discovered so much more about Phillip, and the three of them had grown much closer. They'd learned about and got to know Viola, and Addie and Nicholas had had the chance to extend their knowledge of each other and explore the possibilities of a joint future.

Overall, Kirkwood and Wisthorpe's scheme had given rise to many beneficial if unintended outcomes.

The others joined Addie, all turning their backs on and walking away from the pair of disgraceful and now-disgraced gentlemen.

As she neared the horses, Addie said, "After all that, I believe we deserve to celebrate with a good meal and a comfortable bed in the very best hotel in Harrogate." She glanced at Nicholas, pacing beside her. "That's not far away, is it?"

"Only a few miles." Nicholas met her gaze and smiled. "And I second that motion."

With everyone in wholehearted agreement, they mounted up or climbed into the curricle, and once more in convoy, although this time traveling much closer together, they set out for Harrogate in search of their well-deserved reward.

CHAPTER 16

*T*he company took rooms at Hale's Hotel in Harrogate. Located across the road from the famous Royal Pump Room and with the upper-floor rooms overlooking the town gardens, Hale's was the premier place to stay in the fashionable spa town.

Although, it being the height of summer, it was the spa season, there were not over-many visitors crowding into the town, and despite arriving at a relatively late hour, they managed to secure rooms for their entire party.

It was close to nine o'clock when six of their company gathered in the private parlor that Nicholas and Phillip had organized to partake of their celebratory meal. The grooms, stablemen, and Sally had assured Nicholas that they were more comfortable eating in the inn's main bar, and he'd organized for an extra-special meal to be served to them there.

That left him flanked by Adriana and Devenish, with Dickie beyond Adriana and Phillip and Viola opposite, seated at the circular table in the parlor.

After the long and eventful day, they were famished, and the delicious meal provided by the inn was very welcome and thoroughly appreciated.

They ate, drank, and toasted each other on the successful conclusion of their pursuit of The Barbarian.

For his part, Nigel was deeply grateful to have been saved from parting with further sums for a magnificent horse that, ultimately, he would have had to surrender to the Sommervilles. He waved his goblet.

"If you lot hadn't arrived when you did, that pair would have presented me with The Barbarian, and quite frankly, I would have been blinded by the desire to have him at the family's stud, and when I asked for the papers, odds are they would have spun me some tale about the papers being on their way or some such lie, and with the reality of that horse right there in front of me, I fear I would have weakened and agreed to hand over the rest of the price Wisthorpe had asked for."

"The Kirkwoods maintain that Wesley was born with a silver tongue. I gather he's always been a very persuasive sort." Viola softly huffed. "It seems he's fallen into the habit of using that talent in less-than-acceptable ways."

Nigel shook his head. "This incident will teach me to more definitely suspect any deal that appears too good to be true. Especially when I'm being offered something I will obviously desperately want." He looked at Nicholas and arched a brow. "I don't suppose you'll consider loaning The Barbarian to the Devenish Stable?"

Nicholas reached for his goblet, sipped, swallowed, then met Nigel's hopeful gaze. "There's that Arab mare you have, the one with the white socks and the blinding turn of speed. Perhaps we might manage some mutually beneficial arrangement."

Nigel's eyes widened at the thought. "Oh yes. I'd like to see the offspring from a pairing like that."

Nicholas grinned, and he and Nigel agreed to meet in Newmarket in a few weeks. "Give me time to settle The Barbarian into his new home."

Adriana cleared her throat. "You haven't actually bought the beast yet."

Nicholas smiled at her. "But I intend to, and with your support, your father will sell to me, once we get the horse back to Aisby Grange."

"And if, by chance, the earl decides he doesn't like the look of Cynster's money," Nigel put in, "do bear in mind that the Devenish Stable stands ready to make a most attractive offer."

Nicholas and Adriana laughed, although Nicholas knew Nigel was quite serious.

Adriana's smiling face had drawn and fixed Nigel's attention. "Speaking of being persuasive and pulling the wool over people's eyes," Nigel said, "I have to ask—are you truly Miss Flibbertigibbet?"

Nicholas caught the glance Adriana threw him, and their gazes held for a weighty second before she looked at Nigel and replied, "No. I was, but Miss Flibbertigibbet is no more."

Addie looked at Dickie, then at Phillip and Viola. "As I don't imagine I'll be spending much time in London in the years to come"—she raised her gaze to meet Nicholas's again—"I doubt I'll have reason to summon Miss Flibbertigibbet to the fore again."

Especially not if I'm married and no longer in any gentleman's sights.

She let her eyes and the reassuring tenor of her smile convey that unvoiced thought; from the answering, warm and private smile that lit Nicholas's eyes, he caught her meaning well enough.

Viola asked Devenish about his family's stable, and under cover of the discussion, with everyone's attention on Devenish and his reply, Addie felt Nicholas's fingers find hers beneath the table. His hand engulfed hers, then his thumb drew circles over the back of her hand.

She felt her lips curve irrepressibly, felt a warm glow spread through her. She'd wanted to know how strong, how powerful, his feelings for her truly were. While she hadn't been conscious when he'd found her, that he'd carried her out of that field and, in doing so, had faced the all-but-insurmountable difficulty of convincing The Barbarian to allow him on his back and, subsequently, had accepted the undeniable risk and succeeded in his rescue of her told her a great deal about the unbending nature of his devotion to her.

And she knew The Barbarian. From the first time the horse had seen her and she had seen him, they'd connected in a way she would be hard-pressed to explain. She'd put it down to similar natures—a recognition of like to like. They were both reckless, impulsive, and unpredictable.

Perhaps it was illogical to put faith in an animal's instinctive insight, yet The Barbarian, a horse that trusted rarely, trusted Nicholas.

It might seem ridiculous to others, but she felt beyond reassured. Beyond confident that Nicholas was, indeed, a gentleman she could trust. With herself, with her life, with her future.

She tried to convey all that with her eyes and her smile, and the intrigued and eager look she received in reply suggested that he divined something of her feelings.

Devenish turned to Nicholas with a question about some other mare that the Cynsters had, and the conversation once more turned to breeding racehorses.

Addie listened, drinking in the talk of bloodlines and the discussion of various markers of performance.

The serving girls came in and collected the dessert plates. Their company had made short work of a delicious trifle.

Once the table was clear and the door had closed again, Addie seized the moment of distraction as the gentlemen passed around a bottle of whiskey to whisper to Nicholas, "Clearly, I'm going to have to brush up my understanding of all things breeding."

She saw him blink. Saw the question of whether she was alluding to horse or human reproduction rise in his mind. Before he had a chance to voice that query, she smiled across the table at Viola and Phillip. "Now that this business has been resolved, and in doing so, we've all got to know each other, what are your plans?"

Phillip and Viola shared a glance, then Phillip took Viola's hand and looked at Addie and Dickie. "Obviously, we intend to marry, but exactly when..."

Addie nodded briskly. "You'll have to tell Papa and bring Viola to the Grange and introduce her to Papa and Mama and everyone else she needs to know."

Phillip's eyes widened, and he looked more uncertain than he ever had. "I don't know—"

"I do." Addie glanced at Dickie, and he nodded, and she returned her gaze to Phillip. "We do. You need to make your peace with Papa. After that, all else will fall into place easily enough."

"Now Viola knows us"—Dickie smiled encouragingly at Viola—"and we know and approve of her, as we definitely do, she won't be walking into a completely unknown situation or be without supporters on the ground, and in truth, everyone will welcome her with open arms."

Phillip frowned. "I'm not sure it will be that easy."

Addie heaved an exasperated sigh. "Phillip, Papa has been waiting all these long years for you to come to your senses." She glanced at Viola, then returned her gaze to her half brother. "Now you've fallen in love yourself, you know what it's like. The same compulsion that drives you to marry Viola is precisely the same force that drove Papa to marry our mama. You understand now, and you can't pretend otherwise."

"And if you think Papa—of all men—won't understand why you want so very much to marry Viola..." Dickie shook his head. "That's just nonsensical."

When Phillip still looked unconvinced, Nicholas stirred and said, "They're right, you know. I only met the earl and countess for one evening, but the connection between them?" He dipped his head to Viola and Phillip. "It's exactly the same connection all of us can see between the pair of you."

Addie considered saying more, but with Devenish present, decided against it. She would have her chance when they reached Styles Place. By then, she hoped to have her own future decided, and if she was to leave the Grange and live with Nicholas in Newmarket, her latest, brightest, and most-desired goal was to leave her family united, with Phillip and her parents reconciled and Viola welcomed as the future countess. Now that the chance to achieve that had arisen, she wasn't about to let it slip through her fingers. The Sommerville family needed to come together to weather the difficulties that would inevitably arise from her father's slow decline.

"Think about it." She caught Viola's gaze. "Both of you. This is the time to seize your future and craft it into the life you want to lead."

Truer words...

She felt that reality resonate inside her.

Soon after, with the brandy glasses drained and the impact of their long days in the saddle making itself known, they rose from the table and, smothering yawns, made their way upstairs.

With her advice to Phillip and Viola still echoing in her ears, rather than make for her room, Addie walked to the end of the first-floor corridor, where an alcove looked out over the town's gardens. Nicholas's room was close, while her room was around the corner and down a further corridor.

She didn't turn around but listened to doors softly close here and there, then footsteps neared. A second later, Nicholas joined her.

He settled beside her, looking out at the night. "You and Dickie seem to have buried your differences with Phillip." She felt his gaze touch her face. "Was that because of Viola?"

She tipped her head. "Indirectly. Presumably due to his association with Viola, Phillip has changed, significantly and dramatically, and that raises the prospect of a reconciliation between him and Papa." She drew breath and added, "And for everyone's sake, that needs to happen sooner rather than later."

After a second's hesitation, he quietly asked, "Because of your father's failing faculties?"

Startled, she looked at him. "Was that a guess or...?"

He met her gaze and raised one shoulder. "Mostly a guess, but I've seen the signs before, in other aging men. Physically, they're hale and hearty, but their minds drift. Their focus meanders. After speaking with your father, I wondered."

She grimaced and looked out once more. "Phillip learning of that is no longer the threat we once thought it would be. Based on his previous behavior, we all believed that he would seize the chance to take over the estate and get rid of...well, everyone. But now... Aside from all else, as Papa's heir, he needs to know. He and Viola will need time to prepare for what's to come. They'll need to marry soon and take up residence at the Grange, so Phillip can properly learn the ropes and the staff can come to know Viola and she, them."

Nicholas wholeheartedly agreed. Family dynamics, especially the changes brought about by the succession of the generations, was familiar territory for him. So many adjustments, some more easily made than others. He glanced at Adriana. "It helps if people know what they want of life."

Do you know? Have you made up your mind?

Those questions prompted him, for once, to surrender to impulse. "This afternoon, when I found you thrown and lifeless on the ground..."

He didn't know where the words were coming from, only that he needed to say them. That he had to utter them, and she had to hear them. "It felt as though my world had ended. I had no idea I would feel like that —that I *could* feel like that. It was as if my heart had been torn from me, and only black nothingness remained."

She turned to him, concern in her face, solace in her eyes. She put a hand on his arm. "I hadn't left you."

He nodded. "Realizing that, and that you needed my help, was all that kept me anchored." Carefully, because he wasn't sure he could control the forces he'd allowed to rise, he raised a hand and, with one finger, traced the curve of her luminous cheek. "I realized then—fully and completely —what it was I felt for you. I knew before, but only theoretically. In that moment, my feelings for you became entirely real. Manifest and undeniable." His finger stilling, drowning in her blue gaze, he slowly shook his head. "I can't walk away. If you deny me—"

She seized his finger. "I won't." She searched his eyes. "I don't."

To him, it felt as if the world stood still. "Are you sure?" It was all he could do to get the words out. He didn't want to question her decision. He wanted to seize her and never let go.

She nodded. "I wasn't certain until today. I've been waiting for signs, but today I realized that I don't need any other signs. I know what I want"—she tapped her fist to her chest—"in here. And I'm not going to change my mind any more than you are."

He felt his features ease, his expression lighten, as the weight of uncertainty lifted from his shoulders. "In that case, I suppose that, along with all else we're celebrating, we should celebrate that, too."

Her smile was radiant. "Yes, we should." And with no more ado, she framed his face, stretched up, and kissed him.

He took several seconds to savor the moment, then he slid his hands around her waist, drew her to him, and kissed her back.

He wasn't entirely sure when—or how—they reached his room, but then he was closing the door on the world, and his awareness shrank as he focused solely on her.

On the delights of her passion and the joy of her wordless declaration.

His heart swelled, and he seized her, lifted her, and swung her about, then backed her against the door.

And felt her lips twist beneath his and sensed her breath catch.

Alarmed, he drew back and searched her face. "What is it?"

She wrinkled her nose and raised one hand toward the back of her head. "I'm still a little sore."

All desire effectively doused, he drew back, lowering her to her feet and holding her steady. "You need rest. Not"—he glanced at the bed —"what we were thinking."

She frowned. "We're supposed to be celebrating."

He released her and stepped back. "Not tonight. At least, not like that." Seeing the mulish protest forming in her face, he sternly stated, "Not while you're in any sort of pain."

She thought about forcing the issue; he could read that much in her eyes. But then she seemed to take stock of herself, of how she was truly feeling, and grimaced and frowned even more darkly. "All right," she conceded. "You might be right. I'm too new to the activity to judge. But"—she fixed him with a near-pleading look—"can we still share a bed? It won't feel like a celebration at all, otherwise."

He felt himself nod. "Of course." It might kill him to share a bed with her and not... But if that was what she wanted and needed, he would grit his teeth and bear it.

Her glorious smile dawned. "Good." She stepped to him and draped her arms about his shoulders. "Kissing doesn't hurt."

So they indulged and drew out the minutes as they divested each other of their clothes. With lips and tongue, he paid homage to her curves, to her slender yet lush body, and hungered.

He had to draw back, pull back on their reins, or she would have stampeded him into the act. Discovering the bruises decorating the backs of her shoulders, along one arm, over one hip and down that thigh—in all the places on which she'd landed heavily—gave him the strength to insist that tonight, they would sleep in each other's arms and no more.

Eventually, they settled in the big bed. In truth, tiredness was dragging on his limbs as well as on hers.

She snuggled against him, her head on his chest, her arm and one lithe leg draped across him.

He dipped his chin and pressed a kiss to her forehead. "Sleep," he whispered. "We have a long ride south over the next two days."

She replied with a sleepy groan. Within minutes, the tension drained from her limbs, and he heard her breathing slow as she slid into slumber.

He smiled into the darkness, savoring the warm weight of her, the soft promise of her body pressed to his.

This was what being in love was about—when the well-being of the one loved mattered more than anything else.

Experienced as he was, he knew of any number of ways they might have celebrated in the way she'd expected, but the truth was that, contrary to his long-held belief, he was, at heart, just the same as his father's generation of Cynster males.

She had been hurt. She needed proper rest. She needed to recover.

She needed all those things far more than she needed another bout of lovemaking. He and she would have the rest of their lives to indulge in the latter.

His obsessive protectiveness—a force he was willing, now, to own to—was unwavering and immovable in its absolute insistence that ensuring her well-being was his first and principal duty.

His smile deepening, he closed his eyes.

In the moments while he waited for sleep to claim him, he dwelled on the rosy future unfurling before them.

He was a Cynster in love, and all that was essential to him and his future was, inexorably, falling into place.

Two afternoons later, still buoyed on a wave of triumph, their company clattered back into Sleaford.

Devenish had left them at Harrogate; his family's stud was located south of Chester, and his way home lay in a more westerly direction. The rest of their company had ridden south, this time via the major roads, and had spent the previous night at a pleasant inn in Gainsborough.

Eagerly, they trotted down Northgate, and as the walls of Styles Place came into view, Addie couldn't imagine feeling more delighted with her world. She'd spent the past night in Nicholas's arms, but this time, they'd been most pleasurably exhausted after a lengthy and wholly satisfactory bout of lovemaking. Her attitude to traveling the countryside had substantially altered; now, she could readily imagine accompanying Nicholas to the race meets and major horse sales that, she'd learned, he occasionally needed to attend.

During the journey south, he and she had ridden together, without others close enough to hear, and had made considerable headway in discussing and shaping the details of a joint vision of their shared life.

She was increasingly confident that being Nicholas's wife would suit her to the ground. That Mrs. Nicholas Cynster was the role she'd been waiting to find and make hers.

Their return to Styles Place with The Barbarian in tow was colored with relief; they'd succeeded in accomplishing all they'd set out to achieve and more.

In furtherance of one of those unlooked-for achievements, Addie chose her moment, and in the late afternoon, half an hour before they would gather in the drawing room prior to dinner, she went looking for Phillip.

After the celebratory evening in Harrogate, she hadn't again alluded to the need for Phillip to make his peace with their father and introduce Viola to Addie's parents and the household at the Grange.

She found her half brother sitting behind the desk in the small library. The door was open, and when she looked in, Phillip was absorbed in dealing with what appeared to be estate matters. That he was shouldering that burden for Viola came as no surprise. Smiling, Addie walked in.

Phillip looked up, and a faintly wary look stole over his autocratic features.

She smiled more widely. "Yes, I know. You'd rather walk over the proverbial hot coals, but we—you and I—need to talk." She tipped her head at the French doors that stood open to the terrace and the gardens beyond. "Come, walk with me."

Phillip studied her, then sighed, laid aside his pen, and pushed back from the desk.

Without a word, he joined her, and together, they walked out onto the lawns.

Looking ahead, she softly said, "There are things you need to know."

Phillip frowned. "About the Grange?"

"No. About Papa." Her gaze on the distant rose garden, she drew breath and plunged in. "He's well physically. Mentally…" She explained how his mind wandered and what that sometimes led to. "We've hidden it as well as we can, at least from those outside the estate, but of course, everyone in the household, and I'm sure on the estate as well, will know by now that the earl isn't always…"

When she gestured vaguely, Phillip supplied, "Compos mentis."

His tone was bleak. She glanced at him. He was looking down, but what she could see of his expression was starkly sad.

After several moments of staring at the grass before their slowly pacing feet, he sighed. "I should have been there. To help." He met her eyes. "To help you all shield him."

Lightly, she gripped his arm. "Never mind the past. It's today, tomorrow, and the day after that matter. He needs you, Phillip. The rest of us can and will help, but he needs *you*."

When Phillip didn't respond, she released him and went on, "This estrangement was instigated by you. Through the years, it was driven by you, fueled by your resentment of what you interpreted as Papa turning his back on your mama. On her memory." She shook her head. "It was never that way, but Papa couldn't reach you, couldn't bridge the chasm and make you see the truth, but now, you've learned what love truly is— what it means."

Phillip made a sound that might have been reluctant agreement.

She went on, "You want a future with Viola. This is your path to seizing and securing that. No matter what happens between you and Papa, you're destined to become the earl eventually, and I have no doubt whatsoever that Viola will fill the role of countess admirably, and she'll stand by your side and support you in this as well. You know she will. And we will, too."

She halted, and when Phillip stopped and faced her, she met his eyes. "Please, Phillip. Come to the Grange and talk to Papa. He'll be so happy to see you again, it will give him heart and, very likely, give him the strength to hold back the fog that encroaches on his mind, at least for a time."

Phillip searched her face, his rising hope and burgeoning longing etched in his features. "Do you really think I can just walk into the drawing room and behave as if the past decades of separation didn't happen?"

She imagined that, then nodded. "Yes." She searched his eyes. "If you will walk to him, he'll meet you more than halfway. He loves you, Phillip. He always has."

Phillip looked down. A moment passed, then he hauled in a huge breath and exhaled. "All right. I'll try it." He refocused on her face and gently smiled. "You've become a surprisingly good judge of character. Is that a consequence of your years as Miss Flibbertigibbet?"

She thought, then admitted, "Very likely. I learned to judge men by what is in their hearts."

Phillip arched his brows. "And Cynster?"

She beamed and, turning to the house, linked her arm with Phillip's. "I definitely know what's in his heart."

Phillip chuckled, and with her smiling delightedly, they started walking toward the house.

"Speaking as the older brother you've just challenged to seize and secure his most-desired future, what of you?" When she looked up, Phillip caught her eyes and arched his brows again. "Are you set on seizing and securing your most-desired future, too?"

Addie allowed her answering smile to fill her face and eyes. "I am. Rest assured, brother mine, I intend to do just that."

Emboldened by her exchange with Phillip, after dinner, Addie inveigled Nicholas into walking in the gardens with her.

"I've yet to investigate the rose garden." With her arm twined with his, she nodded toward the walled garden on the far side of the lawn across which they were strolling.

They reached the archway in the gray-stone wall and walked on along a flagstone path that ran down the middle of the garden to end in a small alcove. Built into the rear wall, the alcove hosted a stone bench with a seat cushioned by a thick layer of creeping thyme.

The sun had just set, and the light had softened into a rose-gold twilight. The evening air was balmy and heavily perfumed, scented by the profusion of roses bobbing on long canes. The beds were thick with bushes and blooms, the denseness creating the ambiance of a secret place cut off from the rest of the world.

As they approached the alcove, Addie reviewed what she wanted to say. There weren't any more questions she felt compelled to ask. No pertinent facts she didn't know or couldn't, with confidence, guess. They'd achieved what might be referred to as a complete understanding.

Buoyed by that thought, on reaching the space before the alcove, she halted, drew her arm from Nicholas's, and swung to face him. Eagerly, she took his hands in hers and, smiling delightedly up at him, asked, "Nicholas Cynster, will you marry me?"

He stared at her for a second, then laughed. As his laughter faded, still smiling hugely, he looked into her eyes. "Is this Miss Flibbertigibbet?"

"No." She shook her head vigorously. "This is just me."

His features softened, and his eyes held all the love she could desire. "In that case…" He turned his hands in hers, wrapping his fingers about hers, and went down on one knee before her. Looking into her eyes, his unwavering gaze locked with hers, he said, "I had assumed that I ought to wait and speak to your father first, but of course, I should have known that the usual path wouldn't be the one you would choose to follow. So here we are." He paused, then, his voice deeper, went on, "Adriana Sommerville, you are the lady I want as my wife. I'll gladly marry you if you will consent to marry me."

She laughed, then tugged him to his feet and went into his arms.

Their lips, curved with laughter, met, and joyful and eager, their mouths merged, and passion, that familiar sweet rush, rose, sank in, and took hold.

She raised her hands and framed his face and held him to the soul-searing kiss. Between them, some barrier had fallen. Was it because they'd finally declared themselves out aloud, in words? She didn't know, yet the connection that had always been between them, that had grown and swelled with every kiss, every caress, with every shared interaction, had solidified into a force so powerful, she knew it would link them, now and forever.

Determined to seize all she offered, Nicholas tightened his arms about her. "To have and to hold" was the Cynster motto, and with her in his arms, he felt the full meaning of that maxim resonate inside him.

The kiss, full of passion and laden with desire, spun out and on. The promise inherent within the exchange welled and drove them. Lured them to seize the moment and make that promise real.

The compulsion mounted, but...

He raised his head and, on a gasp, said, "Let's get back to the house." To a room, his or hers. To a bed.

Her lids rose, revealing brilliant blue eyes overflowing with giddy delight. Then she smiled exuberantly, stepped free of his arms, and seized his hand. "Yes. Let's."

Laughing anew, he joined her in hurrying—almost running—to the house. They slipped through the open French doors into the thankfully deserted library, paused to share another scorching kiss in the middle of the room, then she broke away and tore for the door, dragging him with her.

Feeling giddy—as giddy as she seemed to be, as effervescent with happiness—he was by her side as, holding their breaths, they crept into the hall. Avoiding the drawing room with its open door and the sounds of conversation emanating from within, they rounded the newel post and quickly, silently, hurried up the stairs.

"Your room," Addie whispered and headed in that direction.

He wasn't about to argue. When they reached the end of the corridor, he set the door swinging wide and swept her inside.

Following on her heels, he barely had time to shut the door before he had to catch her. She'd flung herself at him, reckless, impulsive, and so very determined.

He staggered back and fetched up with his shoulders against the door. Apparently delighted, she framed his face between her hands, drew his head down, and pressed a fiery—incendiary—kiss on his lips.

She called, and he answered. She incited, and he responded.

He returned the kiss in kind, and they both went up in flames.

Desire soared, passion exploded, and hunger roared.

Heat spread, insistent and demanding. Their hands raced over each other, assured now, knowing and confident. Every touch, every passionate caress only drove the flames higher.

In a flurry of need, they stripped away their clothes, blindly flinging garments away or letting them fall to the polished floor.

Then they were naked, skin to heated skin, and hunger swelled to ravenous heights.

He hoisted her in his arms, and eagerly, greedily, she wrapped her slender thighs about his hips, wriggled her lush bottom, now clasped in his hands, and as he positioned the head of his turgid erection at her entrance, she drew her lips from his and, eyes closed, concentration in her face, pressed down and took him in.

Smoothly, steadily, he filled her, thrusting deep to penetrate that last critical inch.

Finally!

They both exhaled, breaths tight, almost quivering with expectation as she leaned close and settled, then she clamped her inner muscles about his length.

His lungs locked. Overwhelmed by sensation, for a finite instant he couldn't breathe, then instinct took over, and he lifted her. She eased her hold on him, then claimed him anew as he filled her again.

They settled into a rhythm they now knew well, one of retreat and return, of swelling heat and rising, mindless, driving passion.

Soon, all they knew was the building, blinding urgency to race to completion.

To be one.

To attain the nirvana of intimacy.

With her arms draped over his shoulders, Addie clung to him. Her thighs and hips rhythmically shifting in time with his urging, increasingly desperately, she moved her torso against his, glorying in the heat and the delicious friction. The tight peaks of her breasts were on fire, and the fullness inside her, the molten heat pooling low and spreading, held her awareness in complete and utter subjugation.

He'd introduced her to this position the previous night, when she'd insisted that they shouldn't waste another opportunity for her to expand her horizons, but he'd been concerned over the bruises still decorating her back and side.

This had been his solution, and she'd embraced it wholeheartedly.

Enthusiastically.

Yet, as it always seemed in this sphere, she wanted more.

More of him, more of the delicious pleasure.

Her breath was already coming in soft gasps. Her lips were hungry and swollen. Determined on securing her "more," with her lids simply too heavy to raise, blindly, she found his lips with hers and, with complete and utter devotion to her cause, plunged them both into a searing kiss, one of rapacious demand.

He responded instantly, as she'd known he would.

He angled his head and, with lips and tongue and an experience she still lacked, wrested control of the kiss from her and, ruthlessly deploying said experience, turned the exchange into a fiery clash that consumed every iota of her awareness. Demanding, commanding, through the kiss, he seized her senses and drove her into ever more mindless wanting.

When, desperate, she broke from the kiss to drag in some air, she discovered that he'd walked them to the side of the bed. With her in his arms, he turned and, before she realized what he intended, toppled backward to land on his back on the thick coverlet.

On a smothered shriek, she rode him down, instinctively splaying her hands on his chest and tightening her body around the intrusion of his.

She landed atop him, her knees buried in the bed on either side of his hips, her calves flanking his thighs. Her hips slammed down across his, and he closed his eyes on a groan.

They hadn't tried this before. Poised over him, her hands spread on his chest for balance, she straightened her arms and slowly sat up, sat back, glorying again in the feeling of him inside her, filling her, alive and throbbing at her core.

She looked at his face. His expression appeared faintly pained.

"How does this work?" seemed her most pertinent question. She was surprised to hear her voice so sultry, so breathless.

Experimentally, she shifted her hips slightly side to side, and his chest rose as he drew in a deep yet tense breath.

She caught the glint of brilliant caramel-brown beneath the fringe of his lashes.

"It's simple," he ground out. His jaw seemed impossibly tight. His hands, which had fallen to either side, rose to clasp her hips, and he urged her up—just a little. "Ride me."

She blinked, then followed his directions. She rose up, feeling the glide of his erection within her slick channel, then before she lost him from her body, she reversed direction and slowly slid down.

Oh my Lord.

With avid enthusiasm, she flung herself into mastering this new form. Into exploring and implementing whatever little tweaks incited the most pleasure for her and for him.

The flames that had earlier roared and gripped them had cooled a trifle, but now passion and greedy desire returned in full measure and combined with their surging hunger to whip them both on, into the beckoning conflagration of their senses.

The delirious delight of being completely in charge quite went to her head, and impulsive and reckless to the last, she flung her every passionate effort into the moment.

Breathless, close to mindless, balanced upon him, she drove them on. Eyes closed the better to absorb the delights of their joining, with her hair loose and whipping about her shoulders, with him, metaphorically hand in hand, she strove to reach the ineluctable end while, furnace-like, their bodies burned with need and with the overwhelming yearning to claim and be claimed.

The culmination was intense—more intense than she'd experienced before. She came apart, and she would have sworn her mind shattered into a million shards of impossibly brilliant and pure sensation.

Pleasure spiked, and ecstasy took her, and glory filled her veins.

Only her grip on his wrists kept her anchored to earth. The desperate clenching of his fingers on her hips as he drove into her melting body, the low groan that racked him as he reached his release, and the warmth of his seed flooding her womb completed her joy.

This was true intimacy.

Her heart swelled with happiness, gladness, and unadulterated joy. She'd found him, and with him, this was and forever would be within her reach.

Surely this was earthly glory; this was paradise on earth.

Love had claimed her and shown her the way, and now she'd found him, she would never, ever, let go.

As she sagged and slowly slumped forward, helped by the soothing stroking of his hands, she knew only thankfulness and gratefulness that she had finally found her true home.

Her lover. Her soulmate. Her place.

Nicholas gathered her to him and nuzzled a kiss to her temple.

She was exhausted, wrung out, and so was he. After that performance, he couldn't summon the strength to rearrange their limbs, and luckily, with the summer night so warm, there was no urgent need to do so.

He could lie there and allow quiet triumph to fill him.

Could let the glow of success wash through him.

Getting them to this point had required a degree of finesse he hadn't been sure he possessed, yet apparently, he'd found the right way, the right path. He'd eschewed pursuing her—an impulse that was so very much a part of him—and instead, allowed her to come to him in her own time.

He'd allowed her to make the running, and she'd obliged and brought them to this point.

To where fronting an altar lay in their immediate future.

From the first moment of meeting her, he'd known she was the one for him, and now that she'd freely chosen him as hers—hers for evermore —he was beyond convinced that nothing in life could possibly be more wonderful. No other moment would ever be so sublime. No other achievement would ever mean as much.

Equally, of course, nothing in his life would ever be the same, yet with her by his side, he welcomed that future, filled with impulsive uncertainty though it would surely be, with open arms and a ready heart.

CHAPTER 17

$\mathcal{T}$he following morning, Nicholas rode beside Adriana, perched once more on Nickleby, as their small cavalcade rolled up the drive of Aisby Grange. Astride his chestnut, Dickie trotted on his sister's other side, while Phillip and Viola followed in Phillip's curricle.

Adriana had argued forcefully that Phillip needed to return to the Grange immediately—that very day—and bring Viola to meet the earl and countess as well, and no one had been in any position to disagree. There'd been an insistence to her fervor that suggested that, having gained the chance to steer Phillip and her father to a reconciliation, she was determined not to allow anything to get in the way of achieving her purpose. So powerful had been her persuasiveness that Phillip and Viola had surrendered, packed bags, and climbed into the curricle.

Behind the carriage came Rory and Young Gillies, the former leading The Barbarian. To everyone's surprise, the huge stallion had behaved himself, more or less, since they'd retrieved him from the field outside Scriven. The grooms and stablemen had suggested that the surprise of losing Adriana from his back had sobered the beast.

Whatever the cause, they were all grateful for his compliance in returning peaceably to Aisby Grange.

As they approached the portico and slowed, Nicholas glanced over his shoulder and saw Viola, head tipped back and holding onto her hat, scanning the width of the front façade. Her expression suggested she found the sight intimidating.

Having noticed the direction of his gaze, Adriana flicked a brief glance that way. Facing forward once more, she murmured, "Viola will be fine."

Nicholas merely inclined his head, then drew sharply on the reins to halt Tamerlane as the three younger Sommerville siblings burst through the open front door yelling "You're back! They're back!" at the tops of their lungs.

Adriana and Dickie managed to wrestle their horses to a halt without trampling any of the trio, who exuberantly danced about the leading horses.

Then the three saw the curricle, which Phillip had drawn to a standstill.

"Hello." Angie tipped her head. She'd noticed Viola first, but then her gaze had passed on to Phillip and come to rest there.

Mortie stopped beside Angie. After a second of staring frowningly at Phillip, clearly puzzled, Mortie challenged, "Who are you?"

Nicholas and Dickie dismounted. Nicholas rounded Nickleby and lifted Adriana down before she could jump. He set her on her booted feet, and they turned to see Benjamin walking up to the curricle, with Mortie and Angie falling in behind him.

Like his siblings, Benjamin had his gaze locked on Phillip's face.

That the three younger Sommervilles recognized the familial resemblance was plain.

Benjamin halted beside Phillip and, after a fraught moment, simply asked, "Are you our older brother?"

Phillip shot a glance—a pleading one—at Adriana and Dickie, then looked at Benjamin, hesitated for a heartbeat, and somewhat carefully, nodded. "I am. I'm Phillip."

Nicholas sensed that Adriana was torn between rushing forward to intervene and standing back and allowing matters to play out by themselves; she all but teetered beside him. He closed his hand about one of hers. "Wait," he advised, then even more quietly added, "The four of them have to find their own way."

After several seconds of silently studying each other, Phillip offered, "I'm here to see...our father."

That, apparently, reassured the trio.

"Good-o." Benjamin offered his hand. "I'm Benjamin. Please don't call me Benny or Benjy—just Benjamin. I'm pleased to meet you."

"I'm Angie." Angie pushed forward to offer her hand as well. "Don't call me Angela, or I might not answer."

"And at home, I only answer to Mortie." His gaze still scrutinizing Phillip, Mortie also shook hands, then he stepped back and, including Viola with his gaze, waved to the house. "Welcome to Aisby Grange."

Taking that as a signal that her siblings were predictably curious and not about to make a fuss over this being the first time any of the three had set eyes on their half brother, Addie exhaled with relief. She handed her reins to Rory, and still leading The Barbarian, he and Young Gillies, who had Nicholas's and Dickie's mounts in tow, turned the horses and, with Jed and Mike, headed around the house and on toward the stable.

Sally had already scrambled down from her saddle, and she gave her horse's reins to one of the two stable lads who came rushing up to take charge of the curricle and pair. Phillip stepped down to the gravel and surrendered the ribbons, then rounded the horses to help Viola down.

After stepping carefully from the carriage, Viola looked at the three younger Sommervilles, who had followed Phillip. Shyly, she smiled at them. "Hello. I'm Viola."

As, with Nicholas, Addie joined the group, the trio's gazes were shifting from Viola to Phillip and back again.

It was Angie who asked, "Are you Phillip's wife?"

Phillip squeezed Viola's hand and replied, "No. Viola is my fiancée. We plan to marry soon."

"Oh!" Angie's eyes brightened. At her most angelic, she inquired, "Can I be a bridesmaid?"

Addie quickly stepped in. "We'll have to see about that, but first, Phillip needs to see Papa." She met Phillip's eye. "And Mama, too." As Dickie came up, she glanced at the younger three. "Do you know where they are?"

"They're in the conservatory," Angie said. "It's cooler there," she informed Viola.

Merriweather was hovering in the doorway. Unlike Addie's younger siblings, he'd recognized Phillip and wasn't sure what was afoot.

Addie saw the butler's uncertainty and smiled reassuringly, then beckoned the others to follow and started up the steps. "Merriweather, we have guests, who I expect will be staying the night. At least." She passed into the front hall and paused, waiting for the others.

Merriweather bowed. "Of course, my lady." He straightened to his full imposing height. "I will ensure suitable rooms are prepared."

Phillip and Viola reached her. Phillip met Merriweather's eyes and nodded. "Merriweather."

Merriweather bowed again. "Lord Phillip." Still bent, he slanted a questioning sidelong glance at Addie, who nodded encouragingly. Reassured, Merriweather straightened and, with a small yet transparently sincere smile, added, "It's a pleasure to welcome you home to Aisby Grange, my lord."

Phillip's expression gave little away, but Addie sensed he was touched. Merriweather hadn't needed to say that. Phillip duly introduced Viola to Merriweather.

Then Dickie swanned in with a "What-ho, Merriweather?" to which the long-suffering butler merely arched a brow.

Nicholas walked in, ushering Benjamin, Angie, and Mortie ahead of him.

Merriweather's expression turned openly approving. He bowed. "Mr. Cynster. It's a delight to welcome you back, sir."

"Thank you, Merriweather." Nicholas locked his gaze on Adriana, wondering what her plans were.

As if in answer, she collected everyone with a glance—one severe enough to ensure no one tried to get away—and stated, "Dickie and I will lead the way into the conservatory, with Phillip and Viola following a few yards behind, and the rest of you should bring up the rear."

Nicholas inclined his head in agreement, as did everyone else. He thought Adriana was wise not to allow anyone to put off the fraught moment.

She duly led the way down a long corridor giving off the rear of the hall, eventually reaching double glass doors, which she opened and set wide. With Dickie beside her, Adriana swept down the central aisle of the long conservatory, passing between ranks of large palms and banks of exotic plants to reach a seating area bounded by the curved glass wall at the end of the long room.

There, her parents were seated in wicker chairs, angled toward each other but also facing up the room.

"Mama, Papa," Adriana declared. "We're back, as you can see, and we have The Barbarian once more in our hands."

"Excellent!" Her father had turned his head to regard her and Dickie, but now, faintly puzzled, his gaze slid past them. "Who...?"

His voice trailed away.

Addie caught her mother's eyes and shifted to the side so that her mother, too, could view the visitors. "We also met some others and invei-gled them to come on a visit."

Her father had paled. Using his cane, he levered to his feet. He stared at his heir, then, his voice a bare whisper, said, "Phillip?"

Phillip looked equally shaken, but he managed a rather stiff nod. "Sir." He shot a pleading look at Addie. "Addie and Dickie..." Phillip looked at his father, then simply said, "It seemed it was time."

For a second, no one breathed.

Slowly, Addie's mother got to her feet, but made no move to intercede.

Then her father sighed—a long, relieved, contented sigh—and stepped forward, one arm coming up to draw Phillip near. "My boy. I'm so glad to see you."

As Phillip moved forward and returned their father's embrace, Addie blew out a surreptitious breath.

What followed were lots of careful words and introductions, which elicited several shaky laughs, tentative smiles, not a few rapidly blinked-back tears, and ultimately, massive relief on all sides.

Nicholas stood back and observed the reunion. The Sommerville family gathered around, the younger children eager to be part of such a momentous occasion.

It soon became apparent that everyone was of a mind to let bygones be bygones. Nicholas watched approvingly as, leaving Viola speaking with his eager and interested father, Phillip made his peace with the countess.

Once the talk turned to Phillip and Viola's plans, Adriana detached from the family group and walked to where Nicholas had halted at the end of the aisle. She met his eyes and smiled. "Thank you for giving us time to reconnect."

He inclined his head. "This is what should be. How a family should be." He took her hand, raised it to his lips, and holding her gaze, gently kissed her knuckles. "You've done well."

She all but glowed, then looping her arm with his, turned to face the others. "Be that as it may, it's our turn now."

She walked forward, and he readily went with her.

Smiling—he suspected in besotted fashion—he stood beside her and left it to her to break their news. After she had, and congratulations had rained down upon them—the same congratulations that had earlier show-ered Phillip and Viola—Nicholas seized a quiet moment to speak directly to the earl. "My apologies, my lord. It was my intention to speak to you and ask your permission to pay my addresses to Lady Adriana, but she jumped the gun and insisted we exchange our troths and, in what I suspect will be the story of the rest of my life, I discovered I couldn't deny her."

The earl—who looked younger and fitter than he had before—laughed and clapped Nicholas on the shoulder. "Don't worry about it, my boy. You'll soon learn to appreciate the ever-changing delights of living with an impulsive woman." The earl's gaze had shifted to rest on his countess. "I thank my stars every day for the joys such a lady brings."

Nicholas heard the love that thrummed so strongly beneath that simple statement and felt an answering chord vibrate inside him.

Then Merriweather arrived to announce that luncheon was served, and the entire party adjourned to the dining room, where the meal turned into a joyous celebration, with numerous toasts—to the two affianced couples and to their successful journey culminating in the retrieval of The Barbarian and to the exposure and rousting of those behind his removal—before, inevitably, the countess turned the talk to the two impending weddings.

To Nicholas's mind, Phillip and Viola got off lightly, with everyone agreeing that a small private ceremony in the Grange's chapel would allow Viola to feel her way into the role of future countess without having the spotlight of the ton shone upon her too soon.

For Nicholas and Adriana, however, there was to be no escape.

"After all," the earl said, "you are your parents' elder son, and Adriana is my elder daughter. You're a Cynster, and she's a Sommerville. The ton will expect a major event, and in light of Phillip and Viola's quiet affair, your nuptials will need to generate a great to-do to satisfy the hordes."

The countess smiled up the table. "Not the hordes, dear. It's the hostesses these two will need to placate." Her twinkling eyes met Nicholas's. "Especially as dear Nicholas numbers several of the ton's most senior hostesses among his close relatives."

Sadly, there was no arguing with that.

By dint of pointing out that, as yet, his family knew nothing about his impending nuptials, Nicholas managed to put the question of their wedding to one side and turn the conversation to The Barbarian and the sale of the horse to the Cynster Stable.

"Yes, indeed." The earl beamed at Nicholas. "I'm entirely content to see the beast pass into your hands, and I daresay the horse will be only too happy to be going with Addie, to whom he seems quite attached."

"There's an understatement," Dickie murmured.

With the fruit platters decimated and the meal at an end, the children asked if they might be excused, and the earl and countess smiled and waved them away. The younger trio left the room, leaving the earl, Adriana, the countess, Dickie, Phillip, Viola, and Nicholas to discuss the details of the sale.

Somewhat to Nicholas's surprise—perhaps because of them having to chase after the horse and reclaim him—the others evinced real interest in hearing about how the huge stallion would be used at the stud and what options that raised in terms of the conditions of his sale.

The earl, Phillip, Adriana, and Dickie were, predictably, most invested in the details, and all contributed to the arrangement on which Nicholas and the earl eventually settled.

With the sale agreed and all details defined, the earl and Nicholas shook hands on the deal.

Joining in the toast Dickie subsequently proposed, Nicholas felt a weight he hadn't known was there lift from his shoulders. What with all the excitement over chasing and reclaiming The Barbarian compounded by the distraction of falling in love with Adriana and securing her hand, he'd actually forgotten just how much, in terms of the Cynster Stable, had rested on him buying the stallion.

His gaze drifted to Adriana, the biggest distraction he was ever likely to meet. He smiled, sipped, and when she glanced his way, raised his glass to her and drank.

Pru will cackle herself into fits.

Later, after the company adjourned to the drawing room, Nicholas found himself standing with the earl at one of the long windows that looked out over the rolling fields.

For several moments, they drank in the sight, then without looking at Nicholas, his voice quiet, the earl said, "One thing, my boy, that you really have to promise me is that you'll watch over my Addie in the years to come."

Nicholas comprehended that the request was prompted, at least in part, by the earl's acceptance that he would, very likely, not live all that long. "On my honor, I will be her strength and shield throughout the rest of our lives. Until death do us part truly means that to me. I will never let anything harm her."

The words had come readily to his tongue.

The earl cast him an assessing glance, then gently smiled and looked back at the view. "The vow of a Cynster. I couldn't ask for more. Thank you, my boy."

His gaze on the green fields, Nicholas softly replied, "Living up to that vow will be my life's pleasure."

On the other side of the room, Addie found herself standing with Phillip and watching her mother and Viola, seated side by side on the sofa.

"They're getting on like a house on fire," Addie murmured.

Phillip had been smiling more than she'd ever imagined he could. "Your mother is…very motherly."

Addie smothered a snort. "Well, she's had five of us to practice on. If you'd come home earlier, she would have practiced directly on you as well." She met Phillip's gaze. "As it is, she's being very cautious with you, but Viola is a lady of a type Mama recognizes and knows how to deal with, how to support and encourage her. And she will."

"For which I'm extremely grateful." After a second more of watching his wife-to-be and his stepmother, Phillip turned his gaze on Addie. "But what of you?"

When, uncertain what he meant, she looked at him questioningly, he went on, "At no time in the recent days have you behaved as Viola or I imagined Miss Flibbertigibbet would."

"Ah." Addie nodded. "That's because, when Nicholas first arrived here, he found me dealing with a minor disaster involving flying flour bombs. I didn't have the option of donning my alter ego, and"—she shrugged—"once he'd seen the real me, there was no point in doing so."

Phillip frowned. "So he never saw you as she?"

Addie shook her head. "We'd never met before. And of course, as from the first he saw me as me, he…dealt with me directly." She thought, then added, "He didn't try to step in and control me." She glanced at Phillip. "And yes, I'm aware that I'm impulsive, but he seems to have a knack for knowing how to rein me in without overstepping the mark."

Phillip's lips twitched. "I'd noticed." He studied her for a moment more, then quietly asked, "So Miss Flibbertigibbet truly is no more?"

She thought about that for some moments, imagining what situations might cause her to resurrect her alter ego, but then she remembered that Nicholas would be there, by her side, and even if he wasn't, she would be his wife and, in that role, she knew to her soul that she would always have his support.

Slowly, she shook her head, then met Phillip's eyes. "Yes. Miss Flibbertigibbet is dead."

~

Later, as the afternoon waned into evening and a rosy wash painted the sky, Nicholas walked out with Adriana, seeking privacy in the extensive gardens of Aisby Grange.

Her arm in his, she drew him toward the rose garden. Smiling, he paced beside her.

As they passed under the archway leading into the large rectangular garden, Adriana stated, "We need to decide how we want our wedding to be, or before we know it, all the arrangements will have been settled, and it will be a massive social undertaking commencing in Hanover Square."

Her tone declared that she wasn't the least attracted by the prospect, which reassured him. "Perhaps we can manage to limit the size of it."

"But how?"

"I think our first step should be to write to my parents and give them our news." A plan was taking shape in his mind. "They're in Ireland at the moment, waiting for my sister Prudence to have her second child, and I'll urge Mama and Papa to remain there until after the happy event, as they'd intended." He met Adriana's eyes. "That will stall any decision-making and give us a chance to make up our own minds—"

"And marshal the necessary arguments to support our stand." Adriana nodded decisively. "Yes, let's do that."

Nicholas glanced toward a small fountain playing at the path's end. The heady scents of roses in bloom wreathed about them as they slowly strolled. "Looking further ahead, beyond the wedding and settling at Newmarket, have you had any thoughts about how you would like our marriage to evolve?"

She tipped her head and rested it against his shoulder. "Well, children, of course, if we're blessed."

His heart leapt, then settled, even more deeply content.

"As for the rest, I thought..."

He listened as, based on their earlier discussions, she verbally sketched her vision of their married life. He added a touch or two here and there, tweaking her notions, giving them substance.

As the evening enfolded them in its perfumed embrace, they moved on to sharing their hopes and their dreams, and beneath their words, buoying them, ran the confidence that, together, united, they could and would achieve every goal.

∾

Arm in arm, the earl and countess stood in the bay window of the earl's apartments and, with fond affection, looked down on their elder daughter and their soon-to-be son-in-law and counted their blessings.

"I never imagined," the earl confessed, "that not only would Phillip come to his senses and return to us but also that he would have the sound sense to choose a lady like Viola to be his wife."

"When he walked in with Viola on his arm, you could have knocked me over with the proverbial feather." The countess went on, "She is exactly the sort of steady lady Phillip needs to anchor him and provide... well, ballast to his character. With her by his side, he'll make an excellent earl." She glanced at her spouse lovingly. "When the time comes."

The earl chuckled. "I haven't felt so well—so much myself and confident in that—for longer than I care to think. It's happiness, I believe." His gaze on the couple ambling through the rose garden, he patted the countess's hand where it rested on his sleeve. "They'll be happy, too." His lips lifted in a gentle smile; turning his head, he directed that smile at his wife. "Just as we've been."

Her smiling gaze on Adriana and Nicholas, the countess nodded. "For all these long years." After a moment, she added, "Perhaps Phillip returning and bringing Viola with him was our reward for working so diligently to bring Addie and Nicholas together."

"Even though he wasn't the brother we'd expected?"

"Indeed. But they're so very right for each other, which is another thing we couldn't have foreseen, so I do think we got the correct brother as well." The countess tipped her head, then amended, "Or Fate did. After all, it wasn't by our actions that Nicholas came instead of Tobias, but clearly, Fate decided to take a hand, and as ever, she knows best."

After a moment during which they watched the ambling couple pause beside the fountain, then, laughing, come together in an embrace, the earl murmured, "Despite us gaining Fate's blessing, my dear, I rather think we should keep our part in fostering Addie and Nicholas's romance to ourselves."

"Oh, indeed." The countess looked surprised that he'd imagined anything else. "Now and forever, our lips should most definitely remain sealed." With her free hand, she gestured to the couple kissing in the rose garden. "Why create questions about something that is so patently meant to be?"

The earl patted her other hand. "Just so, my dear. Just so."

For several more minutes, with pleasure, delight, and hope in their hearts, they remained at the window and looked down upon what Fate, with their help, had wrought.

EPILOGUE

AUGUST 26, 1854. AISBY GRANGE, LINCOLNSHIRE.

The Earl of Aisby got his wish and, smiling proudly, walked his elder daughter down the aisle.

The wedding was celebrated in the beautiful old church of St. Michael of All Angels, the local parish church located not far from the gates of Aisby Grange. Early in the planning, the chapel at the Grange had been dismissed as far too small to accommodate the necessary number of guests. Although that number proved significantly larger than Nicholas and Addie had hoped, the event was nevertheless deemed to be "select," meaning that the guest list was restricted to the families, connections, and close family friends.

With that, Nicholas and Addie had decided to be content.

Indeed, once Nicholas's mother had returned from Ireland with not just her husband but also Nicholas's sister, Prudence, and the ladies of the wider Cynster family had become involved, all of whom knew Addie as Miss Flibbertigibbet, she'd greatly feared that their wedding would become something of a cause célèbre.

To her eternal relief, Nicholas's mother had taken pity on her and Nicholas and had acted as a bulwark of sorts against the tide that had pressed for the wedding to escalate to major-event status.

Consequently, when Addie had paced down the aisle, preceded by an ecstatic Angie and Nicholas's younger sister, Meg, as bridesmaids, followed by his older sister, Pru, in the role of matron of honor, it was under the eyes of only four hundred or so people—three hundred guests and about a hundred staff and locals who'd crowded into the church to see a well-known local young lady wed.

Now, with the ceremony, the wedding feast, the speeches, and the first two waltzes behind them, on Nicholas's arm, Addie circulated among those three hundred guests in the ballroom of the Grange. In between the inevitable chatting, the teasing comments, and the rapturous envy generated by her exquisite gown, she found herself looking back with joyful if quiet delight on those moments when she and Nicholas had stood before the altar, painted by the jewel-toned sunbeams which had poured through the stained-glass windows, and exchanged their vows firmly and intently.

Her father had surprised her and the rest of the family as well. Ever since Phillip had returned to the Grange and he and their father had reconciled, and at Addie's mother's insistence, Viola had come to stay as well, her father's mind had remained steady. He hadn't suffered another bout of vagueness, which was a huge relief. He'd insisted on walking her down the aisle and been so pleased to be able to do so that it had been plain that the action had meant something special to him.

She'd made a mental note to ask her mother about that later.

But for now, all was unalloyed joy and happiness as everyone about them—Cynster, Sommerville, connection, or close friend—joined them in celebrating their big day and the promise of all to come.

"No matter what your inclinations," Louisa, Marchioness of Winchelsea, warned, "you will need to come up to London occasionally." Louisa's look was polite yet pointed. "Because you're so observant and courtesy of your four Seasons, your knowledge of the ton is extensive, and your insights have already proved illuminating. At least to me, which, I'm sure all will agree, is quite a feat." Her pale-green gaze ensnared Addie. "We can't afford to lose such a source of sound intelligence."

Having learned that Louisa's husband, Drake, was deeply involved in ensuring the security of the realm, especially when plots involved members of the ton, and having also, by then, taken Louisa's measure, Addie merely smiled, inclined her head, and stated, "We'll see."

Moments later, as she and Nicholas moved on, Addie leaned close and whispered, "I never before thought of myself as 'a source of sound intelligence'!"

Nicholas laughed and squeezed her hand. "I should have warned you. I truly can't see the Cynster ladies—our generation as much as that past— allowing you to molder in Newmarket all year. They of all groups will value your talents and the contributions you'll be able to make to their social plans."

"Hmm." Somewhat to her surprise, Addie discovered that the notion of being one of a coterie of ladies who supported each other socially wasn't as off-putting as she would have thought.

One thing of which she was certain was that, despite the limited guest list, with the avid interest of the wider ton focused on her and Nicholas, Miss Flibbertigibbet was now well and truly dead, buried, and never to be resurrected. No matter that she still looked the part and always would, no one would ever believe that the lady who had married Nicholas Cynster and was intent on becoming his partner in all things was a featherbrain.

Another waltz was in progress. Addie and Nicholas paused at the edge of the dance floor. Surveying the swirling couples, Addie saw her parents dancing. Her mother's face was tilted up, and the happiness investing her features made Addie's breath catch.

There'd been so much worry and anxiety over recent years, to see her mother—and her father, too—made so happy by this day brought tears to her eyes.

Nicholas noticed. Gently, he squeezed her hand. "You've lifted the cloud that hung over the Grange."

She met his eyes. "We have." She looked back at the dancers, finding Phillip and Viola in the crowd. "And now Phillip and Viola will keep the cloud at bay."

Given that Addie and Nicholas's wedding had needed to be at least this size and, inevitably, would garner much social attention, it had been agreed that Phillip and Viola—their connection, now formalized in an engagement, made widely known through this event—would marry in a few weeks, in early September, in a private service in the chapel at the Grange, essentially allowing the ton's focus on Addie and Nicholas's event to divert attention from theirs.

By the time the majority of the ton caught up with the changes, Viola's installation as the future Countess of Aisby would be a fait accompli.

His gaze still on the dancers, Nicholas dipped his head to Adriana's and murmured, "I heard you promise Viola that you would be in London next Season to hold her hand."

Adriana shrugged. "I could hardly leave her to manage on her own." Glancing sideways, she met his eyes. "And as you just heard from one of the younger major hostesses, no less, I possess a great deal of useful social intelligence."

Nicholas laughed. "True."

He still found himself amazed by how everything had worked out. It was as if the universe had simply been waiting for him to find her and persuade her to be his. So much had just fallen into place, without them having to fight or even push to make things happen.

When he'd left the Grange to take The Barbarian to the Cynster Stables, Adriana had elected to come, too. In the end, her mother and Sally as well as Rory had accompanied them and Young Gillies, the intention of the ladies being to inspect the farmhouse that Adriana and Nicholas would call home. For his part, he'd been glad to have Adriana along to keep The Barbarian in line.

That first visit of hers to the Cynster Stable and the house had been an unmitigated success.

Her second visit, a few weeks later, to meet his parents and siblings, had been even more heartening. His parents—and Pru and Toby, too—had been hugely impressed by Adriana's connection with The Barbarian, so much so that his mother and Pru had immediately moved to test whether Adriana's talent extended to other skittish Thoroughbreds.

And so it had proved.

Everyone had been utterly delighted. "She's a natural," his mother had declared.

His father had clapped him on the back. "Trust you to find such a rare lady to marry."

To say his family had welcomed Adriana with open arms and taken her to their hearts would be a gross understatement. They were utterly captivated by her and in awe of her ability with horses.

As a wedding present, Nicholas's parents had formally deeded the Newmarket farmhouse to him and Adriana. Despite that, Adriana had made it clear that she expected his family to use the residence exactly as they previously had. The Lord knew, it was large enough to accommodate everyone easily.

When, tomorrow, they left Aisby Grange as a married couple setting out upon the journey of their shared life, he felt confident that the road ahead of them—while not necessarily smooth all the way and doubtless strewn with their fair share of challenges—would be one they would conquer. That the future that lay ahead would be one they would successfully shape and negotiate.

The previous waltz had ended, but now the musicians played the introduction to another. He looked at Adriana—his wife, his helpmate.

His heart.

"Mrs. Cynster." When surprised and delighted, she looked up at him, he raised her hand to his lips and kissed her fingers. "Can I persuade you to dance with me, my love?"

She smiled radiantly, joy dancing in her eyes, and simply said, "Always." She stepped toward the dance floor and, still beaming, tugged. "Come on."

He laughed and followed her, then swung her into his arms and whirled her into the throng.

Later, when the merriment of the wedding breakfast was inevitably sliding toward its end, Nicholas fetched up beside several of his married male cousins and cousins-in-law, who were standing in a loose group to one side of the ballroom. He'd left Adriana in deep conversation with what he thought of as the gaggle of his married female cousins and cousins-in-law. Among others, the group included Louisa, Antonia, and Therese; a more powerful gathering of younger major hostesses was difficult to imagine.

"Welcome to the fold, old man." Michael thumped Nicholas's shoulder.

"Took you long enough," Christopher observed.

"This," Drake said, tipping his head at the gathering around them, "is now something of a tradition."

Nicholas frowned. "What tradition?"

"Where we guess who'll be next to fall into matrimony's loving arms," Devlin, Therese's husband, explained.

Gregory grinned. "It might interest you to know that, at my wedding, I correctly foretold that you would be the next of our company to fall at Fate's feet."

Nicholas stared at him. "You're joking."

"He's not," Drake said.

"But the question before us now," Christopher said, "is who do we think will fall next?"

"Justin, Evan, Aiden, and Julius are the most likely," Michael pointed out.

They were tossing around names when Toby wandered up and joined them. He listened for several minutes, like the others, his gaze raking the crowd, then Drake looked at him and asked, "So, speaking for the younger group, who do you think it'll be?"

Toby tipped his head. "You always concentrate on the males. What of the females?"

"Too hard to predict," Devlin said, and by their nods, he spoke for the rest of group.

"Hmm, possibly," Toby allowed. "But for what it's worth, my suggestion would be that, in keeping with Nicholas's choice of wife being utterly unexpected and that he wasn't really looking when he found her, I've got my eye on Meg as being the most likely to give rise to the next Cynster wedding."

"Meg?" Nicholas located his and Toby's younger sister in the crowd. She was talking avidly with several other young ladies of her age. Puzzled, Nicholas frowned. "She's been immersing herself in the social round since she came out. Surely her finding a husband shouldn't come as any surprise."

"Ah, but," Toby said, "for all that she enjoys gadding about socially, if you watch closely, you'll discover that she's not really looking for a husband. In fact, I suspect she's grown rather disillusioned with what's on offer and isn't sure anymore what she's going to do." Toby glanced at the rest of the group. "Looking at all of you, it seems to me that Fate has a definite liking for swooping in at such times."

Devlin, who'd been studying Meg, slowly nodded. "Stepping in to correct our misapprehensions. In that, you're not wrong."

The others looked across the room at Meg and wondered if Toby would be proved correct.

∽

Seven months later…

Feeling much as she imagined a beached whale would, Addie was folding shawls and placing them in the new oak chest in the freshly painted nursery in the attic of the farmhouse when she heard her husband's steps as he climbed the attic stairs.

She dropped the last shawl into the chest, then shut the lid and turned to sit on it. Her hand resting on her distended belly, she smiled when Nicholas appeared in the doorway.

"There you are." His smile held pride, relief, and the glow of love. Then he glanced around before bringing his now-frowning gaze back to her face. "I worry about you being all the way up here alone."

She pointed to the new bellpull dangling beside the door. "Withers insisted on setting that up. If I need help, I only have to pull it."

Withers was their new butler, a younger man keen to please his master as well as his mistress.

Nicholas considered the bellpull and nodded. "Good man." Then he looked at the letter he held in his hands. A grin flitting about his lips, he walked to where Addie sat. "Here." He offered her the sheet. "This came by courier. You'll want to read it."

As, mystified, she accepted the letter, Nicholas added, "It seems that Toby, as he often is, was right."

Frowning, Addie scanned the sheet. "Right in what way?"

"At our wedding, Toby predicted that Meg would be the next Cynster to marry."

Addie frowned, then focused on the script. As she read, her lips parted, then she reached the end of the missive, and her jaw dropped. Stunned, she looked at Nicholas.

Grinning, he nodded. "Toby suggested it would be unexpected."

"Unexpected?" Addie looked back at the letter, then waved it at her husband. "This… This…"

Nicholas arched a brow. "Is certainly one way to get engaged."

∿

∿

Dear Reader,

Nicholas Cynster's sister, Pru, met her match over Thoroughbred racehorses in 1851 and left the family's home in Newmarket to live at Glengarah Castle in Ireland. Since then, Nicholas has buried himself even more deeply in Newmarket, tending the Cynster Racing Stable and keeping well away from any ballrooms and, even more, from the young ladies who inhabit them. He has little time for dalliance and none at all for romance. Even more than Pru, his attention is all for horses. Consequently, it's hardly a surprise that it's a horse that leads him to his fated lady.

And because Fate has a definite sense of humor, that lady is the last lady he would ever have willingly approached. As remarked by Therese Cynster in the Epilogue of the previous book (*The Time for Love*) this is one romance that no one foresaw.

Writing romance is often most fun when the characters are not instantly and obviously compatible, when there's real reluctance to engage on both sides. We, author and readers, then get to watch as two people are forced by circumstance to learn more about each other and unexpectedly discover the traits, strengths, and vulnerabilities that make each the perfect match for the other.

Recognizing that and acting on it is, after all, the essence of romance.

I hope you enjoyed reading about Nicholas and Addie's pursuit of the Barbarian that, ultimately, leads them into love and marriage.

As is now my habit, the Epilogue ends with an indication of which Cynster is next to front the altar, and it is, indeed, Nicholas's younger sister Meg, whose entirely unexpected romance is the second of the two matches referred to by Therese in *The Time for Love* epilogue. *Miss Prim and the Duke of Wylde* will be released in August 2023, and Toby's tale is slated to follow in early 2024.

With my very best wishes for an abundance of happy reading!

Stephanie.

For alerts as new books are released, plus information on upcoming books, exclusive sweepstakes and sneak peeks into upcoming novels, sign up for Stephanie's Private Email Newsletter https://stephanielaurens.com/newsletter-signup.php

Or if you don't have time to chat and want a quick email alert, sign up and follow me at BookBub https://www.bookbub.com/authors/stephanie-laurens

The ultimate source for detailed information on all Stephanie's published books, including covers, descriptions, and excerpts, is Stephanie's Website www.stephanielaurens.com

You can also follow Stephanie via her Amazon Author Page at http://
tinyurl.com/zc3e9mp

Goodreads members can follow Stephanie via her author page https://
www.goodreads.com/author/show/9241.Stephanie_Laurens

You can email Stephanie at stephanie@stephanielaurens.com

Or find her on Facebook
https://www.facebook.com/AuthorStephanieLaurens/

COMING NEXT:

MISS PRIM AND THE DUKE OF WYLDE
Cynster Next Generation Novel #14
To be released in August, 2023.

*In the leadup to her tenth Season, Meg Cynster—known to the ton's
bachelors as Miss Prim—retreats to her cousin Christopher's home
ostensibly to help him and her close friend, his wife, Ellen, with their
growing brood, but in reality, to dwell on what Meg wants of life. Clearly,
there is no Mr. Right for her so what else is she going to do? She has yet
to come to any conclusion when she happens on an elegant curricle
drawn by a pair of fabulous horses with a drunken lord unconscious on
the box seat. Others present know where the gentleman is staying but are
unable to manage the horses. Reluctantly accepting the responsibility,
Meg takes change of the reins and drives the inebriated gentleman home.
What she doesn't know is that the gentleman is the notorious Duke of
Wylde and that her driving him home is going to seal their fates.*

Available for pre-order in June, 2023.

RECENTLY RELEASED:

THE TIME FOR LOVE
Cynster Next Generation Novel #12

*#1 New York Times bestselling author Stephanie Laurens explores what
happens when a gentleman intent on acquiring a business meets the*

unconventional lady-owner, only to discover that she is not the biggest or the most lethal hurdle they and the business face.

Martin Cynster arrives at Carmichael Steelworks set on acquiring the business as the jewel in his industrialist's crown, only to discover that the lady owner is not at all what he expected. Miss Sophia Carmichael learned about steelmaking at her father's knee and, having inherited the major shareholding, sees no reason not to continue exactly as she is—running the steelworks and steadily becoming an expert in steel alloys. When Martin Cynster tracks her down, she has no option but to listen to his offer—until impending disaster on the steelworks floor interrupts.

Consequently, she tries to dismiss Martin, but he's persistent, and as he has now saved her life, gratitude compels her to hear him out. And day by day, as his understanding of her and the works grows, what he offers grows increasingly tempting, until a merger, both business-wise and personal, is very much on their cards.

But a series of ever-escalating incidents makes it clear someone else has an eye on the steelworks. The quest to learn who and why leads Martin and Sophy into ever greater danger as, layer by layer, they uncover a diabolical scheme that, ultimately, will drain the lifeblood not just from the steelworks but from the city of Sheffield as well.

A classic historical romance, incorporating adventure and intrigue, set in Sheffield. A Cynster Next Generation novel. A full-length historical romance of 100,000 words.

FOES, FRIENDS, AND LOVERS
Cynster Next Generation Novel #11

#1 New York Times bestselling author Stephanie Laurens returns with a tale of a gentleman seeking the road to fulfillment and a lady with a richly satisfying life but no certain future.

A gentleman searching for a purpose in life sets out to claim his legacy, only to discover that instead of the country residence he'd expected, he's inherited an eccentric community whose enterprises are overseen by a decidedly determined young lady who is disinclined to hand over the reins.

Gregory Cynster arrives at the property willed to him by his great-aunt with the intention of converting Bellamy Hall into a quiet, comfortable, gentleman's country residence, only to discover the Hall overrun by an eclectic collection of residents engaged in a host of business endeavors under the stewardship of a lady far too young to be managing such reins.

With the other residents of the estate, Caitlin Fergusson has been planning just how to deal with the new owner, but coming face to face with Gregory Cynster throws her and everyone else off their stride. They'd anticipated a bored and disinterested gentleman who, once they'd revealed the income generated by the Hall's community, would be content to leave them undisturbed.

Instead, while Gregory appears the epitome of the London rake they'd expected him to be, they quickly learn he's determined to embrace Bellamy Hall and all its works and claim ownership of the estate.

While the other residents adjust their thinking, the burden of dealing daily with Gregory falls primarily on Caitlin's slender shoulders, yet as he doggedly carves out a place for himself, Caitlin's position as chatelaine-cum-steward seems set to grow redundant. But Caitlin has her own reasons for clinging to the refuge her position at Bellamy Hall represents.

What follows is a dance of revelations, both of others and also of themselves, for Gregory, Caitlin, and the residents of Bellamy Hall. Yet even as they work out what their collective future might hold, a shadowy villain threatens to steal away everything they've created.

A classic historical romance set in an artisanal community on a country estate. A Cynster Next Generation novel. A full-length historical romance of 118,000 words.

RECENTLY RELEASED:

THE MEANING OF LOVE
A spin-off from Lady Osbaldestone's Christmas Chronicles

#1 New York Times *bestselling author Stephanie Laurens explores the strength of a fated love, one that was left in abeyance when the protagonists were too young, but that roars back to life when, as adults, they meet again.*

A lady ready and waiting to be deemed on the shelf has her transition into spinsterhood disrupted when the nobleman she'd once thought she loved returns to London and fate and circumstance conspire to force them to discover what love truly is and what it means to them.

What happens when a love left behind doesn't die?

Melissa North had assumed that after eight years of not setting eyes on each other, her youthful attraction to—or was it infatuation with?—Julian Delamere, once Viscount Dagenham and now Earl of Carsely, would have faded to nothing and gasped its last. Unfortunately, during the intervening years, she's failed to find any suitable suitor who measures up to her mark and is resigned to ending her days an old maid.

Then she sees Julian across a crowded ballroom, and he sees her, and the intensity of their connection shocks her. She seizes the first chance that offers to flee, only to discover she's jumped from the frying pan into the fire.

Within twenty-four hours, she and Julian are the newly engaged toast of the ton.

Julian has never forgotten Melissa. Now, having inherited the earldom, he must marry and is determined to choose his own bride. He'd assumed that by now, Melissa would be married to someone else, but apparently not. Consequently, he's not averse to the path Fate seems to be steering them down.

And, indeed, as they discover, enforced separation has made their hearts grow fonder, and the attraction between them flares even more intensely.

However, it's soon apparent that someone is intent on ensuring their married life is cut short in deadly fashion. Through a whirlwind courtship, a massive ton wedding, and finally, blissful country peace, they fend off increasingly dangerous, potentially lethal threats, until, together, they unravel the conspiracy that's dogged their heels and expose the villain behind it all.

A classic historical romance laced with murderous intrigue. A novel arising from the Lady Osbaldestone's Christmas Chronicles. A full-length historical romance of 127,000 words.

THE SECRETS OF LORD GRAYSON CHILD
Cynster Next Generation-Connected Novel
(following on from The Games Lovers Play)

#1 New York Times *bestselling author Stephanie Laurens returns to the world of the Cynsters' next generation with the tale of an unconventional nobleman and an equally unconventional noblewoman learning to love and trust again.*

A jilted noblewoman forced into a dual existence half in and half out of the ton is unexpectedly confronted by the nobleman who left her behind ten years ago, but before either can catch their breaths, they trip over a murder and into a race to capture a killer.

Lord Grayson Child is horrified to discover that *The London Crier*, a popular gossip rag, is proposing to expose his extraordinary wealth to the ton's matchmakers, not to mention London's shysters and Captain Sharps. He hies to London and corners *The Crier's* proprietor—only to discover the paper's owner is the last person he'd expected to see.

Izzy—Lady Isadora Descartes—is flabbergasted when Gray appears in her printing works' office. He's the very last person she wants to meet while in her role as owner of *The Crier*, but there he is, as large as life, and she has to deal with him without giving herself away! She manages—just—and seizes on the late hour to put him off so she can work out what to do.

But before leaving the printing works, she and he stumble across a murder, and all hell breaks loose.

Izzy can only be grateful for Gray's support as, to free them both of suspicion, they embark on a joint campaign to find the killer.

Yet working side by side opens their eyes to who they each are now—both quite different to the youthful would-be lovers of ten years before. Mutual respect, affection, and appreciation grow, and amid the chaos of hunting a ruthless killer, they find themselves facing the question of whether what they'd deemed wrecked ten years before can be resurrected.

Then the killer's motive proves to be a treasonous plot, and with others, Gray and Izzy race to prevent a catastrophe, a task that ultimately falls to them alone in a situation in which the only way out is through selfless togetherness—only by relying on each other will they survive.

A classic historical romance laced with crime and intrigue. A Cynster Next Generation-connected novel—a full-length historical romance of 115,000 words.

THE GAMES LOVERS PLAY
Cynster Next Generation Novel #9

#1 New York Times *bestselling author Stephanie Laurens returns to the Cynsters' next generation with an evocative tale of two people striving to overcome unusual hurdles in order to claim true love.*

A nobleman wedded to the lady he loves strives to overwrite five years of masterful pretence and open his wife's eyes to the fact that he loves her as much as she loves him.

Lord Devlin Cader, Earl of Alverton, married Therese Cynster five years ago. What he didn't tell her then and has assiduously hidden ever since—for what seemed excellent reasons at the time—is that he loves her every bit as much as she loves him.

For her own misguided reasons, Therese had decided that the adage that Cynsters always marry for love did not necessarily mean said Cynsters were loved in return. She accepted that was usually so, but being universally viewed by gentlemen as too managing, bossy, and opinionated, she believed she would never be loved for herself. Consequently, after falling irrevocably in love with Devlin, when he made it plain he didn't love her yet wanted her to wife, she accepted the half love-match he offered, and once they were wed, set about organizing to make their marriage the very best it could be.

Now, five years later, they are an established couple within the haut ton, have three young children, and Devlin is making a name for himself in business and political circles. There's only one problem. Having attended numerous Cynster weddings and family gatherings and spent time with Therese's increasingly married cousins, who with their spouses all embrace the Cynster ideal of marriage based on mutually acknowledged love, Devlin is no longer content with the half love-match he himself engineered. No fool, he sees and comprehends what the craven act of denying his love is costing both him and Therese and feels compelled to rectify his fault. He wants for them what all Therese's married cousins enjoy—the rich and myriad benefits of marriages based on acknowledged mutual love.

Love, he's discovered, is too powerful a force to deny, leaving him wrestling with the conundrum of finding a way to convincingly reveal to

Therese that he loves her without wrecking everything—especially the mutual trust—they've built over the past five years.

A classic historical romance set amid the glittering world of the London haut ton. A Cynster Next Generation novel—a full-length historical romance of 110,000 words.

PREVIOUS CYNSTER NEXT GENERATION RELEASES:

THE INEVITABLE FALL OF CHRISTOPHER CYNSTER
Cynster Next Generation Novel #8

#1 New York Times bestselling author Stephanie Laurens returns to the Cynsters' next generation with a rollicking tale of smugglers, counterfeit banknotes, and two people falling in love.

A gentleman hoping to avoid falling in love and a lady who believes love has passed her by are flung together in a race to unravel a plot that threatens to undermine the realm.

Christopher Cynster has finally accepted that to have the life he wants, he needs a wife, but before he can even think of searching for the right lady, he's drawn into an investigation into the distribution of counterfeit banknotes.

London born and bred, Ellen Martingale is battling to preserve the fiction that her much-loved uncle, Christopher's neighbor, still has his wits about him, but Christopher's questions regarding nearby Goffard Hall trigger her suspicions. As her younger brother attends card parties at the Hall, she feels compelled to investigate.

While Ellen appears to be the sort of frippery female Christopher abhors, he quickly learns that, in her case, appearances are deceiving. And through the twists and turns in an investigation that grows ever more serious and urgent, he discovers how easy it is to fall in love, while Ellen learns that love hasn't, after all, passed her by.

But then the villain steps from the shadows, and love's strengths and vulnerabilities are put to the test—just as Christopher has always feared. Will he pass muster? Can they triumph? Or will they lose all they've so recently found?

A historical romance with a dash of intrigue, set in rural Kent. A Cynster Next Generation novel—a full-length historical romance of 124,000 words.

A CONQUEST IMPOSSIBLE TO RESIST
Cynster Next Generation Novel #7

#1 New York Times *bestselling author Stephanie Laurens returns to the Cynsters' next generation to bring you a thrilling tale of love, intrigue, and fabulous horses.*

A notorious rakehell with a stable of rare Thoroughbreds and a lady on a quest to locate such horses must negotiate personal minefields to forge a greatly desired alliance—one someone is prepared to murder to prevent.

Prudence Cynster has turned her back on husband hunting in favor of horse hunting. As the head of the breeding program underpinning the success of the Cynster racing stables, she's on a quest to acquire the necessary horses to refresh the stable's breeding stock.

On his estranged father's death, Deaglan Fitzgerald, now Earl of Glengarah, left London and the hedonistic life of a wealthy, wellborn rake and returned to Glengarah Castle determined to rectify the harm caused by his father's neglect. Driven by guilt that he hadn't been there to protect his people during the Great Famine, Deaglan holds firm against the lure of his father's extensive collection of horses and, leaving the stable to the care of his brother, Felix, devotes himself to returning the estate to prosperity.

Deaglan had fallen out with his father and been exiled from Glengarah over his drive to have the horses pay their way. Knowing Deaglan's wishes and that restoration of the estate is almost complete, Felix writes to the premier Thoroughbred breeding program in the British Isles to test their interest in the Glengarah horses.

On receiving a letter describing exactly the type of horses she's seeking, Pru overrides her family's reluctance and sets out for Ireland's west coast to visit the now-reclusive wicked Earl of Glengarah. Yet her only interest is in his horses, which she cannot wait to see.

When Felix tells Deaglan that a P. H. Cynster is about to arrive to assess the horses with a view to a breeding arrangement, Deaglan can only be grateful. But then P. H. Cynster turns out to be a lady, one utterly unlike any other he's ever met.

Yet they are who they are, and both understand their world. They battle their instincts and attempt to keep their interactions businesslike, but the sparks are incandescent and inevitably ignite a sexual blaze that consumes them both—and opens their eyes.

But before they can find their way to their now-desired goal, first one accident, then another distracts them. Someone, it seems, doesn't want them to strike a deal. Who? Why?

They need to find out before whoever it is resorts to the ultimate sanction.

A historical romance with neo-Gothic overtones, set in the west of Ireland. A Cynster Next Generation novel—a full-length historical romance of 125,000 words.

The first volume of the Devil's Brood Trilogy
THE LADY BY HIS SIDE
Cynster Next Generation Novel #4

A marquess in need of the right bride. An earl's daughter in search of a purpose. A betrayal that ends in murder and balloons into a threat to the realm.

Sebastian Cynster knows time is running out. If he doesn't choose a wife soon, his female relatives will line up to assist him. Yet the current debutantes do not appeal. Where is he to find the right lady to be his marchioness? Then Drake Varisey, eldest son of the Duke of Wolverstone, asks for Sebastian's aid.

Having assumed his father's mantle in protecting queen and country, Drake must go to Ireland in pursuit of a dangerous plot. But he's received an urgent missive from Lord Ennis, an Irish peer—Ennis has heard something Drake needs to know. Ennis insists Drake attends an upcoming house party at Ennis's Kent estate so Ennis can reveal his information face-to-face.

Sebastian has assisted Drake before and, long ago, had a liaison with Lady Ennis. Drake insists Sebastian is just the man to be Drake's surrogate at the house party—the guests will imagine all manner of possibilities and be blind to Sebastian's true purpose.

Unsurprisingly, Sebastian is reluctant, but Drake's need is real. With only more debutantes on his horizon, Sebastian allows himself to be persuaded.

His first task is to inveigle Antonia Rawlings, a lady he has known all her life, to include him as her escort to the house party. Although he's seen little of Antonia in recent years, Sebastian is confident of gaining her support.

Eldest daughter of the Earl of Chillingworth, Antonia has abandoned the search for a husband and plans to use the week of the house party to decide what to do with her life. There has to be some purpose, some role, she can claim for her own.

Consequently, on hearing Sebastian's request and an explanation of what lies behind it, she seizes on the call to action. Suppressing her senses' idiotic reaction to Sebastian's nearness, she agrees to be his partner-in-intrigue.

But while joining the house party proves easy, the gathering is thrown into chaos when Lord Ennis is murdered—just before he was to speak with Sebastian. Worse, Ennis's last words, gasped to Sebastian, are: *Gunpowder. Here.*

Gunpowder? And here, where?

With a killer continuing to stalk the halls, side by side, Sebastian and Antonia search for answers and, all the while, the childhood connection that had always existed between them strengthens and blooms…into something so much more.

First volume in a trilogy. A Cynster Next Generation Novel – a classic historical romance with gothic overtones layered over a continuing intrigue. A full-length novel of 99,000 words.

**The second volume of the Devil's Brood Trilogy
AN IRRESISTIBLE ALLIANCE
Cynster Next Generation Novel #5**

A duke's second son with no responsibilities and a lady starved of the excitement her soul craves join forces to unravel a deadly, potentially catastrophic threat to the realm - that only continues to grow.

With his older brother's betrothal announced, Lord Michael Cynster is freed from the pressure of familial expectations. However, the allure of his previous hedonistic pursuits has paled. Then he learns of the mission his brother, Sebastian, and Lady Antonia Rawlings have been assisting with and volunteers to assist by hunting down the hoard of gunpowder now secreted somewhere in London.

Michael sets out to trace the carters who transported the gunpowder from Kent to London. His quest leads him to the Hendon Shipping Company, where he discovers his sole source of information is the only daughter of Jack and Kit Hendon, Miss Cleome Hendon, who although a fetchingly attractive lady, firmly holds the reins of the office in her small hands.

Cleo has fought to achieve her position in the company. Initially, managing the office was a challenge, but she now conquers all in just a few hours a week. With her three brothers all adventuring in America, she's been driven to the realization that she craves adventure, too.

When Michael Cynster walks in and asks about carters, Cleo's instincts leap. She wrings from him the full tale of his mission—and offers him a bargain. She will lead him to the carters he seeks if he agrees to include her as an equal partner in the mission.

Horrified, Michael attempts to resist, but ultimately finds himself agreeing—a sequence of events he quickly learns is common around Cleo. Then she delivers on her part of the bargain, and he finds there are benefits to allowing her to continue to investigate beside him—not least being that if she's there, then he knows she's safe.

But the further they go in tracing the gunpowder, the more deaths they uncover. And when they finally locate the barrels, they find themselves tangled in a fight to the death—one that forces them to face what has grown between them, to seize and defend what they both see as their path to the greatest adventure of all. A shared life. A shared future. A shared love.

Second volume in a trilogy. A Cynster Next Generation Novel – a classic historical romance with gothic overtones layered over a continuing intrigue. A full-length novel of 101,000 words.

The third and final volume in the Devil's Brood Trilogy
THE GREATEST CHALLENGE OF THEM ALL
Cynster Next Generation Novel #6

A nobleman devoted to defending queen and country and a noblewoman wild enough to match his every step race to disrupt the plans of a malignant intelligence intent on shaking England to its very foundations.

Lord Drake Varisey, Marquess of Winchelsea, eldest son and heir of the Duke of Wolverstone, must foil a plot that threatens to shake the foundations of the realm, but the very last lady—nay, noblewoman—he needs assisting him is Lady Louisa Cynster, known throughout the ton as Lady Wild.

For the past nine years, Louisa has suspected that Drake might well be the ideal husband for her, even though he's assiduous in avoiding her. But she's now twenty-seven and enough is enough. She believes propinquity will elucidate exactly what it is that lies between them, and what better opportunity to work closely with Drake than his latest mission, with which he patently needs her help?

Unable to deny Louisa's abilities or the value of her assistance and powerless to curb her willfulness, Drake is forced to grit his teeth and acquiesce to her sticking by his side, if only to ensure her safety. But all too soon, his true feelings for her show enough for her, perspicacious as she is, to see through his denials, which she then interprets as a challenge.

Even while they gather information, tease out clues, increasingly desperately search for the missing gunpowder, and doggedly pursue the killer responsible for an ever-escalating tally of dead men, thrown together through the hours, he and she learn to trust and appreciate each other. And fed by constant exposure—and blatantly encouraged by her—their desires and hungers swell and grow…

As the barriers between them crumble, the attraction he has for so long restrained burgeons and balloons, until goaded by her near-death, it erupts, and he seizes her—only to be seized in return.

Linked irrevocably and with their wills melded and merged by passion's fire, with time running out and the evil mastermind's deadline looming, together, they focus their considerable talents and make one last push to learn the critical truths—to find the gunpowder and unmask the villain behind this far-reaching plot.

Only to discover that they have significantly less time than they'd thought, that the villain's target is even more crucially fundamental to the realm than they'd imagined, and it's going to take all that Drake is—as well as all that Louisa as Lady Wild can bring to bear—to defuse the threat, capture the villain, and make all safe and right again.

As they race to the ultimate confrontation, the future of all England rests on their shoulders.

Third volume in a trilogy. A Cynster Next Generation Novel – a classic historical romance with gothic overtones layered over an intrigue. A full-length novel of 129,000 words.

If you haven't yet caught up with the first books in the Cynster Next Generation Novels, then BY WINTER'S LIGHT is a Christmas story that highlights the Cynster children as they stand poised on the cusp of adulthood – essentially an introductory novel to the upcoming generation. That novel is followed by the first pair of Cynster Next Generation romances, those of Lucilla and Marcus Cynster, twins and the eldest children of Lord Richard aka Scandal Cynster and Catriona, Lady of the Vale. Both the twins' stories are set in Scotland. See below for further details.

BY WINTER'S LIGHT
Cynster Next Generation Novel #1

#1 New York Times *bestselling author Stephanie Laurens returns to romantic Scotland to usher in a new generation of Cynsters in an enchanting tale of mistletoe, magic, and love.*

It's December 1837 and the young adults of the Cynster clan have succeeded in having the family Christmas celebration held at snow-bound Casphairn Manor, Richard and Catriona Cynster's home. Led by Sebastian, Marquess of Earith, and by Lucilla, future Lady of the Vale, and her twin brother, Marcus, the upcoming generation has their own plans for the holiday season.

Yet where Cynsters gather, love is never far behind—the festive occasion brings together Daniel Crosbie, tutor to Lucifer Cynster's sons, and Claire Meadows, widow and governess to Gabriel Cynster's daughter. Daniel and Claire have met before and the embers of an unexpected passion smolder between them, but once bitten, twice shy, Claire believes a second marriage is not in her stars. Daniel, however, is determined to press his suit. He's seen the love the Cynsters share, and Claire is the lady with whom he dreams of sharing *his* life. Assisted by a bevy of Cynsters —innate matchmakers every one—Daniel strives to persuade Claire that trusting him with her hand and her heart is her right path to happiness.

Meanwhile, out riding on Christmas Eve, the young adults of the Cynster clan respond to a plea for help. Summoned to a humble dwelling in ruggedly forested mountains, Lucilla is called on to help with the difficult birth of a child, while the others rise to the challenge of helping her. With a violent storm closing in and severely limited options, the next generation of Cynsters face their first collective test—can they save this mother and child? And themselves, too?

Back at the manor, Claire is increasingly drawn to Daniel and despite her misgivings, against the backdrop of the ongoing festivities their relationship deepens. Yet she remains torn—until catastrophe strikes, and by winter's light, she learns that love—true love—is worth any risk, any price.

A tale brimming with all the magical delights of a Scottish festive season. A Cynster Next Generation novel – a classic historical romance of 71,000 words.

THE TEMPTING OF THOMAS CARRICK
Cynster Next Generation Novel #2

Do you believe in fate? Do you believe in passion? What happens when fate and passion collide?
Do you believe in love? What happens when fate, passion, and love combine?
This. This…

#1 New York Times *bestselling author Stephanie Laurens returns to Scotland with a tale of two lovers irrevocably linked by destiny and passion.*

Thomas Carrick is a gentleman driven to control all aspects of his life. As the wealthy owner of Carrick Enterprises, located in bustling Glasgow, he is one of that city's most eligible bachelors and fully intends to select an appropriate wife from the many young ladies paraded before him. He wants to take that necessary next step along his self-determined path, yet no young lady captures his eye, much less his attention...not in the way Lucilla Cynster had, and still did, even though she lives miles away.

For over two years, Thomas has avoided his clan's estate because it borders Lucilla's home, but disturbing reports from his clansmen force him to return to the countryside—only to discover that his uncle, the laird, is ailing, a clan family is desperately ill, and the clan-healer is unconscious and dying. Duty to the clan leaves Thomas no choice but to seek help from the last woman he wants to face.

Strong-willed and passionate, Lucilla has been waiting—increasingly impatiently—for Thomas to return and claim his rightful place by her side. She knows he is hers—her fated lover, husband, protector, and mate. He is the only man for her, just as she is his one true love. And, at last, he's back. Even though his returning wasn't on her account, Lucilla is willing to seize whatever chance Fate hands her.

Thomas can never forget Lucilla, much less the connection that seethes between them, but to marry her would mean embracing a life he's adamant he does not want.

Lucilla sees that Thomas has yet to accept the inevitability of their union and, despite all, he can refuse her and walk away. But how *can* he ignore a bond such as theirs—one so much stronger than reason? Despite several unnerving attacks mounted against them, despite the uncertainty racking his clan, Lucilla remains as determined as only a Cynster can be to fight for the future she knows can be theirs—and while she cannot command him, she has powerful enticements she's willing to wield in the cause of tempting Thomas Carrick.

A neo-Gothic tale of passionate romance laced with mystery, set in the uplands of southwestern Scotland. A Cynster Next Generation Novel – a classic historical romance of 122,000 words.

A MATCH FOR MARCUS CYNSTER
Cynster Next Generation Novel #3

Duty compels her to turn her back on marriage. Fate drives him to protect her come what may. Then love takes a hand in this battle of yearning hearts, stubborn wills, and a match too powerful to deny.

#1 New York Times *bestselling author Stephanie Laurens returns to rugged Scotland with a dramatic tale of passionate desire and unwavering devotion.*

Restless and impatient, Marcus Cynster waits for Fate to come calling. He knows his destiny lies in the lands surrounding his family home, but what will his future be? Equally importantly, with whom will he share it?

Of one fact he feels certain: his fated bride will not be Niniver Carrick. His elusive neighbor attracts him mightily, yet he feels compelled to protect her—even from himself. Fickle Fate, he's sure, would never be so kind as to decree that Niniver should be his. The best he can do for them both is to avoid her.

Niniver has vowed to return her clan to prosperity. The epitome of fragile femininity, her delicate and ethereal exterior cloaks a stubborn will and an unflinching devotion to the people in her care. She accepts that in order to achieve her goal, she cannot risk marrying and losing her grip on the clan's reins to an inevitably controlling husband. Unfortunately, many local men see her as their opportunity.

Soon, she's forced to seek help to get rid of her unwelcome suitors. Powerful and dangerous, Marcus Cynster is perfect for the task. Suppressing her wariness over tangling with a gentleman who so excites her passions, she appeals to him for assistance with her peculiar problem.

Although at first he resists, Marcus discovers that, contrary to his expectations, his fated role *is* to stand by Niniver's side and, ultimately, to claim her hand. Yet in order to convince her to be his bride, they must plunge headlong into a journey full of challenges, unforeseen dangers, passion, and yearning, until Niniver grasps the essential truth—that she is indeed a match for Marcus Cynster.

A neo-Gothic tale of passionate romance set in the uplands of southwestern Scotland. A Cynster Next Generation Novel – a classic historical romance of 114,000 words.

And if you want to discover where the Cynsters began, return to the iconic
DEVIL'S BRIDE

the book that introduced millions of historical romance readers around the globe to the powerful men of the unforgettable Cynster family – aristocrats to the bone, conquerors at heart – and the willful feisty ladies strong enough to be their brides.

ABOUT THE AUTHOR

#1 *New York Times* bestselling author Stephanie Laurens began writing romances as an escape from the dry world of professional science. Her hobby quickly became a career when her first novel was accepted for publication, and with entirely becoming alacrity, she gave up writing about facts in favor of writing fiction.

All Laurens's works to date are historical romances, ranging from medieval times to the mid-1800s, and her settings range from Scotland to India. The majority of her works are set in the period of the British Regency. Laurens has published more than 80 works of historical romance, including 40 *New York Times* bestsellers. Laurens has sold more than 20 million print, audio, and e-books globally. All her works are continuously available in print and e-book formats in English worldwide, and have been translated into many other languages. An international bestseller, among other accolades, Laurens has received the Romance Writers of America® prestigious RITA® Award for Best Romance Novella 2008 for *The Fall of Rogue Gerrard.*

Laurens's continuing novels featuring the Cynster family are widely regarded as classics of the historical romance genre. Other series include the *Bastion Club Novels*, the *Black Cobra Quartet*, the *Adventurers Quartet,* and the *Casebook of Barnaby Adair Novels.*

For information on all published novels and on upcoming releases and updates on novels yet to come, visit Stephanie's website: www.stephanielaurens.com

To sign up for Stephanie's Email Newsletter (a private list) for heads-up alerts as new books are released, exclusive sneak peeks into upcoming books, and exclusive sweepstakes contests, follow the prompts at http://www.stephanielaurens.com/newsletter-signup/

To follow Stephanie on BookBub, head to her BookBub Author Page: https://www.bookbub.com/authors/stephanie-laurens

Stephanie lives with her husband and a goofy black labradoodle in the hills outside Melbourne, Australia. When she isn't writing, she's reading, and if she isn't reading, she'll be tending her garden.

www.stephanielaurens.com
stephanie@stephanielaurens.com